The Secret Box

A Story of the South

By
Sharon Griggs

Dedicated to my true love, Ron

Chapters

Stamper Family Genealogy

Powell Stamper and Mary Margaret Copeland

Joel
Polly Bowman
*James
Melmath
Stillborn daughter

John
Catherine Coble
Premature Son
Unnamed Son
Alex
Gilbert
*George
*Ellen

*Susannah 'Susan'
Rebecca (died in childhood)

Margaret

Hugh
Cassie Waggoner
Lewis F.
Joseph H

Mary E.

James Brooks
Nancy Coble
Mary Elizabeth
Margaret.
Sarah Jane
Martha
Nancy
Susannah

James Stamper
Annie O'Brien
Riley
Heath
Carolina 'Lina'

George Stamper
Sarah 'Sallie' Allen
Dolly Saline
Stillborn twins
Gilbert Abraham 'Abe'
Stillborn infant
James Columbus 'Lum'
Ernest Elmo
Mamie
Naomi
Lula 'Lou'

Ellen Stamper
Josiah Stamper
Jamie
Jonathan
Margaret 'Maggie'

Susan Stamper
Lafayette 'Fate' McAlpine
Amanda Grayson
Lucinda 'Luci' - twin
Oliver - twin
Catherine 'Reiny'

*See chart below

Prologue

North Carolina 2005

Memories of my paternal grandmother always make me smile. She was a prim and proper farm wife; always neatly groomed, she smelled of teaberry gum and cinnamon. Grandmother walked with a cane placing the blame on my father's birth, claiming she heard her bones crack when he was born and that her hip had not been the same since. Deeply religious, she lived her life with faith with prayer, however she was not above listening in on the telephone party line.

As I age, my mind seems to draw me closer to the family farm along with pleasant memories of time spent with my grandmother. She generously shared her passion for her heritage and strong pride in her family's history. Occasionally I look in the mirror and catch a slight glimpse of her reflecting in my face, especially the eyes. There is a realization that a part of her lives within me, especially the part about pride in heritage and ancestry.

Once my own children were grown, and gone from the nest, I began looking around for an activity to exercise my mind, something interesting. What I discovered was a driving force to know the people who had passed along the color of my hair and eyes, the shape of my chin, my somewhat large hands and feet. Embarking down this path would lead me into a romance with the past and that of my family history. My future turned into literally years of camping out in libraries, searching for long forgotten cemeteries, and scrutinizing ancient wills, deeds and land grants; this would become my love affair.

My days off from work became a secret life, that of a research junkie. Visiting every location where relatives had once lived and searching out distant cousins became more than a hobby, looking more like an obsession every day.

Remembering the times I visited my grandmother's birthplace, always gave me a sense of peace that seemed to cover me. On one of my first research trips to Iredell and Alexander Co, I visited Concord Baptist Church, a small country church, with a neatly trimmed and well-kept cemetery. Walking through the rows of graves, familiar names appeared on most of the stones. Not that I actually knew any of these people but their names had passed before my eyes on census readings, for literally years as I searched for my descendants.

There is a stone there with the carved name 'LACKEY', that is large, and has withstood the elements for over ninety plus years. This is the grave of my great grandparents Thomas Preston Lackey and his bride, parents of my beloved paternal grandmother,

My quest began over ten years ago, at this very cemetery with a single name engraved on a stone, Margaret "Maggie" Stamper Lackey. The family Bible had only her name and nothing more. My grandmother had left me a family photo showing Maggie with her spouse and all their children, taken around the year, 1904. Occasionally I look at the photo and study Maggie's eyes. What had she seen? Who were her parents? Where had she lived? This was a mystery that would not soon be solved and would lead to a search that would last more than a decade.

The quest for answers had suddenly turned from months into years and my family tensed whenever they heard the words 'guess what I found'. Another boring genealogy story was on the way and they prepared with stonewall faces trying to generate interest. Obviously, the saying is true that there is only one person in each family, per generation, born with the genealogy gene, and it was my turn.

The result of searching would result in a large collection of history. My history. There were rewards beyond knowing the various branches of the family. The excitement of the chase had sucked me in and I finally have all of the pieces and can now fit them together.

With all the information gathered through the years, I began to imagine how life would have been for the people beneath those gravestones I visited, strangers who shared my blood. Though my imagination inserts itself into this story, most of the circumstances surrounding the family are factual events, then, there are some not so factual. The majority of characters are actual people who lived in the 18th and 19th century and were either in my family, a neighbor or associated with them. Some of the happenings you will read have some historical background. My fascination of how things were and how to put them on paper became my love.

And now I know who I am.

"....Fear not, for I have redeemed you;
I have called you by your name;
You are mine.
When you pass through the waters,
I will be with you;
And through the rivers, they
Shall not overflow you.
When you walk through the fire,
You shall not be burned.
Nor shall the flame scorch you
For I am the Lord your God...."

Isaiah 43:1-3

Chapter 1
Learning to Survive

Lord Edgar Falsworth fell madly in love with the beautiful daughter of a wealthy French merchant. He was nearing the end of his European travels when he first spotted her being gently assisted into a carriage. France had not been on his travel agenda but hearing of fine wines available in a region called Champagne he decided the investment might be worth the travel. One week in France turned into six months with the first two weeks spent trying to gain an introduction to the beautiful young French girl. Tall and handsome, it was not impossible for Edgar to meet this beautiful girl. After months of courting, there was a decision to marry.

After their marriage ceremony, Edgar sailed for his home in England with his beautiful bride, Laurent, and settled into Falsworth Manor. How proud he was at showing off his wife. Elegant, she turned heads wherever she went and fascinated all with her beautiful French accent. Her dark blonde hair was worn in the latest fashion and her pale skin was flawless. She had striking green eyes that drew attention away from her very round face. Constantly smiling and greeting all of Edgar's friends enthusiastically, it was evident to everyone that she was madly in love with her aristocratic husband.

At the end of the first year of their marriage, Laurent craved a child for her husband. She wanted a strong son to carry on his father's name. Soon she announced to Edgar that a child was expected. He was filled with joy but quickly became alarmed at her physical condition. The first five months found her too ill to leave her bed except for short periods of time. Frantic, Edgar sent to London for the best physician that could be found. After examining Laurent, the doctor pronounced that she was undernourished, and that she would be fine.

Despite the doctor's prognosis the sickness would stay with her until the birth of the child. Frail and weak the hard labor was too much and Laurent's life slipped away as another life took their first breath. Holding the lifeless pale hand of his wife Edgar was inconsolable. As soon as the funeral was over he stepped into his carriage shouting for the driver to leave immediately. Only once had he even looked at his newborn daughter Elizabeth. His only thought was that the infant had killed his beloved Laurent. The care of the infant was given over to a nanny and as she became older, servants and a governess became her companions. Elizabeth's father was too involved in business to pay much attention to his daughter and preferred staying in his London home rather than the countryside where there were only painful memories.

In truth Edgar could not bear to see the child, as her face was a replica of her dead mother, but with his dark hair and blue eyes. Years began to pass with Edgar spending all his time in London or Paris to avoid his daughter. With each birthday Elizabeth grew more beautiful and with each year the resemblance to her mother was more evident. The minor difference was Elizabeth's shorter stature, yet even the smile was undeniably her mother's.

For many months, Elizabeth would go without seeing anyone, with the exception of the household staff. Under the care of a governess she was taught how a lady comports herself in the company of gentlemen, how to dress and what was expected of her. She was tutored in French and German, embroidery, painting, flower arranging, and the running of a large household.

During a rare outing to a county fair, Elizabeth was introduced to one of her father's tenants, Mr. Charles Coble and his son George. She was immediately smitten by the younger man. Having just turned twenty George was of average height with a stocky build. His deep-set blue eyes crinkled when he smiled, showing less than perfect teeth.

Shortly after Elizabeth turned sixteen she began slipping away to clandestine meetings with George. They would sit and talk for hours. As days led into weeks their love for one another grew until only after three months they secretly traveled to London telling the magistrate that Elizabeth was nineteen and orphaned, and so they were married.

Travel tickets for a ship, bound for America, were purchased by selling pieces of Elizabeth's family silver, which she considered an inheritance from her mother. Standing at the railing she watched as the last trace of land disappeared along with the thought that never again would she see her family or home again. Slipping her hand into her pocket, she felt for the tiny object. Nestled inside was dirt that was scooped from her mother's rose garden. It was a small piece of home she would carry forever.

Their journey across the ocean brought countless hours to discuss their plans for living in this new land and they listened carefully to other young families describe the area where they hoped to settle. Privately they prayed for guidance. Arriving in Baltimore, they decided that the land in the south would be their final destination. Traveling to North Carolina, they found the area reminiscent of their homeland. It was here in the year1802 that Elizabeth learned to survive. Life was not easy on this new land, but Elizabeth learned and excelled in her accomplishments.

This western section of North Carolina abounded with large farms yielding acres and acres of wheat and potatoes. Animals grew fat grazing on the rich green grasses. At the beginning of 1820 the Cobles were farming a moderate spread in the Shiloh section of Iredell County near Buffalo Shoals Creek. Husband, wife, two sons and five daughters enjoyed the solitude of the countryside and had no desire to ever stray from their quiet little corner of the county.

Quite suddenly in 1828 Elizabeth Coble found herself to be the widow Coble raising two young daughters and owing money that would deplete all her holdings. The older Coble children, now all married, had settled in Tennessee taking advantage of land opportunities. Moving to Tennessee was not something Elizabeth wanted to do. She loved North Carolina and wanted to remain in the area. There was nothing to do but search for employment.

Elizabeth would see that her girls were fittingly provided for. Catherine was almost 15 years old and the younger girl Nancy was 12. Their destiny would be in the hands of whoever would hire their mother and hopefully take them also. Both girls were bright and had been schooled by their mother in reading and writing; each had some knowledge of music, art and etiquette.

A visiting neighbor told Elizabeth about a recent widower named Vanderburg, living on a plantation, located in the southern part of the county at Coddle Creek. The planter's wife had died in childbirth last year, leaving behind many small children to be cared for by the housekeeper. Then the housekeeper up and died of old age, which left house servants caring for the children. Mr. Vanderburg was in desperate need of a housekeeper and governess for his children. It was at this moment that Elizabeth set her sights on traveling to Vanderburg plantation and obtaining a job. Within two days she had packed a small bag, settled her affairs and with her daughters, began walking to what Elizabeth hoped would be a future for herself and her daughters.

Their neighbor, Thomas Bowman, came upon Elizabeth and her girls walking along the side of the road, on his way to the mill. Stopping, he offered them a ride as far as the turnoff to the mill. Reaching the fork in the road, Thomas pulled on the reigns and the wagon rolled to a stop. Elizabeth and the girls climbed down from the wagon while Mr. Bowman pointed them in the direction of Vanderburg Plantation. Waving farewell, they began their walk the remaining miles to the area of Coddle Creek. Elizabeth's husband had not yet been dead two months but the time for mourning had to be put behind her. Once their debts were paid, the money was exhausted. Even so, the law of the day was to assign guardianship of minor children, but Elizabeth would not have someone else accepting responsibility for rearing Catherine and Nancy just because she was a widow and might not remarry. George Coble had distant cousins living in Virginia but Elizabeth had no desire to ask for their assistance. She meant for her girls to stay with her and that was the end of it.

Elizabeth and her girls were once again walking toward Vanderburg Plantation, with renewed determination, but not the promise of a job. There had been no thought given as to what they would do if the position had been filled. The road was dusty with high weeds on either side, with the sounds of a creek not far from the road. In the distance, smoke from a chimney could be seen, so they left the road to wash off the dust of the road before walking the remainder of the way to the big house.

Vanderburg Plantation stood nestled among huge old Oak trees. The house was large but not as big as some they had seen along the way. A separate building housing the kitchen stood close to the back of the house with black smoke spewing from the chimney bringing the smell of burnt bread in the air. Behind the house Elizabeth could see a smokehouse along with several storage buildings. A barn of decent size with a pigpen on one side could be seen in the distance. To the left, nestled among shade trees, were several small cabins and more small storage sheds. A duck pond with water glistening in the sun lay on the right. At the back of the pond behind a stacked fence, a large ewe grazed with her lambs. The entire scene was the picture of serenity.

There was a large expanse of front lawn with children, both black and white, playing chase near the front porch, along with several dogs in hot pursuit, yapping at their heels. Racing up and down the steps, the giggling children ran from one end of the porch to the other end.

Spotting Mrs. Coble walking across the lawn the children scattered in every direction seeking places to hide. Peering from behind bushes, they watched as the three females stepped onto the porch and rapped on the door.

Opening the door, Amos Vanderburg was the picture of a country gentleman. Short in stature and portly, he was dressed immaculately with the exception of his muddy boots. He listened politely to Elizabeth's inquiry about a position in his household but he refused to discuss any position with Elizabeth. Clasping his hands behind his back, he explained there were more than enough little ones in his home without adding to the number with children, brought in by a housekeeper. But Elizabeth Coble stood her ground and pointed out in a refined English accent that she knew he was a smart man and if he would look very closely he would see that Catherine was in her teens and Nancy not far behind.

–My daughters are not very tall, but old enough to work like grown women and you would be getting four extra hands at no additional expense. Catherine and Nancy come as part of the bargain. There would be three for the price of one. You strike me as an astute man and can surely see the merit of this deal. Smiling, she slipped a hand in her pocket, feeling for the small object.

It was a proposition he could not turn down.

–Then I'll begin immediately.

Elizabeth smiled as she brushed past him, headed toward the back of the house and out to the kitchen and the burning bread.

With his mouth hanging open, Mr. Vanderburg rubbed his balding head and moved aside as Catherine and Nancy stepped into the house.

–Now, if you will point us in the direction of the children's rooms, sir, we will begin there.

Catherine smiled sweetly as Mr. Vanderburg gave directions to the rooms above. As the sisters went up the steps Catherine looked over her shoulder and told him that a child is happiest when they are nurtured in orderly surroundings. Amos Vanderburg stood at the open door, his mouth still hanging open.

Their adventure at Vanderburg Plantation had begun and the first week the children wanted nothing to do with Catherine and Nancy. Because the sisters weren't too terribly much taller than the oldest child, they struggled with appearing to have authority. Getting the children to behave was going to be a challenge.

-*You're not my mother, let go.*

'Whack.' Right across the backside and then there was no more backtalk. As the children settled down Catherine winked at Nancy and whispered.

-*I think I bruised my hand but there'll be no more trouble now that they know who's in charge.*

Chapter 2
Becoming A Family

The Cobles had now worked for two years at Vanderburg plantation and were treated more like family than hired help. Always demanding perfection, Elizabeth kept an inventory of the linens, household items and stored goods. Making sure that there would always be enough provisions to keep the house and kitchen running smoothly.

The household staff consisted of Aunt Sukie, Lucy and Jencie. Elizabeth had grown to deeply love Aunt Sukie and considered her a friend. There were a few field hands on the property but Amos Vanderburg hired most of his fieldwork so as to not overwork his own men. Then there was Uncle Jake, who they claimed was close to ninety years old. Black as coal and just slightly over five and half feet tall, his frizzled hair had turned snow white and stood almost on end, giving him an added inch or two in height. In a hundred wrinkles, his face bore the years of his trials and tribulations

Jake had come to the attention of Mr. Vanderburg many years ago. A neighbor had abused Jake severely and when word of the beatings reached Vanderberg Plantation the master of the house immediately went to the neighbor's farm. There he found Jake in a miserable state. Amos stormed into the main house and in a firm tone asked the price for Jake.

Standing stiff and looking stern, the neighbor shouted at Amos.

–He is not for sale so you can leave right now. Jake has been in this house since before I was born and here is where he will stay.

Firmly rooted to his spot, Amos tried to stretch himself to the same height as his neighbor but he was about six inches too short. Not one to be bullied or pushed about, Amos took one step closer.

–My money is in my pocket and I will gladly wait until you draw up the necessary papers of transfer. Jake will be at my house today, or tomorrow I will return. If he is not with me then, I will return again and again, one day after another until he is. Do you understand me? Do not doubt me. If I have to come again tomorrow, I will not be alone.

On the way home Jake asked Amos why he had come to his rescue.

But his only answer was a smile.

–Today you are free my friend. And you shall live on my land till the end of your days. Your job from now on will be to bounce the new born babies on your knee and to sit in the shade and whittle while you tell stories to the children.

A radiant smile was on the face of Jake and pretty much stayed there from then on out.

Amos Vanderburg had held ownership papers on six adults and twelve children. The slaves were a part of his bride's dowry. Ownership papers meant nothing to him as he considered them part of his family and under his protection. Though Amos received much criticism from the neighbors, he had long ago given them their papers and set them free. Everyone believed that the darkies would bolt and that Amos would be left with land he could not work alone; they were surprised by the loyalty of the men and women and at the sight of them working the fields at Vanderburg Plantation.

At Christmas and in June he gifted each one, including the children, one dollar along with new clothes and shoes. Household items where distributed to the adults as were needed. They were treated with respect, paid for their work, given decent living quarters, and medical attention when needed. Many evenings would find the plantation owner sitting on the porch at Uncle Jakes cabin sharing a pipe. In a sealed envelope in his desk, Amos had written the name of each worker along with instructions that if they still lived on his property at his death, they were to be given ten acres of land.

Uncle Jake had ample time to watch the Coble sisters as they tended to the Vanderburg children, and what he saw pleased him. Many evenings he would sit on the porch smoking his pipe with Catherine and Nancy sitting at his feet along with the children, listening to his stories of the past. He could remember sailing on a large ship far from his home to a place called Wilmington where he stood on a block in the town square and was sold into slavery.

One year while traveling with his former master, Jake saw men from his village that were also slaves and laughed at the surprised look on their faces at seeing someone from home. He told the children of how the stars looked at night shinning over his village and of sitting on a big rock, high above his village, watching the sun set with brilliant colors of orange and red. The children were fascinated by the stories and description of his far-away homeland that seemed magical.

Nearly every morning Catherine would rise early and go to Uncle

Jake's cabin to start his fire, making sure there was enough wood for his fireplace and that he was well. This very old man was respected and admired by both Catherine and Nancy. One Saturday Catherine baked a cake and with the children in tow started for Uncle Jake's cabin. The children, laughing, pounded on his door, calling his name. When the door opened the children broke into song and sang loud and long. Sitting in his chair with a big grin he asked what this was about.

  -We've decided that today should be the day we celebrate your birthday.

  And with that Catherine leaned down and kissed him on the forehead. For the first time in many, many years, Jake cried.

  The Stampers settled into a routine at Vanderburg Plantation. The girls tended to the children and their schooling. House servants cared for a three-year-old boy and a four-year-old boy. In Catherine and Nancy's care there were two sets of twins' ages six and eight, a boy and a girl in each set. In addition, there was a boy five-years-old and a seven-year-old girl. The oldest child was a tall gangly girl of ten and almost as tall as Nancy. A grand total of nine children! Each one had bright red hair, fair skin and freckles, echoing their mother's Irish roots.

  The sisters were constantly hovering over their charges. The experience was one they relished. And books, oh the house had hundreds of books and they were allowed to read all of them. The children loved both Catherine and Nancy and were attentive to their instructions. There were fields and woods to be explored. The countryside held beautiful landscapes with streams and rolling pastureland. There were caterpillars to watch, bugs to collect and their favorite pastime, spending hours in the woods exploring, finding and cataloging wild herbs and flowers.

  Catherine found that she could walk with the children for hours on end, just breathing in the beauty of the land. There was a small-pooled area in the creek where the children were allowed to play in the heat of summer. Sitting on the rocks, Nancy and Elizabeth read while the children splashed and played. Wild ferns and Galax, along with laurel, grew lush on the banks. The children would wander the banks gathering bee balm, which they pressed in a large book. Each adventure was a learning experience and Mr. Vanderburg looked on approvingly as his children were taught and cared for by the Coble girls. He had made a good decision about hiring Mrs. Coble. Yes, indeed.

Chapter 3
Changes of The Heart

It was near the beginning of their fourth year at the plantation when several new men appeared for spring planting. George Campbell, the brother of the deceased Mrs. Vanderburg, had delivered men from his plantation to help with seeding. He had been a widower for many years but remained busy with his land and enjoyed occasionally visiting with his nieces and nephews. Brothers John and Joel Stamper were among the men hiring on for spring planting.

The first time Catherine saw John Stamper he was pitching hay with his shirt tied around his waist, which she thought was scandalous. She gasped and turned her head but when she realized he was not aware of her presence, she looked at him again. He was tall and lean with a broad muscular back. His hair was black and he had a dimple in his chin. Beautiful blue eyes with thick lashes were the first things she noticed about his face.

The Stamper brothers had previously worked at Vanderburg and on occasion returned when work became scarce in their part of the county. John was only a few years older than Catherine but exhibited wisdom far beyond his years. Hard work he said, at least that is what Catherine thought she heard him say to his brother. Hard work was what would make a man successful in John's eyes. Catherine secretly loved him from that first day and always seemed to make herself visible within his sight whenever he was near.

For lodging, food and a few dollars a month, John hired on for the season. With a good year he would also receive a small percentage of the crop once sold. In the evening by lamplight, he tooled leather goods that he used for trade. It was several days after his arrival that John first noticed Catherine, though seeing her only as just a young girl working at Vanderburg.

Catherine seemed to find an excuse to take the children outside whenever she thought it was time for the workers to come in from the field. Every time John turned around Catherine was smiling and swinging some child around and laughing followed by the joke....

–You best be good or I'll throw you in the haystack!

This was always followed by giggles and lots of hugs.

Then one evening John joined Catherine on the back porch steps and they talked for hours. She was definitely different from any female he had ever known. This young girl was intelligent and mature far beyond her years.

Interested in everything about John, Catherine wanted to know about his childhood and his family. John gave Catherine a brief glimpse of his family. He was eighteen when his father, Powell Stamper, fell from a wagon had died. There were six children in his family beginning with the oldest brother Joel, then John, Margaret, Hugh, Mary Jane and Brooks. It had been some months since he had seen his family but wrote to them often.

Smiling, he told Catherine how beautiful his mother is and what an industrious woman she was to run a large farm while raising a family. Of course his mother was thinking of selling some of her land, now that the oldest son had married and John was no longer at home. Both of his sisters were now married and had moved to Kentucky. The two younger brothers, Hugh and Brooks, were only fifteen and thirteen and not quite old enough to truly manage the work of grown men around the farm.

A few days later Catherine and John were sitting together at church, listening to Preacher Icenhour, who came every third Sunday. On the other Sundays they would sit in the parlor together as Mr. Vanderburg read scripture and had prayer. Afterwards they would walk the land and share their dreams and hopes.

Talking about the farm where he was raised, John told Catherine about the land he hoped to have one day. He had begun thinking about a helpmate in making that dream a reality. It was not that John had never thought of taking a bride, he just did not think it would be so soon. If he was to have his own plot of land, he would need help in making it a reality, and having sons is essential for a landowner. Deep inside he knew his heart was slipping away to Catherine and that had not been his plan. Six months later they would be married at Vanderburg Plantation, standing under the big chandelier in the front room.

Walking beside her groom Catherine wore her mother's periwinkle blue wedding dress, which had long fitted sleeves, edged with delicate handmade lace, dyed to match the dress. This embellishment had been a birthday present, tatted for Elizabeth by a great aunt. The matching hat, adorned with flowers and feathers, set off the deep blue of Catherine's eyes. Her sandy brown hair had been pulled back and braided with blue ribbons, then coiled at the back of her head. Catherine was truly a beautiful bride.

John felt his heart racing. Here he was saying vows while Mr. Vanderberg held the ring and his mother softly crying in the background. Standing beside his mother was Mr. Campbell, brother-in-law of Mr. Vanderberg, along with John's brothers, Hugh and Brooks slightly behind them. John's sisters, Margaret and Mary, were now living in Kentucky, could not attend but sent the bride a new quilt. John's older brother, Joel also absent, as he awaited the birth of his first child due any time. Wiping her tears, Nancy listened intently as the vows were repeated.

When the minister pronounced them husband and wife, John gently kissed Catherine on the lips. The men in the room hooted and clapped, and managed to see John's face turn red as Catherine hid her blushing face. While the couple greeted their guests and accepted best wishes, Elizabeth was busy with the kitchen staff laying out a feast in the dining room. Fresh greens cut from the shrubbery circled the bottom of a large silver punch bowl placed in the center of the table. Platters of food including sweets, graced the long dining room table. Silk bows with ribbon streamers were attached to each corner of the table and the chandelier overhead was festooned with ribbons and dried white flowers.

Hours after the wedding guests had departed, Elizabeth stood on the porch and watched as John and Catherine stepped into a carriage, bound for their first home. Mr. Vanderburg had offered a small cabin used by a former overseer to the couple that was in sight from the main house. Living close by John would still work the farm and Catherine would continue to tend the children.

Many evenings they sat quietly, listening to the pop and crackle of the fire; other times they chatted the evening away. Occasionally John would bring out his fiddle, which was one of his most prized possessions. Catherine would sing and the sound of her voice in harmony with the fiddle, carried over the night air.

Once they heard giggles after one such singing session. Quietly opening the door and stretching to see around the corner, John found four pairs of eyes staring back at him.

-I got 'cha now!

There was high-pitched laughter and the chase was on. Little feet flying in every direction with both John and Catherine on their heels, laughing as they ran. The mystery of love had lured the spying eyes of four little girls, barefoot and in their nightclothes. Tomorrow Nancy would surely hear about this as she had let them slip by her door unnoticed. As for Catherine, she loved all the children and often daydreamed of motherhood and what it would feel like to hold your own child.

When John and Catherine's one-year anniversary rolled around there was enough money saved to move out on their own. Leasing land was not the goal that John had in mind, but it was a start. When the word spread that John and Catherine were leaving to farm on their own land, a date was set-aside for a pounding. Neighbors came to wish them their best and to give them a pound of this or a pound of that. Supplies and staples were not the only gifts: A nice set of feather pillows, two quilts, a new cast iron Dutch oven, candles and a beautiful blue plate. Mr. Vanderburg held his gifts, a saw and hammer, three hens with a dozen biddies, till the last. He also sold John a cow due with calf at a low price, and promised to bring several sheep in the fall.

Their destination was Sharpesburg Township in the northwestern section of Iredell county. John liked the idea of starting their farm there. They would be close enough to his mother and Mrs. Coble, but still out on their own. There were mines and mills nearby, and if needed he could always hire on for extra money. The land was there for the taking if you worked hard and long and did not look back.

In May of 1833, Elizabeth Coble stood at the end of the lane, with her arm around Nancy and watched as Catherine climbed aboard the wagon that would take her to their first home some fifteen miles away. Timidly turning around several times, blinking back the tears, Catherine raised a small hand in good-bye. Before their last good-byes, Elizabeth took Catherine aside. Telling her again about her own mother's death, she also revealed the object, explaining where it came from and what it represented. It was her connection to her mother and now Elizabeth surprised Catherine with placing the object in her hand, as a parting gift. Almost at their destination, Catherine reached into her apron pocket, wrapping her hand around the tiny box, and knew that her mother would always be with her in spirit.

With their cow tied to the back, the wagon moved slowly. Their belongings were piled high and tied to secure their safe transport as well as the crated chickens. Elizabeth had given Catherine a beautiful silver-serving spoon that had belonged to her mother, Lady Laurent Falsworth. The spoon was now carefully wrapped and tucked in with the dishes among the linens and herbs.

As soon as cold weather arrived, John's brother Joel would bring his wedding gift, a young hog with several piglets. When freezing weather arrived, they would slaughter the hog and put the pork up in barrels full of brine, smoke parts of the meat and cure hams. Life was going to be good.

Sighting the land for the first time, excitement began building in

John's chest. Jumping from the wagon seat he stood and just took in the land around him. Far in the distance he could see the beautiful Brushy Mountains. Stooping, he scratched the ground scooping up a handful of dirt. It was wonderful dark, rich dirt. Letting out a whoop he reached to hug Catherine. They were finally home.

The land had previously been used as a home site and the remains of a burned cabin could be seen on the ground along with a partial rock chimney still standing. Looking around, Catherine saw signs where flowers had bloomed and then faded. She made mental notes of how she could transplant them and use them around her new house.

Setting up camp would take the remainder of the day. Until their cabin was completed, they would sleep under the wagon on pallets. John backed the horses until low-lying branches of the trees to give them some protection from the elements. Several yards out from the wagon, Catherine dug a fire pit and lined it with rocks. All of their cooking pots and supplies would be left in the wagon. Catherine spent an hour arranging the wagon so that she could easily get to her supplies. She carefully tucked away her precious supply of salt and herbs, safe from the elements and anything else that might go snooping around in the wagon, then pulled an oiled cloth over the back of the wagon.

For the first cooked meal on their land Catherine fried bacon, roasted potatoes and baked biscuits. She proudly set her new Dutch oven on the ground next to the fire pit. Mixing her dough, she pinched off pieces and placed them inside the greased pot. Setting the three-legged pot at the edge of the fire she placed the lid on tightly and laid hot coals on the lid. Soon the aroma of baking bread filled the air.

Sitting by the fire they ate their meal and watched the sunset. Catherine told John that she was anxious to get started.

–*I just want to do everything right and for it to be perfect or at least almost perfect.*

John hugged her and laughed, as he was just as impatient.

–*You'll get your chance. Just be patient.*

Later that night they pulled their pallets from under the wagon looking at the stars. The air smelled clean and fresh and a huge moon shone in the sky.

The next morning John took care of the animals while Catherine fixed breakfast. The crated hens had produced three eggs that were quickly put to use. Soon they were eating eggs with leftover bacon and biscuits. Though, as yet, there was no roof over their heads, it felt so good to be out on their own. Catherine wanted John to be proud of her strengths, knowledge of cooking and keeping house that she brought to the marriage.

As John was returning from fetching water from the creek, he spotted horses in the distance. He waved and received a like greeting. David and Alexander Lackey had come to welcome the Stampers to the neighborhood. It was their land that John was leasing with hopes of buying. The brothers lived just across the county line in Alexander County which adjoined Iredell.

Much to Catherine's delight, they brought with them two small apple trees ready to be planted, a good-sized cutting from a rose bush and a cloth filled with flower seeds. Also wrapped in a cloth was fresh apple cake from Alexander's wife, Margaret. Both men were well respected in the community and experienced farmers who proved to be highly successful in whatever endeavor they chose. Being second generation in America the men spoke as most in the area but accented certain words with a slight Irish brogue acquired from their father, which Catherine loved to hear. Carefully unwrapping the cake, Catherine inhaled the sweet smell of apples and cinnamon, a mouth-watering mixture.

The brothers were short, with bowed legs with and Alexander walked with a cane. Their Irish heritage was evident in their light strawberry blonde hair, streaked with silver. Each man sported a short beard and both bragged of having a large family. They loved to tell the stories about their 'triple' cousins. Their father was one of three Lackey brothers; Thomas, William and George; who married three Stevenson sisters; Ann, Nancy Agnes and Margaret. They referred to all the children from these marriages as triple cousins. Laughing, they often told stories of all three families gathering together with nearly thirty children among the brothers.

As they walked the land with John, the brothers made suggestions for the best location of the barn in relationship to the cabin, corncrib and storage building. Alexander seemed to be the most vocal about locations.

–Ye'll not be wanting water runoff from the barn headed down a hill toward your water source.

Nodding, John agreed that this was a wise observation. A spot was pointed out as the best place to locate the cabin so that it would be within sight distance of the creek. And the smokehouse should be near the cabin.

Looking over the cow and checking out the crate of chickens and biddies, on the back of the wagon, all met with the brother's approval and with a slap on the back and a handshake they were on their horses and headed home. Giving a final wave, they promised to send their womenfolk to visit.

The second night on the land was spent sitting side by side staring into the fire and talking for hours of all their plans. As soon as the cabin was under roof, John would tackle building a table and chairs during the evening hours. They were fortunate enough to have brought a bedstead along with a mattress.

After breakfast the next morning, Catherine began gathering supplies for some much-needed items. She had already seen several small, spindly oak trees nearby. Kneeling by the first small tree she began stripping the bark and peeling the fleshy wood into strips for weaving baskets. Once there was enough, they were placed in a bucket of water to thoroughly soak, making them pliable. After dinner, she would begin the task of weaving baskets.

John sat by the fire mending a harness while Catherine began weaving the reeds in and out to form an egg basket. The night air was cool and on the breeze came the scent of honeysuckle. Far away a dog could be heard barking and John stood and looked in the direction of the sound. Finally the night grew quiet and they lay down in exhaustion quickly falling asleep. At sunrise John opened his eyes to see Catherine stoking the fire and putting on a pot of water for tea. Another day had dawned bringing them one day closer to living their dream.

Working from sunrise to sunset with his new wife by his side, John began the chore of cutting trees for their home. Catherine led the horses, pulling the logs from the field. A week had passed since they moved onto the land and there were almost enough logs for the cabin. Several logs were laid aside for milling as John had promised Catherine a wooden floor.

Standing and looking at the growing pile of logs, Catherine breathed in the scent of freshly cut wood. It was a wonderful smell, fresh and sharp to the senses. Looking down at her apron she could see spots of sticky sap covered with dirt and stretched out her arms to look at the sticky sap on her hands, now filthy and black. Her palms were covered in blisters and her back ached. Tonight she would bathe her hands in salve and then cover them in strips of rags.

Scrapping in the dirt, John laid out the size of the cabin, marking where they would begin digging the root cellar. After three days of constant digging, a nice root cellar, with walls that went straight down, was completed.

Several days later, neighbors came to help with notching the logs. Gideon Solomon, who came to work the logs, also brought his wife to visit with Catherine and officially welcome her to their community. Jemima Solomon was almost as wide as she was tall. Catherine bit her lips in hopes of keeping the smile from spreading across her face at seeing the size of the woman. Climbing down from the wagon Jemima's backside hid the entire wagon wheel and the side of the wagon dipped low as she stepped to the ground. Poor Gideon almost disappeared beside his large wife. Standing only an inch taller than Jemima, Gideon was slender, small boned, but wiry. He was neatly dressed and smiled as he turned to join the other men, his hat bouncing on his head, two sizes too big.

As the men placed logs Jemima chattered away. Soon it became quite clear that if you wanted to know what was happening in the area, just ask Jemima. Catherine smiled sweetly as she watched Jemima's triple chin flap and wiggle as she talked.

–Miz Catherine, you can call on me for any favor you might need. You'll soon find that I'm well respected within the neighborhood and my husband is held in the highest regard. And I'm pleased to be able to advise you on certain unpleasant people. Now take Katie Stewart for example....

Speaking rapidly Jemima only stopped long enough to take a breath. Bubbles of spit collected in the corners of her mouth and she wiped her mouth every few minutes with a plain white hanky. As the afternoon wore on and on the low hum of Jemima's whispered advisements continued. Catherine tried to smile only at the appropriate times but the exaggerated body movements and the flapping chin and occasional dribbling of spit had made it difficult. Sitting very erect it was evident that Jemima was cinched in as tight as poor Gideon could pull on the corset. Catherine smiled as she mentally envisioned the size of the corset stretched to its full length. Jemima reached over and patted her on the hand, thinking the smile was a form of acknowledgment.

Trying to keep her eyes directly on the face of her guest was proving to be almost impossible. The top of Jemima's head had only slightly more hair than some balding men. It was quite evident that she had dusted crushed charcoal on her scalp to try and hide the thinning hair. It looked just awful and she smelled of wood smoke. That afternoon Catherine heard about each and every family in the area and had yet to make a statement on her own, only to smile and nod.

Later, as the Solomon's drove off, Catherine waved with one hand while placing her other hand over her mouth. Once they were out of sight, she burst into laughter. John soon joined in her mirth. While moving the logs, he would glance in the direction where the two women were seated and chuckled inwardly at seeing the look on Catherine's face. With a big grin, Catherine looked at John.

−Ask me anything. Ask anything about anyone. Oh, I can now tell you everything about anyone within ten miles. And I also know what not to do if my hair starts thinning!

Within a few months of arriving on their land, a decent sized cabin stood in a clearing with a small barn and smoke house not far behind. John took great pride in the glass windows that he had carted all the way from Salisbury, which was by far their biggest expense. It was his first gift to Catherine, and one she desperately wanted.

John paced off an area for the kitchen garden, then sliced through the untouched earth with a sharp plow while Catherine gathered rocks from the freshly turned earth. They hoed the ground, laid out the rows and established a modest, but practical garden. They would plant beans, corn, beets, onions, carrots and potatoes. In the fall turnips, greens and cabbage with an area kept separate for herbs that Catherine would use not only for cooking but also medicinal purposes.

Rounding up and tending to the chicks was a chore every day, though spreading corn out beside the cabin helped keep the chicks in that area. Hopefully they would lay their eggs in nearby weeds and be easy to find. At night they roosted in a small open chicken coop safe from predators. As soon as they saved some money for building supplies, a more permanent enclosure could be built for the chickens.

The milk cow, due with calf any day was another responsibility. Allowed to graze freely, the cow was rounded up at the end of the day to be put in the barn. Milk from the morning and evening milking was placed in a crock and set in the cool creek water, shaded by low hanging branches. Next summer they would build a small springhouse, divert the creek to run through the bottom of the house and have a place that would not only be cold for their staples but safe from animals. John also had an idea for a small pond just large enough to raise carp and catfish.

On the left inside cabin wall, John began digging a root cellar. There would be a trap door in the cabin floor with a ladder leading down into the cellar. Here they would keep their stored vegetables cool, safe and preserved. John had also cut wood for a stacked fence he would build around the kitchen garden to keep the cow at bay.

At first light, John was up and out the door plowing and planting. Seeing his dream of a big farm, he worked most days on only a few hours of sleep. With Catherine always at his side, John worked with the determination of ten men. Things were going well.

On Saturdays their pace quickened. Sunday would be their day of rest and worship so they worked harder and longer on Saturdays, thinking it would make up for the coming day off. At sunset they would go to the creek walking the banks until they came to a small-pooled area. Here the weekly pleasure was soaking in the creek and Catherine especially looked forward to washing her hair. Just being able to scrub her skin all over was a long awaited pleasure. Both John and Catherine considered bathing a necessity so during the week they washed their face, hands and arms in a basin at the cabin. At night they used a basin to wash away the daily dust on their feet before climbing into bed.

John helped Catherine into the wagon on Sunday morning for the thirty-minute ride to the nearest church. It was the third Sunday of the month and Preacher Icenhour would be there today. Catherine enjoyed meeting everyone and the women especially made her feel welcome.

After the service they shared a meal together with the women eating together. Just being with women, sharing food and catching up on news was something Catherine truly looked forward to. There were two other young brides in the group which helped Catherine feel less shy. But the person who made her feel the most welcomed was the widow, Nanny Grindstaff. There was something about the elderly widow that drew Catherine. Nanny was short with stooped shoulders and walked with a cane, which she claimed was not for support but more for protection.

-I can fend off dogs and old men with one whack of my cane.

Nanny's eyes crinkled at the corners when she laughed and her tiny white teeth showed. Although she had lived the life of a farm wife, her skin looked like that that of a lady of leisure, smooth and pink. Never had anyone seen Nanny without a small, ruffled cap framing her face. She looked exactly like what you would imagine the perfect grandmother to be and she always smelled of lemon balm. Yes, Nanny was someone that Catherine definitely liked.

The men gathered in groups, discussed the weather, crops and local politics. Offers would go back and forth for barter or trade; seed, tools, animals and labor. Often they discussed the latest methods of building and clearing the land. Their new community was close-knit and there were many offers of help whenever a harvest was in progress or a need was voiced.

The churchyard was filled with playing children, carefully watched over by their mothers. Most times a fiddle and guitar would appear and there would be music and singing. Catherine enjoyed listening to the women talk about tending their gardens, preserving their food and rearing children. Maybe one day she would be able to brag on a child.

It was usually late afternoon by the time John and Catherine got home from Sunday meeting leaving only a few hours left till milking time. Catherine changed into her work skirt and shirt, slipping her arms through her apron and putting on her everyday bonnet. Together they walked the woods usually not far from the cabin, searching out herbs, roots and berries. Of course it was the Sabbath, and they would not dig or pick but merely look and remember the location. There were times that they just sat on the rocks by the creek to watch the water flow past. Catherine would hold these memories close in her heart.

Chapter 4
Unexpected Catch

Early one Saturday morning several neighbors asked John to join them fishing on the Catawba River. The idea of fishing was great but he just felt there was too much to do around the farm. Finally, Catherine had to just push him out the door. He was not sure that he even remembered how to fish since it had been so long. Reluctantly, he saddled his horse and was off for a morning of fishing and fellowship.

The group rode for an hour before sighting the river. One of the men, Simon Oliver, had a favorite spot and led them to a shady spot on the bank. The men spread out and John went to sit beside Andrew McClelland. The McClelland family was well known throughout the county and each McClelland family consisted mostly of men. Andrew was the oldest of twelve children, and had only two sisters. Standing nearly six feet tall, he had a large barrel chest and long blonde hair that he pulled to the nap of his neck and tied with a cord, and large hat that shadowed his face.

Digging into a bag Andrew drew out a plain wooden box filled with dirt; large pink worms crawled out. Within a few minutes the two men were sitting on the bank with their lines in the water. It had been months since John had felt so relaxed and now he was glad that he had come. The men talked about their land and families. It was interesting to hear these older, more experienced farmers share with John their knowledge of the land.

It was such a relaxing day that John was just before dozing off when he happened to spot what looked like a large piece of paper moving rapidly with the current. Andrew spotted it at the same time but thought it looked like cloth. Both men watched as the object floated down stream and became caught on low-lying tree branches. Just out of curiosity they walked along the edge of the stream toward the branches.

-Ha! I was right. It is cloth and it looks like a piece of someone's shirt.

Andrew hopped down in the water and started to wade over to the spot and pick up the cloth. Suddenly he made an odd noise and jumped back.

-There's a dead body caught in these limbs!

Quickly John called to the other men and they came running. With Andrew still standing in the water the others tried to find a position on the bank that would give them a good view of the body. Finally they all were in the water and pulling at the tree limbs. The body broke free and John grabbed at the sleeve to keep it from floating away. Pulling, John and Andrew brought the body to the bank and the other two men helped pull the body onto the grass.

Slowly turning the body over they looked into the face of a young girl, probably no more than thirteen or fourteen-years-old, with her throat cut from ear to ear. The fabric of her clothing showed signs of slashes and her undergarments were gone. Quickly Simon Oliver took his jacket off and laid it over the lower part of the girl's body. Andrew volunteered to ride into town and find the constable.

Two hours had passed and finally the men sighted Andrew in the distance followed by four other riders. It had been a long and tense two hours. John could not help but think about Catherine at home, alone and he wanted nothing more than to get on his horse and leave.

The local constable was Addison McLain, who was in his early fifties, tall and wiry with a dark bushy mustache and dark bushy eyebrows. He walked toward the men with a worried look on his face. After introductions had been made all around; McLain stooped down to look at the body. The girl lay on her back, eyes and mouth open with the slit in her throat gaping open.

The constable lifted the coat from the lower half of her body and then dropped it back in it place. Shaking his head he stood and faced the men.

   -This girl is Frances Woodward and she's only thirteen years old. Her parents have been looking for her the last two days and we've had men out scouring the countryside looking for a clue as to where she went. Guess we know now. Oh how I dread facing the Woodward's.

The men were quiet and just watched as the sheriff and his men searched up and down the creek banks. A wagon was seen approaching the group and one of the constable's men identified the wagon as being part of their group. Gathering the men around him, McLain dropped his head and cleared his throat. When he looked up his eyes were watery and he began to speak in a shaky voice.

   -Gentlemen, we surely have a madman in our midst. We've tried to keep it quiet but this is the fourth child found in this condition

within three counties and now everyone needs to know.
John felt a tingling in his extremities and recognized the feeling of
fear.

The fishing party watched as the girl was wrapped and tenderly placed in the wagon. They began the hour-long ride home and in silence. At the crossroads John separated from the group and headed home.

Catherine was in the yard digging around her flowerbed when John arrived. Nanny Grindstaff had walked over to visit and was sitting on the ground at the edge of the flowerbed. Running across the yard John reached down and pulled Catherine to her feet not even seeing Nanny sitting there he held her close and tightly. Catherine, somewhat embarrassed, began pushing him back and asking what was wrong. It took several minutes before John could tell her all that he had seen that afternoon.

Refusing the request to stay at the Stamper farm, Nanny insisted on going home and walking was just fine with her. She had not expected such a loud "No! You're not"! Catherine had grown very fond of Nanny and she felt a kinship she could not explain. Nanny was in her mid '70's and had no kin. All were dead – her husband, son, brothers and sisters. Living alone in a modest house half way up the road, she managed to scratch out a small garden and survive.

Before sunset John hitched the horses to the wagon, and they took Nanny home. Helping her down from the wagon John told Nanny that he had to make sure her house was empty before she went in. Not one to be easily spooked, Nanny announced that she would handle anyone who stepped on her porch and showed John a large rifle she could barely lift. Satisfied that Nanny's house was secure, the Stampers headed back to their farm.

Even though all of the victims had been very young girls John still would take no chances with Catherine's safety.

–You can't go anywhere unless you have someone with you.
Promise me that you'll do that.

Smiling, she promised and hugged him around the waist.

Chapter 5
Going to Town

It had been weeks since John and Catherine had been to town. On Saturday they were planning a trip to buy supplies and just look around. The week crept by slowly for Catherine and she wanted Saturday to come quickly. All morning she had been cutting herbs and binding them in small bundles for drying. The loft was a perfect place to hang them to dry and there were forty bundles hanging, already dry and part of these they would sell in town.

The day before, Catherine had baked bread and cooked a stew. She planned to stop on her way to town and to check on Nanny Grindstaff taking her food and a few bundles of herbs. Climbing down the loft's ladder Catherine's mind was filled with thoughts of all she had to do before they left. Outside on a rope strung between two trees, she was airing their quilts. Still deep in thought as she headed for the quilts, she pulled them from the rope, folding each one carefully.

Twenty feet away John stood watching Catherine and realized she was so deep in thought she had not even seen him. Very quietly he came behind her and put his arms around her waist. To say he was surprised was an understatement. With lightning speed a fist was thrown over Catherine's shoulder smacking him in the right eye, then a backward kick to the shin. Letting out a yelp in pain and hopping on one foot, John lost his balance and hit the ground hard. Catherine was almost back to the porch before she turned around.

–Oh! Oh!

Then she sat on the steps and laughed holding her sides as the tears rolled down her cheeks.

–It's not funny. Not funny at all Catherine. I think you've cracked a bone in my leg and my eye really hurts.

Trying to stand, John's balance was off but he was able to catch himself before he hit the ground a second time. Sitting on the ground he was holding his wrist and moaning in pain. Catherine reached to help him up, but he pushed her hand away.

–Oh no. I can get up myself. If you help me, I'll probably have

broken ribs next.

Sitting at the kitchen table, John let Catherine place a cool cloth on his eye. Pulling up his pant leg, he inspected the large bruise growing on his shin and examined his swelling wrist. Catherine tried to keep a straight face but could not control her smile.

–It's not funny Catherine you could have really hurt me.

Seeing John limp out the door Catherine started to feel badly but not enough to avoid seeing the humor in the whole event.

Saturday morning broke with a bright sun and the promise of a beautiful day. John could smell biscuits baking and ham frying. John thought, "It's not Sunday," wondering what was up. Greeted by a table set with Catherine's best tablecloth and good plates, a feast was spread; fried potatoes, ham, biscuits and gravy, even a pot of strong coffee. Seeing the confused look on John's face, Catherine dropped her head.

–I'm sorry about yesterday.

Breakfast was a treat as they both cleaned their plates and lingered over the coffee. While Catherine cleaned up their breakfast dishes, John limped out to the barn to hitch the horses to the wagon. Waiting on the porch Catherine thought of all the places she needed to go in town. Buying buttons and thread were at the top of her list.

It was a beautiful day; on the ride to town John and Catherine chatted about the day ahead of them. They stopped briefly at Nanny's house to leave food and to make sure she was OK. Thirty minutes later they were in Statesville and trying to decide where to go first.

Standing on the corner a group of men were speaking with a very nicely dressed gentleman and keeping their voices low. Seems that the visitor had just heard of the tragedy several blocks away and had stopped the men to inquire. Walking in the direction of the corner John heard his name called. Looking up he spotted Andrew McClelland waving and walking towards them.

–Guess you've come to town because of all the news? Don't blame you. I'll be glad when this is over. John looked puzzled and told Andrew he had not heard any news.

Motioning for John to step away from Catherine so they could speak privately, Andrew walked a few feet away and then stopped. Lowering his voice, he began to tell John that two more girls had been found dead. One of them not three miles from John's farm and another in an alley two blocks away.

-She's still up there in the alley and they're waiting for Addison McLain to show up. He's been out in the county at the other murder spot.

Watching the men at the corner Catherine studied the nicely dressed gentleman. Slim and of a small build, his blonde hair was tucked neatly beneath his beaver hat. He turned so that Catherine could now see that he had a straight and pointed nose and that his face was long and narrow. Speaking loudly, he began telling the men that he was relocating to Statesville and opening a clothing store. Constantly pulling at his shirt cuffs, he fiddled with gold cuff links. He said that he had lived on a plantation just outside of Richmond and that he had decided to start his own business and leave the farming to his older brothers and father. Turning to look at Andrew and John huddled together speaking softly, Catherine noticed that John looked pale. What could Andrew be telling him? Walking over to the men Catherine placed her hand on John's shoulder and he jumped.

-What is wrong? You look as if you've seen a ghost.

-I don't think we can stay in town today after all. We'll go to the mercantile for your supplies and then we need to go home.

As John spoke he was held Catherine by the top of her arm leading her away from the men and down the street.

Sensing that something was terribly wrong Catherine did not question him. At the mercantile several women were discussing the murders and for the first time Catherine heard that another body was found not far from her home.

Once outside the mercantile John saw Andrew, smiling and walking briskly toward him.

-We're going to get help. That fancy dressed man is Lacy Reynolds and he knows of a man we can hire that will find this murderer in no time. He's even going to put up half the money. Says he wants to be a good neighbor. Addison can't handle all this and he needs help. Maybe we'll be able to rest easy again. John agreed they needed help, but the news made him feel no better.

John gathered their supplies and helped Catherine up on the wagon and headed home. Once out of town John began telling Catherine all the news of the murders. Both felt uneasy and Catherine slid closer to John on the wagon seat. They traveled back to their farm, silence but thinking about the families who had lost children. They stopped at Nanny's house and told her all they had heard. Catherine pleaded with her to come stay with them but the old woman would not budge. She insisted that she could handle trouble and shooed them out of the house and on their way.

Chapter 6
A Hanging

Two weeks after John and Catherine were in town there was another murder, just over the county line in Alexander County. A farmer had found a girl dead in his field, slashed from head to foot. The killer was no longer making any attempt to hide his victims. This weighed heavy on John as his land extended right to the county line and gave him concern that the killer might be too close. Most of the women in the neighborhood were near hysteria and kept their children within sight at all times. Catherine was also scared even though they had no small children; she feared for those around her, insisting that Nanny stay with them until the murderer was caught. Finally John convinced Nanny to come but was quick to be told that she would be back at her house the day the devil was caught. Knowing that a murderer was possibly walking on their land terrified Catherine.

Sitting on the porch one Sunday afternoon, John spotted Cabel McIntosh, who owned a small spread several miles away, riding up the road. John invited him to come and sit on the porch but Cabel said he was just out spreading the news.

-Lacy Reynolds was good to his word and has hired a private detective from Raleigh, Mr. Holland, and they're all out at the last murder site looking around. Most of the men in the neighborhood have agreed to help in any way they could and I thought you'd like to know.

John thanked Cabel for the information, but said he could not leave just now, but would ride over to see him soon.

There really was no reason that John could not go and join the men he just did not want to leave Catherine and Nanny alone at home. The last victim had been in her late teens John was taking no chances, as the killer appeared to be working his way up to older victims.

Tuesday brought about a beautiful day and Catherine had extra butter and eggs laid out on the table, while waiting for John to come in from feeding the animals. She told him they had to go to town, as the butter and eggs would not keep and besides, they could use the money for supplies. Hesitantly John agreed and hitched the horses to the wagon, and they were on their way. Nanny wanted to return to her house and begin her weekly wash. John left Nanny standing on her porch as he drove down the road. Looking back several times he could not shake an uneasy feeling.

Seeing Main Street in the distance they could also see a large crowd gathering and heard voices raised in angry tones. Stopping about two blocks away John helped Catherine from the wagon and gathered her baskets from the wagon bed. The crowd had started to quiet and John stationed Catherine at the door to the mercantile telling her to go inside and then he headed over to see what was happening.

Not being able to see over the crowd, John stood on a hitching post and stretched to see what all the commotion was about. Lying in the street, bloody and with his clothes torn, lay Lacy Reynolds. Nearby stood the fancy detective Mr. Holland holding a large barreled gun and pointing it in the direction of Lacy. Then a shot was heard and the men started to scatter. Addison McLain came pushing through the crowd with five other men.

–*You have no right to this man. Not now. Not ever. He'll be tried fairly and the first man to think that he won't be, had better think again.*

Several of the men who accompanied Addison began picking up Lacy and heading for the sheriff's office. A new jail was still being built and the cells had no doors yet so they would put him in the storage room located in the back of the office and would take turns guarding the door. But first they poured buckets of water over his head and watched the water wash the blood from his face and hands.

People were everywhere on the streets talking about what they had just seen and how it had come about. Angry voices proclaimed there should be immediate justice. John began pushing his way through the crowd making his way back to the mercantile.

Lacy's money had brought the finest detective money could buy to solve the murders of seven people. Foolishly he had thought that by being in the middle of the investigation and hiring a detective, they surely would not look in his direction. The first victims had been small children, then an older child, then two girls in their early teens and the latest a girl seventeen–years–old. Mr. Holland took notes from everyone as to what they had seen or heard. Only one thing had been left behind at one of the murders. The fourth girl to be killed was clutching a fancy button possibly pulled from a coat or vest. This is where he started his search.

Early that morning, unable to sleep, Holland decided to walk through the town and just clear his mind. So many thoughts ran through his mind of how the crimes were committed and what clues he felt might lead him to the killer. An uneasy suspicion was growing within him about who committed the crimes and he needed to sort things out. Cutting through the alley and heading for the stables, Mr. Holland stumbled upon a sight that took his breath away. Lacy Reynolds was sitting astride a female and holding a bloody knife. He was covered in blood and just as the detective saw him Lacy dipped his hands in the slashed neck of his victim and began bathing his face in her blood. Not hearing anyone behind him Lacy went down without a fight, when the billyjack struck the back of his head. Mr. Holland grabbed both of Lacy's arms and proceeded to drag him out to the street.

Soon shopkeepers began arriving and discovered Lacy tied to a porch post at one of the shops. Before long there were dozens of men gathered round. Then someone shouted about justice, then another shouted back about justice now and before he knew what hit him Lacy's bonds were cut and he was drug to the center of the street. Boots kicking in all directions as they aimed for his stomach, sides, back and head; within seconds he was unconscious. When constable appeared the crowd began moving away from their intentions.

Down the street Jesse Weisner was running, waving a paper and calling to the constable, that a notice had been received from Richmond, Virginia.

"WARNING of one Lacy Reynolds, gone mad, and now identified as a murderer. He could now be in North Carolina or Maryland. Having murdered several of his Negroes he is suspect in the torturing and killing of one certain eight-year-old girl from Richmond Proper. Several counties, with their borders joining Henrico County, all within riding distance of Mr. Reynolds plantation, have produced other children found slashed and dead. All with their throats cut and their bodies were found to have slashes. Beware as Lacy Reynolds is The Richmond Slasher.
Sincerely, upholding the law, your servant,
Henry Lippard, Sheriff, Henrico County VA."

John and Catherine had completed their business, loaded up their supplies bought with the butter and egg money and headed back to the farm. They had managed however, to hear how Lacy was caught and all the gruesome details.

Several days later with the scene still fresh in his mind, John took grain from the storehouse and headed for the mill. Far in the distance he could see a black ribbon of smoke in a clearing. Thinking there could be someone in trouble he headed in the direction of the smoke. Pulling to the side of the road he headed through the thin band of trees running beside the road and stepped into the clearing. Seven men stood in a group staring at a ball of fire swinging from the limb of a huge oak tree. Burning flesh soon filled the air and John gagged at the smell, backing away.

Townsmen had stormed the sheriff's office in the middle of the night, over powering the night guard and dragging Lacy from the storage room. Throwing him into the back of a wagon tied and gagged, they headed for the countryside and an isolated meadow. Here they stripped him of his clothes and cut away his manhood, doused him with oil and put a rope around his neck. But before they pulled the rope to lift him off his feet they set him on fire. The Richmond Slasher would never kill again. It was not the way to do things and John felt sick at the sight but he also felt a sad sense of relief.

Chapter 7
Preparing for Winter

With the mystery of the recent murders solved, although it ended in such a disturbing way, life could again return to normal rhythms and there was much to do. When not in the fields with John, Catherine would work in the kitchen garden hoeing to keep the weeds under control. She had carved out a small square of dirt next to the front porch where she carefully planted the flower seeds given by the Lackey brothers on their visit. If all went well, there would be flowers of all colors. As this year's blooms turned to seed, she would gather some seed for another season. Maybe next year she could add a flowerbed to the side of the cabin.

June and July saw lush growth spring forth everywhere with vegetables making their first appearance. Wildflowers grew at the edge of the field and yielded color and fragrance. The ground was rich and the yield was great. It seemed they worked nearly round the clock caring for this bounty, falling exhausted into bed every night. John seemed to be asleep by the time his head hit the pillow but Catherine would listen to the night sounds of crickets. She always smiled when the breeze brought in the fragrance of honeysuckle and with it sweet memories of her first summer knowing John.

August was almost at an end and September would signal the beginning of harvesting grain. Wheat was most precious and would be needed to see them through the winter. Neighbors would help with the threshing and sacking the grain for storage. The men would gather an armful of wheat and with a scythe cut it off about three inches from the ground. With one slashing stroke they would have the perfect size shock of wheat.

The heads of wheat were piled in a circle on a wooden pallet. The pair of horses were led, walking round and round, tramping on the wheat. The men would turn the wheat with a fork constantly making sure all the grain was exposed to the horse's hooves. Occasionally a flail would be used, beating the grain until the grain fell below the straw onto a canvas.

The seeds could then be separated from the chaff. Filling a winnowing basket with seed the women would throw the seed in the air allowing the breeze to blow the chaff from the seed, which fell back in the basket.

Beans were strung together and then hung to dry in the hot air, turning them into what was referred to as leather britches. Annie and Margaret Lackey, Jane Stevenson and Cynthia Lackey came from their farms to help Catherine prepare for the drying. Catherine truly enjoyed their visit; she liked Annie and also Margaret as they were open and friendly, talking constantly and laughing. Cynthia was their niece and Jane was Margaret's cousin. They made Catherine feel as if she had known them for years. With them came the gift of apples that would be sliced and dried for a treat in the middle of the winter.

The women sat directly on the ground in a circle and spread the beans in their laps. In the center a large cloth was laid out and as the beans were strung they were tossed on the cloth. Once the beans were sufficiently dry they were hung inside the cabin. Next year if they continued to prosper, John would build a drying house.

Near the end of harvest, a Saturday evening was set aside for shucking corn which was a big event in the neighborhood and was something everyone looked forward to attending. Most families in the community rotated to each farm helping with the huge job of shucking.

Nanny Grindstaff had come to help Catherine with the meal they would serve after the shucking. Most of the women brought bread or sweets and someone always had a fiddle or banjo, for dancing afterwards. Shucking was left to the men as they sat around a fire pit. Most sat with a huge chew of tobacco in their cheek; a spit can was passed around the circle. Part of the women busied themselves with carrying the shucked corn back to a wagon and a few carried off the corn shucks. Songs were sung and stories were told that had been handed down for generations. Jugs of cider would be passed and there was always much laughter and the telling of tall tales.

One of the men, Rupert Deal, told the story of his uncle Cyrus Deal. Born into a family of traders Cyrus decided early on that traveling the back roads trading goods just was not what he wanted. Oh he liked the trading but being lazy it was just easier to sit on the porch whittling away and watching the day go by. As luck would have it Cyrus had a huge mule named Glory and that is how he decided to make his living, by selling the mule.

One thing he knew about animals; they were loyal to one thing.... food. And this he had learned by mistake. Mrs. Deal had baked an apple cobbler for Cyrus' lunch and promptly took the hot dish to the barn. Calling to him Mrs. Deal gently laid the hot dish on a sack of grain and went back to the house. Up in the loft Cyrus could smell the apples and cinnamon. Pitching another forkful of hay he stopped and climbed down the ladder with his mouth watering at the smell of the cobbler. Turning around his mouth dropped open and his eyes widened. There stood Glory up to his eyeballs in cobbler. Sitting on the ground Cyrus laughed and laughed but Mrs. Deal did not think the happening funny at all.

The next time she baked a cobbler Cyrus took Glory a small bowl and watched as the mule licked the bowl clean. What a funny thing.

Several weeks later Cyrus decided to sell Glory and rode the mule over to the next county where he knew animals were being bartered and sold. That day he received top dollar for the mule. Leading him over to the new owner Cyrus reached into his pocket and unwrapped a piece of apple that had been dusted with sugar and cinnamon which the mule quickly snatched. It was a long walk home but Cyrus made it there by dark.

The next morning when Mrs. Deal went outside to milk there stood Glory. And so the adventure had begun. Cyrus would sell the mule but not before feeding him apples laced with cinnamon and the mule would leave in the middle of the night, finding its way back to the Deal farm.

–My Uncle Cyrus sold that mule fifty times before folks caught on! Everyone laughed at the story even though they had heard the same a dozen times before. The men continued to shuck the corn and swap tales.

At the end of the day the wagon was full of corn. Gathering around makeshift tables the men heaped their plates full of food and sweets then sat on the ground enjoying the meal together. Nanny Grindstaff busied herself pouring milk for the men and Catherine made sure there was enough on everyone's plate. Later they visited and sang songs and several of the men showed off dance steps their parents had brought with them from Ireland. The women clapped and kept time to the rhythm and they all laughed. The evening ended with many hugs and handshakes as their neighbors made their way back to their homes.

Part of the corn would be used for feed and part would be ground for cornmeal. The potato cave was now almost full with Irish potatoes, sweet potatoes and onions. Straw was laid in layers among the vegetables separating them and helping to keep them preserved. A barrel full of sauerkraut now stood ready inside the cabin along with a small barrel of flour and dried herbs hung from pegs on the wall. Looking about at this bounty Catherine felt safe and secure.

When the weather tuned cold, John's brother Joel was expected to bring them a hog for slaughter. The meat, brined in barrels, or smoked would last through the cold winter.

Chapter 8
Atlee

John was now beginning to think of setting traps for rabbits and walked the woods looking for the best spots. He had walked far from the cabin and needed to turn back. Fresh meat in the middle of the winter was very appealing so he would just check out one more spot. Pushing his way through the brush he squatted down to touch a faint print in the dirt. Rabbit? Maybe. The air was crisp and cool with the smell of fall in the air.

Before he could straighten back up he heard it. Wailing. He held his breath so as not to have the sound of his own breathing in his ears. Then a scream cut through the silence. Now John had a direction to follow as he picked up the sound again.

Slowly he rose to a half-stooped position and quietly pushed aside brush, weeds and small trees. Stopping he listened again. Now he could hear sobbing, talking and pleading. Walking a few more feet he listened and then dropped back down to a squatting position as soon as he saw him.

A small clearing lay about fifty feet away and it appeared to be a burial place. John could see mounds with big rocks marking their spot. Off to one side there was a young boy who looked to be possibly no more than fifteen. With frenzied motions the boy dug into the ground with hands that were unusually large. His face was round with wide set eyes, a full mouth showing large yellow teeth with big spaces in between; sheer madness in his eyes.

His dirty blonde hair stuck out all over his head and looked dry as straw. Stopping his digging, he took his fist and pounded the side of his head, then ran his fingers through his hair. Sitting on his knees in the waist deep hole he screamed again pulling at his hair and showing his large teeth. Moaning and wailing loudly, the boy began digging again.

Just as John decided to back away from his hiding place the boy suddenly shrieked and started pulling something out of the dirt____ pulling an arm, then a shoulder and finally a head appeared.

Frozen by such a horrible sight, John stared, not being sure if the body was that of a man or a woman. Then the boy shifted and he saw the head better and it looked like a man with open eyes full of dirt.

John continued to stare, his mouth open. The boy began wiping the face of the rotting body with his hands and skin began to slide off revealing muscle. Then he began cradling the head and shoulder rocking back and forth, speaking softly. John's nostrils filled with the smell of the corpse. This was not a situation he wanted to investigate nor did he want to get caught looking.

The sound of voices drifted over with the wind and a voice could be heard calling out "Atlee". What was an Atlee? That was a word John had never heard before. Stretching up and shifting to get a different view from the brush he saw the first man walking toward the clearing.

There were four men in all and they motioned to one another to spread out while still making their way toward the clearing; the last man led a horse and followed slightly behind. The first man stepped into the clearing and looked relieved when he saw the boy. He spoke softly to him.

-You come on now Atlee. Everything will be all right. We're just going to help you out of that hole.

Hearing that, the boy stood and started swinging blindly at the air screaming and standing on the arm and shoulder of the corpse. Digging his feet in for balance he dislodged the arm from the body. Then the four men were on him, wrestling him out of the hole and pinning him on the ground.
The boy they called Atlee was screaming and fighting for all he was worth. One man produced a rope and they began tying Atlee's hands and feet. Next they dragged him to the horse and laid him across the horse's back. Then holding the reins and leading the horse, one of the men started walking back the way they had come with Atlee screaming, "Daddy! Please don't let them take me."

The air was still and rank with the smell of rotting flesh. Pulling small pieces of cloth from their pockets, each man tied the cloth around his face to block the pungent odor from their nostrils. Rolling up their sleeves they started digging out the body. At this John stood up, making his presence known and objecting to what they were doing.

Abram Crouch separated himself from the other men and slowly approached John identifying himself and holding his arms out, palms up.

-Now we've got a problem here but I think you see the wrong thing. This here rotting man is Atlee's daddy. The boy is now an orphan with no family except across the water. When the fever

looked like it was going to take his father, Atlee lost all reason. His Ma and brothers had just died from the fever. We'll have to burn the body this time and bury the bones where the boy won't find them. Have to. This is the third time he's found the grave and dug up the body. He'll be locked in the smoke house over at the Stevenson's for a few days. He won't hurt you. He's just looking for his daddy.

John was speechless but nodded and turned to leave pushing through the brush. He quickly tracked backwards and was relieved to see home in the distance. The things he had seen today he would keep to himself.

Chapter 9
Biscuit and Pork

Near the end of the month, John's brother arrived with his large draft horses pulling a two-wheeled cart with a wobbly crate sitting in the cart box. A large hog and two piglets snorted and squealed from inside the crate. Joel lived less than five miles away, but with the weight of the animals, the trip had been slow going and took nearly two hours. His gift for John and Catherine was finally being delivered. Now there would be pork for the long winter. A pen had been prepared beside the barn to hold the hog, who would be fattened up with daily feedings of nothing but corn and milk. The piglets would be allowed to run loose and root during the day.

Backing the cart next to the pen John and Joel prepared to unload the pigs. The back of the crate slid up and away leaving three sides standing. Patiently the pigs snorted and watched. Eyeing the distance to the pigpen, Joel said the cart position was just right. John tuned and lifted Catherine to sit on the front of the cart for balance and with both men pushing up on the crate, the pigs spilled out into the pigpen.

Faithfully every day Catherine fed the large hog and each day he grew fatter. After several weeks the temperature had dipped to below the freezing mark and a call was sent out to neighbors for help in slaughtering the hog. The men would handle the butchering while the women prepared the meat.

The carcass was hoisted up between two poles and tied to the cross- bar and left to drain. Next the men seared the hair off the hog by pouring boiling water over the carcass then, scraped the skin with knives to remove the bristly hair. On a long table they laid out the hog and cut off the head and feet, which were put into a large pot to boil and would be used for souse meat, a pickled mixture of pork meat. Next the entire animal was split down the middle on the underside, entrails were removed. Then the hog was turned over and split. The meat was cut into manageable pieces and put into barrels of brine.

What would become their bacon was covered with salt and placed in a cloth bag on a hook in the smokehouse. Two hams were salted and wrapped in cloth then dropped into a cloth bag to hang upside down in the smokehouse. Later that evening they would build a fire in the smokehouse using hickory wood and corncobs. The fat was set aside for soap making; nothing went to waste.

While the men were busy cleaning and packing the meat, Catherine and the other women were making sausage that would be smoked. The Stampers provided a meal for those who helped and Nanny had helped Catherine cook the entire day before. Since the cabin was not large enough to hold everyone, a table had been set up in the barn; they would take their meal there out of the cold. Two large cast iron pots were filled with hot coals from the fire and placed on the dirt floor of the barn. The pots were not meant to heat the large structure, but to take the edge off of the cold.

It was a good time to catch up on all the neighborhood news. Someone had received a newspaper from Salisbury and promised to bring it to the next church meeting to share. They ate their fill and then some. The women, excited to be together, chatted away.

By late afternoon the families climbed into their wagons and headed to their own farms. Catherine stood on the porch and waved until the last wagon was out of sight. John began dismantling the yard table and putting away their butchering tools.

The cabin was filled with the smell of cooking pork. There would be a large meal tonight and leftovers for several days. Calling to John, Catherine placed a tin plate on the step with the steaming bread, for him to sample. She had baked enough bread to last them through several days and carefully wrapped each loaf, placing the extra on a shelf.

Smoke poured out the chimney and John could smell the cooking pork all the way to the barn. Hearing Catherine's call, he put away the last of the tools and headed for the house knowing there would be a full table of food tonight. Looking up John caught movement out of the corner of his eye. There, sitting on the ground licking the empty tin plate, was a huge rough coated dog. As soon as the dog saw John he trotted toward him, tail wagging in all directions. Realizing that his biscuits were now resident in the dog's stomach, John let out a laugh. Reaching down he scratched the dogs' ears and said "come on boy, and meet the cook."

Opening the cabin door, John stepped aside and the dog trotted in.

–Looks like we just might have ourselves a dog. If he stays he'll come in handy with hunting and be a good warning sound here at the cabin. Think I'll name him Biscuit.

Catherine turned to see the large dog sitting, with an expression that looked like a smile.

The dog walked over to Catherine and sniffed at her apron. Reaching down she rubbed the top of his head.

—My goodness, he feels like a brush, rough and stiff, and he's so big.

Long ago John had seen another dog that resembled Biscuit and he remembered the breed was called Wolfhound.

In the darkness of the cabin with only light from the fireplace, John and Catherine snuggled beneath the quilts on the bed. It would be a somewhat sleepless night for John; he woke several times to feed the fire. Biscuit, snoring, made himself right at home in front of the fireplace.

As Catherine was frying up side meat for breakfast, Biscuit had kept her company. In fact he had decided that by her side was the best spot in the whole room. Tail wagging and eyes begging, she finally gave in and gave him a leftover biscuit. With his prize clenched tightly in his teeth he trotted to the door, patiently looking back at Catherine.

—Oh, so you're too good to eat in the house are you? Out the door you go.

Biscuit seemed particular about where he ate and still a little skittish, so he took the food and headed off to the porch. Catherine left the door cracked to let out some of the heat from cooking.

Smiling she went back to preparing breakfast; it might not be a bad idea to have a dog, especially to let us know when someone was coming. Throwing another log on the fire sparks popped out, and Catherine quickly moved back bumping into Biscuit.

—Finished already? Well, there's no more for you this morning. Smiling at the dog Catherine checked on the biscuits in the Dutch oven. Riiippp.

—Why you..... Biscuit had his teeth firmly planted on the back of Catherine's skirt and was pulling.

—Let go! Let go you bad dog! Biscuit hung on to the skirt and was pulling backwards with Catherine trying to twist to swat him on the head. Determined, the dog put all his strength into pulling and Catherine fell on the floor.

The door banged open and John grabbed her by the arms and

continued pulling Catherine out the door, then picked her up and ran to the yard. John pointed to the roof. Cinders had dropped from the chimney onto the roof, smoldered and then flamed.

Rushing over to the rain barrel, John dipped one bucket in and then another. Catherine was dragging the ladder, then propped it up against the cabin wall and John was up the ladder in a flash. Swoosh. One bucket then the other bucket. Catherine filled another bucket and handed it up to John. One more bucket. Now there was just smoke and the smell of burning cedar.

Relieved, John and Catherine sat quietly on the grass and surveyed the damage. Biscuit was nowhere to be found.

Finally, John stood up and crawled back up the ladder to the damaged area. Pulling off the burned shingles, he tossed them into the yard. Next, he examined the area around the burned spot. He split wood for twenty new shingles and carried both tools and shingles up the ladder with him to make repairs.

While John was busy with the roof, Catherine was hunting for Biscuit, who was now hiding and would not come when she called. Now she wished she had not swatted and hollered at him. Finally out of desperation, Catherine went into the house and brought out some biscuits and side meat. Placing the plate on the porch and wrapping up in a quilt, she sat down under a tree in the yard. Lowering her chin to her chest made her look as if she was asleep. Playing possum just might bring Biscuit out of hiding.

Just as she thought, within a few minutes Catherine could see out of the corner of her eye the big dog pulling himself along on his belly. As soon as he grabbed up the meat Catherine grabbed him by the scruff. Hugging him tightly she talked soothingly to him and stroked his neck. Soon the tail was thumping on the ground and she was covered in wet kisses.

–I think I love you Biscuit. You saved the house and me today. That surely deserves a piece of meat every day.

Chapter 10
Going to Court

Coming in from the field John saw Catherine standing on the porch speaking with a man. Coming closer he recognized the constable. Dropping his tools at the edge of the yard he headed toward the cabin to see if something was wrong.

The constable had been riding to various farms in the county since early morning. Court would be in session next week and he was handing out jury summons. John would be serving on a jury next week. Catherine assured John that she could handle things while he was gone and besides she had Biscuit for protection.

On Monday morning, John rode to Statesville and reported for jury duty. Here he saw a few of his neighbors, also enlisted for duty. Never having served on a jury or even been inside the courthouse for that matter, John felt a little awkward, but knew that jury duty service was an honor.

Sitting with eleven other men, John watched as the constable brought before the judge the docket for the day: theft and more than one divorce. Now this was something that John did not look forward to hearing. This was going to be a long day.

John looked around the courthouse room; it was very official looking. He had ridden by the building many times but never thought he would find himself inside and part of the procedures. There was a commotion at the back of the room and the judge called for order. Turning, John saw three gaudy dressed women settling down on one of the benches.

Court was called to order and the first case, Bently vs. Bently was called. Caroline Bently was primly dressed wearing a black frock and black hat. She fanned herself and tucked her dark hair under her hat. Trying not to look directly at the judge she kept her face lowered, hiding her features. Everyone could see her blushing. Speaking softly she told how her husband, Ephram, had taken up with three Miller sisters who were all working on a neighboring farm. She claimed that when her last child was being born, almost at the very minute, that the sisters came to her house and enticed her husband to go to the barn with them. He now had a disease of which she could not speak and she could no longer allow him in her house and certainly not around the children.

The defense called one of the loudly dressed Miller sisters to the stand. At the back of the court room one of the women stood and walked to the front to take the witness stand. Clarinda Miller was short and round with a huge bosom. Smiling she displayed discolored teeth and she looked as if she had rouged her cheeks heavily to match the color of her hair which looked none too clean. She told the court that yes, they did go to Mr. Bently's farm but he had invited them to come and see about some work.

—When we went to the barn to see what was needed he pounced on us all. Being afraid of not getting the job, well, we naturally let him do what he wanted. But he told us he would not have touched us if his wife had not been involved with some darkie.

A loud 'thunk' was heard and everyone turned to see Mrs. Bently prostrate in the floor with her lawyer fanning her face with some papers. The judge called for a recess and the lady was taken from the courtroom.

John stared as Mrs. Bently was carried out through the doors of the courtroom. This case might be about the worst thing he would have to sit through and it was certainly not something he would tell Catherine. Of course, if Jemima Solomon was within ten miles of this place, everyone would surely hear about it anyway. Standing to stretch, John spoke with the other jurors and then sat as the judge returned to the bench.

At this point in through the back doors came Mrs. Bently escorted by her father Elijah Blankenship, who helped his daughter back to the prosecution table. When the judge called the court to order once again, Mr. Blankenship took the stand.

His testimony was that his daughter had fled to his house with her children. His son-in-law was a drunkard and failed to provide properly for the children. Elijah proceeded to tell the court that the son-in-law had gone to Kentucky to work and when he came back he brought a darkie with him who had a newborn mulatto child. He put the woman right in his own house and dared Mrs. Bently to say anything. Then Mr. Blankenship looked between the judge and the jurors and lowering his voice explained that he wanted no further scandal; his other daughter's husband was going to run for State House of Representatives.

Now the defense had their turn and they called Ephram Bently to the stand. Tall and impeccably dressed he sat and crossed his legs, saying that his wife was a cold woman with him and that he had

suspected she had taken up with one of the darkies on his farm. At this Caroline Bently stood and screamed he was a liar and was quickly restrained by her father and the lawyer. Banging the gavel on the bench the judge called for order. Ephram grinned and looked at her and said she shouldn't be ashamed of where her desires go. Then the entire courtroom erupted and the judge beat his gavel again on the bench calling for order and threatening to clear the courtroom.
During all the testimony gasps could be heard and women hid their faces behind their fans or dipped their heads so that their hats covered their faces. Men looked at their feet and sat very still.

When all was said and done the jury went to a side room to talk things over. John did not like being put in this position and said as much to the other men. But he knew that he would have to decide with the others what needed to be done.

After only thirty minutes the jury returned to the courtroom and the judge read the verdict and rendered the penalty. Ephraim Bently was guilty of lying with a prostitute and adultery. He was ordered to pay for the support of his children and would be allowed to see them until they were old enough to tell him they did not want to see him anymore. Caroline Bently would be granted the divorce. The final part of the verdict brought a verbal curse from Ephram as the judge ordered him to sell forty acres of his land and give the money to Caroline Bently for her keep. Then as if to add salt to the wound the judge fined him $10.00 for profanity in the court room.

The gavel banged again and the judge called for the next case.

Sliding into the seat at the plaintiff's table was Adolphus Gwaltney a short, frail looking little man with an accent. He had come to court to sue Joseph Hoke who appeared to be three times the size of Mr. Gwaltney. Lumbering in from the back of the room Mr. Hoke took a seat at the defense table and it was quickly noted that he was more than half the size of the table. His lawyer scooted over; his nose wrinkling, cutting his eyes toward Mr. Hoke.

The plaintiff's attorney stood and addressed the judge explaining his case. Next he called Mr. Gwaltney to the stand to testify.

-Well, it was like this. I had a big old sow that was just before having her babies. I had let her roam around my property rooting out nuts and such, but always put her in a pen at night. The old sow was so big that she could not go far, was slow and had never wandered before. On a piece of paper, I had marked the days, keeping track of when the sow should give birth.

On the very day that the piglets should arrive, Adolphus left his house to go slop the hogs and the sow was gone. He looked everywhere and finally went over to Mr. Hoke's farm to see if he had seen the sow.

But what he found was his sow nursing twelve little pigs right inside Mr. Hoke's pigpen. He knew it was his pig as she had a black spot on the underside of her chin. Banging on the door of Mr. Hoke's house, Adolphus demanded that Hoke open up the door.

Joseph Hoke opened the door and Adolphus hauled off and socked him in the stomach hollering that he had stolen his sow. Then Mr. Hoke got his gun and ran Adolphus off his land.

–And I ran like the devil was after me until I got home. But he's still got my sow and now the 12 babies are getting big. I need those animals to feed my family. He stole my sow.

The next witness was Simon Olivett a neighbor to Mr. Gwaltney. Yes, he had seen the sow and yes it did have a big spot on the underside of its chin. There was no mistaking that the animal belonged to his good neighbor and not to Mr. Hoke.

Finally Joseph Hoke was called to the stand. Walking toward the witness stand the floor creaked under his massive weight. The platform visibly sagged when he stepped up. His huge size swallowed up the chair and he appeared to be just sitting on air as his wide legs hid the chair legs and his backside hung over all sides of the chair. Sweating profusely, he mopped his face with a dirty cloth he pulled from his pocket. He had a distinct odor of cooked cabbage and general filth, all of which could be smelled ten feet away.

Now that he had everyone's attention he proceeded to tell how he just looked up and saw the sow standing beside his pigpen. Being a good Christian and not wanting to see any animal mistreated or starved, he put the sow in the pen. Seeing as how the sow found him and decided to have the babies in his pen he figured they all belonged to him. Why, he was always a good neighbor but that Adolphus Gwaltney had hit him in the stomach, and hard. There was not even enough time to say hello.

–Looking at him I could tell he had gone mad, so I got my gun.

Shifting his eyes right and left John could tell that the men on either side of him felt just like he did. It took all his willpower to keep a straight face. This man actually thought they would believe that he feared little old Adolphus Gwaltney and that he was just rescuing a wayward animal. Whew! John could smell him all the way to the jury box.

This time the jury was out an hour. But what they were deciding was if any one of them had ever smelled anything quite like Joseph Hoke. Snickering they tried to get serious and discuss the case but all the laughter just was not out of them yet. Finally they sobered up enough to talk about the testimony. No one had actually seen Mr. Hoke steal the animal; they decided to take a vote.

The judge asked for both men to rise and then he read the verdict. The jury finds for both the plaintiff and the defendant. The sow and eight of her piglets will be turned over to Mr. Gwaltney and Mr. Hoke will keep the remaining four piglets. Since there was not a witness to theft, both of you will share. Turning to look directly at Joseph Hoke, the judge told him that he was a lucky man to have neighbors who were fair.

—We can't actually prove that you stole the sow but if it had been left up to me, I would have put you in jail for theft.

The gavel banged once again and the next case was called.

Next was the case of Bolick vs Bolick. It seemed that Barnard Bolick had known that his wife was pregnant by a Mr. Caldwell of Rowan Co. After his wife had the child, he chose to raise the boy as his own and not let the facts be known. But now his wife was prostituting herself to several men in the community, mainly Addison Kerley, James Yount and William Gabe. Barnard wanted his wife put out of the house but he wanted to keep the boy.

After Mr. Bolick left the stand, the three men named in his testimony were each called, one after the other and asked if what had been stated was true. Each man took the stand and admitted they were involved with Mrs. Bolick and on a frequent basis. One man proceeded to volunteer that she sometimes sought him out twice a day. Mrs. Bolick sat unaffected by their testimony and merely smiled. An audible gasp could be heard from two women seated on the third row.

This case went by quickly as no one fainted or shouted accusations. The jury was out only twenty minutes and the judge read the verdict. Divorce granted in favor of Mr. Bolick and he could keep the boy. Mrs. Bolick was to leave the house immediately and could not see the boy unless Mr. Bolick gave his permission. The judge told Mrs. Bolick that she needed to seek soul cleansing.

Martha Etta Gaither was the plaintiff in next case of Gaither vs Gaither. The defense table was empty and Mr. Gaither was nowhere in sight. Martha took the stand and told that her husband drank and gambled their money away. He had been seen selling off her family heirlooms to purchase whiskey. The children were terrified of him and took to hiding whenever he came into the house.

The final insult came when told her that an animal would be more desirable that her. All this had taken place in front of Mrs. Gaither's sister, Miranda Crouch. Mrs. Gaither then hit her husband with a cast iron pan and forced him out of the house. He was now living in Tennessee and had written to say he would never be back and was going to marry a woman who pleased him. She wanted a divorce so that she could marry Alex Sherrill, a God—fearing man. And she also wanted the farm, which she would sell to help make a new start in another state for her and Mr. Sherrill.

This last bit of testimony was just simply too much for some to deal with in a public place. Several women and even a few men stood and left the room when Martha gave voice to her husband's crimes. Even the judge seemed affected at hearing the man's crimes spoken out loud. The jury was not out of the courtroom five minutes. It took only a moment to gather their thoughts, whispering back and forth. Back in court they passed a note to the judge and the verdict was read. Mrs. Gaither was granted her divorce and the judge declared to her the farm and the rights to sell. With a final 'bang' of the gavel the judge mopped his forehead with a handkerchief and stepped from the bench

With court adjourned, John was now free to go and was greatly relieved that his duty was over. He hoped to never ever hear of such happenings in the community again, not to mention how thankful he was that he did not actually live near any of those folks.

Arriving home several hours later, John could smell supper cooking and was glad to be back in familiar surroundings. Before he could get the horse unsaddled he heard Catherine calling to him, running from the house to the barn and completely out of breath.

 —*Is it true? Was there really something said about Mr. Gaither and his   animals?*

John just stood with his mouth open.

Chapter 11
Missing

The wind was cold and the trees looked stark with a never-ending blanket of leaves covering the ground. The killing frost had been early this year and the weeds around the cabin were brown, dying to the ground. Catherine loved mornings like this, when you could see your breath and it was so still you could almost hear your heart beat. Pulling her cloak tightly together she stepped softly through the weeds, looking for eggs. The chickens had been making a ruckus for the last hour but now had scattered.

The air was silent and Catherine picked up her last egg and turned to go back to the cabin. The arm around her throat cut off her air and she tipped the basket, eggs rolling in all directions. Grabbing at the arm around her throat she pulled, gasping for breath. She could see the sky as she was dragged backward then crumpled as her eyes swam in the black.

John had been busy in the barn and was now taking the milk to the house. Catherine would take the cream and set it aside. Within a day or two she would have enough to churn and fresh butter would be on their table. Pushing open the cabin door John opened his mouth to tell Catherine of the large pail he had gotten that morning. The cabin stood silent and empty and the fire was dying out.

Quickly John placed the pail on the table and went out the door standing on the porch calling for Catherine and then listening. Silence. Panic began to rise in his throat and he started around the corner to check the west side of the cabin. And his first thought was to see if the eggs were still there. Quickly looking around he saw indentations in the weeds where the hens had sat to lay their eggs.

Now his heart began pounding and he scanned the area, suddenly seeing a path through the weeds leading toward the woods and up to the hills.

Following the path he came across the egg basket. His voice betrayed his emotion as he called Catherine's name. Only silence. Biscuit was also gone and hopefully was with Catherine, safe somewhere.

He was now wet with sweat, more from emotion than exertion. An hour had passed and his searching had yielded no other clues as to where Catherine had gone. His throat was raw from calling. Exhausted, he could not think of what to do next. Collapsing on the ground he sat with his head in his hands. Help. He had to have help. Looking up he prayed out loud, "Help me Lord".

John rode over to the next farm and the alarm went out from there. Within the hour neighbors quickly responded to the need. Now he had help and they would find Catherine. It was now after one o'clock and the late afternoon would bring colder air.

Several men gathered together to look and discuss the area and what their next move should be. One man stepped from the group, who John recognized immediately. Abram Crouch. This seemed to unsettle John and he took one step back.

-Mr. Stamper, do you remember me? Abram Crouch? We'll find your wife. We've let this thing go too long and we're going to fix it today for good.

At this John just stared at Abram wondering what in the world he was talking about. Catherine had only been gone a few hours. How could he say it had been going on too long? Then the weight of the words hit John, with as much force as a punch to the stomach and his face went white. Atlee! That's what he meant. Atlee had taken Catherine.

John grabbed Abram on each arm and demanded to know what exactly he knew about the situation. Then the story unfolded.

Atlee took to the hills after the death of his father. Some say they saw him go in and out of a small cave. Others saw him among the rocks, sleeping. But they knew exactly the area where Atlee had been seen.

Several of the men spoke up telling of how Atlee had stolen chickens right in front of them. Another claimed to have found a piglet, half eaten raw. Then there was the grabbing of a woman. A few weeks back he grabbed Jocasta Alexander when she was hanging out her wash. Dragging her away, all the while calling her mama but the Alexander's dog rounded the corner and attacked. Jocasta fainted when the dog latched on to Atlee.

They weren't sure what happened from there except the boy was gone when they found Jocasta out cold on the ground, with the dog standing guard.

Then there was the recent grave incident. Atlee had definitely crossed over a line of reason and would probably never return. He was most likely insane and could now be dangerous. At hearing these things John began shouting that they needed to find him now before he hurt Catherine.

The men spread out so as not to miss any signs that Atlee had passed through with Catherine and started making their way to the hills. One man shouted that he had found pieces of eggshells and the group switched directions to where the find was made. Off to the right they could see a wide path through the weeds. Atlee was most likely dragging Catherine.

Now John was panicking. He raced ahead of the others following the flattened grass and weeds. Then there was nothing. No trail. Not a sign, only a steep hill with trees and rocks. Faintly in the distance a dog could be heard barking. Abram Crouch knew exactly where to go.

–There's a very small cave just top of the hill right where the large trees stand and that's where he'll be.

Men began advancing on the hill with John leading three paces ahead, with Abram close on his heels. The sound of the barking dog grew louder. Near the top they suddenly saw a small opening in the hill. Rocks partially covered the entrance but it could be seen. And just sticking out the opening was a pair of bare feet, black with dirt. Atlee's feet. Biscuit was bouncing back and forth, barking and nipping at the bare feet.

Abram called Atlee's name, but the feet did not move. He called again and started slowly walking toward the entrance to the cave calling softly to the boy. Still no sound could be heard except for the dog. Then Abram began shouting for the men to come quick. Large rocks had dislodged from the hill striking Atlee on the back and blocking the entrance. They could hear Catherine calling for help inside the cave. Atlee was mashed flat from the middle up. Only his legs and feet could be seen.

Quickly they began looking for something to use as a lever on the rock. Biscuit danced around the men whining, then running back to the cave entrance. The men advanced up the hill and stood balancing between the hill and rocks. With one foot on the ground and the other on the rock, they wedged a tree limb between the rock and the ground and began to move the rock slowly back and forth. With a last push the rock started to roll. Down it rolled, first over Atlee's legs and then straight down the hill. Now Atlee was now completely flat.

John stepped over Atlee's body to gain entrance to the cave. Catherine was sitting up against the cave wall not four feet from the entrance, her cloak held tightly around her. They reached for each other and John held her tightly. She was not harmed, only scared. John quickly scooped her up and stepped back over Atlee's body.

As the men gathered round, Catherine quickly began telling the details of her ordeal. Atlee had come from behind, grabbing her around the neck and then dragging her from the field. At first she could not breathe and passed out. He stopped and tried to shake her awake and as she came to she began kicking and screaming, while being dragged through the weeds and grass. Suddenly Biscuit appeared, snarling and racing in circles around them. Atlee kept telling her, "It's all right mama, I'm going to take care of you."

When they got to the cave, Atlee shoved her in and sat down in the entrance with Biscuit crouched behind him ready to spring. Catherine said she began praying out loud. At the sound of her praying, the boy backed to the entrance of the cave, just sitting, and staring at her with Biscuit growling in the background. Suddenly there was a rumbling noise and then splat. Atlee was flat under a big rock. God had answered her prayer.

John turned to the men giving his thanks. He watched as they went to gather the body of Atlee from the cave entrance. They would bury him on top of his father's bones hidden away, deep in the woods. John could not help but feel sad for the boy. Poor child did not have a chance, but he would have been dead sooner if he had hurt Catherine and the rock hadn't got him. Even if he had to borrow he would somehow get the money to build a fenced-in chicken coop near the cabin.

The next few days were hard for Catherine. She had been brave and dry-eyed during the entire ordeal but now that it was over, she cried off and on during the day and was afraid to go outside. Biscuit was her shadow, never leaving her side. Nancy Lackey and her niece Cynthia Thompson, came to visit and brought a stew, bread and apples. John had to drag Biscuit from the cabin as he would now growl and stand in front of Catherine.

Seeing Nancy and Cynthia was a blessing to Catherine. In the absence of her mother Elizabeth, she was grateful for the company of the two women. The afternoon passed with pleasant conversation and Catherine did feel better. It would be weeks before she would feel safe gathering her eggs.

Chapter 12
Unexpected Joy, Unexpected Sorrow

Plans change. John had not counted on any babies right now, and was quite disturbed at the thought. This would certainly slow them down, but children were bound to come, sooner or later. And when the child came four months early, it was so tiny. The baby was bluish grey in color, and slightly shriveled. The pain that seared deep within John was almost unbearable. A tiny face that looked like his own but cold and pale in death.

Out in the barn, he pieced together a tiny wooden casket; Biscuit lay whining, sensing something was wrong. Catherine lay weeping being comforted by several of the neighbor women, each having experienced this sorrow. Alone at his own request, John chose a tranquil spot near a large water oak tree and laid his son to rest, quietly crying as he tossed each shovel of dirt in the hole.

Later that night after Catherine had fallen into an exhausted sleep, he marked the date in his Bible and searched the scriptures for comfort.
"I will lift up my eyes to the hills,
From whence cometh my help
My help cometh from the Lord,
Which made heaven and earth."

Two days later the sound of a wagon could be heard in the distance. Catherine's mother, Elizabeth was arriving to care for her daughter. Guiding the team of horses was George Campbell who had been visiting his brother-in-law Amos Vanderburg. Hearing of the recent tragedy he offered to deliver Elizabeth to her daughter. George Campbell's visits had grown more frequent to Vanderburg Plantation and his thoughts were now leading him toward making Elizabeth the next Mrs. Campbell.

At the sight of her mother Catherine began to cry uncontrollably. With arms folded tightly around her daughter, Elizabeth rocked back and forth giving the comfort that was so desperately needed. Whispering in her ear that God would bless her again with a child, she gently brushed away her tears.

With Elizabeth caring for Catherine, George Campbell offered his hand in helping with the chores. It had disturbed him greatly to see Mrs.

Coble so distressed at the news of her daughter's loss. George followed John around, helping with the chores, but both men worked in silence, each with his own thoughts.

As was the custom of the day when death visited a home, the women of the community came and took over the running of the house. This included cleaning, laundry, cooking and literally anything that was needed. The house seemed to be full of females. At lunch the women from the church arrived with food. Preacher Icenhour had driven over from his fourth week church and arrived shortly after the women. When prayers were said over the food, he also prayed for John and Catherine's peace.

Before leaving, the preacher offered to say a prayer over the baby's grave. Against the advice of every woman in the room Catherine insisted on seeing the grave and hearing the preacher's prayer. John picked her up from the bed and carried her to the tiny grave. Standing, he held her tightly, feeling her tears drop on his arm. Preacher Icenhour read scripture from the book of Job.

> *"Naked came I out of my mother's womb,*
> *And naked shall I return thither:*
> *The Lord gave, and the Lord hath taken away;*
> *Blessed be the name of the Lord."*

And then reading from II Samuel.
> *"...Can I bring him back again?*
> *I shall go to him, but he shall*
> *not return to me."*

By evening all had left. Catherine now dry-eyed, was sitting up in bed. Reaching for her Bible on the bedside table, she opened the book to Psalms. Here is where she would begin her healing.

Five days later Catherine rose from her bed claiming that she wanted to be beside John in the field. All John ever knew about women having babies was that you did not see them out of bed for weeks. But she would not be dissuaded. John watched as she tied on her bonnet, grabbed her apron, pulled it around her still protruding belly and marched out the door.

Only four full moons passed before Catherine was once again leaning over the nightjar losing her insides. Another baby was on the way. John was filled with joy and anxious for this baby. Five months later Catherine collapsed in the garden; John carried her to the house as her blood dripped on his boots.

Within the hour Eliza Harrell, the neighborhood midwife, arrived bringing along several neighboring women. John had insisted that Catherine have a real midwife this time. Standing in the yard he paced and waited, feeling good that Eliza was with Catherine. Shortly before sunset Catherine delivered a son. Eliza tried to prepare John for what would surely happen. This baby was too small to live. Five hours after his birth the Stamper's second son died.

Late into the night John sat beside the bed watching Catherine's exhausted sleep. Rubbing his rough hand over her smaller one, he looked at the calluses on her palms. Catherine was forever misplacing her work gloves. John's thoughts went back to the tiny baby. There would be no son this year and a tear fell and landed on the bed.

It was two years later before a healthy Stamper son would finally make it into the world. When he was three weeks old Catherine strapped him to her back to milk the cow and gather eggs. Smiling, John looked on his strong wife as a gift from God and one he had never expected. Three times she had tried to give him a son and the third time they were blessed.

As soon as they received word, John's brothers and mother came to see the newest family member. Brooks and Hugh had been waiting for another male to carry on the Stamper name. Catherine's mother arrived not far behind them and wept with joy at seeing the baby. God had answered their prayers and had given them a tiny soul to love.

Their joy increased when John's younger brother Brooks, announced his intentions to marry Catherine's sister, Nancy. When Powell Alexander Stamper was four months old, he slept on his mother's shoulder as his parents watched with much pleasure the marriage of Brooks and Nancy. The newlyweds leased land that adjoined John's farm; Catherine was thrilled. Now she would get to see her sister often.

Chapter 13
Soap and Tall Tales

Working dawn till dusk, John and Catherine worked their land and each year brought a higher yield in their crops. They had worked their land eight years, and all their hard work was paying off. Catherine tied a rope around the waist of her toddler and attached one end to a tree, leaving him to play with a kitten. Strapping yet another newborn babe on her back she began her chores, keeping her four-year-old by her side and the toddler within view.

With three growing children now in the household an increase of supplies was heeded. Soap was something that Catherine never seemed to have in abundance. Today she would make enough to last for quite some time. Granny Millsap, along with her companion Peaches, would come and watch the children during the soap making. Since Granny was frail, fifteen-year old Peaches accompanied her mistress wherever she went. Small and weak in her body Granny made up for it all in spirit and wit, with stories that would be handed down from generation to generation.

Brooks brought Nancy to help with the soap, stopping along the way to pick up Granny and Peaches. Nancy now had two little girls with another baby on the way. At only thirteen months apart Mary Beth was two- years -old and Peggy was one-year-old. For helping, Nancy would be given part of the soap. The work was easier for two than one, so Catherine welcomed the chance to work with her sister.

The sisters busied themselves preparing all they would need to start the job. Ashes from the fireplace had been saved and Catherine poured them in the ash hopper. Water was poured into the hopper with a pan underneath to catch the liquid that ran out. This process formed the lye that they would use.

Granny Millsap, steadying herself with a cane, led the children over to a large tree in the yard. Peaches carried the smallest child and held the hand of another. John had built a small sitting bench at the base of the tree and Granny plopped down on the bench; one of the toddlers crawled into her lap. It seemed that all children loved Granny Millsap.

Nancy stoked the fire around the big black pot. The first step was to render the fat. Catherine placed a small amount of water along with pork fat in the pot. Throwing more logs on the fire Nancy backed away as the heat became intense. Catherine constantly stirred the fat, which began to melt, then boil. With a long wooden paddle Catherine scraped the bottom of the pot, bringing the fat at the bottom to the top. More wood was placed under the pot. By now Catherine and Nancy were wet with sweat. Both hoped that one day they could rely on daughters to do this chore.

Looking around the yard Catherine spotted Granny sitting on a bench, one child curled in her lap, the others sitting at her feet. Storytelling had made her famous in the community and the children sat very still listening to every word. With a voice that had a singsong quality Granny began telling about her childhood. Before she was ten years old, she was burned out of the family cabin by Indians and washed away in a river and trapped in a tree by a charging bull. Each tale was vividly described. Gazing up at her the children could see the twinkle in her eyes.

Granny, of course, had not been born Granny. Her name was Rebecca Stikeleather Millsaps, and she had been born in October of 1766. Her father had been one of the first settlers in the area. Jacob Stikeleather and his wife Martha settled in Rowan County, North Carolina and began their family eventually having nine children. They were a jovial and close-knit family. Being one of the local cordwainers, Jacob was always in demand and was now teaching the oldest boy the craft of shoemaking.

Indians, still living in the area, were always a concern so a small fort was built in a centralized area. Here the settlers would find shelter from Indian raids, which came with more frequency as the Indians struggled to keep the white man off their land.

It was a beautiful late spring day and the Stikeleather children were helping bring water from the river to the cabin. Jacob had gone to a neighboring farm, to sell a calf. Margaret was preparing to do the family wash and the children were laughing and singing silly verses back and forth as they carried their water from the river. Once the pot was full and a decent fire was started, the children scattered to play in the yard.

Rebecca had decided to go back to the river, walking further down from where they had gathered the water. It would be nice just to sit with shoes and stockings off, feet dangling in the water. She was tired from hauling the water and wanted to just sit quietly. In the distance were sounds of her brothers and sisters playing.

The water flowing over Rebecca's feet felt good still dangling her feet in the water, she leaned back on the grass and was soon asleep. Her eyes popped open as she thought she heard her named called. Listening for the call again, she heard only silence. Lulled back to sleep by the sound of the water Rebecca continued to lie on the grass. Later she awoke with a start and realized that everything around her was now very quiet. Pulling her feet out of the water she turned and listened for her brothers and sister's voices in play. Standing she decided it was best to go and see why everyone had gone inside.

With her stockings and shoes in her hand, Rebecca turned to see rolling black smoke in the distance. The cabin was on fire and she could see Indians in the distance. Squatting in the tall grass at the edge of the bank, with her heart pounding, thoughts of what to do swirled with through her head. Unfortunately, it had been decided for her as wet grass pulled her feet from under her and into the river she went, headfirst.

Although the river was not deep at this point but swift as Rebecca flapped her arms wildly as the current pushed her toward the bank, she grabbed a low-lying branch. Clinging and shouting for help over and over, she suddenly remembered the Indians. Afraid to shout again she clung helplessly, struggling against the rapid water. Finally realizing that she had to save herself, she pulled herself from one branch to another until she could finally plant her feet on the bank of the river and pull herself ashore. Drenched and with scratches from head to toe she sat down on the bank and cried.

There was nothing else to do but try to find help. Suddenly she remembered Fort Dobbs. That must be where everyone had gone when Indians began raiding. Scrambling up the bank and through the tall grass, she stopped only to get her bearings. Fortunately, she had not drifted too far away from home and could soon identify her surroundings.

Fort Dobbs was well constructed with a ten-foot high wooden wall topped off with sharp points. A huge double gate stood open allowing people to freely come and go, trading and visiting. If Indians attacked the settlers an alarm went up and folks ran to the fort seeking shelter before the large gates were slammed shut. On a walkway four feet from the top of the wall men walked and watched for settlers, quickly shouting orders to open the gates if they spotted a neighbor running toward the fort.

Rebecca could finally see the fort in the far distance and slowly walked through the trees. Without her shoes it was painful walking over acorns, rocks and roots. The stillness yielded only her soft padding along the forest floor, all except for the snort. Rebecca stood frozen and listened. Then another snort and a sound that sent her heart to her throat, hooves that were hitting hard on the ground.

Quickly she ducked behind a tree and peeked around to see a huge bull headed her way. Screaming she was frantically grabbing at lower limbs, trying to pull herself up, finally gaining about six feet between her and the ground. The bull snorted and pawed the ground. Then with a loud bellow and a burst of power he rammed the small tree shaking the limbs all the way to the top.

Holding on for dear life Rebecca began screaming for help. The bull continued to circle the tree stopping to paw the ground and looking like he was not going to leave. A new sound could now be heard in the distance, the sound of dogs barking and coming closer. The bull shifted its focus and slowly trotted away as if he suddenly remembered he was needed elsewhere. Rebecca watched but was too terrified to move. Soon the base of the tree was swarming with dogs, barking and jumping up on the tree trunk.

Within minutes several men were running toward a screaming Rebecca. Strong hands snatched her from the tree, turned and began running toward the fort. There were men leaning over the fort wall hollering," run faster, run faster". The fort's huge gates were partially opened and the men squeezed in with Rebecca in hand.

All those gathered at the fort began cheering at the safe return with one voice louder than all others. Margaret Stikeleather was running and crying out Rebecca's name. She grabbed her daughter and held on tight, as they both cried. Soon all her children surrounded their mother crying hanging onto Margaret's skirt. The tears were of joy but also of fear. Jacob Stikeleather had not come to the fort and Margaret feared the worst.

Then just as they thought that Jacob might never return, a shout went up from the wall to open the gate. Running at top speed, dragging a calf on a rope behind him, Jacob Stikeleather reached the gates of the fort. Once through the gates the exhausted calf collapsed.

With both Margaret and Rebecca crying, along with all the children, crying, they ran to Jacob. Joyous shouts went up and all gathered round to slap Jacob's back in welcome and relief. He laughed and hugged his wife and children. Jacob told them he had spotted the Indians a little over a mile away from his house. But there were more of them than there was of him so he dropped to the ground behind a fallen log dragging the calf down with him. Holding his hand on the calf's muzzle to keep her quiet he listened. With a muffled mooing the calf tried to wiggle free of his grip so he stuck his thumb in her mouth and just like a baby she quietly sucked.

Soon he saw the smoke and knew it was his cabin. Staying just within the tree line he walked quietly, pulling the calf behind him, until he could see the flames jumping onto the shingle roof. The Indians were nowhere in sight and he raced toward the cabin calling for Margaret.

But he could see that no one was there. Toys and wash were dropped in the yard and he knew they had heard the warning and were now probably at the fort. But first he checked an area behind the house. Here was a small ravine with heavy brush that would be their hiding place, if they could not make it to the fort. There was no sign of Margaret and the children.

Knowing he was at great risk he grabbed the rope around the calf's neck and started running in the direction of the fort. Why he kept holding on to that calf even he did not know.

Leaning back, Rebecca concluded her tale.

–And that was how my house was burned and I fell in the river and got treed by a bull, all within a few hours.
Granny Millsap grinned a mostly toothless grin and hugged the child sitting in her lap. The little ones sitting at her feet smiled back at her and Peaches sat grinning with the other children at Granny's tales. She had heard this same story a dozen times, only it was a little different each time she heard it.

Nancy and Catherine had been listening to Granny also as they stirred the melting fat. And they both knew it to be true. Almost.

Soon there was more liquid than fat and Catherine began dipping out the liquid pouring it into another pot which Nancy stirred. An hour later all the fat had melted and there were only crisp pieces floating on top.

Nancy poured the lye into the fat as Catherine stirred the mixture, ever so often raising the paddle to see how the mixture ran. If it ran off the paddle like water, Nancy would add more lye. Once the mixture was cooked it was poured into pans and pails and set to cool.

A small flat pan of soap was set aside and Catherine swirled rose-water in the mixture, giving it a pinkish tint. Once cool, the soap was dumped out and cut into chunks. A few pieces of the pink soap would be sprinkled with water and rolled between their palms until nice and smooth. Both women would keep one piece of the pink soap but the rest would be bartered or sold in town.

On Saturday there would be fresh soap for their bath and Catherine looked forward to the newly made scented soap to wash her hair. Sunday morning she and Nancy would smell like roses.

Resting on the porch steps the sisters surveyed their handiwork. Soap making was no small task by any means and both were grateful it was over. Brooks would soon be back to pick up Nancy and take Granny and Peaches back to their farm. Catherine gave some of the pink soap to Peaches and for Granny a jar of honey from John's beehives, some of the best in the county.

In the remaining hour before resuming their separate lives, the sisters just sat enjoying each other's company.

Chapter 14
Bad Times, Sad Times

Catherine seemed to have boundless energy. One-by-one she gave John the family that would help him gain his dream; land, family and a home. She was the most valuable thing that John had and he told her often.

When John and Catherine's fourteenth anniversary rolled around, there were three sons and two daughters: Alex, Gilbert, George, Mary Ellen and Susan. All were born screaming their way into the world, with a head full of black hair. Three small grave markers were now the only reminders of children that would for always be a bittersweet memory. The last marker was for a little girl named Rebecca, who was not quite two-years old at her death. With three growing boys and the two girls to help, John knew the need to increase their land was just over the horizon.

The years of struggle had rewarded John and Catherine with a comfortable lifestyle. Food was plentiful and money had been saved. A new glass window was now on the back wall of the cabin and two rooms had been added. On one anniversary, John had given Catherine a store-bought rug for the bedroom floor. At Christmas they could afford to buy fruit for the children and every fall and spring they bought new shoes for everyone. This past year they were able to send the two oldest children to school.

The Stamper family could lay claim to having one of the first cast-iron cooking stoves in the entire area. With abundant wildlife in the area, John trapped, hunted, and tanned leather in the winter months, selling his leather and furs, saving the money he made from the sales. It just seemed that life could not get any better. Life, though, would soon change and not for the better.

Drought and bugs ate at the crops two years in a row and on the third year the extended winter freeze nearly killed the Stamper family. A pig they had fattened all spring and summer was dragged from the pen in the middle of the night and killed by animals they could hear but not see. That pork would have carried them far through the winter, but now that was out of reach. John was worried. Time to rethink things before another freezing winter was here again and killed them all. Most of the money reserves had been spent just to survive.

The mines in the area were just about played out and could not be considered for extra work and mills in the area were not hiring workers. The Stampers were not the only farmers to feel the effects of the drought. Because they had saved money, John knew they were better off than many others facing the same situation.

In the middle of this new struggle word came that John's brother Hugh, had died. Hugh's young wife Cassie was only eighteen years old, with one baby crawling and another in her belly. Grief stricken she held her baby Lewis close and would not let anyone take him from her. Catherine was numb; she could not help but think that this tragedy could have happened to her.

Both John and Hugh were talented with their hands, and both could whittle a piece of wood into the shape of any creature in the forest. Hugh especially enjoyed working with wood. With a another baby on the way, he wanted to make a small toy for Lewis, something to occupy him while Cassie cooked. She was forever saying how Lewis clung to her skirts and it was difficult to cook while carrying him on her hip.

One evening Hugh took a small block of wood and began carving. He sat in front of the fireplace, taking off his shoes enjoying the warmth of the fire. Several hours passed and he had finally carved the desired shape. Feeling the need to stretch he stood dropping the knife on his foot. There was not much blood and hardly any pain. After looking closely at the cut and considering it minor he took a rag, dipped it in water, cleaned the cut, then put his sock back on and went to bed.

Within a few days Hugh could hardly walk. The foot was painful and swollen. Cassie placed hot, wet rags with crushed herbs on the wound. The area around the cut was discolored. The entire foot was hot to the touch, swelled and red all the way to his knee.

Two mornings later Cassie rolled over in bed only to see her husband's dead eyes staring at the ceiling. Hugh had died at twenty years old. And now they were burying him.

As dirt was shoveled into the hole, covering the casket, John held his mother close as she wept. Brooks and Nancy stood with Catherine and watched until the last shovel full of dirt was thrown on the grave. Older brother Joel stood alone at the back of the crowd. Cassie's father had come and insisted on taking his daughter back to his home. There was no way she could stay on the farm, broke, with a baby on the way and without a husband. The farm would be lost and Hugh's children faced an uncertain future.

Several weeks after Hugh's death, John and Brooks stood among the crowd of men as Peter Waggoner, Cassie's father, fulfilled his duty as administrator of Hugh's estate. What little had been accumulated during two years of marriage was now being sold to the highest bidder. John's eyes misted as Hugh's work tools were put up for bid. How hard he had worked to establish his home and to begin gathering what was needed to survive.

Looking around him, John saw neighbors from near and far. Brothers, Thomas and Burton Cook, Jonathan Goodman and George Robinson who had come from just over the county line in Alexander County. Local neighbors attending were James and Robert McNeely, David Kistler and Peter Waggoner's brothers, Lewis and Jonathan.

The Waggoner family loaded up the household goods that Cassie had chosen, and Brooks who could no longer watch this sad departure, quietly left. John stayed until the last wagon had disappeared down the road. Looking around at Hugh's farm, there was no trace of his brother; no tools, no animals. Even the hay set aside for feed had been sold. John reflected on this terrible event for a long time and thought of what Catherine would do if this tragedy ever came to her door.

Chapter 15
Scared

Several times during the next month John would ride over to Hugh's cabin, sitting empty and still. He sat on a tree stump and just looked around. There was such a sense of loss in his heart. What if it had been him? Would Catherine have been able to keep the farm and feed their children? He could not seem to shake these morbid thoughts.

John wrote a long letter to a Stamper cousin living in the Blue Ridge mountains, asking if there was work available there. Logging and brick making in Ashe County were abundant and times did not appear as hard in the mountains. Just before the first hard freeze, an answer to John's letter arrived. Quickly reading the letter, John told Catherine that a cousin had work for him. Before she could utter a word, John was out the door, headed over to see his brother Joel, hoping to persuade him to go along. Within twenty-four hours the brothers rode off, headed for the mountains.

Catherine was prepared to do what she had to do in order to see her children through another tough winter. And she worried about others in their family. Brooks and Nancy had moved to Catawba County to be near his mother, Mary Stamper. Being the youngest Brooks was fiercely protective of his mother. The last time Catherine had heard from them, she had learned that they too were having it hard and Nancy had yet another baby on the way.

Old man Locklear, a nearby neighbor, stopped by one morning and brought a letter from Hessie Stewart, the postmistress. Too scared to open the letter for fear it was bad news Catherine placed the letter on the mantel and went about her daily chores. Every time she came in the door she would glance at the letter propped on the mantel.

After the children had gone to bed Catherine took a deep breath and opened and read the letter. Laughing, tears ran down her cheeks in sheer relief. Hugh's wife Cassie had her baby. Another boy and she had named him Joseph Hugh Stamper. Cassie went on to write that she would stay permanently with her parents. Her mother needed help and she needed someone to help raise her boys. The letter ended with warmest wishes and an invitation to visit. Then near the bottom of the letter was an additional note stating that she was putting a keepsake for John in the letter in a small folded piece of cloth. Catherine took the tiny folded piece of cloth and carefully began to unfold it. Inside she found a lock of hair with "Hugh's hair" written on the inside of the cloth. Placing the lock of hair back on the cloth she carefully folded and placed it inside her Bible.

The days flew by and Catherine stayed busy. She was now doing double duty on many of the chores, but the children also pitched in with the chores. Alex, at ten years old was trying to do all that he could. He kept the fireplace well stocked with wood, just as John had done. . Behind Alex was Gilbert at nine and then George who was eight. They knew to rise every morning and feed the animals. The girls, Ellen and Susan, were six and four. The boys could milk the cows and slop the hogs and even at six Ellen could gather eggs. Susan mostly whined and wanted to stay on the porch with her doll. Most days Catherine depended on Alex and Gilbert to watch after the others and the dogs to watch over the boys.

Work was plentiful and as quickly as John made the money he bought what little supplies he needed, then sent all the rest to Catherine. At least his family would still be alive this spring instead of frozen or starved. Carefully watching his money, John planned to have enough for a hog and seed for the spring planting.

He wrote Catherine as often as he could to tell her how much he missed her and the children. In one letter he told her of dreaming about the farm.

   –There were acres of golden wheat swaying in the wind. People were coming to me asking to buy the wheat because it was so good. Everything on my farm was bursting forth with more fruit than anyone in the county had ever seen before.

Ending his letter, he told Catherine that he wanted the dream to become real for his family; he wanted a bounty of food. Promising he would be home soon, he signed his letter, 'your loving husband, John Stamper'. Sitting with his letter in her lap Catherine pictured how he looked the day he left. Before he was out of sight, he turned and raised a hand in farewell.

Chapter 16
Unwelcome Guests

John had been gone from home for three and a half months. Catherine had wanted to believe that within a month of leaving he would return. But she also knew how stubborn John could be and how terrified he was of losing everything, and if need be, he would work twenty-hour days to ensure the success of the farm and survival of his family.

Weeks after John and Joel left, Polly Stamper arrived at Catherine's cabin with her two boys in tow. Catherine had a deep affection for Joel, however she was not overly fond of his wife Polly. But she would hold her tongue as Polly had lost a baby girl not six months back and Catherine knew exactly how painful that could be. Joel's boys were always welcomed.

Polly's parents were George Bowman and Cornelia Adams Bowman, and both born into wealthy families. Cornelia came from English aristocracy and traveled to America to visit her uncle, Joshua Adams and see this new country.

George Bowman was the only child of an industrious merchant from Pennsylvania. When he was in his teens, his father moved the family south for even greener pastures. Father and son were soon setting up business and making themselves known in the area. Eventually the Adams and Bowman families would become partners in various ventures. After Cornelia had been in residence for a few weeks, Jacob Adams decided to give a party and introduce his beautiful niece to the neighborhood. The first invitation for the party to honor Cornelia's visit was sent to the Bowman family.

George Bowman saw Cornelia Adams for the first time at the party. Trying not to be too obvious, he studied her; beautiful, delicate, and oh, so lady like. Even most favored girls George had known back home in Pennsylvania, paled in comparison to Cornelia. She was taller than most girls and rather large through the top of her body, wearing her dark hair loose, hanging down her back and tied with ribbons, which matched her blue eyes. Of an open and friendly nature, Cornelia attracted people with her charming smile. Finally introduced, George stood eye to eye with this beautiful girl; oddly he did not feel intimidated by her equal height.

Years later George and Cornelia would laugh about how shy they were with one another, but both would admit that it was love at first sight. When they married, there were many parties and dinners in celebration. George would become part of his father's business dealings and they would lead a comfortable life

George found himself in complete control of all business after the death of his parents. He also soon discovered how unprepared he was to run the business. Always knowing how to spend the money, he now found out he not only did not know how to make it nor how keep it. Within six months all was lost. George and Cornelia sold all their belongings and headed for Wilkes Co. to establish a farm on land given to them by Joshua Adams. Here they would learn how to provide for themselves and survive. It was a hard lesson to learn and even harder to swallow.

After having three sons, Polly would be their only daughter and both George and Cornelia pampered and spoiled her. When the family fortune was lost, there was no consoling Polly. She stubbornly refused to accept the fact that she could not have one or two dresses made every month. Tantrums became her normal routine. Straining against her parent's strict guidelines, Polly decided she desperately needed to get away and be free of them. If she had to live in poverty, then she would rather live away from family and be the mistress of her own home, poor as it would be. Barely sixteen years old, she was headstrong and stubborn, beyond belief.

Sometimes what you see is not what you get. And that is how Joel Stamper felt within one week of their marriage. Polly had turned on all her charms and Joel was smitten with her, blind to her real personality. Much too soon they were married and not with total approval of Joel's family.

A month into the marriage brought a shock to Polly that would remain with her forever, never to give her peace, for years to come. The Bowman house had burned to the ground taking both parents and two of her brothers. The remaining brother, who inherited the land, wanted nothing to do with Polly.

During their years of marriage Joel Stamper had honored Polly as his wife, even during her 'spells'. Two boys were born to them and a tiny daughter who did not live. At times Joel was the sole parent when Polly would withdraw into herself, into a dream-like state.

Now here she stood on the Stamper's doorstep; Catherine could not imagine Polly as anything but useless. On the other hand, her boys could be enjoyable at times. They had always helped on their own farm so Catherine could certainly use their help with chores.

The cabin would be cramped but somehow it would just have to work out. The oldest boy, James, had driven their wagon loaded down with their belongs to John and Catherine's farm while Melmath the youngest, bounced around in the wagon bed. Polly could not cope without Joel being at home.
So now it was three months later and Polly and her boys were still at Catherine's with their welcome wearing thin.

Chapter 17
Carrying On

Rising before dawn Catherine dressed quickly. In the kitchen she set out leftover fried streaked meat and cold biscuits. She checked the sleeping children in the loft; here pallets covered the floor and seven little lumps strewn about under the quilts.

Downstairs consisted of a large main room and two sleeping rooms. In Catherine's room the beds were crammed into the tiny space along with a small table with one drawer. Pegs on the wall held clothing. Shoes were neatly stacked in one corner and a nightjar peeped from under one of the beds.

Catherine picked up a pair of old mud-encrusted boots that belonged to John. No sense wearing out her only pair of shoes when boots were right there for the taking. Stuffing rags into the toes of the boots, she quietly crossed the main room to the other bedroom. Standing beside the bed she lightly shook the shoulder of the sleeping Polly.

—Time to get up and see to the children and tend the cows while I get the plowing started. We'll be needing butter so don't forget to skim the cream off. Oh, and don't forget the chickens.

Then out the door, across the yard and to the shed. Daylight was breaking.

Leading the horses out of the lean-to, Catherine began placing a blind bridle and bits, then putting on the collar with hames and hame strings on each horse, then the girth. Catherine threaded the lines through the girth. The horses stood still as she double-checked all the tack. Standing in front of the plow, she maneuvered Burt back into position, then Simpson. Now she was ready to attach each trace to the collar and then back to the plow and then hook up the singletree. Checking the reins, she hooked them over the plow handles. Burt had seen better days but hopefully he would last one more growing season. Next year John said they would find a way to buy more horses. Two of their horses had been sold when times became hard, but they had held on to old Burt and Simpson. It just made sense to sell what would bring the most money. John had taken their mules when he left and the plowing would be left up to these two old horses.

Most of the rocks had been cleared from the field years before and there would be only two large stumps she had to maneuver around. She could do it and when John came home, he would be proud of a wife who worked like a man in his stead. Leading Burt by his harness with Simpson following, she began at the corner of the field. Tying her lines in a knot she slipped one of the lines over her shoulder, she placed the other line under her arm and prepared herself to plow.

The sun was slowly making its way higher in the sky and the warmth was being felt. Sweat began to run down her face and in between her breast as she guided the plow. It was unusually warm for this early in the season. Catherine called out 'Gee" and Burt and Simpson turned at the end of the row and then seemed to pick up speed. By tomorrow she hoped to start dropping seed and the little ones could help cover them over. Her thoughts were on keeping as straight a line as possible because old as he was, Burt still had power and constantly veered to the left.

Holding on to the plow while guiding it straight pulled at the muscles in her arms and shoulders and neck.

–I can do this, long as I don't cramp in my arms or I don't blister up too bad on my palms.

Sweat was now dripping off the end of her nose, and she could feel it running between her shoulder blades down to her waist.

She'd have to find a way to trade for a length of cloth before the summer was out. Next year they would plant cotton and spin and weave their cloth. In late May they would shear the lambs and once her loom was fixed, she would weave their winter cloth.

Huge clumps of dirt turned as the plow sliced through the soil, here in the foothill country in North Carolina; the land in Iredell County was dark and rich, not the red clay found further north, closer to the river. Only here there were rocks. If it had just rained a few days before, the earth would have turned easier.

Calling to the horses she pushed further into the field. The sun was moving higher in the sky when James, Polly's oldest boy, came stepping over the clods left by the plow. Carrying a gourd of water, he carefully watched for arrowheads and shards of broken rock. His special trove, hidden down near the creek, wedged in between the rocks was a box holding his precious collection of arrowheads. James did not want anyone to know he still held on to such things.

Lost in his thoughts he stared at his feet moving over the freshly plowed earth. His daddy had told him he once knew a man who had seen a real Indian.

One time long ago, Indians lived all over this land. But his daddy was not here now to tell him these stories. He and his Uncle John had gone off to work and his mama would not be the same 'till he came back. She just could not get over her baby girl dying of fever. The baby had been gone six months and she still grieved like it happened yesterday. That was why he was here at Uncle John and Aunt Catherine's place.

The land they had lived on had just about played out and with no relatives left to help he certainly could not work the whole farm by himself with the way his mama was and no help to him. And the next thing he knew his mama said, "Load up the wagon" and he was on the road to Uncle John's house.

Catherine spotted James hopping from one furrowed row to another sloshing water from the gourd as he went. At 14 James should be the one plowing, but a busted arm that was only now showing signs of healing, held him back. It would be better to save the boy for things she would not be able to do. In a few weeks when his arm was mended, the logs could be dragged from the woods to the house for chopping. Hopefully James would be the one to complete that chore.

That was how he had hurt the arm in the first place. Catherine had told him a dozen times to stand clear when the large oak started making cracking noises. It had taken the two women and the boy all morning sawing away at the big oak. They had marked a tree they felt would be easy to handle and they worked tirelessly to saw through the middle. As the tree began to fall, James was hit by a large branch across his arm. Falling to the ground he was passed out cold, on the spot. Catherine could hardly get to the boy for his mama hovering over him screeching and hollering that he was dead.

But the logs would keep. Catherine and Polly had made three trips into the woods to saw the branches off. Then a neighbor, Jacob Moser along with his son, had ridden over and sawed the tree trunk into workable lengths. Now if Catherine did not work the life out of Burt or Simpson, they would be able to pull the logs to the house. Maybe John would be back in time to see to that job. There had been no money delivered from him in weeks so he was probably on his way now. But Catherine felt she just could not take a chance and let the plowing wait.

Balancing a gourd and several nice arrowheads he had spotted,

James jumped the last furrowed row and thrust the half empty gourd toward Catherine.

—Thought you might want to wash the dust away. I'm going to go over to Barnett's pond and try to catch us some catfish for supper. Arm's feeling really good. Thought maybe I'd try my hand at the plow tomorrow if there's any land left to turn.

Left? Catherine now realized that she'd be lucky to turn even half the land for the corn crop and that was not even a start on all that had to be done.

James was not fooling Catherine. Fishing was not what he wanted to do. No sir, she had that all figured out. Polly did not have sense enough anymore to see where her son was headed but fishing was the last thing on his mind. It was Ada Barnett that he was fishing for, and her only thirteen years old. Why, old man Barnett would skin him alive if he knew that they had been sneaking around meeting. Catherine had seen them at the edge of the woods staring at each other holding hands.

Standing and staring at Catherine, James slowly moved the toe of his boot back and forth over the sandy soil, pushing at small clods. He was a head taller than Catherine and would soon be fifteen years old. In his mind, he was old enough and big enough to make his own decisions.

A slight breeze kicked up stray locks of hair around his face, a reflection of Joel's face. He had large beautiful eyes with long lashes, a true Stamper trait.

—There's nothing for me to do here. I've got to do something to help feed all these people sitting at your table.

Catherine, stunned by his statement, whirled around to face him, disbelief revealed on her face.

—My mama and me pull our weight and don't you say we don't. She's just about worked down to a nub trying to do around here and with you always pushing at her.

Catherine was too tired to argue, especially with a headstrong boy like James.

—If old man Barnett catches you, don't come crying to me. Your mama's not going to like me telling her about that Barnett girl though.

Seeing the red spread across James' cheeks, Catherine saw that her comment had struck a nerve.

Sweat seemed to be pouring from every pore in her body as she wiped her apron across her face and pushed stray hairs away from her face. Pushing back her bonnet she looked at James squarely in the eye daring him to sass her. Watching his face color up was almost as much fun as finding that colored ear of corn at the corn shucking last year.

Yes sir, you could not get around Catherine, not today anyway.

-You had best be saving that arm for another week at least. I'll get this land plowed. You go see that your mama watches all those children and tends to the chickens and cow. And don't you go giving me that look. You know how she gets when you're not right where she can see you. Scared to death something's going to happen to you. Go on. Get back to the house. And stay away from Barnett's. If he catches you taking any more fish out of his pond, he'll shoot first and ask questions later, then have his boys string you up in a tree. Now go home! Do like I tell you.

Turning, James slammed his hat on his head and started in the direction of the house. Just to make sure she was in control Catherine called after him.

- And make sure your mama checks those bushes around the side of the house for eggs. I don't want to find rotten eggs there next week. Last time she did not look good and there were at least a dozen rotten eggs.

Turning his head slightly to glance over his shoulder, he gave Catherine the best glare he could manage and still keep walking.

-Dumb old woman. Thinks just because it's her place, she can boss everybody around. Treats me like a two-year-old. And she's always hinting that we don't do anything around here, like we're guest or something. What about all them nice persimmons I 'bout broke my neck getting? And all those times I walked forever trying to sell that extra butter she churned that did not taste all that good to me anyway. And how I helped build that hog pen? Well, if she thinks telling mama lies about me liking that Ada Barnett will keep me from going fishing then she's just going to have to think again.

At the edge of the field Catherine watched as James stomped dutifully back to the house making sure that he slammed the door loud enough to be heard in three counties. Turning, Catherine spoke to the horses.

–Come on horses. We've got a field to finish and I aim to finish it with you alive or dead. And you best stay breathing because I'm not going to pull those logs out of the woods without you both on the front end.

Chapter 18
James Takes Charge

Sitting at the kitchen table Polly stared into her cup. The children ran in circles giggling and playing chase. The older boy, who usually ignored them, now participated in the game and made silly noises as he chased the children.

Melmath was nearly twelve and in the midst of a growth spurt; his pants were inches too short and his shirt stretched over his back to the point of ripping. Barefoot, he had ceased wearing shoes altogether, mainly because there was not a pair in the house that would now fit. After the last bout of blisters on his feet, he announced that somebody was just going to have to die and leave him some shoes. The only pair that he could hold on his feet were his uncle John's boots, the ones that Catherine had worn to plow.

With the same light brown hair as his brother, Melmath bore a resemblance to his father Joel but carried more of his mother's features with prominent cheekbones and an oval face. Although he had grown several inches in the last year, he already knew that he would never be as tall as his brother. Glancing away from the children and looking at his mother, Melmath became very still. Polly just sat staring but not really seeing.

Crossing the room, he laid a hand on his mother's shoulder and shook her gently. Vacant eyes stared ahead and she mumbled something he could not truly understand. Some days she was real bright and talked and acted normal but other days she would sit, staring and mumbling about her dead baby girl and how Joel was gone. Shaking her again Melmath was just about ready to shout to try and get her to look at him when the door slammed rattling the window.

James stood and looked at the mess in the room. Then looked at his mama and Melmath. His face glowed red and his fist clinched at his side. Breathing deep he brushed his hair out of his eyes.

-Don't you think you could get her up and start fixing up this mess? You know you have to watch her when she's like this. The little ones don't even have their clothes on. What is the matter with you? Do I have to do your job and mine? I told you when I left to do the milking to get her up and get those little one's cared for. Catherine's out there in the field plowing like a man and with me *half– laid up with this arm and here you are running round playing. How's this family going to survive the winter if we   don't work together and get the crops in the ground and the wood stacked up to keep us from freezing? And here you are playing.*

–Like I just told Catherine, it'll take the both of us to do it because the others don't have enough brains to think of what needs be done. And you've gone and let the fire go out in the fireplace. Guess my thoughts were right all along. You aren't smart enough to think like a man and   make sure things gets done.

Rooted to the spot Melmath felt a stinging in his eyes. But he held the tears at bay.

–You shut your mouth. I am helping! These little ones needed looking after   and that's what I'm doing. It's not up to me to clear up any cooking mess or dress children.

With lightning speed James swung and cuffed Melmath behind the ear, knocking him to the floor.

Turning he walked slowly to the door then stopped. His hand hurt and his chest felt tight. Hitting his brother in anger was something he had never done before and it made him feel sick to his stomach. Without looking back, he crossed to the porch.

–Get britches or something on those children. I'll go draw the water and then start the fire again. Find that egg basket and start looking through the bushes and make the little ones help you. Mama's no good today so leave her alone. Don't let me find you still in this room when I come back.

Chapter 19
Tears of Joy and Pain

Almost faint from exhaustion Catherine steered Burt and Simpson back toward the house. A small ribbon of smoke could be seen coming out of the chimney. Polly was sitting on the porch with the children playing at her feet. In the distance storm clouds were gathering. If only the plowing had been done yesterday, the seeds would be in the ground today to get their first drink of water. Still a good way off though, maybe we could get a few rows planted by torchlight.

Burt picked up speed and rounded the side of the house and headed for the barn with Simpson not far behind. James appeared carrying a small sack of grain and finished leading the horses the remainder of the way. He removed the collars and harness, leading them into the barn where he proceeded to rub them down. Melmath came from around the corner of the shed carrying two buckets of water and headed for the water trough.

A faint smile crossed Catherine's lips as she watched the two boys tend to the horses. Right now, all she wanted was a cloth dipped in cool water to bathe her face and a biscuit to nibble on and to take off the boots. Her dress and apron were filthy and her hair hung loose from the bun at the back of her head. Wisps of hair stuck to her sweaty face, smudged with dirt and she no longer smelled like the rose petal soap she had used in the past. Her reward, though, was that a third of the field lay in nice deep furrows. It had taken the best part of the day but it had to be done. Tomorrow she would take Melmath to the field. James could watch things at home while she showed Melmath what they needed to do.

She crossed the remainder of the yard and sat on the porch steps fanning herself with the bottom of her apron. Polly sat in a chair on the porch rocking back and forth with George and Alex sitting at her feet. Melmath crossed from the shed to the yard and up to the porch carrying a bucket with a small amount of water.

–I saved some of this cool water. Want I should get some more?
Just as she reached for the bucket, Melmath's hand opened and down it went, turning upside down, water splashing her entire right side. Before she could react Melmath struck off in a dead run toward the road.

Dust was flying from the wheels of the wagon as it turned off the road and onto the lane leading to the cabin. Melmath almost collided with the horses as they came to a halt. Henry Dagenhart, a nearby neighbor, took his hat off and wiped the sweat and dust from his face and slowly made his way off the wagon seat.

The ride from Statesville had been none too pleasant but seeing as how he was the only one at the mill who had an empty wagon he was quickly elected for the errand.

–Got Polly's man in the back of the wagon sick as a dog. Some rover found him north of here and slung him in his wagon and kept on going where he was going. Guess he figured somebody at the mill swould know who he was.

Henry hopped in the wagon bed and uncovered Joel. Catherine looked at the boys and told them that they needed to get water, lots of it and clear off the table inside. James grabbed two buckets from inside the house and as he was leaving, swiped the dishes from the table. Jumping from the porch he set off at a run toward the creek.

Polly rocked back and forth and seemed oblivious to all that was happening around her. Melmath's lip quivered as he backed away, slowly inching his way to the front of the wagon. His daddy lay still as death in the wagon bed. When Henry thrust his arms under Joel's back and hips to lift him, he shook violently. Carrying him was no problem as Joel had just about wasted away to nothing. Gently Henry moved up the steps and onto the porch passing by Polly and through the door.

Poking at Polly, Catherine leaned up into her face.

–Joel has come home. Can you hear me, Polly?
Not getting any response, she stepped into the house and over to the table. Joel was burning with fever. His cheeks were sunk in and his coloring looked grey. Sweat rings covered his head and his lips were dry and cracked. The clothes he wore smelled of urine and filth and one pant leg was ripped from thigh to knee. Showing through the rip was a wound that was discolored with pus oozing out the edges. The stench of the wound was almost overpowering. Staggering back Catherine stared at Joel and knew the sign of death when she saw it.

Polly stood in the doorway, screaming, "He's dead!" Stumbling back on to the porch she flopped back in the chair. Flailing her arms she continued to scream and pull at her hair until it lay in tangles around her shoulders. Instantly Catherine reached out and slapped Polly on her check. The stinging in her cheek stopped the flailing but she continued to scream. Catherine smacked her again, only this time harder, leaving her handprint on her cheek.

–I haven't got time for any of your crazy ways. Get up from there. Get up from there right now and help your husband. If you sit in that chair one more minute and leave me to take care of him I swear on my father's grave I'll set you off the place. So help me I will. And I'll keep James and Melmath. Get up, you hear me?

Shaky and drying her eyes, Polly rose from the rocker and followed Catherine into the house. Henry stood by the table and just stared at the two women. Never had he seen anything like this in all his years. Miz Polly standing tall with the print of Miz Catherine's hand on her face. Miz Catherine acting like nothing happened, standing rigid and smelling like a field hand. It would be best to back away and return to his farm where the women do not hit each other.

–Beg your pardon Mister Henry but sometimes if Polly's having one of her spells the only way to get her out of it is to let her feel your hand. I never had to do this but once before and did not want to do it now but there just was not any other way. I hope you will tell your womenfolk that I did only what had to be done. Polly has been poorly all week and I had been plowing since sun up. Usually if I'm in the house, I can get her out of her spell but like I said, I had to do the plowing today.

Henry looked from one woman to the other then to Melmath. How was this woman going to do all that was needed to run this farm? Plowing should have been left to the boys. Tomorrow he would send one of his sons to finish the plowing. At least that would get them ahead and they could get their seed in the ground and not starve over the winter. By the looks of Joel, he might need to send someone out tomorrow to see if there was need for a burial.

At a loss for words Henry put his hat on and said he would leave the women to tend to Joel and strode from the room. Once at his wagon he pulled off a sack of meal and placed it on the porch. His family had more than enough to go around and with the looks of things here, this family was going to need help. He shouted in the direction of the door that he was leaving now and climbed aboard the wagon. Within minutes he was on the road again heading home. He felt it best to find the preacher and ask him to check the Stamper place; there's going to be a grave that needs praying over.

With quick strides James bounded onto the porch with two buckets brimming with water and then into the house. He swung the cast iron pot on to the stove and filled it to the top with water. There were still the remnants of a few coals and throwing in large slivers of wood, he began stoking the fire. Behind him through the silence he heard the ripping of cloth as Catherine and Polly tried to free up the pants from Joel's swollen, discolored leg.

Polly was now starting to act alert. Tears rolled down her cheeks as she helped Catherine ease the pants from Joel. Only the sound of James' labored breathing and the sound of water beginning to boil could be heard. Catherine leaned into Joel's face and asked where he had left John but Joel just moaned.

The gash on the leg was not deep, but it was infected with faint red streaks going up his leg. This kind of wound was something that Catherine could not deal with and she knew it. Busted arms and small cuts she could handle, but not red streaks. Looking at James she told him to hitch up Burt and find Doc Stewart. And for his daddy's sake that he'd better ride like the wind and find Doc quick.

It was now four o'clock; James had been gone over an hour. Catherine checked the clock on the mantel once again. Doc did not live that far away so James probably had to go looking for him. Polly paced around the table constantly touching some part of Joel's body.

Catherine had sent Melmath for cool water from the creek and dipped rags in the water and laid them all over Joel. Once he was covered she dripped water into his half open mouth and soon he was swallowing. Joel had stopped moaning and did not look quite as gray in the face, but his leg still oozed with every beat of his heart

With the heat of the day, still trapped inside, the room was unbearable; the boiling water made the room feel like an oven. Both women were afraid to take the pot off the fire for fear that Doc would need it so they kept adding wood to the fire.

Melmath stood off to the side and watched with quiet fear. He'd heard about red streaks before and always it was when somebody died. The two youngest children lay directly on the floor just inside the front door and slept in spite of the hard surface. No one had paid much attention to the little ones since the arrival of Joel. Now tired and hungry, they lay on the rough wood floor and slept as if on feather beds. Alex, Gilbert and George sat quietly taking it all in around them. Occasionally Alex would go stand by Catherine, placing his hand on her arm, but saying nothing.

Checking the clock once again Catherine began to pace around the table behind Polly. She began praying out loud and asking the Lord to save this woman's husband and the boys daddy. Another hour went by and still no sign of James or Doc. So they reapplied the wet rags to Joel, as it seemed to ease him.

Joel opened his eyes and saw the splintered wood of the beams above his head. He could see the cobwebs and a place that he had helped patch just last summer. He must be home. Turning his head he saw Catherine just as she lifted another rag from the bucket of cool water. She glanced up and seeing Joel looking right at her, she smiled in relief. But before she could move or even acknowledge to Polly that Joel was awake, he raised his head, keeping his eyes even with hers.

–John's dead.

The color draining from her face, Catherine fainted away in a heap, landing hard on the floor. Doc strode through the door and asked who was dying here. Joel passed out.

Chapter 20
Empty

The evening was unusually cool this time of year and the air felt moist. Lightning flashed in the distance; occasional thunder announced a storm was on the way. The wind was blowing stronger now, and moved the homespun cloth away from the window, making shadows in eerie patterns on the bed. Catherine lay quiet and listened to the muffled voices in the other room.

Turning on her side she found her youngest child Susan, lying quietly asleep and clutching at her sleeve. The child looked frail and poorly kept. She tenderly laid her hand on the child's tangled hair and ran her fingers through it as if to try and bring some order to the dark brown mass. This was her last gift from John, lying here sleeping like nothing had happened. How could that be?

Still clutching her mother's sleeve, the child opened her eyes and then closed them again, sinking deeper in sleep. Catherine touched the small hand on her sleeve and ran her calloused hand over the tiny fingers. She's hanging on for dear life waiting for me to do something. But do what? What can I do to feed and clothe all these people?

Quietly and slowly she eased herself up to a half sitting position and loosed the child's grasp on her sleeve. She felt chilled from the cool breeze blowing in the window. Rising from the bed she crossed to the pegs on the wall and drew down her shawl, placing it around her shoulders. A fine thing if I were to come down with the fever. Who'd look after my little ones? Alex was big enough to do some work in the field and George and Gilbert would have to help. How were they going to get by without John?

Standing at the window she held back the cloth and watched the rainfall in big splats. Rain, so peaceful and sweet smelling, reminded her that John always loved the rain. She could almost see him, cleaning or repairing tools. Sometimes he'd just whittle or carve a piece of wood while telling the children stories that his father had told him. Sadly, the porch was empty now and bright flashes of light filled the sky as the thunder rolled once again. With each streak of lightning she could see the plowed field. Her arms ached and her shoulders felt stiff. The blisters on her hands and feet needed lancing. She stared into the darkness, wondering if all this was worth living for after all. Closing her eyes, she could still see him.

Quietly, Catherine left her room, crossing to the front door and out to the porch. Sitting and rocking, Catherine suddenly thought of Nanny Grindstaff. If ever there would be a comforting word that is where she would find one. Standing up, she pulled her light shawl around her shoulders and stepped from the porch. Walking in the dark had never bothered Catherine. She had traveled the dirt road to visit Nanny a thousand times. Feeling the drops of rain, she picked up her skirt and her steps quickened. Lightning soon lit up the sky and she could see Nanny Grindstaff's house in the distance. Loving arms were just a few steps away.

Chapter 21
A Healing

The side meat hissed and spit in the cast iron pan causing little streams of smoke wherever it hit. Polly turned the meat and checked the cornbread she'd made from the bag of meal Henry had left. Her hair was neatly pulled back and fastened with pins at the back of her head. Finally there was color in her cheeks and her eyes were bright and clear.

Turning to the kitchen table she broke six eggs in a bowl and threw in a splash of milk.

–Those chickens are hiding their eggs but not after today because I'll find every single place and then that will be that. We can't feed all these people on six eggs every day so they had best be doing more than this.

Beating furiously at the eggs with a wooden spoon she debated over whether to throw in a pinch of Catherine's precious salt. After a moment's pause, she turned to a crock on a shelf and very carefully took only a small pinch and surely Catherine won't miss such a small amount. Good food is what will help him get strong again, good food with salt added.

Doc and his son had carried Joel to a pallet in the corner where Polly had stacked layers and layers of quilts for comfort. Better to watch him here where he could catch the cross draw of air between the door and the back window. Not to mention that the entire house now needed a good airing as it reeked of the odor of Joel's festering leg. Doc had cleaned the leg as best he could but had to stop when the offensive odor caused Polly to vomit on the floor. Sending her outside with Melmath, Doc ordered James to clean it up. Working until all the dead flesh was removed and the wound was clean, Doc began packing the open gash with medicine and wrapped a bandage around Joel's leg.

That first night Doc stayed by Joel's side, not leaving until his son came for him the next afternoon. One of the Gilbert brothers had just about sawed his hand off and was in danger of bleeding to death, so Doc hurried out the door and was on his way. By this time Joel felt cool and was peaceful now that his leg had been cleaned and tended.

Once Joel had slept for a few hours, he woke and asked for water. Polly carefully held the cup trying not to pour the liquid directly on him. Seeing the anguish in Joel's eyes, Polly sent the children outside to play. Joel slowly began telling how John had died.

John and Joel had left home well over four months earlier. Their cousins had started a large building project and both brothers could earn good money laying brick. Then they heard about a lumber dealer who would pay big money for driving a team through the mountains. This opportunity sounded like easy work until they found out the shipment was logs. Working a team of horses through the mountains with such a heavy load would be slow going and logs had a way of shifting on the curves no matter how they were tied down. Broken wheels were common and especially dangerous when the load was so heavy. A wealthy lawyer, living just over the state line, had contacted the dealer for oak that he wanted in building his house. When the dealer saw that they might be having second considerations, so he doubled his offer of money and they accepted. Bricks could wait.

The first day went by quickly and without incident and they started to relax. The winding mountain road had not been nearly as bad as they had heard and the view was something to see. The brothers could not figure out why this lawyer fellow went on and on about wanting only oak, and they discussed it all day on the second day. By the third day they knew that they were only a few hours away from making their delivery. Around noon, they pulled to the side of the road intending to relieve themselves and eat. Joel was first off the rig and headed for the woods. Before he got very far he heard John call for him to come quick, so he turned back around and headed back to the wagon.

Squatting down beside the wheel John looked underneath the wagon. Just as Joel came near a loud crack sounded as the wagon axle snapped and John caught the brunt of the logs as they began falling. Scrambling backwards, Joel caught only the ragged edge of a log on his left thigh and in the process he was knocked unconscious. Joel lay for hours until a lone rider found him. As the stranger poured water on his face, slapping both his cheeks, Joel awoke to a burning pain in his leg, and not knowing where he was. Once his head cleared, the man helped him stand to see if his leg was broken. He could walk but still did not know where he was or why he was there. Finally. the man asked why he would try to bring such a load over the mountain alone.

Standing to the side of the road, Joel stared at the crumpled heap of logs. Turning he looked at the man.

–My brother's under that pile and we need to get him out.

Two hours later and with six men and ten horses, the logs were all pulled from the wreckage to reveal the body of John Stamper. Joel stooped down and gently touched what once had been a man he had loved like life itself. Tenderly turning him over he stared at John's face, now unrecognizable and covered in blood.

Joel told the men that he was taking him home and would need their help with something to pull the body on. Everyone stood with mouths hanging open and staring at this crazy man.

–*You can't have him. He'll stink by tomorrow and he's mashed so bad he's in different parts. You got to bury him right here. Right up in the woods, deep so the dogs don't dig him up.*

Standing and staring at John's body, Joel felt sick. Minutes passed and finally he turned facing the men.

–*I'll do it myself so you go on back to your business.*

No one moved. Joel turned to lift John's body and felt himself drifting into black. His next memory was of being in the back of a wagon heading east, his leg throbbing in pain with each heartbeat. He could not even remember where he had been or why he was in this wagon. Then he was seeing Catherine's surprised grin.

Stunned by the details of John's death, Polly mechanically wiped his brow with a cool cloth. Sitting there, heavy with the weight of their sadness, Polly was nonetheless content to just sit by Joel, wiping his brow. Hearing the dogs, she turned to see Catherine coming in the door.

–*Where have you been? I thought you were in your room.*

–*This morning I suddenly realized I hadn't checked on Nanny in days, so I went to see her and to tell her about John.*

–*Well I certainly would not be leaving to go see that old woman.*

Lowering her head, Catherine felt the sting of Polly's words and turned to leave the room.

Catherine had arrived at Nanny's in the middle of the night and sat on the porch calling Nanny's name. Had she not recognized the voice, Nanny would not have opened the door. Finding Catherine sitting there and soaking wet, she brought her inside, and helping her out of wet clothes, Nanny wrapped her in a quilt. Catherine sat on a low stool as Nanny stoked the fire in the fireplace and watched as she pulled a chair closer to the fireplace. Nanny listened as Catherine began telling her of

John, laying her head in Nanny's lap, crying until she had no more tears. Gently stroking her hair Nanny talked quietly to Catherine and quoted scripture and prayed aloud. Soon Catherine sat sleeping with her head still in Nanny's lap. At daybreak she had walked back home, her thoughts filled with visions of seeing John for the first time. Then she thought of how her mother had died from fever just two years ago. Feeling the loss of her mother Elizabeth, all over again, the tears began to flow again freely. If only her mother was here, she could face the next part and living without John. Her hand closed around the object in her pocket and she immediately felt comforted. At least she had Nanny and that was a reassuring.

With these thoughts, and not looking back at Polly, Catherine opened her bedroom door and quickly went inside. With the door closed she sat on the bed and just stared.

–I need to know what to do and how to do it.

Sliding off the bed she came to her knees, bowed her head and began praying.

Outside the door, Alex sat with his ear to the door listening to his mother praying. At hearing her words, he knew that everything was going to be all right. He was still anxious and decided to stay at the door until she came out.

Chapter 22
Better Times

The sun had been shining the last three days and sunshine made everyone want to be outside. George and Melmath were gathering eggs when they heard what sounded like a herd of horses coming up the road. Quickly putting their baskets on the porch, they ran to the end of the lane hoping to see who was coming down the road. At seeing the line of wagons Melmath turned and started running toward the house while George just stood and waited.

Bursting into the house Melmath announced to everyone that all of the neighbors were coming up the lane. Polly moved to the door and then on to the porch to await their arrival.

Henry Dagenhart had checked several times on the family but today he came again and this time brought several neighbors. The men pulled their wagons into the yard and started unloading. Sacks of grain and meal, quilts, crocks and several dishes covered with cloths, digging tools and seed. Then they began unloading plows from a wooden sled that Henry's son had pulled with six mules. Polly stood on the porch and watched, wondering why they brought all these things and dumped them in the yard. Behind her the door stood open and Joel rose up on his elbows leaning to see through the door.

-We've come to plant your crop and get your land ready for when Joel heals. Then he and the boys can do the harvest.

Polly nodded but stood with her mouth slack and watched as Henry turned and motioned to the other men to hitch the mules to the plows and cross over to the field. Before they reached the field another wagon pulled off the road. This time the driver was black as night, as was the woman sitting beside him. Amos and Luella belonged to Hiram Campbell who lived not two miles up the road. Hiram had purchased land from the Lackey brothers and now it was his land that the Stampers leased.

Amos jumped from the wagon with a smile that showed very white teeth. His clothes were homespun but clean and his boots looked almost new.

Reaching into the bed of the wagon, Amos began pulling out tools and supplies, motioning to the woman, Luella, to climb down and help him. Not more than thirty years old and black as coal, she barely weighed ninety pounds.

Catherine moved to the window to see what all the noise was about. The large gum tree in the yard cast shadows on the porch and no one could see her peeking out the window. What are those folks doing here with all those supplies? Taking her bonnet from the peg, she stooped to pick up her shoes thankful that Nanny had cleaned them of mud from last night's walk through the rain. Sitting on the edge of the bed she slipped her swelled, blistered feet into the well-worn shoes. Outside she could hear Amos talking to Polly. With his biggest smile he began telling her that the Campbell's, being good Christians, wanted to help and had sent him and Luella over to help get the kitchen garden in the ground. Chuckling he slapped his leg and said that Mr. Campbell was a fine man and glad to help anyone.

Catherine stood at the door with her jaw clinched and felt indignation rising in her chest. She could certainly take care of her own family. Pushing past Polly on the porch Catherine stood and glared at Amos giving him her most disgusted look while pushing up the sleeves of her dress. Waving her hands in a 'shooing' motion, she started toward Amos.

−You just go on and get out of here right this minute Amos Campbell. Go on. I don't need any help. This family will make it just fine and we really don't need pity, especially the Campbell's. Go on. Get right back in that wagon and get yourself back on home and tell Mr. Campbell that he'll surely get his share just as soon as I can get the seed in ground and harvest. I can take care of it all so you just get on back home.

Standing at the foot of the steps Amos turned and told Luella to keep getting the tools out of the wagon. Then smiling and looking at Catherine and Polly, he asked if she wanted any turnip seeds put in her kitchen garden and did she know if there was enough manure piled up so they could work it in before they set to seeding. And could she bring some buckets for water as they plumb forgot to get theirs and not to worry about feeding them because Miss Campbell would be over shortly with food. Turning he went to help Luella drag all the tools over to the side of the house where the kitchen garden was located.

Catherine moved to go down the steps to stop him when Joel appeared hanging on to the doorframe, pale and shaky.

−Catherine, don't. Please. We need this. Think of the children and how they're going to need this food.

Stopping she turned and looked at Joel knowing he was right but swallowing that big lump of pride in her throat almost made her choke. Without a word she stepped from the porch and followed Amos around the side of the house and picked up a hoe and looking him in the eye said she'd take the right side so he'd best take the left and Luella could take the middle. If they worked together they could probably get the seed in by sunset.

Out in the field Henry Dagenhart, Moses Lackey along with James Thompson called to their mules. Plows sliced through the rich earth revealing dark brownish gray dirt. The rain several days ago had sweetened the earth even more making the plowing easier. Within two hours what had taken Catherine almost an entire day to finish, was now duplicated twice over. The field was finished and ready for planting. Leading their mules by their harness they crossed the road and began plowing the field across from the house. By lunch time all the plowing was complete. Unhitching their mules they tied them under a shade tree in the yard and gave them buckets of water and grain. More neighbors began arriving for the planting.

Late afternoon saw the completion of the kitchen garden. Tired, Catherine sat on the ground under the big gum tree. Frances Campbell, one of the older Campbell daughters, had brought food for their noon meal and was now loading the last of her supplies back into the buggy. Reaching under the seat she removed a small item wrapped in cloth. She smiled and walked toward Catherine glancing up briefly to see the breeze rustle the leaves on the big tree. She smiled down at Catherine and extended her hand offering the cloth wrapped item.

Slowly unfolding the cloth, Catherine revealed a small book entitled "Encouraging Bible Verse for Everyday Living – In Joy and in Sorrow". Her voice was almost a whisper as she spoke to Catherine.

–*You are so strong and brave and I hope if I were to ever be faced with tragedy I could act just as you have and be an example to all around.*

Not waiting for any answer or sign of acknowledgment for the gift she turned and walked to her buggy, mounted the step and settled herself on the seat. Calling to the horses she steered the buggy out on to the road and toward her home. Catherine sat looking at the book of verse and feeling the heat in her face. All she could hear were the words "be an example" and she felt ashamed at how she had greeted Amos and Luella that morning.

The day had been almost more that Catherine could physically bear. She could not remember ever being so tired. Pausing she sat on the steps, looked around at all those still hurrying about the yard and house. George and Gilbert had latched on to one of the neighbor men, and had spent the afternoon following him around. The girls were on the porch, playing. Suddenly realizing that Alex was missing, Catherine scanned the yard again. Walking around the yard she asked if anyone had seen Alex. How long had he been out of sight? Where could he be?

Knowing his need for privacy, Catherine headed in the direction of the creek. Even as a toddler, she recognized that Alex would have times he wanted to be alone. Growing older he would handle disappointment or worry by disappearing. He would always turn up several hours later and be back to the same sweet Alex.

Walking just a short distance from the house Catherine could hear the water and stopped to look up and down the creek banks. Not too far to the right she spotted a pair of legs sticking out from behind a bush, dangling over the creek bank. Quietly she called Alex's name. The feet immediately were drawn up out of the water and into the bushes. Calling again, she heard him answer, "over here".

Making her way through the foliage, Catherine slid down and sat on the ground beside her oldest son. Pulling her skirt up, she pulled off her shoes and slipped her feet into the creek. Alex dangled his legs over the edge, swishing his feet back and forth in the water. They sat quietly for ten minutes before Catherine finally spoke.

–Your daddy knew that you loved him and he was so very proud of you. Before he left he talked about how much you had learned this past year and he told me he felt good knowing that you would be here to help me.

Sitting still, Alex stared into the water. Then his lip trembled and the tears ran down his cheeks but he was still silent. Placing her arm around him, Catherine gathered him to her and finally he cried out–loud, trying to push her away. Catherine told him,' no let all of it out'.

–Your daddy would not want it any other way.

An hour later mother and son slowly walked back to the house. Alex felt he could now face the rest of the family and begin planning as to what they should do.

That night after everyone had gone to bed Catherine sat on the porch with a small lantern near her feet. She rocked slowly back and forth holding the small book Frances Campbell had given her, gripping it with both hands in her lap. She thought that Frances was much like the oldest daughter she had cared for at Vanderburg Plantation. Reading to them from a book of poems written by a man from Virginia, Catherine remembered how hard it had been for her to ask Mr. Vanderburg if she could borrow the book of poems. With the newly borrowed book, she sat by the fire reading over and over again the beautiful, melodic words.

There would be a scripture in the Bible that would tell her what needed to be done. Just sitting here, quietly rocking, holding on to the book, she finally felt peaceful and hopeful. Next fall she would see about getting her children some books. Their education would be foremost from this day on.

Placing her hand in her apron pocket, Catherine felt for her treasured object. Wrapping her hand around the tiny item, she slowly moved her thumb back and for, comforted by the stroking action. Leaning back in the rocker she began humming quietly a hymn her mother always sang, rocking slowly, letting the words of the song roll through her mind.

> *Rock of Ages, cleft for me.*
> *Let me hide myself in Thee;*
> *Let the water and the blood,*
> *From Thy riven side which flowed,*
> *Be of sin the double cure,*
> *Save me from its guilt and power.*

Melmath eased out the door, quietly crossing the porch. He slowly slipped into a sitting position at Catherine's feet. Moving closer to her skirt he laid his head against her knees feeling her warmth through the dress.

–Guess you could not sleep either?

With book in one hand and the other hand stroking Melmath's hair, she rocked and hummed and looked at the stars.

When the eastern sky broke with the dawn Catherine was still sitting and rocking on the porch.

Chapter 23
Fellowship

By the end of the week all the crops had been planted; the kitchen garden was in the ground and a small lean-to had been built on the side of the horse shed, housing extra grain and hay. The logs were dragged from the woods, split and stacked. One of the men insisted on adding two new shelves in the kitchen to hold the extra supplies. Members of the community and church had come in large numbers to help. John and Catherine had been well respected.

Someone had brought a new dishpan and a fairly new cast iron wash pot. One neighbor brought quilting needles and thread and had lovingly collected enough cloth scraps to make a quilt. Catherine's loom was now repaired and sat beside the spinning wheel at the front window. Along with a new shirt, Melmath had new shoes that fit his feet. The flour barrel was full and various staples including dried fruit now lined the shelves. Horace Crouch, who lived a few miles away and was very poor, had come to give the only thing he felt he could give. He offered his bull for service on the cow so a calf would now be in the future. Everyone had been so kind, but the best gift was that all of the red streaks on Joel's leg were almost gone.

Outside the cabin, under the gum tree, wooden saw horses stood with planks placed on them to form a makeshift table. Mismatched cloths covered the planks and a huge pot of stew was placed in the center of the table along with a platter of fried chicken and ham. There was a large bowl of potatoes boiled in their skins along with onions and a bowl of greens. Cornbread, biscuits with fresh butter and jams, and a jug of cider rounded out the meal. Lanterns were placed on the table for light. Rough-hewn benches were on either side of the table and pewter plates along with a knife, spoon and a cup marked each spot. Preacher Icenhour stood at the head of the table and gave thanks for what they were about to receive and thanked the Lord for the strength and courage of this family and of those who helped them. Everyone said "Amen."

Seated at the table were the Campbell's and the Stampers. Isabel Campbell sat beside Catherine, smiling she placed her smooth delicate hand on top of Catherine's calloused stained hand.

    —Hiram and I were so pleased that you allowed us to help get your seed in the ground. We so admire your strength and wanted to

give you our love during the time of John's passing. He was such a kind man and Hiram was deeply disturbed when he heard of the accident. Why, we've never had a tenant as hard working as John Stamper and anything that we can do to help his family is our pleasure. God surely blessed him with you Catherine because we know John would not have made it without you here. I told Hiram that you had fine children, God fearing, and respectful. Preacher Icenhour cleared his throat and asked that everyone help themselves.

Plates were piled high and no one spoke for concentrating on eating. In the background there was the music of crickets and other night sounds. Luella appeared carrying a cake with real sugar icing, something not everyone could afford. Several sets of small eyes lit up at the sight and they immediately stopped eating, begging for cake. Catherine smiled as she watched the children dig into the sweet taste and relaxed knowing that tonight their bellies would be full not only when they went to sleep but also in the days ahead.

After the meal Hiram and Isabel sat on the porch with Catherine while Polly and Luella cleared the make–shift table. The children sat in the grass listening to Amos tell of seeing a cougar when he was a boy. Clearing his throat and staring into the night, Hiram told Catherine that as soon as harvest was over he would ride to the mountain and find John's grave and place a marker. With only the sound of Amos telling his stories, and the occasional squeak of the rocker, Catherine slowly allowed a tear to run down her cheek.

The next few weeks found the Stamper household working through the freshness of their grief, throwing themselves into everyday tasks. At the end of the month, a letter arrived from John's mother.

To my dearest daughter Catherine,
My heart is broken and I grieve not only for my loss but the loss of your husband and the father of your children. John was a good man and loved his land and his family. There are so many things about him that were like my husband, Powell. Carry on and stay strong in your body and your mind, placing your faith in God. My grief has aged me and I feel as if I cannot travel to see you and ask that as soon as you can that you visit and let me hold and kiss John's children. Brooks and Nancy send their love and best wishes and they hurt in their hearts for John. Please write to me and let me know when you are coming.
Your loving mother by marriage
Mary Stamper

As soon as the newly planted seeds had sprouted, Catherine loaded up the children and headed for Catawba County. Following behind the wagon were Joel, Polly and their boys in a borrowed buckboard. Mr. Campbell, ever the helpful neighbor, had agreed to send Amos over to the Stamper farm to care for the animals and tend to the milking each day. Catherine would spend three days with Brooks and Nancy. The children were thrilled to see their cousins and visit with their granny. At first sight Catherine almost did not recognize John's mother, who had grown thin and frail; her hair was now completely white.

When they first arrived, the children could not contain their excitement at seeing their granny Stamper and gave her many hugs. Brooks remained by his mother and expressed anger at the lack of letters from his sisters, nor was he happy with his brother Joel, whose only concern seemed to be Polly. Joel saw his mother only occasionally and seemed to blush when she showed her excitement at seeing him. Granny Stamper was crushed by this show of uncaring. The pain of losing John went deep within her as he had visited his mother every two or three weeks without fail, usually letting one of the children ride with him.

Now surrounded by her grandchildren Granny Stamper smiled and continuously reached out to touch each one of them. Watching her visiting with her grandchildren, hugging them and telling them stories, it was difficult to believe that this was the vibrant woman of just a few years past. Upon seeing all of this Catherine was determined that her children would see their granny at least once a month. The time to return home came all too soon. Catherine held Granny Stamper in a farewell embrace, promising that the children would write and visit and that she would come as often as she could.

The ride home was slow for Catherine and the children, with each mile seeming to drag on and on. The beginning of their trip had held excitement, knowing that they would soon see their Granny Stamper. Now they were headed back to their own farm and the emptiness of knowing that John would not be there to greet them. sArriving at home, they all pitched in to unload the wagon and settle in for the night. The house was now dark, with everyone sleeping but Catherine. Sitting on the porch she rocked and thought about Granny Stamper. John would have been so hurt to see how his sisters and brother Joel ignored their mother.

Listening to the night sounds and feeling a soft breeze, Catherine closed her eyes. It was at times such as this that she missed John the most. Next month Lord willing, she would see that they visited Granny Stamper again and the children would begin writing to her. Laying her head back she closed her eyes.

-Dear Lord I thank you for precious Granny Stamper

Chapter 24
Time Races By

With the passing of John Stamper, a new determination formed within Catherine. She surveyed all around her and pledged to God above that the dream she and John shared would become a reality. She would raise their children with a switch in one hand and a Bible in the other. Truly, she would give them a legacy to be proud of and keep their father fresh in their memory.

Joel decided to move to the Blue Ridge Mountains, to settle near his uncle, Josiah Stamper. Polly seemed to care for nothing except keeping Joel within her sight as her mental state slowly deteriorated. Joel knew that Polly needed him more now than ever and she hardly acknowledged their boys any more, acting as if they were strangers. Settling in the mountains with the quiet scenery would give her peace. This move would allow Joel to be near older members of his family and hopefully provide some rest from the daily turmoil of Polly's angry outburst one day and withdrawal the next.

As the date drew close to the move, James and Melmath gathered up their courage and asked to stay behind with Catherine. James was first to explain that they could not just leave Catherine helpless with children. They were truly not big enough to completely run the farm even though Alex was just three years younger than James; he claimed that Melmath needed to stay with him. Actually, James did not want to leave and miss a chance at courting Rosa Bogle. Inside he felt little connection with his mother and leaned heavily on Catherine for attention and advice.

Strangely Polly did not seem to care that her boys would not be with them in the mountains. Joel tried to convince them to go, but then remembering how John had sacrificed for him, he relented and told them to stay. The land he and Polly would live on would only yield a garden big enough for their survival and a few acres that would be used for crops to sell. There would be no more rolling acres of land with cattle to tend with dozens of pigs and chickens. Joel was tired and his hope was that life would be simple.

Keeping James and Melmath felt more like keeping sons, than nephews and Catherine was very glad they were staying.

....

The years rolled by and one September morning James came running into the kitchen waving an advertisement for Catherine to see.

WANTED: Strong, trustworthy men. Paying $5.00 per week, with room and board. Ten weeks guaranteed work. Clearing a rich 20 year stand of Carolina pine to be milled on site. Apply to Angus O'Brien, Erin Mavournin Plantation, Wilkes County, North Carolina.

Immediately Catherine voiced her displeasure that James would even think of working logs after John's tragic death. Twisting the bottom of her apron, Catherine paced back and forth showing her frustration.

–How could you do this?

–Aunt Catherine, I'll be fine. Look at the words again. "Milled on site" means that there will be no heavy loads of logs, to travel for miles and miles. This man, O'Brien, has a large plantation that has its own mill. The pine is not over twenty years old in the area he's clearing so there is no hard wood like Uncle John hauled. Please Aunt Catherine.

Dropping her hands to her side, Catherine turned and left the room. James knew that he could not go if she said "no." All he could do was wait to see if she was still speaking to him later on.

Out in the barn, James moved the cow to her stall. Tying her to a side rail, he set a stool down beside the milk pail. Quietly he worked with only the sound of the milk hitting the pail. He was hungry and wanted this chore to be behind him so he could join the family for supper. Deep in his thoughts, James did not hear Catherine enter the barn.

–You'll have to leave early tomorrow so that you can be assured of the job with O'Brien. I know that you're right and I know that you are going to be fine. I've prayed, asking God to keep you safe and bring you back to us.

–I promise I'll come back safe. Thank you Aunt Catherine.

Walking over to James, Catherine embraced him, holding him tight.

–You're like my own son and I want you back on this land as soon as you can.

The job at the O'Brien Plantation was an excellent opportunity for quick money and with Catherine's blessing James headed for Wilkes

County. With Melmath still in residence, she could manage the farm.

....

The seasons began to change and cold weather was upon them. Thursday afternoons found Catherine at Mattie McClain's house sewing quilts. Over the last two months eight women had turned out seven quilts and by the end of their next session each woman would take home one heavy quilt. These gatherings gave Catherine a time to catch up on news, exchange recipes and keep in touch.

Catherine sat remembering the good time she had quilting with the other women in the neighborhood. Looking out the window, she looked at the clouds and thought they looked likely to drop the season's first snow.

Turning from the window, she heard a loud knock at the door. When Catherine answered the knock at the door, there stood James looking handsome and tall, and with a wide grin. James announced that he would like for Catherine to meet his new wife, Annie O'Brien Stamper. Beside him stood a tiny young girl with beautiful auburn hair and large green eyes. Her smile was wide and bright and there were freckles across her nose and cheeks. Annie had defied her father, Angus O'Brien, and married James without his permission. They had traveled over the state line to Virginia and became man and wife. Hiding their marriage for a month, they finally made the announcement and faced the wrath of Angus.

Dumbfounded could not describe the expression on Catherine's face but she stood aside and welcomed them home.

Extending her hand Annie told Catherine how proud she was to finally meet her as James talked of her constantly and fondly. So now, the family had expanded once again.

Annie's parents visited the following month and it was not pleasant. Father Angus was gruff and let everyone know that he thought the couple should be on his land and not on this, as he called it a "shabby excuse for a farm". Catherine merely smiled and asked if he would like some tea and cakes. Everyone, including Annie, breathed a sigh of relief when the O'Brien's left.

The next year flew by and Annie settled in as Catherine's right hand. Shortly after the first planting James and Annie welcomed their first child, a son they named Riley Madigan Stamper, after Annie's paternal grandfather. Hoping this gesture would help to cool Angus Obrien's temper, but unfortunately honoring a family namesake had no effect.

The farm was bustling with activity and Catherine could now look back over the past few years and smile at how well they had managed. With Joel's sons to help with the heavy work, the farm had prospered. She knew that John would have been proud. The children were strong and healthy and for that she was doubly thankful. The oldest two boys, Alex and Gilbert were close to their daddy's height and both bore a striking resemblance to John and also to a small portrait of their grandfather, Powell Stamper. George was catching up to his brothers and although he had the Stamper markings in his features Catherine could see some of herself in his face. The two girls, Ellen and Susan truly looked like sisters and reflected Alex and Gilbert's features.

In the spring, Catherine gave permission for Ellen to visit with cousins in Ashe County not far from Joel and Polly's home. Letters had been exchanged and it was arranged for her to ride with Preacher Icenhour as he passed through Ashe on his way to Tennessee to see his brother. For weeks Catherine and Ellen prepared. Not only did she need clothes but they also wanted to send presents to their relatives. Several jars of honey and a ham would be sent along with a nice blanket that Ellen had woven from wool, from their own sheep.

Had there been any hint the visit would be life changing, Catherine would definitely have had second thoughts. Three weeks into Ellen's visit a letter arrived from John's uncle Josiah Stamper. He praised Catherine on raising such a fine and spirited young daughter and repeated throughout the letter how pretty she was. Reading back over the sentence again Catherine began to feel uneasy.

"We have been so blessed to have this visit with Ellen. She is so much like my mother in her manner and movement that it brought tears to my eyes. How proud John would have been of this daughter. Our son, also named Josiah and your cousin, has asked me to write to you. We find him to be in love with your Ellen and ask that they be allowed to marry. I write this to ask your permission for him to speak to her. Seeing them together I believe that they are a good match"

So it was that four weeks later the Josiah Stamper Sr. family traveled to Iredell County, bringing with them kin that Catherine and her children had not seen in many years. It was a joyful time but also a sad time. Standing ramrod straight and never taking her eyes off her daughter, Catherine was dry-eyed as she witnessed the marriage of this precious child. The deep sadness came when Ellen gathered her belongings and holding her husband's hand climbed aboard the wagon. Ashe County, would now be their home.

As the wagon was lost in the distance Catherine thought of how this must be the feeling her mother had when she married John and left. Now she shared the pain that Elizabeth surely must have felt. At least she still had Susan, and Annie, who was just like a daughter to her.

Chapter 25
Gift of Love

Years had passed since John died and times were still not easy but Catherine had all the essentials needed to live comfortably. Bartering had become a way of life or her, and she was better at it than most men. There were household essentials she could offer, for old widower men or single men that would be needed in the way of household goods. Her quilts were known for their thickness and warmth and no one could match the quality of her dried herbs and fruits. For a sack of grain, she would hem pants, or sew on buttons, or mend the tears and then wash and iron their clothes. She had bartered for a pregnant sow, though the man who traded had not realized there would be twelve piglets instead of one pig. Being an honest woman she gave him half of them. Now there was smoked sausage along with hams hanging in the smoke house along with a salted barrel of pork. The sheep in the pasture were growing fat with thick, wooly coats and there would be mutton on the table in the fall; Catherine would have wool to spin and weave.

In 1855, Catherine thought her life was settled forever in Iredell County, however, life could abruptly change. For her, the change brought about a move to Concord Township in the northern section of Iredell County. The move was brought on by good fortune and also deep sadness. Nanny Grindstaff had died and having no living kin, she left her entire estate to Catherine. Nanny wrote in her will that through the years Catherine had visited weekly and cared for her better than most daughters.

The entire family was very excited about this newfound gift. Nanny's land was rich with many more acres than what they were presently farming. They truly needed more room as James and Annie now had two little boys, and the loft was growing crowded. If only they had truly understood the depth of Nanny's gift.

Shortly before Nanny's husband Grier had died, his only living relative, a brother named Perin had been killed in an accident. Perin had made a small fortune in trapping, trading and owning a sawmill. Extremely frugal, he saved practically every penny he earned. He became smitten with a beautiful girl in the neighborhood almost twenty years his junior. Her father gave his blessing to the union but with the stipulation that Perin would have to wait two years before marrying in order to build his bride a new home.

Using his savings Perin began building an enormous house. Six days a week he labored right beside his workers, until the house was finished. He stood and surveyed all that he had created and could envision bringing his bride to the house and filling the large house with children. Six weeks before his wedding, and having lived in the house only a few weeks, Perin was killed, gored by his bull. Grier Grindstaff inherited his brother's estate. Still grieving over Perin, Grier was walking his fields when a bolt of lightning struck him dead burning off the soles of his boots. And then Nanny became the sole survivor of this family.

Perin's plantation was named Grindstaff House and had never been mentioned in all the talks that Catherine and Nanny had on their visits. Several times Catherine had described to Nanny the size house she would one day like to have in order to finish raising her family. The seed was planted in the old woman's mind, as she never forgot about Catherine's dream.

The Campbell family was sad to see them move. Isabel Campbell gave Catherine a fine shawl she had knitted and one that Catherine wore proudly on the day they left.

This new home was not only larger but much nicer, a true house and not a cabin, with a large barn, smokehouse, springhouse, several sheds and a very large privy. There were four chimneys visible from the outside. The layout of the house consisted of five rooms downstairs and four large rooms upstairs, each with a fireplace. There was even a large attic with windows. The kitchen was modern for its day and had a separate stair- case that led to the second floor and then to the attic.

Two covered porches in the front with one on ground level and one on the second floor, gave ample shade in the heat of summer. The porches made for a pleasant place to sit and visit or just relax, to enjoy the sounds of the evening. The porch at back of the house ran the length of the house.

Opening the front door revealed a large staircase with two landings leading to the second story. To the left was a parlor nicely furnished in hopes of one day bringing a bride to this beautiful home. The room had been given every attention to colors and patterns. The finest silk draperies hung from the window but were now dusty and faded from years of neglect. Down the hall behind the parlor was a small library that Perin had built to use as his study.

The kitchen was furnished with a large cast iron stove and a few cabinets along with a dry sink lined with tin. Water released from the sink ran under the house on crushed rock into a reservoir. Gathering their water would be easy as the well was located on the back porch.

Entering the kitchen from the outside there was a door on the left that led to a cellar. Another door led to a laundry washroom complete with its own fireplace for boiling water.

Furniture from the previous owner had also remained in each room. Catherine not only managed to obtain a much larger home but one that was mostly furnished. The one piece of furniture that thrilled her most was a huge table in the dining room. Seeing the large table brought back memories of her childhood when her parents had a separate room for eating with a table that would seat ten. A dining room was the one thing that Catherine's mother had wanted most, something to remind her of home. Although her parents' home was very modest, the family enjoyed eating together in the brightly lit room. Reminiscing, Catherine thought of the beautiful table that had been lovingly made by her father as a gift to her mother and was the first thing sold after he died. Catherine could picture her family around this large table on Sundays sharing a meal, while laughing and talking.

The Stamper household now consisted of eight adults and two children and with plenty of room for more in the big house. Everyone would have his own space. Upstairs the brothers George, Alex and Gilbert would share a large bedroom with their cousin Melmath. Next to their room James and Annie had their own room. Across the hall Susan had a small room to herself and next to her room Riley and Heath shared a bedroom and had enough space for several more people in their room. In the upstairs hallway there was a small sitting area giving additional room to sit and read or just rest. There were glass doors that opened to the upstairs porch. Downstairs Catherine had decided to use the library as her own personal bedroom. There was still space to move all throughout the house. This is where Catherine had wanted to be in life, with family all under one roof. There would even be room to house Ellen and her family when they came to visit.

Acres and acres of land surrounded the large house. Special areas had been laid out for a blacksmith shop and the beginning of a sawmill. The land was rich and had been kept active by allowing tenants to farm and their cotton was standing in the fields ready for picking. To the side of the kitchen was an herb garden and beyond that were a kitchen garden plot, grapevines and a small orchard.

On the first day of the move the women washed windows and the men rolled up rugs, taking them outside, and draping them over chairs. The children took small brooms and beat the backside of the rugs throwing up clouds of dust. Catherine tackled the kitchen and dining areas keeping Alex busy, drawing water to boil. Upstairs Annie placed clean sheets on all the beds while Susan mopped the floors.

James and George worked the barn removing decaying straw and replacing with fresh hay for the animals. By the end of the second day they were able to lead the cows and horses into the barn, now their new home.

Amidst all the work, a lone rider comes up the lane and ties his horse at the steps. Inside Catherine was putting out leftover biscuits and ham for their evening meal when she heard Annie calling that a stranger had come and was now on the porch. Lewis Day was Nanny's solicitor, and had ridden out to see Catherine and finalize his duties of turning over the estate to Catherine.

He requested to see Catherine privately. There was one particular bit of information that had been withheld from the family. He had been instructed to place in Catherine's hands a small, carved box, within the week of reading Nanny's will. Along with the box was a sealed letter of instruction. Because Mr. Day had been so secretive about the entire business, Catherine placed the box in her bedroom, then walked with Mr. Day to the front door. Hurrying back to her bedroom, she closed the door. The box was heavy and it would be best to see the contents alone.

Turning the key in the lock until she heard the 'click', she cautiously lifted the lid then fully opened it, Catherine's knees gave way and she dropped to the floor. Gold. Lots of pieces of shiny, gold coins. Immediately Catherine closed the lid on the box and placed it under her bed. It would be best to go about her daily duties and deal with the box in private when the house was quiet.

As the day wore down, evening found the entire family sitting quietly in the kitchen, all very tired. Although they had managed to clear away enough dust to sleep on clean sheets, walk on clean floors and have a spider web free kitchen, there was still much to be done. A full hour before they would normally go to bed everyone was fast asleep. Everyone that is, except Catherine.

Dumping the contents of the box on the bed Catherine picked up each item. There was a brooch that looked very old, one small ring, some old letters tied with a white ribbon, more papers tied together and what looked like a gold wedding ring. And gold coins, many, many gold coins.

–Jump back Jehosophat!
Timidly reaching out, she touched several of the coins and then uttered "Jehosophat" one more time.

Sitting on the bed she just stared at the contents of the box for a long time. Finally, she reached for the sealed letter, tore it open, immediately recognizing Nanny's handwriting.

To my Dearest Catherine, Friend and Loved one,
As you read this letter I am resting in the arms of our Savior, safe
and peaceful at last. You are in surprise of my gift, I am sure, and it
is my wish to let you know that you have truly treated me as a
daughter would treat a very beloved mother. It is not important
what you have on earth as my beloved Grier and I knew all too well.
And Perin would have wanted to see his house filled with children
and laughter, which you will surely provide. There is one condition
to accepting the contents of the box and that is you must keep its
contents hidden using them only when necessary. There are many
people who would be a false friend to obtain money. The   coins
do not come from what I gained at Perin's death, but rather what I
have saved over the years. I do ask that you take one coin and
*   purchase books for the little ones in your house, but that the*
remainder be guarded and used as you see fit. Also in the box you
will find a gold ring. This was my mother's wedding ring and was
also placed on my hand by my most beloved husband. It is my wish
that you pass this along in your family, as it is evident by my gift
that you are now my family. You will see there is also a brooch that
I wish for you to wear as this belonged to my grandmother who
was born and lived in Scotland. The letters and   documents I leave
for you to read and hold safe. I could not bear the thoughts of
these writings being mislaid or given up to be burned. My last days
on this earth have been made joyous by your visits and your
thoughtful gifts of food. Being able to be with you and your family
every Christmas has made my heart very light. I kiss you now and
bid you farewell and will wait to see your face one day in heaven.
Your loving and faithful neighbor
Abigail Grindstaff (X)
Letter drawn this 10th day of October 1853
Lewis Day, solicitor

Laying the letter aside Catherine reached into her apron pocket, brought out a handkerchief and blew her nose. How easy it had been to love Nanny. She touched the coins and began counting how many pieces there were, figuring in her mind the total amount. Counting again as she was sure she had made a mistake. There was enough here that she could sit on the porch doing nothing and still feed her family, pay taxes and give to the church for years on end.

Not one to overlook Nanny's instructions nor her own sense of thrift, she laid her skirts on the bed and began ripping out the hems. Looking through her cloth scraps Catherine selected several fabrics and cut them into tiny squares. Carefully she began sewing small pockets inside the hem. Next she searched through the quilt cabinet for her old worn out blanket and began cutting and tearing strips from the blanket. Wrapping the jewelry and coins in a small piece of torn blanket she placed one item in each pocket and then sewed shut. Hours passed and Catherine had managed to sew the items into practically everything she owned. Putting on one of the skirts, she walked back and forth across the room. She could feel the weight of the objects but the blanket pieces cushioned them so there was no noise as they brushed together as she walked.

Cracking her door and seeing no one around, Catherine quickly left her bedroom and headed for the kitchen. In the small hallway between the kitchen and the dining room there were cabinets filled with china. As the household slept Catherine quietly selected plates and carried them to the dining room table. Calling up her memories on etiquette she laid the dishes out one by one. Then standing back she admired how grand the table looked. Tomorrow morning her family would be greeted with their first breakfast in the house that would become their home for many years to come. Catherine wanted this particular morning to be one that they would all remember. Returning to her room she laid on the bed and thought about her day. As she relaxed, her body felt the ache of the long day and she slept.

Early the next morning Alex awoke to the smell of freshly baked bread. Leaving his bed he opened the door and looked down the hall at that same time another door opened across the hall. Soon the entire family was awake and headed down the stairs seeing Catherine standing in the doorway to the dining room, welcoming them to their first official mean in their new home.

Stepping aside she revealed the dining room table set with Perin's finest china and silver. A gasp could be heard from the girls and then giggles.

–*Today we are having Christmas. It is truly a day of blessings to us all.*

Sitting at the head of the table Catherine watched and listened as her family talked and laughed, as they passed the platters of food. The sun was shining through the lead glass windows and the room appeared rosy and sparkling.

–*Thank you Nanny for your gift of love. Thank you Lord for your gift of Nanny.*

Chapter 26
Talk of War

Even though Nanny Grindstaff made it possible for Catherine and her family to have a better life, everything was not rosy. Each time Catherine went to town, all the men could talk about was war. Walking home she talked aloud to herself about the possibility of war.

> –Well there better not be any war because I don't have time to be worrying about a war. I'm just not going to waste time talking about it either because it's not going to happen. The boys at the house have better things to do than fight some Yankee they don't even know.

Nonetheless, Catherine did agree that certain conditions and taxes, which mostly applied to products from southern states, were unfair especially since the northern states were not suffering from this situation. All she wanted to concentrate on was how much salt she would need for the slaughter of hogs in the fall and how much corn she would need in the corncrib.

In 1861 the talk became more specific. There was going to be a vote on secession. James, now eligible to vote, listened to all the discussions. At home George and Alex asked questions that James did his best to answer. Melmath listened in nervous anticipation to all the talk of war.

One afternoon Catherine's oldest daughter Ellen suddenly appeared with her children announcing that her husband had gone to Virginia to be with his brothers. If there was going to be a war, his family was sticking together, and they would all go together, meeting up on the Virginia side of the mountains to confer about their decisions.

Small in stature like her mother, Ellen was fourteen when she married her twenty-year-old cousin, Josiah Stamper, and with her mother's blessing. By fifteen she had given birth to her first son Jamie, followed two years later by another son, Jonathan. Determined to keep her family together Ellen hitched up her team and drove for two days before she arrived in Iredell County. Now she was home and that meant three more mouths for Catherine to feed.

Embracing her mother, Ellen finally cried.

-Mama, I'm so scared.

Her deep blue eyes shone with tears and there were dark circles under her eyes. Ellen was not concerned about her appearance and had let her long dark hair hang down her back, laying in tangles from the windy ride. Catherine held on to her daughter and ran her hand down her hair to smooth out the tangles. Crying on her mother's shoulder Ellen held tight and took comfort that she was in her mother's arms.

As the weeks passed Ellen and her boys slipped into the routine of the household and it seemed as if they had always been there. The boys were moved into Riley and Heath's bedroom and Ellen moved in with Susan. The large house was now filled with children and adults. The only vacant bed in the house was the preacher's bed in the parlor where the traveling preacher would occasionally sleep.

Looking at the four young boys, now living in the house, it was hard to tell which boy was which in the distance, unless they were standing. All four of the boys had the same dark brown hair and each had deep set eyes with dark brows and long lashes. They looked like brothers and often teased visitors who did not know they were actually cousins. Heath and Jamie could pass for twins except that Heath was inches shorter and several years younger; Jonathan and Riley even shared the same crooked smile. Several times during that first week Annie and Ellen both caught themselves calling to the wrong child.

As more talk of war surfaced the days became filled with tension in Iredell County. The state had sent word that every county would vote to determine whether the state would secede. Within weeks the polls were opened in the county; 191 men voted for, with 1,818 men voting against. Iredell County did not want war. There was to be a State Convention and the county would send two delegates, Anderson Mitchell and T.A. Allison.

Soon the delegates were on their way to Raleigh to register the votes of the citizens of Iredell County. Finally the day arrived for the voting at the State Convention. Votes were cast, and tallied by each county representative. The citizens of North Carolina had spoken 46,672 had voted for and 47,269 had voted against, with 85 delegates casting "no" votes and 35 delegates casting "yes" votes. North Carolina wanted no part of secession. Before the ink had dried on the final tally of votes, a shot fired in South Carolina was heard around the world. War had begun.

The Stamper household was in an uproar. Ellen had cried for days when they heard the news, because she knew that Josiah was with his brothers signing papers to join in the fight.

James and Annie had recently discovered their third child was on the way. James felt that he needed to follow the men in the community and enlist in the fight since war was a sure thing. But seeing the beginning of Annie's growing stomach, he worried. Foremost on his mind was the farm and how the family would survive with a war going on around them.

Catherine's youngest daughter Susan, though flighty and a daydreamer, helped some in the house, but at every turn complained about the housework and working outside. Alex, George and Melmath helped work the farm with James taking the lead. Gilbert had gone to stay with Brooks and Nancy to help out on their farm. With three daughters and another baby on the way, Brooks needed all the help he could get.

Frequently Catherine walked up on the boys as they had their heads together talking about the war. She had even caught them making excuses to visit neighboring farms saying they were needed to help with this or that, when in truth they were hoping to find news of the war.

But Catherine knew what they were up to and she was determined the war was not going to include any of the boys in her house. No sir. She had fought too hard and long to get this family where they were and she was not going to let them fight in a war that didn't concern them, possibly being killed. If necessary, she would hide them in the woods to keep them from serving.

Preacher Icenhour now only came to their community every three weeks to serve in the small neighborhood church. On those Sundays the wagon was hitched for the ride to church and with her Bible clutched tightly in her hands, Catherine sat beside James as Annie placed the food baskets in the bed of the wagon. Susan and Ellen helped the children climb up. At a steady pace the ride to Concord Baptist Church would take almost thirty minutes.

The day at church held a predictable routine. Families from miles around gathered early to visit and see friends and then to hear the preacher's message. After the service everyone would spread their food on make shift tables and settled in for the afternoon. Women would sit on quilts under the trees and to talk and watch their children. The would break up in small groups, balancing their plates while discussing the latest crops. After the meal, fiddles and banjos would appear and the remainder of the time would be spent with a singing. How the Stampers loved seeing friends and singing. Church day was always Catherine's favorite day of the month.

Once Preacher Icenhour arrived, the church bell was rung, and families took their places on rough benches inside the tiny church building. Standing on the wooden platform the preacher bowed his head in prayer. Then looking around at all who came today he started his message.

−Today's message will look at what we owe our God and what we owe to each other. And what do we owe our state? You've all heard the talk of war. Where do you stand? Are you willing to stand and fight? The Bible is full of stories where God sends his people to fight, outnumbered, and against all odds they won. And sometimes they came up against impossible situations.

Catherine felt the hair on the back of her neck stand up and gripped the Bible in her lap. She felt her heart beat faster as she listened and fear settled in the back of her mind. Glancing to her right, Annie sat listening to the preacher's words as silent tears ran down her cheeks. James was taking in each word the preacher spoke as well as George, Alex and Melmath. Ellen sat quiet and pale with her youngest child resting in her left arm and her right arm pressing her oldest to her side. Seemingly unaware of the impact of the preacher's words Susan adjusted the folds of her skirt and checked her new shoes for scuff marks.

The day at church held a predictable routine. Families from miles around gathered early to visit and see friends and then to hear the preacher's message. After the service everyone spread their food on make shift tables and settled in for the afternoon. Women spread quilts on the grass under the trees and sat with their children, enjoying the food. The men congregated in small groups balancing their plates, discussing the latest crops. After the meal, fiddles and banjos would appear and the remainder of the time would be spent with a singing. How the Stampers loved seeing friends and singing. Church day was always Catherine's favorite day of the month.

With the church service completed, families scattered as the food was spread and children pushed and shoved while mothers tried to steer them away from the table. With the blessing of the food the meal began. Now everyone could visit with friends as they shared this special time together. Catherine sat with her family but barely touched her food. Sometime later the first sounds of a fiddle tuning up could be heard and voices were raised in singing. But the Stampers were in their wagon heading home, solemn and quiet.

Chapter 27
Facing Duty

Brilliant splotches of color could be seen in the distant hills, hinting at the beginning of fall. Standing in the kitchen, taking inventory, Catherine's mind was racing with thoughts of what needed to be done to prepare for winter. It would not be long now before hog killing. The past growing season had brought an abundant crop with no drought. Ten cords of wood were stacked and ready for winter; more wood was waiting to be split.

The barn was full of hay and the corncrib was bursting at the seams.
Trays of fruit and beans were on the shelves in the drying house. Several bushels of corn and wheat had been set aside and would be traded for salt from old man Crouch, the neighbor down the road. The storehouse held several barrels of sauerkraut along with several kegs of vinegar. Trading had been very good this year.

Catherine checked the shelves on the kitchen wall and peeked inside each crock. Next she checked the flour barrel in the corner and made a mental note to see if Crouch had any extra flour on hand that she could barter for.

She was satisfied that her family would not starve during the winter but her mind kept going back to the letter that had just come this morning. Taking the letter from her apron pocket, she unfolded the sheet and read again.

Dearest Sister Catherine,
I beg your forgiveness in not writing these last few months but my heart is just hurting with all that is going on around us. Lewis and Joseph are grown and can do as other men but they are all I have. Both are determined to enlist and have even defied my daddy when he tried to talk to them. They are all I have left of Hugh and I could not live if something happened to them. My preacher told us that for the next few weeks they would be signing up boys at Paul Payne's store, not far from where you live. Lewis and Joseph have both said they are going to be there. I know that we have not been as close as I would have liked, but our boys are of the same blood. Will you send James to Payne's store and tell them they need to stay at home with their mama? Catherine, I cannot live without my

boys and ask that you please help me keep them at home. I told them that you wrote to me and told me that your boys were not going. I beg you to write to Lewis and Joseph and tell them they do not need to do this. My mother died last month and this is a heavy burden on me to run the house. My grief keeps me in tears at the sight of her things and I cannot bear to touch them or pack them away.. Daddy is beside himself as my brother Paul has enlisted. We are not sure how we can work the farm and there are still four children at home, besides me and mine. I know that you will pray for me and ask that you pray for my daddy and my boys also. Please come to see me when you can.
Your sister by marrying Hugh Stamper
Cassie Stamper mother of Lewis and Joseph

Slipping the letter back in her pocket Catherine made a mental note to speak to James and see if he knew when the sign up would be held at Payne's store. Hugh's boys had visited several times and both were very fond of James. He surely could make them see they needed to stay with their mother.

Across the road from the house, George and Melmath walked through the field making their way among the drying corn stalks until they were within sight of the house.

–She's going to have a fit when she finds out what we've gone and done.

–There's no turning back now and just look at the kind of men that's joining up with this company.

–Why, you'd think she'd be right proud that her kin would be serving with the Tomlinsons, Stewarts, and the Moose boys. The best men in the county are going to be in Company E or Company A and we'd be stupid not to get in on it first.

George listened as Melmath boasted on and on about getting to fight alongside men from the most respected families in the county. But George who had eyed Sally Jane Allen for almost two years now, was waiting for her to grow up and now she was almost grown. What if she did not wait for him to come back or what if her daddy made her marry some deferred man while he was away? No, he had to figure out a way to get her daddy to hang on to her till he could get back and marry her. Melmath was still talking big as they emerged from the cornfield and crossed the road. Walking slowly through the yard they both felt relief at seeing that Catherine was not on the porch waiting for them. Supper would be soon enough to tell them all about this great news.

Earlier in the day James watched from behind a tree outside Paul Payne's store when he spotted George and Melmath walking towards him. Men in spiffy new uniforms showing their rank on clean new jacket sleeves, sat on barrels behind a table signing up new recruits. George and Melmath waited in line to sign their names to the roster.

Just as he thought, they've snuck in here to sign up without letting anyone know, thinking they were so smart. Well by the time they make their way through that line the page in the book will be full. They'll turn the page to start a new list of names and the name of James Stamper will be on the back side so they'll never even know unless they ask.

Walking from the barn James carried the evening supply of milk and stepping over to the gate he placed the buckets on the ground. Looking around at how the place was shaping up he thought of how he was going to miss all this. Across the yard he spotted George and Melmath slowly walking toward the house. He'd beat them home by a good hour just in time for milking. The smell of fried ham shifted in his direction as he started for the house. Well, supper is as good a time as any to tell them.

The long table was set and Catherine was busy dishing up turnips. Annie carefully lifted the cast iron pot that was filled to the brim with potatoes. Ellen placed a platter of ham and another of biscuits on the table. Everyone started toward their usual place at the table and James blessed the food.

On the average day the chatter at the table went from local gossip to crops. Tonight there was a loud silence. Catherine looked from one face to another only to see the tops of heads. Everyone was bent over their food.

-The food can't be so good that you have to root like a pig on your plate.

Still no one looked up and finally James spoke up.

-Why don't we let George and Melmath tell us what they saw when they went to Paul Payne's store today.

Gilbert sat up straight and Alex ducked his head continuing to eat. At hearing this news, Catherine frowned because she knew that men were signing up at Payne's store today.

George, red-faced and stammering, glared at James wondering how he had found out?

—Me and Melmath joined up today. Lewis and Joseph were there and they   joined too.

And before the final drop of blood drained from Catherine's face James threw in a "Me too"; Annie started to cry, all the while cradling her protruding belly. Alex pushed his chair back from the table and without a word left the room. Turning to look in Gilbert's direction Catherine's face showed fear.

—I'm sorry mama but I was there before George and Melmath, so I'll be going too.

The room was so silent Catherine could hear their breathing. She pushed back from the table, turned and grabbed her shawl from the peg by the door and was outside before anyone could say a word. Cool air hit her in the face and she drew the shawl tighter around her shoulders. Pushing open the barn door, she stepped into the dark, pausing for her eyes to adjust. Feeling for the lantern she lit the wick and hung the light on a nail, protruding from the wall.

How could they do this to her? What had she done to make them leave? Would they have enough food to get through the winter? Who would help her? All these thoughts flying through her mind made her dizzy and she sat down in the hay. Finally tears began to roll down her cheeks and her nose began to run. Falling on her face in the hay, Catherine began to pray out loud, pleading for peace in her heart, for her fears to abate.

Inside the house James stared out the window.

—She's still in the barn and would not be surprised if she stayed there all night.

George, Gilbert and Melmath, pressed close to James' back, tried to see out the window.

Before the sun rose, James eased from his bed and dressed. Better to milk early and start on chores. Coming down the steps into the main room, James stopped and held his breath. Was he seeing something unreal? Catherine sat in a rocker by the fire. Her head was thrown back and at first James thought she was dead. Coming closer he could see the short rise and fall of her chest. Sleeping. But in her lap was the beginning of a shirt.

Slightly nudging her shoulder, James smiled as her blue eyes popped open and she smiled.

-Guess I'm not much for staying up all night sewing, but just wanted George to have at least a decent shirt ready. Next I'll make Gilbert and Melmath a nice shirt.

She had lost the battle. Her boys were going to war and she could not have them leaving thinking she was against them. No, she would hold them close for the next few days. Three days and James would be gone. Six days till Gilbert, George and Melmath would be gone. Although she did not want to watch, she could not deny herself a last look at them as they marched off to war.

When James left to do the milking, Catherine went to the kitchen to begin making provisions for the boys to carry in their haversacks. Taking cups of flour she stirred in baking powder and salt. Gradually adding water, a dry dough formed.

Rolling the dough out, she carefully began cutting the dough into three by three inch squares. Taking a ten-penny nail, she dotted holes into the dough. There would be enough hardtack to last the boys for weeks. Slipping the pans into the oven she stoked the fire with more wood chips, and the kitchen became almost unbearable with the heat. Leaning against the table, Catherine fanned herself with her apron, waiting for the dough to finish baking.

Taking the pans from the oven, she laid them on the table to cool. Today the hardtack was soft, but by tomorrow it would dry out and the boys would soak it in their coffee before eating. Laying out several cloths, she began distributing the hardtack and then folding the cloths to cover. Each bundle would now ride safely in their haversacks; at least they would have some food.

Wanting them to have an occasional sweet she decided to put together vinegar candy. A few cups of sugar along with butter and a small amount of vinegar completed the recipe. Placing a pot on the stove she began stirring the mixture to dissolve the sugar. The fire was still hot, so it did not take long for the mixture to boil. Dipping a wooden spoon into the mixture she then let the liquid drip off the spoon into a cup of water. As soon as the liquid hit the water, it formed small balls and sank to the bottom of the cup. It was ready to pour onto the table and begin pulling and cutting. Soon there was a growing pile of pieces of candy. Divided and wrapped this treat would also be placed in their haversacks.

Preparing food was not all that Catherine wanted to do. She wanted to stop them from going, but knew that would be impossible. At least when they took out their hardtack they would know that she had thought of them as she baked. Whenever they ate their candy, they would think of the sweetness of home.

Later that evening Catherine wrote a note to each of the boys that she would place in their haversacks. She would send words to encourage them, to let them know she was praying for them, a Bible verse and finally, words that told them how much she loved each one. With the notes in her lap she laid her head back against the chair, closed her eyes, and silently pray

Chapter 28
Farewell or Goodbye?

The morning air was fresh and crisp for early October. When Catherine rose that morning, Annie had already been about building a fire and mixing dough for biscuits; she hadn't been able to sleep since her husband James had left three days before. Rolling through her head was the reminder to keep busy and think on the new baby, soon to come.

Catherine placed a hand on Annie's shoulder to show her support.

–Time will come when you can sleep.

Smiling, Annie patted Catherine's hand on her shoulder. Moving to her room Catherine sat in the rocker as she finished sewing buttons on two shirts and then rolled them for stuffing in the knapsacks.

It was just after dawn and already there were families huddling in groups about Payne's store yard. Horses sensing the excitement in the air, moved and twitched as their saddles were checked and saddlebags were double-checked to make sure nothing had been forgotten.

Sights of women fretting over sons and husbands, lightly touching faces and placing hands on the arms of their loved ones, mothers staring into eyes filled with anticipation and mentally fixing their faces in their mind. It might be months before they were able to again touch the one they loved so dearly. The thought of never seeing them again was etched on every female face in the crowd. Catherine stood with Agnes Moose and watched as George, Gilbert and Melmath compared provisions with David Moose. Catherine watched as Alex talked with his brothers. Seeing his face told her that the men were questioning why he was not riding out with them. Seeing that her son and nephews were questioning Alex made her uncomfortable and it was evident that her first-born was not giving them answers they wanted to hear. Turning to see who bumped her, Catherine turned back to see George and realized that Alex was gone.

Agnes Moose was quick to tell Catherine that the boys would be back in just a matter of weeks, no more than a few months.

–The Yankees don't stand a chance against our fine men. Why my

David can shoot the feathers off a hen a hundred yards away.

This was not exactly comforting to Catherine. George and Gilbert were not experienced at shooting and James was not too much better. She was not sure that Melmath had ever fired their gun more than twice. The boys were so small when John had died and the gun was there for hunting and nothing else. It had never entered her mind that the boys should practice to be crack shots. Other young men in the crowd had fathers that they regularly hunted with, and Catherine now felt fear well up in her throat. Her boys were very ill prepared.

Although they had only been awake a few hours it felt like days to Catherine. Annie had stayed at the house with the children and Susan the youngest daughter, was now standing at the edge of the crowd. Smiling sweetly at an older man, she was telling him how sorry she was that he would not be able to join his neighbors in this grand adventure.

Beating on a drum, a young boy gained everyone's attention. Standing on the steps to the store, Preacher Icenhour raised both his arms and called for everyone's attention.

–We cannot send these men off without our blessings and prayers.

Silence spread among the crowd and they waited till all the men had gathered around the preacher. Holding his arms outstretched toward the men, he began praying for safety and for victory. Catherine stood dry-eyed and staring, watching the preacher's lips move but truly not hearing his words. At the sound of "Amen", someone in the crowd raised their voice in song and soon others joined in, voices harmonizing.

> *We are a band of brothers,*
> *And native to the soil,*
> *Fighting for our Liberty,*
> *With treasure, blood, and toil;*
> *And when our rights were threatened,*
> *The cry rose near and far,*
> *Hurrah for the Bonnie Blue Flag, that bears a*
> *Single Star!*
>
> *Hurrah! Hurrah! for Southern Rights Hurrah!*
> *Hurrah! for the Bonnie Blue Flag that bears a*
> *Single Star!*

Men began mounting their horses, while others fell in line to march, whooping and hollering they waved their hats as they fell in line behind their leader, beginning their journey out of the small community. Men and boys, standing by the road, cheered and shouted to "Go and get them Yanks". Smiling and waving young boys ran alongside the horses. Bringing up the rear were three young boys in their early teens, shiny new drums hanging by straps around their necks, tapping out a marching beat. Women wept as sons rode to a fate unknown. At seeing her loved ones ride off to face possible death, Catherine certainly could not share in the cheers around her.

They rode for an hour before coming to the outskirts of Salisbury, where they would divide into two groups. Half were going to join Company A, 33rd Regiment and the remaining to Company E, of the 49th. Standing and facing each other, George and Gilbert shook hands and wished each other well. Then George and Melmath raised a hand to one another. It would be a parting they would keep in their hearts and memory forever.

Melmath walked silently, glancing over his shoulder, until all he could see of George was just a black speck. Gilbert stood beside Melmath, staring straight ahead. A deep crease forming on his forehead, he occasionally shifted his eyes to the side, secretly catching glimpses of his cousin. Running through his mind were memories of all the times they had been together, hunted together, talked and laughed. This moment however, was too somber for any smiles or laughter. After an hour the tension began to ease as the men relaxed. Several of the men finally began talking, discussing how they were going to win the war. Melmath was silent, listening to all the bragging and posturing, while feeling sick in his stomach. He could still see the look on his aunt Catherine's face as he walked past and at that very moment realized he was probably made a mistake, but he could not turn back now.

Chapter 29
New Life

The one thing left to do for supper, was pick the greens from the kitchen garden. Moving slowly down the row in the garden Annie felt her child stir in protest. She'd been on her feet since sun up and there were still chores to do before she could even think about sitting down.

Seeing how slow Annie was moving, Susan offered to pick the greens. Remembering that the last time Susan picked, and knowing she was not very careful which leaves were picked, Annie had just as soon do it herself. It was high time that Miss Susan found herself a man and started making her own way. She could have been married by now if she hadn't been so picky.

–Always had her head in the clouds thinking that something better was just around the corner. Well I can tell her now it's not going to be better and she had best be looking around at what is left, if anything.

The stems of the greens felt prickly even on Annie's rough hands She pulled off the outside leaves so the plant would keep growing new leaves. At this rate we'll have greens clear up through February, maybe even March. Squatting and shuffling her way down the row she picked till the basket was past full. Standing she touched her lower back where the ache had been since early this morning. Thinking it would ease off once she sat down, she reached for the basket and placed it against her huge belly, walking slowly toward the porch.

Jamie was sitting on the steps plucking the feathers from one of two doves he had caught and Jonathan, sitting on the ground, was blowing the discarded feathers. Riley was chasing the floating feathers and blowing at them trying to keep them afloat.

Stepping around the boys, Annie made her way to the kitchen where she shook the basket of greens down in the small wash barrel already filled with water. They did not look nearly as dirty as she first thought and probably would not have to wash them more than three or four times. The water felt cold as she pushed the greens down to the bottom of the barrel and then released them to float to the top again. She sprinkled salt on top so that any bugs that held on would separate from the leaves.

Her sleeves were wet and with her belly out so far she almost could not get close enough to the barrel. Once the greens were sufficiently clean she poured fresh water into the big cast iron pot on top of the stove and stoked the fire. Well if greens and turnips would keep you from being sick then Annie knew they would be the healthiest people in the entire county. Adding a few pieces of wood to the fire, the greens began to simmer and she poured in a splash of vinegar, just enough to take away the bitter taste. At least there would be this much done before Catherine came home.

....

Swinging her basket, as she walked at the side of the road, Catherine thought of all the money in her pocket from selling their butter and eggs. It was worth the six mile round trip walk; besides, she could not afford to take one of the animals away from fieldwork. Going to town gave her the excuse to check to see if there were any letters from the boys at the post office. They had all been gone for some time now and there had only been two letters that made it through so far. How was she supposed to know exactly where they were if they did not write and tell her? Today there was only a letter for Susan, and who would be writing her?

The men at Payne's store said that some of the boys might get leave. Maybe if they made it back soon she would have enough money to buy some buttons for the coat she was making for Melmath. He had gone off without so much as a heavy coat and here with winter upon them. His mama certainly did not worry about him so Catherine felt it was her God given duty to care about him, just like he was her own. Even if Polly and Joel were still living with her, it would be her job to take care of James and Melmath, like a mother would. From what she gathered in Joel's last letter, Polly was doing poorly, and never asked about her boys.

From the road Catherine's home looked cozy and warm and she paused to survey the house and the land surrounding it. They certainly had come a long way. Sniffing the air she could smell the greens all the way to the road and for a split second she felt a slight nausea rise in her throat. There's got to be something else we can grow next year to see us through besides those greens and turnips.

Stepping lightly over the ditch she hitched her skirt up and walked through the yard, wondering why no one was on the porch. The children must still be out trying to catch birds with that trap Jamie had rigged up. Nearing the porch she spotted feathers littering the ground. "How many times have I told those boys that feathers are to be scooped up and put in the sack till we get enough for a pillow?"

Pushing open the door, Catherine opened her mouth to begin complaining over the feathers, but the room was empty. Greens were simmering in the pot and there was bread rising on the table. A chunk of side meat lay on the table beside a sharp knife. Turning to go back outside she heard the first sounds of pain from upstairs and headed in that direction. "The baby must be coming early". Pushing open the door to the bedroom she stepped through and looked at Annie already in the bed covered in sweat.

Looking pale, Susan was wringing her hands and pacing back and forth at the side of the bed. When they saw Catherine they both said together "Oh Mama". Ellen had gone to the next farm over, so Susan had sent Jamie to find Catherine and sent the children to the barn.

Asking how long this had been going on and hearing several hours, she quickly shed her shawl and started rolling up her sleeves; looking at Annie she asked to see how far things had come. Annie held on to the rails at the headboard while Catherine lifted the sheet to see what was happening.

-*This one's coming fast. Better get ready. I can see his head, black hair and all.*

With two writhing painful pushes Carolina Susanne Stamper was born. Catherine felt the sting of tears as she looked on this new life for the first time. The baby was named Carolina, after John's grandmother and they would call her Lina.

Clutching the newborn Catherine quickly looked for something to tie and cut the cord. Running to the kitchen, Susan returned with twine and the butcher knife. Within thirty minutes the baby was tied, clipped, bathed, wrapped and laid in her mother's arms.

-*Guess this one caught you by surprise, huh?*

Snuggling the baby closer to her breast Annie looked at the baby and smoothed her hand over its damp hair.

-*One thing about the babies in this family, they all come with a full growth of hair and eyelashes enough for two people.*

Annie smiled and drifted off into an exhausted sleep with the baby at her breast.

The birth of Lina filled Catherine with thoughts of triumph but also tragedy. Holding the tiny baby girl in her arms Catherine felt tears as they formed in her eyes and seeing features of her son, husband and nephew, looking back at her. All the Stamper kin had the same shaped eye with a deep blue color; this baby was no different. Tiny but strong, the baby emitted a faint mewing sound. Even in times so hard, this precious gift would be well cared for and loved. The Stamper family had literally dwindled to a house full of women and children as the war waged around them. Catherine had two sons and two nephews who had marched off to fight and left behind their women and children in her care. And now here was another one to be fed, clothed, watched over and prayed for.

Seeing movement from the corner of her eye, Catherine turned as Susan suddenly stepped into the lamplight with a letter clutched tightly in her hand. Catherine smiled and asked if another beau had written about his love for her. Dropping her head Susan decided to just blurt it out.

–The letter is from Alex. He did not have the heart to tell you so he asked me to tell you that he's joined up to fight.

A huge lump seemed to catch in Catherine's throat as she dropped her chin on her chest, as tears rolled down her cheeks. Now there would be three sons gone and nothing she could do about it, but pray for them every day. Silently Susan handed her mother the letter and went to bed.

For what seemed like hours, Catherine sat with the letter clutched in her hand. She folded open the paper and read Alex's words. How unfair had she been to this child that he felt he could not talk to her about his plans? It cut to the bone that he was gone, but also that he could not face her. Alex had always been private and driven, just like his father. Finally she was ready to read his letter.

Mama, I need to do this. Everyone around me showed their loyalty and has gone to fight. I cannot stay any longer, as I am needed. Mama, I love you, but it is killing me knowing my brothers and cousins are out there without me. Do not worry about me, as I will come home and soon. Daddy would not have wanted me to stay home and when I go, I will carry you in my heart and thoughts.
Your loving and devoted son, Powell Alexander Stamper

With the house settled for the night, Catherine leaned over the cradle and brushed the side of her hand along the baby's cheek. In the lamplight she could see the tiny fingers and toes and a mouth so small. Standing straight she looked at the ceiling.

–Oh Lord, we're going to need all the strength you can spare us, so this one can be fed and clothed. We would have never made it if You had not been there for us. You see my boys and keep them

safe and for Melmath and   James too. And Lord, if it's not too
much trouble, would You tell John I still miss him?

Chapter 30
Coming Home

There was a feeling of elation, but at the same time, humiliation as George looked at his discharge papers. He was going home, not as a hero, not as a wounded soldier but as one with consumption. Never had he planned on anything except returning home, having fought the Yankees and maybe just a scratch or two to brag about.

The train slowed and steam poured out around the engine. Screeching brakes finally took hold as the train pulled to a stop. Catherine anxiously searched the faces of the men as they stepped from the train. Then she saw him. Thank God he's home and safe. George embraced Catherine and for a split second had the same feelings he had as a child when he skinned a knee and a soft hug and kiss took away the pain.

Catherine was filled with joy, pure joy, at having George home. She would see that he was well cared for and returned to health. If only she knew how James was getting along and especially where he was right now.

Ellen and Annie were waiting on the porch with all the children to welcome George. Once sighting the house, he could see hands waving and children jumping up and down. Home. He was finally home. Doc Stewart came to listen to his chest and declared that it sounded like bronchitis to him, and was probably not consumption. This good news brought smiles all around.

The week turned into two and then a month. Catherine looked lovingly at George and was pleased at how strong he was becoming. By late summer he should be as healthy as he was before going to war. Spending hours on the porch, he would breathe in the fresh air and sip herbal tea. Catherine was a firm believer in the healing power of herbs. Every few days Doc Stewart stopped by to check on George and was pleased with his progress.

Early one afternoon Catherine and George were sitting on the porch, planning out the crop for mid-summer and fall, mapping out the crops on a piece of paper. Dust clouds on the road signaled a visitor was coming. George Stood and squinted his eyes as if that would clear the dust. Then he saw the flash of a blue parasol and his heart starting pumping. Sarah Jane Alley was on her way for a visit.

When George first came home, he felt terrible and really did not want visitors. Especially Sarah Alley. It would never do for her to see him gaunt and sickly. After the second week home, George had written her a note explaining his situation and that as soon as possible he would visit. In turn, Sarah wrote back, and a flurry of letters went back and forth.

The plan had been for George to visit. But it would seem that Miss Alley could not wait any longer. The buggy pulled up close to the house and Abraham Alley called a greeting as he stepped down and extended a hand to his daughter. Sarah Jane was a tiny little thing, barely five feet tall, with huge brown eyes. She stepped from the buggy and reached under the seat and withdrew a package. Surprisingly Sarah came to Catherine before even looking at George.

–It's so very good to see you Mrs. Stamper. I've missed you at church but know that you were taking care of things at home. You were on my mind last week, so I made a small token for you.

The surprised look on Catherine's face could not be hidden, but she managed a polite "thank you." Sitting back in her chair she pulled the paper open to reveal a crocheted doily with a beautiful design. Catherine stood and clasped Sarah's hand, showing her appreciation, then they all sat down.

The afternoon seemed to just slip away. It was a wonderful visit and they laughed at stories that had been repeated a thousand times. Ellen served tea and Lina was passed around for all to hold and admire. Mr. Alley stood and announced that they would be going and hoped that Catherine and George would visit them soon. At hearing this invitation, the top of George's ears turned red as he helped Sarah back in the buggy. He stood staring at the dust from their buggy, until there was nothing to see.

Catherine or Mr. Alley did not miss the exchanged glances of George and Sarah. Could it be that perhaps she needed to prepare for losing a son in marriage? What George Stamper would want was a secure future for his bride, so there would not be any rush decisions. Besides, Sarah Jane Alley was only sixteen years old and George wanted to be sure she was ready for marriage. Catherine would have him a few more years. Maybe.

Chapter 31
Down but Not Out

The skimpy thin blanket did not quite cover his feet. Any minute now the doctor would probably come and check on him, if he came at all. James looked around the tent at the other soldiers. The smell of blood and human waste was everywhere. Well, at least he was not bleeding. Just freezing.

His fever was going up again and the pain throbbing behind his eyes added to the discomfort. With effort he leaned over the cot and tried reaching for the water bucket. The dryness in his mouth was so bad his tongue felt swollen. Just as he had given up hope a small hand thrust a cup of water his way. Gulping he felt the cool as it slid down his throat.

Lying back he suddenly felt very weak. The nurse was moving among the beds checking on the men and giving out fresh water. Behind her the army surgeon stopped to examine the leg of an older soldier.

–*You need to get this leg healed up and head on back home soldier. Never should have let you get this far at your age. What'd you do, lie about your age?*

The answer came in the form of a slight smile and then a smile showing gaps where teeth were missing.

James felt the cool hand of the doctor on his forehead. Then he winced as his stomach was poked in several places.

–*Sore and tender. Bad sign. Skin is starting to yellow. Very bad sign, very bad.*

Then the doctor moved on to the next bed.

He knew that whatever he had, he felt just awful. No one seemed to take the time to tell him what he had or how it was treated. Yellow skin? What did that mean? He stuck out his hand and looked at the lower part of his arm, and the yellow tinge to his skin. For the first time he knew that he was very, very sick as he was turning colors.

An orderly came and gave him some liquid medicine to swallow. Soon he was drifting to sleep and feeling no pain. He would sleep and mend for the next two weeks.

The field hospital tents smelled awful, filled with men who were almost healed but very dirty. Side flaps were pulled back and secured so that air could flow through the tent. Twelve men lay inside the tent and waited for the next round of medical personnel to arrive. James sat up in his bed and just enjoyed the cool breeze now sweeping through the tent. Two weeks ago they thought he was dying. Now he appeared to be on the mend and had asked to go back to the field. The breeze seemed to be gently blowing the smell of sickness out of the tent. Pulling the blanket up higher and trying to cover his feet, James laid back down.

On the following morning, James Stamper was on his way back to his company. Not quite as strong as he had been, but alive and anxious to move about. Five other men traveled with him, along with a sergeant and a journalist. Hiram Foster, the famous journalist, had traveled all through the South following various companies into battle, then writing an in depth description, sending to his employer in Charlotte, North Carolina. His articles were colorful and spared no detail.

Traveling with Mr. Foster was entertaining as he told stories of where he had been and what he had seen. It was four days after leaving the field hospital that the men arrived at Company E where James would once again connect with friends and neighbors.

The months passed quickly and now there was much excitement in the air. Companies were gathering and there was to be a battle at a place called Gettysburg. James would see some real fighting instead of small skirmishes here and there.

Iredell County was well represented within the Company and James felt more secure having familiar faces around, sharing conversations about familiar places and people. Robert C. Lackey, or 'R.C.' to his friends, was among the group and had stuck close to James. The first land that John Stamper had leased was from R.C.'s great-grandfather, William Lackey, and there had always been a good relationship between the two families. Also in their group were George Dagenhart and his brother, Leander. All these men had grown up on farms within a fifteen-mile radius and had known each other since childhood.

At night there was always talk of family. James thought about his brother Melmath and how he was getting along. But he thought mostly about Annie and the children. He had written three letters, but had not received any word from them in over three months.

The baby would have been born by now and he did not even know if he had another boy or a girl. The thought of his family brought thoughts of how safe there were. The Home Guard, which was the local militia, should be looking after all the women at home but James had heard tales of how they operated, that he just did not want to believe. He would continue to pray for the safety of his family.

The following week there was excitement among the men. Word had reached them that several women from their county were traveling to Camp Hill, at Harper's Ferry, Virginia, and would arrive the next day. George Dagenhart's wife was among them. At hearing this news George cried, not caring who saw him. Bedy, his beloved wife and mother of his child, would be with him for a day.

Many nights James would watch George as he wrote letters to Bedy, his face showing that of a man in pain, pouring out his love for his wife and telling her of the ache of not being home. The loneliness affected them all, leaving most with a deep empty feeling in their gut, knowing they might never see their loved ones again.

Arriving at Camp Hill, George began searching for his wife who had traveled from North Carolina, by train. There were three women in all who made the trip to see their loved ones, bringing with them food, clothes and letters from home. Leander, George's brother was elated to receive a jar of honey from his father and letters from his mother.

Two days passed quickly and the Company was preparing to move on. James stood with R.C. Lackey and watched as George embraced his wife, with Leander standing not far behind him. Soon Leander stood with his arms wrapped around the back of George, who had his arms wrapped around his wife. All three cried and the parting brought a sting to James' eyes. How he wished he could hold Annie for just one minute.

Weeks passed and the group moved farther north. R.C. was the bugler for their company and some time back there had been a drummer also, but one morning when they awoke the boy was gone and never seen again. Each morning at dawn R.C. would play the signal to rise. James, Leander and George would always be together during the day just on the outskirts of the group. They had been on the move for ten weeks. And James felt that every week was equal to a year.

They had marched north for the last three days, finally arriving just before dusk at their destination. Tired and hungry the men flopped on the ground, too exhausted to pitch their tents. James took some hard tack from his bag and chewed on the dried beef. Not much nourishment, but it fooled his stomach into thinking it was being fed. Lying back on the ground, James took stock of how dirty he was and how tired his body felt. He wondered about Melmath. Strangely his head hurt and he felt cold to the bone. Sleep soon covered him.

The full moon shone down illuminating the field dotted with sleeping bodies covered in blankets. Leander could not sleep and sat with his back against a tree, looking out over the scene of sleeping men. How he wished he could be back home. Closing his eyes, he could see his mother as she called them to dinner from the fields. He could smell the sweet aroma of fried apple pies that would be drizzled with honey on top. Looking back at the group he stared at the sleeping hump on the ground that was his brother. There was nothing that he could do to relieve the heartache for George, as his heart ached too.

As the night aged, Leander dozed, still sitting against the tree. This would be the final night that the friends and brothers would be together. Tomorrow would bring a change and much pain to the hearts of their loved ones.

Chapter 32
Heart Felt

Preacher Icenhour had no stomach for delivering letters that soldiers sent to their loved ones telling them how bad the war was, or how cold they were or how hungry. But he had promised.

Leaving the Shaw place he turned his buggy north and headed up the road praying he would not freeze before he got to the Stamper place. The road was frozen solid and the vapor of breath from the horse could be seen as he bumped along the country road. His feet were already feeling the bitter cold, his toes were starting to feel numb.

-I've got to remember to put more paper in the bottom of these shoes before I walk clean through them. Do you think that would help Maybelle?

The horse kept steadily going forward, not acknowledging hearing her name.

-You hear me Maybelle?

At this the horse pulled her ears back and the preacher chuckled.

Reaching down he gathered the edge of the lap blanket into a pile to cover his shoes. He could barely see his own breath as it vaporized in front of his face and fogged his glasses. Wiping furiously at the lenses with his worn gloves as he held the reins in his teeth. Iredell County was blanketed in ice and snow. Ice hung from the trees to form a dazzling and blinding light. Putting his glasses back in place, he gave a small flip to the reins and the horse sped up but only slightly. Stretching forward in the seat he squinted to see if there was smoke in the distance beyond the trees. If there was not rolling smoke, then he'd put off turning down to the Stamper place. Widow Sharpe, who was postmistress in Statesville, would have his hide if he put off delivering the letter.

....

Boiling clothes during February was simply not done. It certainly was not Susan's idea of helping out, especially with wash. But Catherine had shoved her out of the house bundled up saying that it'd been over a month now and the clothes had to be boiled. Watching as Susan hastily opened the door to the washroom on the porch, Catherine called after her.

–Do you want to be itching with bugs and then have to burn everything in sight to get rid of them? I don't care if the clothes don't dry. If they don't dry even this year, I don't care. We're not having any more talk of who did it last time and we're not going to talk any more about why you have to do it this time.

Annie and Jamie had fired up the large black pot, filled up with water and then fled to the house for warmth. The fire hissed and crackled as drops of water hit the flames; then the water began to boil. A small section of the back porch had been enclosed for the purpose of washing clothes and keeping out of the elements. The small fireplace, just big enough to hold a large pot for boiling water, stood on the back wall. To the right was a solid brick wall, which was the backside of the chimney in the kitchen. With a roaring fire in the kitchen, the bricks warmed and the wall gave off warmth, helping to cut the chill. The lone window let in light but was fogged. A large washtub with a scrubbing board, a rinse tub along with a side table and roller took up most of the space, with little room to move around. Grabbing two buckets, Susan dipped them in the boiling water and headed for the washtub. One more trip and there was enough water to begin. Stirring with a whittled hand paddle Susan swished and sloshed the clothes, thinking that any minute her fingers would fall right off her hand, frozen solid.

Grabbing the bar of soap, she began soaping down the clothes and scrubbing them on the washboard. The room was now warm, and her hands were beginning to shrivel from the moisture. Dragging the clothing up by the paddle she moved the wet garments to a narrow table pushed against the wall. There she took the smooth roller and started rolling it over the clothes as the excess water dripped from the edges of the table with a draining trench. It would be too painful to wring the clothes by hand. Steam rising from the clothes told of their heat but disappeared almost instantly as the clothes began to cool. Throwing them in the basket she raced across the porch and into the house.

Annie and Catherine were tying a thin rope to a hook on one side of the kitchen and then pulling the length of the rope, they stretched it to a hook on the opposite wall. Now they were ready to hang the wash over the line and hope it did not take too many days to dry. They would have to keep the fire stoked high all through the night in order to cut through the damp air from the wet clothes. The door banged open and Susan stumbled, dropping the basket on the floor and then rushed to the fireplace where she stretched her hands toward the flames.

Pushing the door closed, Ellen started pulling out clothes and laying them over the chair by the fire. At least they had clean clothes. Susan was mumbling about how stupid it was to wash clothes in the winter. No one she had ever heard of washed when it was this cold. Plus her hands were now chapped and sore and it would probably take a month to get them soft again. Raising an eyebrow and glancing in her direction, Catherine decided to ignore her remarks.

With wet clothes hanging, it did not take long for the windows to fog. Annie moved a pair of soggy pants on the rope to make a space to walk from one side of the room to the other.

Ellen sat at the loom with her feet and hands working together as she continued to weave the shuttlecocks back and forth between the picks. Right foot. Left foot. She pressed one pedal then the other to open and close on the loom while her hands moved above the cloth. Catherine sat near the fire sewing on a shirt, with one foot rocking the low cradle where Lina slept soundly. Catherine hoped that she would not wake until she finished attaching the sleeve.

The dogs sounded the alarm that someone was coming and all the women peered out the foggy windows to see who was coming. Preacher Icenhour stepped from his buggy and carefully eased his way to the icy ground and managed to throw a blanket on his horse. By the time he reached the steps Catherine was standing in the doorway waiting. She knew there must be letters, why else would he come on such a cold and icy day? Stepping aside she admitted the preacher into the midst of wet clothes hanging about the room. He stood waiting to be invited to sit and with a nod Catherine motioned to the rocker by the fire. The three women stood silent as the preacher rubbed his hands and stretched them toward the heat. Jamie and Jonathan came quietly down the steps and sat against the wall near Susan.

Clearing his glasses once again, Preacher Icenhour placed them on his nose and turned to single out Annie.

–A letter, from a Captain in James' regiment has arrived and unfortunately....

Before he could finish Annie was on her knees at his feet, face pale and voice shaking.

–Please don't say the words because I can't bear to hear.

Realizing that she thought James was dead, the preacher leaned over and placing both hands on her shoulders told her that no, he was not dead but very ill and they were sending him home.

The next four days were spent in preparation for the arrival of James. Preacher Icenhour would arrange for Doc Stewart and his son to meet the train in Statesville and transport James home. Annie had to stay at home, both to nurse Lina and to keep the baby out of the cold, icy weather. Annie paced the floor and counted the hours till James would arrive. Seeing how anxious Annie had become, Catherine told her that if she did not stop worrying her milk would dry up and then where would they be? Their two cows, Clovis and Jenny, were struggling as it was to keep up with the family demand.

Neighbors stopped by to wish them well and to ask if they could visit, once James was up to having company. Everyone wanted to know where he had been and what he had seen. Did he see any of their loved ones? Were they well? All Annie knew was that James was coming home. Her children still had their daddy and she still had her husband. With love and care James would be on his feet in no time and if they were lucky, he would be forgotten by the army. Maybe they would hide him until the war was over. She was determined that he would not return and every thought was centered on keeping him home and safe.

George had recently moved to Catawba County to be near the Alley family, hiring on at a large farm and was doing quite well. He was going to marry Sarah in the summer and had been saving his money. The owner of the farm, Mr. Cope, had told George that he would lease him some land. Just thinking about the land made George work harder. Looking up from pitching hay into the barn loft, he spotted Sarah's father, Mr. Alley, coming his way, walking at a fast pace.

–Your mother has sent word that James is very ill and being sent home. Catherine will need your help. I'll square things away with Mr. Cope. You just get on your way.

Dropping his hayfork, George headed for the little shed where he had his belongings. Several hours later George sighted Grindstaff House in the distance. Dismounting he started walking toward the house. Seeing her son coming up the lane leading his horse, Catherine ran to meet him. It had been three months since they had seen one another and now Catherine hoped he would stay awhile. Walking beside his mother, George placed his arm around her shoulders. Realizing that much of his determination and strength came from her, he hugged her close.

–I'm here now, mama, you can rest.

Putting her arm around his waist, Catherine felt great comfort in having George at home. If only she could have all her loved ones with her, but that was not to be.

Chapter 33
Home

Blankets were piled so deep that his chest felt as if a heavy weight was pressing him down. James lay in the bed of the wagon and struggled to breathe. The ice-covered roads slowed the wagon and every bump was agony. Caleb Stewart sat at his feet with his back propped at the side of the wagon. Having just finished his medical training, Caleb was following in the footsteps of his father, and James was his first official patient. Adjusting the blankets around his own shoulders he stared at the pale face of the soldier. Just let him live long enough to get him home.

Their arrival was filled with joy and tears. The men carried James into the house. Caleb checked James over and left medicine for Catherine to give, round the clock, promising to return later that evening. James fell into an exhausted sleep. The events of the week had finally come to a head with his arrival and now everyone felt the weariness of relief.

The parlor held the "preacher's bed" where they would place James. The house was quiet. The fire popped and spit and gave off the fragrant smell of hickory wood. Sleet had begun falling and small ticking noises could be heard as it hit the glass windowpanes. The room was warm and snug. It had been hours since the family had settled in for the night, but Catherine sat in the rocker keeping vigil over James. George had completed all the evening chores and now sat with his mother.

Seeing the distress in Catherine's face, George told her that he was prepared to stay months if necessary. Sally would understand and she would want him to be with his family. They could put off their wedding for a time, as there was really no hurry. Reaching out to place her hand on his, Catherine leaned in and kissed him on the cheek.

–You were always my thoughtful one and you still are. But nothing should put off that wedding and I want you to go back tomorrow. We'll be fine, I see that now, and if I need you I'll send for you.

Annie had been forced to bed, with a promise that if James called for her, Catherine would wake her. A sleepy Riley and Heath sat at the top of the steps, quietly watching their father below, hoping Catherine would not shoo them to bed if she saw them.

Feeling his forehead Catherine knew that his feverish sleep was deep. Caleb Stewart had stretched out on a pallet against the wall and was now snoring. Doc Stewart had assured the family that Caleb's education was superior and that the only reason he was not on the front line caring for dying soldiers was because he was deaf in one ear. James could not be in better hands. James being his first patient though, did not sit well with Catherine. So she sat through the night, watching and waiting, for what she did not know.

At first light Annie was up and bustling about the house. Holding baby Lina, she took a long wooden spoon and stirred the mush while giving instructions to everyone that the cow and chickens need to be fed and the slop carried to the hogs. Not waiting for an answer, she checked the biscuits and threw another log on the fire. Then seeing the first sign of movement from James, she thrust the baby into Susan's arms and rushed to his bed.

Annie was overjoyed to see that James was waking up; she quickly dipped a rag in water, wrung out the excess and gently wiped his face. Seeing Annie's face was the best thing James had awakened to in many a month. He gently laid his hand on her arm and told her he was hungry. Riley and Heath stood staring at their father scared to go near him until James finally turned and saw them. Smiling he motioned them closer.

The remainder of the day the two boys sat watching their father. The fever only went higher and James slipped from consciousness. Once again George asked to stay and once again he was told to go back to Sarah and the farm. With a promise to send for him if needed, he reluctantly rode away. Once at the road he paused and looked over his shoulder, weighing out his options. He could just go back and take charge as the man of the house and stay. "Hah! That's a laugh." Catherine would never ever let him run things. Starting out down the road he mentally made notes of what he had seen so that he could tell Sarah and her father. Everyone was always interested when a soldier returned home.

Chapter 34
Daddy

Angus O'Brien at sixty years old, was short in stature and balding, but setting the pace at a man half his age. He and his wife Hannah had raised nine healthy children, all still living, and he now enjoyed farming with his sons and grandsons.

It had been forty years since Angus had boarded a ship in Ireland bound for the land of plenty. Arriving at Wilmington, North Carolina, he quickly found work and when his savings grew, he set out for Rowan County, NC, with his sights on a land grant. Now the O'Brien's had one of the most prosperous farms in the county. Still in possession of his Irish brogue, he talked to anyone who would listen, of the old country and the luck of the Irish.

When the price for timber climbed, Angus contracted for several acres of his woodland to be cleared and milled. Little did he know that one of the men harvesting the timber would also harvest the heart of his youngest child. But what is done is done. The girl's heart had sent her trailing after a husband who had little to offer but love. Now Angus was here to gather his child to her home again, also her ailing husband and her wee ones. The O'Brien's could once again see all their children settled on their land and this youngest one well cared for under the watchful eye of her father.

....

With the morning chores almost done, Riley and Heath were gathering up the final sticks of wood for kindling when they heard the rattle of a wagon on the road. Dropping their bundles, they moved as fast as possible over the frozen ground toward the house. The woodshed behind the house sat on a slight incline and Riley's boots lost their grip. Landing on his backside he laughed as he slid past Heath.

Once aright, they made their way toward the front of the house. Seeing his grandfather, Riley slipped and slid his way to the wagon. Reaching down, Angus grasped the boy and pulled him up and hugged him tight. It had been nearly a year since he had seen this one and was surprised at his growth. With arms slung over the shoulder of each boy, Angus made a slow and slippery path to the house.

Annie stood with her mouth open when the door banged open and in strode her proud Irish father. Rushing to him she embraced him trying hard not to nearly mash the baby between them. Laughing Angus stood back and quickly reached for the grandchild he had never seen.

-Ah,' tis the look of me father I see in the wee one's eyes and the color of me Uncle Peter in her hair. Truly an O'Brien, through and through.

Smiling at his antics, Annie nearly forgot about James until she heard him call to his father-in-law. Dropping to his knees beside the bed, Angus looked at James with a look of pity.

-I've come to fetch you both home. There'll be no argument on the matter as me mind is already made up. Mrs. O'Brien will be expecting us before the end of the week. And since I brought the big wagon, you will all be comfortable on the journey home. Once you're up and about, we'll start building your home on the east side near the river.

James struggled to sit and his face was red, not with fever, but anger. His lips were pressed so tightly they showed a white line. But he was silent. How could he let this man take over his family? He could certainly make his own way and feed his family once he was on his feet.

Gently Annie laid her hand on her father's arm to gain his attention.

-No Papa, we won't be going with you. This is our home, this is where we'll stay. I will love you forever, but I live here now.

Angus struggled to his feet facing his daughter with the beginning of an objection forming on his lips. But he held his tongue. She was truly a grown woman now and although she would always be his little girl, he could see her determination. Annie reached for her father and hugged him, planting a kiss on his cheek.

Unfortunately, Riley did not feel the same way and very loudly announced that he was going with his grandfather. Immediately Angus put his arm around the boy and drew him close.

Although Annie was just barely five feet tall, she stood as tall as she could make herself and stared at Riley.

-No one is going to leave this house to go anywhere, not while your daddy's sick.

Reaching out she grasped the top of Riley's arm and pulled. But she did not count on him balking and hanging on to his grandfather.

Then everyone was speaking all at once.

–I'll take good care of him and bring him back to you in the spring.....

–I'm going, and you can't stop me......

–You mind your tone of voice to me Riley Stamper or my hand on your backside will be a reminder for next time....

–He's of no use to you here Annie and your mother and I grieve so for you and your boys.......

–Let go of your grandfather's arm......

–I'm not staying! I'm not staying!

It looked like they would soon come to blows and Catherine managed to step in between them.

–All of you be quiet!

Catherine's voice raised above all others and the room fell silent. Turning to look at Angus, Catherine looked directly into his eyes.

–You are such a wise man. Look at what you have built from literally nothing. And you could not have gotten this far by making unwise decisions. For that reason alone you will not punish this mother for not coming home, by taking her child away.

Hearing this, Riley ran from the room and up the stairs. Not caring who heard, he wailed and fussed. All below just stood and listened. And then they heard in a loud voice, "I hate you Aunt Catherine"! Angus moved to go to the stairs' and Catherine placed her hand on his shoulder.

–I matter none to that boy, but his mother matters much.

James had been forgotten in all the excitement. Once he saw Riley scoot up the stairs, he quietly laid back on his bed. This exchange had been exhausting for him and emotionally tiring. Never did he think that he would return home, only to lose part of his family.

Chapter 35
Frozen Hog

It had been four days since Angus O'Brien had visited the Stamper farm. Although he argued to the end that his grandson should go with him, he left alone. Shoulders slumped over, plainly showing his pout, he called to the horses and drove away.

Annie did not seem bothered by her father's display, or the rude behavior of Riley. After everyone retired for the night, Annie slowly climbed the stairs and went down the hall. Quietly she opened the bedroom door, across the room and sat beside Riley's bed. Her mother's instinct told her he was not asleep, just playing possum.

Ten minutes passed, then twenty. But still no words were spoken. Annie bent and lightly kissed Riley. Turning to leave she heard a small voice say, "I'm sorry".

Sunrise the following morning brought a show of beauty. Ice sparkled like diamonds on every tree giving the farm a magical look. At breakfast everyone appeared back to normal. Heath was poking fun at his brother Riley, and cousins, Jamie and Jonathan, and they returned the favor. All was well once again.

Shortly after lunch, the pinging on the windows signaled more sleet and the sky was now grey and threatening. Sitting with her face pressed to the window, Susan sat daydreaming.

Somewhere, somehow, I will leave this place. Go to the city where there are shops and things to do and even the theater. All the boys my age are gone to war. Only old men and babies are left. Well, there was one eligible bachelor in the neighborhood, but mamma had already made her feelings known about him, much too old.

Catherine moved to stand beside her daughter and peered out the window at the weather. Something moved in the distance and Catherine strained to see.

–Jump back Jehosophat! The hog is loose!

With that announcement the room came alive with voices and everyone scrambling for the door. Catherine stood on the porch and just caught a glimpse of the hind end of the hog as it moved into the brush. Behind her Jamie and Riley were pulling on their coats and gloves. Jonathan and Heath rummaged through the kitchen and returned with several lengths of rope. Grabbing the rope, Jamie motioned to Riley and the boys were out the door and in pursuit of the hog.

Before closing the door, Catherine laughed at the slipping and sliding boys. Soon they were entering the brush in pursuit of the hog. This particular animal was only a week away from slaughter and the family depended on the pork to finish out the winter.

The boys had been gone only about forty-five minutes when heavy snow began falling. Within minutes the flakes were huge and it was now difficult to see even the barn. With Catherine posted at the window, Annie and Ellen paced the floor.

  -They'll be fine. They are smart boys and they won't do anything to put themselves in danger. Jamie is twelve-years-old now and Riley's not far behind him in age. Both of them have hunted those woods and know their way around.

As she heard her own words, Catherine felt uneasy. Once the boys had been gone over an hour, Catherine turned the dogs out, hoping they would go straight to the boys. With the earth still and white, the sound of the dogs echoed through the woods, growing more faint. Then there was silence. Placing a hand in her pocket, Catherine felt for the small object, wrapping it tightly in her hand.

It had now been five hours since the two boys had bounded off the porch to catch the hog. Darkness had slowly crept over the land and the house was now bright with lamplight. Ellen sat on the edge of the rocker, swaying back and forth. James, weak as he was, had pulled himself to a sitting position and leaned his head back against the wall. Annie sat with him, holding his hand. Catherine went to her room and shut the door. Kneeling beside the bed, she started to pray.

Snow blew drifts to high peaks all around. The sleet had stopped and the snow had dwindled now to a mist slowly floating to earth. Susan went from one end of the porch to the other, holding a lantern high. Calling each boy's name, her voice echoed through the still night. Silence. Taking turns, Ellen and Annie walked the porch, calling the boys names and swinging the lantern back and forth.

At three in the morning the snow finally stopped. James lay sleeping with Annie still sitting by his side, her eyes open and staring. Soon her head bobbed and with her chin on her chest, she fell fast asleep. Ellen had been pacing around the room for hours. At least once every hour she went to the porch, holding the lantern high, and calling for the boys. Susan sat at the kitchen table, her head resting on her arms, asleep. The silence within the house matched the silence outside.

The sound of logs being placed in the fireplace, brought Annie awake and she jumped. Standing she looked around the room to see Catherine stoking the fire. The air felt cold. Turning to check on James, she pulled his cover higher and placed a hand on his forehead. He was still hot to the touch.

The morning brought beautiful sunshine flooding into the room and the air now warmed by the fire. Ellen stood looking out the window refusing to eat. How could this happen? Jamie was her heart and her husband counted on her to keep him safe. She pressed her face against the window and the tears flowed down each cheek. Suddenly she raised her head, squinting into the sunlight. Then she heard the faint barking of a dog. No, two dogs.

Jamie and Riley were slowing making their way through the brush, pulling the hog. The dogs were bouncing around them and barking.

Seeing the boys in the distance, Annie and Ellen both left the porch, making their way across the snowy yard. Waving and hollering, both women collapsed on each other crying. Slowly they made their way to the barn.

With the hog now safely inside the pen, the boys slammed the gate shut, and held on to their mothers, as they made their way to the house. Bursting into the warmth of the room, they quickly crossed to the fireplace and started shedding wet clothes. Everyone began asking questions all at once.

Heath brought blankets, and Jamie and Riley, wrapped from head to toe, sat with their backsides to the fire. Catherine had brought out her healing salve and began examining their hands and feet for frostbite. Both seemed to be no worse for the ordeal.

Riley had first spotted the hog when they were about a half-mile from the house. The huge animal seemed to just glide across the frozen ground, while the boys slipped their way along. Finally catching up to the hog, they slipped a noose around his neck. By then an hour had passed and the snow started pouring, blinding the landmarks around them. Both boys were pulling on the hog traveling a few yards and then realized they could not see which direction they were traveling.

A clump of large fir trees came to the rescue. Limbs over ten feet long and heavy with snow, dipped to the ground. Dragging the squealing hog through the snow, the boys lifted the branches high off the ground, and scooted under to safety. Tying the rope around the base of the tree, the hog was now secure and the boys protected by the tree.

Huddled together, they were dry but cold. The hog rooted out a spot in the dirt and settled in for the night but not before emitting a foul smell. The boys giggled and waved their hands in front of their faces as if to move the air in another direction.

The hours passed slowly and the boys shoved their feet under the belly of the hog. Riley's feet were starting to ache from the cold. Seeing his discomfort Jamie tried to reassure him.

–Just hold on. It won't be too much longer and we can go home.

But Jamie had also begun to feel the cold seeping deeper into his clothes. And there were noises within a few yards of the tree.

Sitting with their backs to the tree trunk, holding their breath, they watched as the shadow of two animals sniffed the top of the snow and then sniffed the air. Jamie squeezed Riley's hand and motioned for him to be quiet. The shadows continued to sniff, then turned and started to walk away. Riley let out his breath with a 'swoosh' and Jamie slapped his hand across the boy's mouth. The shadows stopped to listen. Praying that the hog would not move or make noise, Jamie continued to hold his hand over Riley's mouth. The seconds seemed like hours as they watched the shadows slowly turn and head their way, sniffing the air.

Pressing tightly against the base of the tree, both boys stiffened and prepared for the worst. When the shadows came closer, tails could be seen wagging. The dogs had found the boys and under the tree they went. The hog snorted and wiggled deeper into his spot. Jamie and Riley held on to the dogs and gathered them close. Excited, the dogs licked their faces and made yipping noises. Settling the dogs, they scrunched together and began to feel the heat from the animals.

Peering through the branches of the evergreen, light from the sun rising on the horizon could be seen. Jamie and Riley pulled the hog from under the tree and started for home. The dogs raced through the drifts and then back again. It would be an adventure that would be repeated in stories for years.

Chapter 36
Lost Forever

Doc Stewart and his son Caleb had started checking on James nearly every day. They had tried every remedy and medicine they knew, but as the days grew longer, James grew weaker. Catherine took over the care of Lina, the youngest of James' children so that Annie could give all her time to nursing.

Preacher Icenhour had volunteered to bring in a bigger bed, so that James could be moved upstairs, but Catherine had wanted him to stay in the main room near the fireplace in the preacher's bed. Chills sometimes shook him till his teeth chattered.

The days stretched into weeks and then a month. James slowly worsened with each passing week. He now could hardly hold his head up and had difficulty swallowing. Everything that went in his mouth was soon in the nightjar. The dysentery was as bad as it could get. The family constantly stayed by his side and Catherine, while placing her hands on his head, would often pray out loud, over a sleeping James.

During this time, Susan began going to town, with Heath driving the wagon. Telling her mother that she was glad to help her with errands, so that Catherine could tend to James, she now went to town at least twice a week. The hotel bought Catherine's butter every week and also eggs. With the next slaughter a ham would also be offered for sale.

Catherine could not understand why Susan was so willing to help, but imagined that the constant sight and smell of sickness drove her to be outside. And she was glad for the help as she truly did not want to leave the house with James so sick. Caring for Lina had become her number one priority and Annie was relieved to have the help.

The hotel in Statesville was not large but still could boast of business during such hard times. Although there were few visitors, five local merchants made the hotel their permanent home that kept the hotel alive.

Depending on the local farmers for staples, the hotel dining room manager was thankful for honest trading. Catherine had been fair and did not overcharge because of the war, like some folks were doing.

Walking through the alley to the back of the hotel, Susan lightly rapped on the door and it immediately flew open. Peggy McLain had been cooking at the hotel for fifteen years and greeted everyone with a "you don't say". Something Susan never understood, but she smiled and told Peggy what she had brought in her baskets. Quickly unloading the butter and eggs, Susan pocketed the money and flew out the door leaving Peggy standing with a partial good-bye on her lips.

Walking briskly down the alley Susan came to the street and turned right. Hurrying down the sidewalk until she spotted her destination the Bank of Statesville. Quickly smoothing her skirts and checking her bonnet, she slowly walked in front of the bank's windows, stopping once as if to search for her handkerchief. Almost immediately the bank's door opened and a tall older man called to her.

Lafayette "Fate" McAlpine was tall with an aristocratic look. Having never married he traveled throughout his youth and had lived off his inheritance. When he turned forty, he decided to settle down and start a business. And thus the Bank of Statesville was born. Now at forty-two he actually had thoughts of settling down even further. And the pretty girl walking towards him was the object of his affection.

Shyly extending her hand to Fate, Susan smiled and said she was glad to see him. Fate placed her hand in the crook of his arm, and escorted Susan inside the bank. His desk, was directly by the front window, so to anyone passing, the couple could be seen as if doing business. Somehow Susan found this acceptable and felt comfortable visiting there.

After chatting for a few minutes, Fate asked Susan if she would like to walk with him down to the mercantile. Early this morning a note had been sent notifying him that his special order had arrived. Walking down the street Susan and Fate made a handsome couple. Although some would say that the appearance was more of a father walking with his daughter.

Peering at the jars of candy Heath leaned on the counter. Susan had given him two pennies and now he was making his choices. It was nice, driving Susan to town, and then for a few pennies' worth of candy, he would not mention seeing Fate with Susan. Catherine had already made it known to everyone that Lafayette McAlpine was definitely not for Susan. Heath had the impression that Susan felt differently.

Just as Heath was handing over his money, Fate and Susan came through the door, all smiles. It was not lost upon all in the store when Fate placed his hand on the small of Susan's back as he guided her over to the counter. Unfortunate for them both, Jemima Solomon stood behind a stack of ready-made-dresses and glared at the couple.

   -Why Catherine Stamper would just die if she knew that daughter of hers was throwing herself at Fate McAlpine.

Chapter 37
Facing The Facts

Jamie brought the wagon around to the front of the house. On Sunday it was his responsibility to hitch up the horses to the wagon and see that they left for church on time. Jonathan had the responsibility of helping everyone into the wagon and making sure there were plenty of quilts for everyone. Cold as it was Catherine was determined not to miss church. Annie could not leave James, but the children would all go with Catherine, and that included Lina. As the wagon bumped along the rutted road, the baby snuggled in the blanket close against Catherine.

Once they arrived at the church they hurried for the building and its warmth. Preacher Icenhour had come early that morning to start the fire in the stove. Now a steady stream of smoke drifted out of the chimney. The church was not what one would call warm, but at least it was not freezing like outside.

Everyone moved about, speaking first to one neighbor and then to another, excited at seeing one another. Winter was especially difficult for trying to keep abreast of happenings in the neighborhood. Catherine proudly showed off Lina and the baby smiled with all the attention.

The women crowded around Catherine and continued to touch and talk directly to the baby. Jemima Solomon elbowed her way to the front and started exclaiming over the beautiful eyes of the baby.

-My, what bee-ut-ti-ful eyes this baby has. Then again, all you Stampers have same color and shape of eyes.

Looking directly at Catherine, Jemima continued.

-After Susan and Fate are married, I wouldn't be surprised, seeing many more babies with the same eyes. Why, I was just noticing her eyes yesterday when she and Fate were at the mercantile.

Susan, being on the edge of the circle of women, felt her knees go. She tried to quietly turn and sit on the bench but missed her step and fell flat on her backside. Everyone rushed to help Susan to her feet, everyone, that is, except Catherine. Standing with her mouth open, Catherine just stared at Susan then turned to frown at Jemima. Settling in on the bench, Catherine held Lina close while looking straight ahead.

After a few minutes of silence, Susan touched her mother's sleeve and started to speak, but Catherine cut her off.

 –We have nothing to say in this place. But you will have lots to say at home.

The service began with a hymn. Although there were no hymnals, the songs were memorized and taught through repetition from generation to generation. Even the smallest child knew the songs sung in church. Susan's mouth moved to the words, but no sound came out. Catherine on the other hand sang in her loudest voice.

The time crawled by; Susan felt she would jump right out of her skin if they did not soon leave this building. Her mind weighed out different conversations. She could deny her relationship with Fate, or she could stand up and claim her right to choose her own friends. All these things were well and good, but there would be no explanation she could give for the new pearl ring on her left hand and hidden under her glove. Unaware that Fate had joined the service late, Susan never turned to look at those behind her or she would have seen his smile as he watched her.

Going to the door at the end of the service, Preacher Icenhour spoke to every person as they left. As Catherine stepped from the church, she immediately spotted Fate McAlpine. Filled with excitement, Jemima fidgeted with her reticule and whispered to the ladies around her.

 –You just watch what happens now. Catherine Stamper will give Fate McAlpine the boot, and well she should.

Her triple chin and fleshy jowls jiggled as she spoke and cold as it was, she was perspiring.

Walking directly toward Fate, Catherine extended her hand and spoke loud enough for Jemima to hear, telling Fate they would be pleased if he would join them for Sunday dinner. Flashing a huge smile he accepted and waited for Susan. Quite shocked, but mostly confused, Susan walked toward Fate and he assisted her into the wagon. Turning to Catherine, he asked if he might speak privately with her later that afternoon?

The ride home was silent. Susan did not know whether to shout or to cry. Her mother spoke to no one, only holding the baby close and humming. Occasionally Jamie would glance at Catherine and then back at Susan. One was ashen white and one was red faced. It was going to be a long afternoon.

As soon as the wagon stopped in front of the house, Susan immediately ran to the house, up the stairs and into her bedroom. Deep inside she knew that she could not hide. Listening to noises from the main room, Susan decided she might as well get it over with and face everyone. All her mother would do was scold her in front of the family, which was better than being scolded outside the church for everyone to see.

The meal was being placed on the table by Ellen and Annie; James lay sleeping on his bed in the parlor. Heath and Riley were sitting on the floor playing a game while baby Lina laid pallet beside them. Rising up on her forearms, Lina spread a big grin and gurgled at the boys. Jamie had not yet come in from putting the horses away and Catherine was nowhere in sight.

Coming out of the barn, Jamie spotted Fate driving up in his buggy. This is going to be good and I'm not going to miss out on one word. "Hello there", he called to Fate. Looking out the window Susan saw Fate as he arrived and could see Jamie talking to him. Then from the side of the porch, Catherine stepped out of the shadows and started down the steps. Immediately Susan could feel her face turning red again and she squeezed her eyes shut as if that would make it all go away. Catherine told Jamie he was needed inside and to go feed the fire.

Before long the entire household had their faces pressed up against the windows watching Catherine and Fate. The expression on Fate's face did not change and he was still smiling. His hands though, were behind his back, twisting his gloves. Tall and imposing, Fate stood at a respectful distance and did not interrupt Catherine's speech. All inside wished she would turn so they could see her lips move and possibly know what she was saying. Soon she did turn and headed for the house with Fate behind her.

A commotion within the house could be heard all the way outside, as everyone scattered, bumping into each other, trying to find a spot to look normal. The door opened and Catherine stepped through the door and turned to welcome Fate to their home.

-We're honored to have you for dinner, Fate. And I hope that during the next few weeks you and Susan will be able to select a date for the wedding. Ellen and I will need to start preparing food and decorations ahead of time, so don't keep us waiting.

Hearing those words, Susan dropped into a chair and started to cry. Everyone gathered round wishing her well and congratulating Fate with slaps on the back, as he stood erect and smiling.

Then Catherine asked Susan if she could see her new pearl ring. Running to her room, Susan quickly returned and extended her hand. The women were "oohing" and "ahhing" over the ring, while the boys just stared. All through dinner the conversation was lively with laughter and sharing of ideas for the wedding.

The afternoon was good. Annie had retreated to a chair beside the sleeping James. There just was not any joy that she could drag up, from within, as long as James was so sick.

The house had been quiet for over an hour and a full moon shone through the windows. Quietly Susan slipped from her room, careful not to wake Ellen. Crossing the foyer and then down the hall, she placed her ear to the door and quietly turned the knob. Trying to be quiet she went to the bed and gently laid her hand on her mother's shoulder. Catherine turned and said she was not asleep. Susan immediately began crying.

Sitting on the side of the bed, holding her youngest child close, Catherine kissed her hair and told her what a beautiful a bride she would be.

–But what changed your mind? I know you don't like him, so why?

Susan did not want to have a marriage and lose a family in the process.

–When I was a young girl I dreamed of whom I would marry. We would be rich and my husband would be highly educated and respected. All our children would go to the finest schools, maybe even in Boston, and we would go to Europe in the summer. My mother encouraged these dreams thinking them as no harm. But papa was still alive then and it seemed that the dream could possibly be one day.

Then when we walked away from papa's grave and heard men telling our mother how much they were owed, she knew all was lost. Mother needed for Nancy and me to help her through this ordeal. Papa had wanted to help invest in our community. Several men had put up money to pay a sheriff and to build a school. Not having any savings to speak of, papa borrowed on the land and then proceeded to drop dead before the first payment was due.

I thought about how helpless I felt. But there was always my dream of marrying and being delivered from all I was facing. Now I think about how wonderful I felt when I met John. And he was not anything my mother had wanted for me, not anything I was looking for. But she quietly watched our courtship. One night she told me that although she knew I would probably never have any of the *things she had dreamed for me, she knew for sure that I would have love. And that meant more than prosperity. Guess I lost sight of that thinking how my baby girl someday would settle down. In my mind I always saw you on the next farm over. We would visit and I would help you put up your preserves and be there when your children were born. Fate is more than twenty years older than you and I made him promise to stay healthy and see his children raised. I know that you'll not lack for anything, but always remember that possessions can go away and they do not keep love alive.*

At hearing that Susan smiled and hugged her mother.

–I do love him mama, more than anything, and if he lost everything tomorrow, I would live in a cave if he asked me.

Chapter 38
Feeling Hopeless

July brought stifling heat. The fields lay lush and green with the promise of a big harvest, something that the Stamper family greatly needed. Jamie, Jonathan, Riley and Heath had worked with Ellen and Catherine to set the fields. And now all their work was evident. The boys were bigger and stronger and the job went smoothly, something that Catherine had not expected.

The entire family had worked hard getting through the winter. In the month of April Susan married Fate McAlpine and moved to Statesville. George married Sarah Allen two weeks later. Lina was now crawling about and hanging on to Catherine's skirts. Heath and Riley loved playing with her and she in turn would grin and say "Wiley, Wiley" whenever Riley came into view. Because both the boys called Catherine, Grandma, Lina also took a stab at calling her Grandma. Mostly what came out was Mam Maw. Then Catherine would pick her up and swing her around. What a precious, precious child. And how deeply she loved this little one.

James had arrived home shortly after Lina was born, Annie turned all her attention to nursing her husband. Catherine had taken over the care of Lina and the two had bonded. Although Lina knew that Annie was her mother, Catherine was her heart. Sometimes she would not go to her mother and screamed when Catherine would hand her over, stretching out her little arms, and crying "Mam Maw, Mam Maw".

Doc Stewart stopped by almost every day. But James grew weaker with each passing day. Hundreds of men were released from fighting and sent home each month because they were sick, maimed or had a disease. The army had sent them home to die. Widows abounded throughout the area and fatherless children were at every turn. Though not directly involved in the war, the county had not fared well.

....

War news of a large battle fought Gettysburg reached the community and put everyone on edge. Iredell County had sent its share of sons and husbands off to war, and now every week brought news of loved ones dying. The Stamper family had stayed on top of the news and every day Susan walked to the post office to check for mail. On July 28,

1863, the postmistress handed Susan a letter addressed to Catherine. Seeing the names on the envelope panicked Susan and she immediately went to find Fate. Within minutes they were in his buggy headed toward the Stamper farm, letter in hand.

A huge tree shaded the front porch making that the coolest place around. Lina was playing with a toy while Catherine sat shelling peas. Early planting had brought about an abundance and Catherine could not wait for family and friends to help with shelling, something to do with your hands and keep yourself busy. With the dogs announcing an arrival, Catherine strained to see who was coming down the lane. Recognizing Fate's buggy, she smiled at the unexpected visit.

Before the buggy came to a complete stop, Susan was out and running toward Catherine, waving the letter. Although mail had been brought to the house before, there had never been a time that Catherine could remember such urgency. Then it struck her, and fear gripped her entire body. Someone must be dead!

As soon as Susan was within an arm's length, Catherine grabbed the letter and ripped at the envelope.

We regret to inform you.........

And at that, Catherine fainted.

Feeling a cool cloth on her face, Catherine opened her eyes to see Ellen, Susan and Fate bending over her. 'Mama, it's all right. Gilbert's OK. He's not dead', said three voices in unison. Sitting up Catherine tried to clear her head, to take in what they were saying. Fate handed her the letter and she began again.

Mrs. Catherine Stamper, Iredell County, North Carolina
We regret to inform you of the capture of Sergeant Gilbert N. Stamper, on July 2 or 3, 1863 at Gettysburg. Wounded and transported to Point Lookout Prison, Maryland.
I remain your servant,
Major Jeremiah Dunst

Stunned, and still sitting on the ground, Catherine began to loudly cry. All the pent up emotion of being strong and brave, suddenly left and she did not care who saw or heard. Pulling herself to her feet she headed in the direction of the field, staggering, blinded by her tears. Ellen and Susan were both calling to Catherine and moved to go after her, but Fate held them both.

–Let her go. She needs the time to take all this in and being alone

will help her do just that.

The backfield, stretched almost two acres, adjoined the woods and could not be seen from the house. Sitting on the ground at the edge of the field in a bed of moss, Catherine was mindless to everything around her. Slowly brushing her hand over the soft moss, she thought of the times she had shown the boys how to identify wild herbs and roots. And how as a child, Gilbert pulled up clumps of moss and brought them home, thinking he had found something grand. Catherine would tell him how thoughtful he was and in turn, he would insist that she feel how soft the moss felt. He was probably around four years old but it seemed like only yesterday.

Remembering every cut and scratch along with every hug and kiss, Catherine lay on the ground and cried. She could not think. All that would come to her mind was how much she loved him and how he was so like his father. John would have been so proud of Gilbert, his strength, his honesty and his easygoing ways. So very much like John. Sitting and wiping her eyes on the hem of her skirt, she raised her face to meet a slight breeze.

–This will not do me any good. I've got to get up and do something.

Tomorrow she would go over to the Waugh farm down the road. Three of their boys were in service and one was at Camp Lookout. She had heard that Milton Waugh had traveled to Maryland and had seen his son, even took him some supplies and tobacco. She had to find out more so that she could help her son. She would also send a note to George and Sarah, inviting them to visit for an extended amount of time. She wanted her children around her and it had been months since she had seen George and Sarah.

Walking through the field, Catherine stopped and looked around her. All the crops were lush and green. Dropping to her knees she cried and put her face to the ground.

–Lord, did I not see you all around me? I know your presence is here. I see the crops, the trees, the animals. I see you in everything. How could I doubt that you would not see me and care for me? My heart is burdened and heavy by the loss of this son to a prison, where I cannot go. My heart aches for James. He is like my own son and my love for him is just as great. Lord, I need strength to walk this road and I need You to help me as the load is just too heavy.

Shortly before dark, Catherine walked from the field, renewed and with determination to support her boy through his captivity. First she would write him a letter and find out how he was and what he needed. But tomorrow she would check with Milton Waugh to see if he had plans to go back to Maryland any time soon. For now she would continue to help with Lina, so that Annie could nurse her precious James.

Chapter 39
Child of Fate

It had been two weeks since the Stamper family had received word of Gilbert's capture. It took all of that time for Catherine to seem like her old self. Knowing that her son was in a Yankee prison seemed to occupy her mind constantly; she just was not as aware of things around her. Every time she walked into the house she was instantly hit by the smell of sickness, as James continued to deteriorate.

Sunday afternoon came and went with dusk just on the horizon. Sitting on a bench under a large tree in the yard, Catherine leaned back and just took in the sights and sounds of the evening. Earlier, Fate and Susan had been by the house, staying for several hours. Funny how Susan was acting, staying close to Catherine and looking somewhat mysterious; Catherine was just now realizing that her youngest child must have something on her mind.

The week flew by and Saturday morning brought a beautiful sun and cloudless sky. Lying in bed Catherine looked at the shadows on the ceiling. Her head was pounding and her eyes hurt. Looking around the room she realized that it was way past time to rise and start chores. Slowly she sat on the edge of the bed, holding her head. The bedroom door slowly opened and Annie stuck her head in.

–*Thank goodness you're awake. We were getting worried.*

–*Annie, my head is pounding like the devil's breaking rocks inside. Would you fix me some herb tea? I don't think I'll leave my room today.*

By lunchtime the entire family had checked on Catherine to see how she was feeling. In fact, Annie could never remember a time that Catherine was ever sick. By one o'clock Fate arrived with Susan. Hearing that her mother was ill, Susan flew down the hall and into Catherine's bedroom.

Seeing the distress on her daughter's face, Catherine smiled and said I'm not going to die, just got a bad headache.

–*Are you sure you're all right mama?*

Never had Catherine seen Susan this distressed.

–What is wrong Susan? You're more than upset. Is there something wrong?

Dropping her head, she nodded then looked at her mother and smiled.

–How would you like to have another grandchild?

Grinning from ear to ear, Catherine reached out and hugged her daughter.
Her head was easing and she finally felt like getting out of bed.

It was over an hour before Susan came out of Catherine's room. Entering the kitchen, Susan actually offered to help. Ellen, with her mouth open, just looked back at Susan.

–Are you feeling well Susan?

–Oh I'm fine. I just thought you might want some help since Mama can't help get the meal ready for tomorrow.

Sitting in the parlor the boys challenged Fate to a game of checkers. It was good to distract the boys; their father's sickness was usually all they thought of. Just at the height of the game they heard a squeal coming from the kitchen. Fate smiled and told the boys to sit tight and leave the women alone.

The coming months would be some of the happiest that Catherine had known since James came home. Rummaging through a kitchen draw Catherine was mumbling, "AHA," and finally heading to the yard slamming the back door.

Peering through the kitchen window Annie saw Catherine lugging their smallest black cast iron cooking pot from the barn. Next she built a small fire and hung the pot over the fire then headed for the smokehouse where their hams and salted ham fat were hanging and began cutting off of pork fat in small pieces. Catherine headed back to the fire to place the fat in the pot. Her face directly on the window, Annie squinted to see what was going on.

–Well she's truly lost her mind, Ellen. Your mama is out there getting ready to make soap in the old bean pot.

–What?

Both women quickly went to the door and out into the yard. Looking up

Catherine grinned.

-Bet neither one of you have ever seen this recipe.

-Recipe?

-Yep. I'm making a special rub for Susan to use on her stomach. It will help make the skin stretch. I've been saving some special scent and some oil I bought in town.

The afternoon wore on and Catherine's oily balm was finally ready.

Chapter 40
Final Farewell

Early evening brought about cool breezes and the house finally began to cool. The past few days had been so hot that Ellen had actually fixed several of their meals over a fire outside.

Now it looked like there might be some relief with a faint sound of thunder rumbling in the distance. Catherine sat beside Annie and watched the labored breathing of James. At the foot of the bed, Riley and Jamie stood staring. Thankfully, baby Lina had been put to bed in Catherine's room.

Catherine had sent Jamie in search of Doc Stewart. It was silent except for the sound of James breathing. Quietly the boys slipped out of the room and headed down the hall to their room where they found Heath, sitting, and biting his lip to keep from crying. Climbing on to their bed, they listened to the silence of the house. And waited.

With James in and out of consciousness the day had been long. He talked of places and things that were not real, but he also talked of the war. During one such time, Annie had to leave the room. He barely whispered....

-George Dagenhart is dead. He loved her so much. I saw him die, wife's letter clutched in his hand. Annie, I want to come home. Don't leave me here. I'm cold, so cold.

At two minutes after midnight, the last breath passed from James Stamper and he peacefully stepped into the presence of his Maker. Doc Stewart listened to his chest and then turned to Annie.

-I'm sorry, he's gone.

Throwing herself on the bed she wept, grabbing his hand, holding it to her face, she kissed his pale fingers.

Someone would have to go to Statesville tomorrow and send Joel and Polly a telegram, since the area they had moved at the beginning of the war to a very remote area of Ashe County, North Carolina. Joel wanted to be away from any fighting and knew that if he stayed near Asheville he would be constantly struggling, trying to keep the farm going without help, worrying about fighting on his land and worrying at what the effect of war would so to Polly. She could not survive the waging of war around her. As soon as the war was over, he would move closer, hopefully back to Iredell County and they would be able to visit and see their boys once again.

It would take at least a week for James' parents to come to the farm, if they came at all. Their oldest child now lay cold and pale. Catherine wrote out what she wanted said in the telegram and tucked it into her apron pocket. Next she wrote a note to her son, George. One of her neighbors had offered to take care of both for her.

Later that morning people began arriving at the Stamper farm to pay their respects. Annie sat with a stunned look on her face. People passing in front of her, bent to whisper their sympathy to her, but she made no movement. The yard was full of children and the porch held old men speaking in low voices.

In the bedroom James still lay on the bed, covered by a sheet. A washbowl, towel and clean clothes were on the table by the window. Catherine dipped a cloth in the tepid water and wrung it out. Walking to the bed she pulled back the sheet and began wiping James' face. Next she struggled to free him of his nightshirt. Washing his neck, chest and arms, she gently blotted away the moisture with the towel. This man had carved a spot in her heart that no one else could ever fill. This was just a part of the circle of life and something that Catherine could not get used to. Someone had to perform the task and as difficult as it was for her, she felt honored to prepare James for burial. After all, she was his mother in deed if not in birth.

A neighbor brought fresh lemons from her ponderosa lemon plant, and another neighbor brought a most precious commodity, sugar. Ellen used both to make lemonade for the growing number of people arriving at the house. Moving about the room she served her neighbors as they waited with Annie for Catherine to finish dressing the body.

Working quietly Catherine's mind filled with scenes of James; walking through the fields as a young boy, driving the team of oxen through the shallow ford of the river, watching him grow to become a man, a husband and a father and what a privilege that had been. She had also had the painful pleasure of seeing him pass into eternal life.

As soon as Catherine opened the door to the bedroom, two women quickly moved from the hallway, down the steps and on to the porch. Within seconds six men came through the door carrying a casket and began making their way upstairs. Another behind them carried two wooden braces, on which to set the casket and began setting them up in the main room. Everyone left the room except for Catherine and Annie. They looked to the stairs as they heard the door to the bedroom open and then saw the men carry out the casket. Carefully maneuvering the steps, they came into the main room and gently placed the casket on the braces. Here James would lie until tomorrow. Here his family would spend the last hours before seeing him buried. Now he was finally at peace.

Several neighbors sat throughout the night, keeping the candles lit as they kept vigil over the casket. Twice during the night Annie came into the room. The first time she merely stood and looked at James' face, placing her hand on his cold hand. The second time she bent and gently kissed his lips. The only sound was the ticking of the mantle clock that James had saved for months to buy as his Christmas gift to Catherine.

The dawn came with clouds and showers. The yard was filled with wagons, and buggies. Joshua Hollowell came with his shiny black funeral coach. Glass windows on both sides gave an all-around view of the casket inside the coach. Opening the back of the coach, Joshua stood with quiet respect as six men carried the body from the house to the coach. All was quiet, only Annie's soft sobbing could be heard. They would bury him at the church cemetery, where he would lie among other soldiers, killed from a war still raging.

The ride to the church was muggy. Misting rain settled the dust but now the air felt steamy hot. Women opened their parasols to protect their hats. There were many people already assembled at the gravesite. Annie was surprised at the size of the crowd. Riley and Heath hung close to their mother and appeared numbed by the events of the previous day. Several women from the church stayed behind to care for Lina, as she was just too small to be a part of the funeral.

The men of the church had erected a cover over the gravesite using large posts, with canvas stretched across the top of each post. Catherine stood with Ellen and Susan and watched as George gently led Annie to stand beside them. In spite of being draped in a mourning veil, her swollen red eyes could still be seen. The casket was pulled out the back of the funeral coach and on to strong shoulders. Fate and Abram Alley held the first positions, right front and left front of the casket. Behind them came Jamie and Jonathan, then Amos Lackey and Emanuel Dagenhart. Carefully they maneuvered the casket to the braces.

The scene was one that had been repeated many times in many places since the beginning of the war. Women being crushed at the death of their husband, children struggling to understand. Mostly old men carried out the traditions of burial, as there were no young men. Older boys participated, taking the place of fathers and brothers, still away at war.

Scripture was read from Ecclesiastes. *"A time to be born, and a time to die.....a time of war and a time of peace"*. Next came verses from Psalms. *"The Lord is my shepherd; I shall not want....."*

They sang James' favorite hymn.
All hail the power of Jesus' name!
Let angels prostrate fall;
bring forth the royal diadem,
to crown him, crown him, crown him Lord of all!

Ye seed of Israel's chosen race,
ye ransomed of the fall,
Hail him who saves you by his grace,
and crown him, crown him, crown him Lord of all!

Let every tribe and every tongue
that bound creation's call,
now shout in universal song
the crowned, the crowned, the crowned Lord of all!

Staring straight ahead, Annie took in the words. Her heart was breaking but she also knew the pain and discomfort that James had suffered his last few weeks. The loss was the deepest pain, but she knew that he was at peace. Now it was up to her to raise his boys the way he would have wanted and to keep his memory alive for them.

With the rain still lightly falling, everyone remained in place as they lowered the casket into the ground and began shoveling dirt into the hole. Tears ran down the cheeks of Riley, but Heath stood stone faced gritting his teeth. Annie held on to both boys. Now the only thing left to do was to go home and decide what to do for the rest of their lives.

Chapter 41
Paying Homage

Thankful that the rain had ended, the neighborhood women who stayed at the Stamper farm began laying out a meal while the family attended the funeral. Once the family arrived home after the burial, there would be tables in the yard and enough food for twice the number of people expected. Although a solemn occasion the tension had been lifted and several men could be heard sharing stories about how they knew James and of the times he had helped them. Now it seemed appropriate to speak of him.

Going to the different tables making sure the children were all fed, Catherine overheard comments about James. Scooping up Lina she approached the men who were balancing their plates while they talked.

–James was a fine man and what you say about him is so very true. But his boys need to know that their daddy was special. Will you tell them?

Everyone nodded, mouths full of food, and Catherine left to find Riley and Heath.

Hours had passed and most of the neighbors had retreated to their own farms to care for their animals and do their evening chores. Catherine, with Lina asleep in her lap, sat with Annie on the porch. In the side yard, Riley and Heath sat on the ground listening to the men talk. These were men who had known their daddy since he first came to Iredell County. Occasionally the boys would laugh, then catch themselves and glance over their shoulder at their mother. Annie sat pretending not to notice or hear what was going on. How wise Catherine was to have these men deepen the memory of their daddy to these boys.

Horace Grider and Pinkney Fox, had both been wounded in the war and sent home, each missing part of a leg. They had attended school with James at the old Stewart School. In session only four months of the year, the school held all the students in one room. From six years old to sixteen, they were all together. Julia Stewart was the teacher, as her father had donated the land and the lumber for the school.

As the boys seemed content to keep listening to stories, Horace settled back to continue telling his favorite story about James.

–Your daddy and me had a big crush on Miss Stewart, but him more than me. At the time we were almost sixteen, and why, she was only eighteen but cute as a button, but real snooty. One day James bought her a present. He had been to Statesville helping a neighbor haul some chickens and with the money he got he went to the mercantile and bought a small round mirror with gold color around the edges. Something a lady would put in her reticule. He even had Susan wrap it in paper for him. Of course he told her it was for somebody else or she'd never have wrapped it. The next day after school he approached Miss Stewart and gushed out his admiration. She in turn only remembered the summer before when he had pushed her in the creek while fooling around with some boys. Sticking her nose up in the air she looked like she was going to leave, but suddenly turned and pushed him down. Ha! she said. Now we're even. And off she went. James was embarrassed to no end and to make matters worse the mirror was now broken.

Well, we did not talk about it ever again. But about a year later he came to me one morning and asked if I knew that Julia Stewart was getting married that day and that there would be a big party at her parent's house afterwards. I told him no, I did not know that. Then he said that's not the best part. They're going to spend their first night right there. And you and I are going to help them celebrate.

By this time, I was not real sure if I knew what he was talking about or if I even cared. But whatever he had in mind it did not sound too good. Seeing as how he was my best friend, I agreed to meet him. It was dark and we could see people inside the house eating cake and drinking punch. We slipped behind the bushes at the side of the house and I let James stand on my shoulders as he pried open the window. Once he was in, he pulled me inside. Being as quiet as we could be, we very gently pulled the coverlet down to the foot of the bed. Then took the sheet and pulled it down too. Next we unloaded the sacks we had brought, hundreds of burrs from the sweet gum trees, with sharp thorny stickers on every one of them. Then we short sheeted the bed and pulled the coverlet back up.

Just about to bust we made it out the window and sat behind the bushes giggling. Soon people started leaving and we were getting excited. James knew that Catherine would probably be standing on her head with worry about where he was, but he said this fun was worth it.

It did not take too long for the house to be quiet and soon we could hear movement at the window as the drapes were pulled. We were each sitting there on the ground covering our mouth so no one would hear us laughing. Then we waited. About twenty minutes later we heard this awful shrieking and then a man's voice cursing. At that we took off to the edge of the field.

As soon as we got to the tree line we could see lanterns coming out of the house and going round the side. Julia was standing on the porch crying with her mother holding on to her and her new husband was pacing up and down the side of the house poking at the bushes with a big gun barrel. I laughed till I wet in my pants!

The boys giggled and then laughed, this time not looking back at their mother. Annie smiled, and reaching over, placed her hand on Catherine's arm.

–Thank you.

Once the laughter died down, Pink wanted to add his story.

–Let me tell mine next. Right after your daddy came to stay at Catherine's, James found out that any time there was a preacher around he would be sitting there listening to him. And that did not set too well. He tried making excuses, being sick and what not, but every time there was a service he was forced to attend.

One summer, there was to be a famous preacher from Virginia coming to our area. All the folks were excited and decided to have a brush arbor meeting. My daddy had me go with him to cut the ranches and help form the arbor and soon we had everything set. The platform area was partially shaded by the branches we tied together, and we put hay all–round the front of the platform to make it look neat. Several men had cut some logs and turned them into benches and set them around the area, and we were ready to go.

Most of our friends had been sneaking over to old man Barnette's fishing pond. We'd been caught a few times, but decided that Sunday to try again. Some of the boys hid and their folks could not sfind them when it was time to go to the brush arbor meeting, but me and James weren't as lucky. Catherine found us both and off we went.

All James could think about was how good a time those boys were probably having sneaking around fishing and probably swimming. He hadn't heard one word that had been said from the platform, and really did not care. All of a sudden he turned and told me we were going fishing. I told him he was crazy. We were all the way at *the back, sitting on the ground in the sunshine, and ever so often Catherine would lean out to see if we were still back there. James waited for her to lean out again. He waved at her and she frowned.*

James said she probably wouldn't check again for another five minutes so we've got to act quick. From his pocket he brought out a small piece of magnifying glass. James was forever finding and keeping small pieces of glass, but most were colored. But anyway, back to my story. He stretched out on his stomach bracing his elbows on the ground and had this real interested look on his face. Looking down I saw the glass laying just beside his elbow, and the sun was reflecting off of it and pointed right at the hay near the side of the platform.

Soon there was a little stream of smoke and then a flame. We waited for a few minutes then someone hollered "fire!" and we took off. It was a great afternoon but when he came home, Catherine whipped him with the razor strop.

It was now dark and the last of the families gathered their things and left. Still sitting on the porch, Annie called to the boys to come in for bed. Both boys were giggling and repeating bits and pieces of the stories they had heard about their daddy. Watching them scoot up the stairs, Annie smiled for the first time in months, thinking "I'll do right by those boys and James would be pleased."

Chapter 42
Forced Invitation

Morning brought a stifling heat. So hot that you could not tell there had been any trace of rain the day before. And everyone was moving slow. It was going to be a huge adjustment going about daily life and not having to check on James every five minutes, or keep cold cloths on his forehead. Already this morning Annie had automatically turned to go to the bedroom, and then remembered that he was not there.

Jonathan had been assigned the milking that morning and Heath along with Riley had agreed to help. Catherine walked back to the house with a basket of eggs and looked up just in time to see Angus O'Brien pulling into the yard. A feeling of dread came over her as she watched the little Irishman bound up the steps and into the house. Behind him, left to fend for herself was Annie's mother, Hannah and Catherine hurried to help her down from the wagon.

Red-faced and puffing, she was not too pleased at the actions of Angus.

-You'd think he did all these children by himself. Whenever there's anything wrong, he runs to them first and then thinks of me.

Steadying herself with a cane, Hannah slowly went up the steps. Several years earlier she had fallen and broken her leg. Even though the doctor had set the leg, and it appeared healed, she could not place all her weight on the leg and now needed the cane.

By the time Hannah and Catherine entered the house, Angus was holding his ground insisting that Annie load up her things, along with her boys, as she was finally coming home. And there would be no discussion over the matter.

Standing in the middle of the room Annie just looked at her father. Then she looked at her boys. They were wide-eyed and waiting to see what would happen next.

-Your Papa's right, you know.

Hannah had heard all that Angus said and was now focused on being his ally rather than wishing she had thumped him on the head for leaving her in the wagon.

Catherine would not interfere and quietly slipped back out the door, carrying Lina with her. Heading off to feed the chickens, she felt a heaviness in her heart. Losing Annie and her children would be a blow. Losing Lina would be an even deeper wound, but she had no right to ask them to stay.

Throwing cracked corn in the direction of the chickens, Lina laughed as they hunted and pecked on the ground. It had been thirty minutes since Catherine had left the house.

–Best to go back and get it over with.

Nearing the house Catherine could hear raised voices, and now realized that two of those voices belonged to Riley and Heath. Raising her skirts she hurried to the steps and into the main room.

Everyone was shouting and waving their arms and pointing at one another. Ellen had covered her ears with her hands as she just stared.

Stepping in front of Angus and Hannah, Catherine placed both her hands on Annie's shoulders and walked her backwards away from her parents.

–What is going on here? Why is everyone making all this noise?

At that Angus and Hannah started once again in loud voices, telling Annie what she was going to do. Hearing that, Catherine turned and invited them to sit at the table.

–We'll hash this thing out over some food, but there will be no more shouting.

Putting some gingerbread from the previous day on the table, Catherine asked everyone to take a seat. Even a sweet tooth could not make Riley and Heath leave their mother, standing behind her seat. This surprised Catherine as she assumed that Riley would be packed and ready to leave the second his grandfather made the offer.

–You're in my home now. This is where I live. This is where Riley, Heath and Lina live. It takes all of us to make this household work. And this is where James wanted us to live. So this is where I'm going to live....

Then glancing at Catherine
–....that is, if it's all right with you.

Angus was now blood red and Hannah's mouth hung open.
–This is the way you treat your parents? You break our hearts? There is no tie for you here but we are blood. Your brothers have not deserted us, how is it that you think you do not owe us this?

Very quietly Annie moved to a chair and sat down.

–Papa, I buried my husband not even twenty–four hours ago. I can still smell his scent in this house. All of this is fresh on my heart and mind. The boys need to be near the memory of their father. Be among people who can share their love of James with them. And you ask me how I can be selfish and not go with you? How could I be selfish and rip my boys from this place? How could I be selfish and leave behind a grave that I have not visited since the burial? How can I take my baby girl from the only home and safety she has ever known? And you think I'm selfish?

Immediately at hearing these words Hannah began to cry.

–She is right Angus; we do not have the right.
At that Angus raised his fist.

–No, by all that's holy, they'll go with us today.

Hannah looked at him with disbelief. For the first time in her married life, she faced her husband, whispering her concern, knowing that she would possibly face his wrath.

–How can you do this? You would sacrifice the happiness of your grandchildren for your own selfish reasons?

Looking at Annie and then at the boys, Hannah told them she loved them and she would come to visit them often. Then turning to face Angus she told him that if he did this she would not live in his house after today, and this she swore on her father's grave. Now the red–faced Angus started to sputter and watched as Hannah picked up her skirts and out the door she went.

Running after her, Angus could not believe what he had heard. Catherine stood at the door watching the arguing couple, Angus waving his arms and shouting, Hannah speaking calmly with determination. Finally hanging his head, Angus listened to what Hannah had to say. Walking toward the house Hannah called to Annie to come out on the porch. Seeing her mother standing stiffly at the foot of the steps, Annie came out the door and stood facing her.

*-Your father will be driving me back to our farm now. I am relieved
that you are safe and well cared for and I know that my
grandchildren will grow strong under your hand. Next month I will
visit you and I will write you to let you know when I am coming.
Your brother Ezekiel will drive me if necessary. My heart aches with
your loss and you will be in my prayers.*

With those words Annie moved off the porch to the foot of the steps and
embraced her mother. Then both boys came and placed their arms
around their grandmother.

Angus sat in the wagon, head hanging, but making no motion at
addressing Annie or the boys. His cause was lost and he knew it. Without
acknowledging her father, Annie turned and went into the house,
followed by her boys. Facing Catherine, she immediately began to cry.
Catherine wrapped her arms around Annie and told her it was all right to
cry.

How precious this young woman was and how much she meant to
Catherine. Her independent streak reminded her so much of Susan.
"What I would not give to be holding my Susan," Catherine thought. On
her next trip to Statesville, she would be sure and give her daughter an
extra hug.

Leaving the farm Angus rode in silence and dreaded the arrival at
his own farm. He certainly did not want to face his sons, and admit that
Annie would not obey him and come home. Hannah and refused to look
at him. The surprise of all would be waiting for him at home when
Hannah would lock her door against him.

Chapter 43
Changing Times

The rest of the summer passed more quickly than they all would have imagined. The crops were all now safely stored away in various hiding places and Catherine felt that she could relax. Doing physical work helped to keep the pain at bay over losing James and especially the heartache of Gilbert.

During a period of one week, the family gathered together supplies to send to Gilbert in Maryland. Their neighbor, Milton Waugh was leaving the first of the month to see his sons at Point Lookout and hopefully he would find Gilbert and pass along the supplies. One small package contained tobacco twists, which they hoped Gilbert could sell so that he would have a little money.

Two letters from Gilbert had arrived on the same day, though written weeks apart. Catherine sat and read the letters aloud to the family and they all began to have a vision of how Gilbert was living. Southern families were traveling to Maryland and taking their loved ones everything from food and clothing to items they could sell. Within the prison, the men actually bartered between themselves for goods. There was a village atmosphere as the men began receiving items from their families. It was an extremely tense time also as Gilbert wrote that most of the guards were darkies, put there by the Yankees to further humiliate the Southerners.

The weather began turning cold and the wind blew the last of the colorful leaves from the trees. Along with his father-in-law Mr. Allen, George worked an entire week chopping and splitting wood. The entire back porch was stacked with wood. Of course the cords of wood stacked against the house would be used first, and during storms the wood from the porch would stand ready.

Twice each week Catherine went to Statesville to barter and trade. On each trip she spent several hours with Susan, now toward the end of her first pregnancy. Fate was constantly checking on her, and was the typical new father-to-be; Catherine merely smiled. Her instincts had been correct and Fate was turning out to be an attentive husband, a good provider and would be a doting father. However, the bank was closed now that the war was in full swing. Several times Fate had spoken of moving to South Carolina to be near his oldest brother on their old home place. This idea was definitely not something that Catherine wanted to hear.

On December the seventh Catherine held Amanda Grace McAlpine for the first time, cooing at the baby and holding her close. The new father strutted around the room praising his wife and telling Catherine how brave Susan had been. Ducking her head, Susan told him to hush.

Even with the war escalating, Catherine thought that life was good. The family had a decent roof over their heads and there was food. Yes, they considered themselves blessed, as they saw neighbors not so well off.

The seasons just seemed to blend one into another and another year had passed. The family stayed on alert and continued to prepare themselves for the worst. Twice in one month, they were alerted by the dogs, as Confederate deserters tried to steal chickens and eggs but then quickly disappeared at seeing the end of a rifle.

Catherine longed for everything to be normal again. Even church was now held once every six weeks. Poor preacher Icenhour was worn out traveling and trying to avoid any conflicts. One week he was attacked on a back road, dragged from his buggy and hit on the head. When he woke his pocket watch was gone along with the coins in his vest pocket. Several of the men in the neighborhood tried to track down the attackers, but lost their trail. Now the preacher was more selective about where he traveled and where he preached.

The family was preparing for Christmas and Fate and Susan planned to come on Christmas Eve bringing Amanda Grace and spending the night. George and Sarah had arrived that morning, so the entire family would be under one roof on Christmas morning, which was Catherine's wish. She especially wanted Susan under her roof as she was expecting again and way too soon to suit Catherine. And to say that Susan was large would not quite describe how large. She was huge and could barely walk and the baby was not due for another month or so.

Christmas morning brought rain and wind. Sitting by the fire Catherine read her Bible and said her morning prayers before preparing the morning meal for all the family. Suddenly her name was being shouted and she stumbled as she jumped from the chair. Fate was running down the stairs screaming at the top of his lungs.

-Catherine come quick! The baby is coming and Susan has passed out with pain.

Racing up the stairs Catherine ran down the hallway and into the bedroom where Susan and Fate were staying. By this time both Annie and Ellen were standing in the hall trying to see what all the noise was about.

   -Come Quick. Susan's having the baby early.
All three women disappeared into the bedroom and slammed the door.

   The morning wore on and Fate was beside himself with worry. At ten o'clock Ellen came downstairs and said that Doc Stewart was needed and quickly. George volunteered to go and Fate sat with his head in his hands.

   Fortunately, Doc was at home and came quickly and once he arrived, Annie took him up the stairs to Susan.

   Within the hour the delivery was over and Doc Stewart wiped his hands on a towel and smiled at Fate.

   -Yes sir. They're both good-looking babies. I would not be surprised if they   did not each weigh five pounds. Early though, but they look healthy. I'd keep them near the fireplace for the next week or so.

   Smoke drifted from the kitchen chimney as Annie and Ellen began preparing their Christmas meal. Humming her favorite hymn Ellen nudged Annie and winked. Smiling they lifted their voices in harmony as they peeled the potatoes and turnips. At the end of the song they laughed and then hugged each other.

   -What a beautiful, beautiful Christmas day. And one we'll never forget.

   Fate and Susan named their twins, Oliver and Lavinia. And grandmother Catherine was beaming. What a joyous holiday, just to have the family under one roof. Even the war could not dampen their spirits. They drank spiced cider, ate chicken with hot rolls, gobbled up the turnips and savored the creamy potatoes. As a surprise, Annie had baked flat sweet bread covered in cinnamon, sprinkled with a dash of sugar. The lone cinnamon stick had been saved for almost a year, just for this occasion.

   The cold winter slowly progressed and most folks stayed close to their farms and the Stamper family was no different. There was really no need to go to town as they had supplies put back to carry them till spring.

The arrival of spring brought beautiful flowers and lush green trees. But not everyone was reveling in the beauty. Fate McAlpine stood before Catherine and told her how sorry he was but that he was taking Susan and the children to South Carolina to be with his older brother. The family there was failing and he was desperately needed. The following week Catherine stood and watched Susan ride away to a new home, hours and hours away.

That night, lying in bed, Catherine cried for this youngest daughter and all that she would face. As Susan had leaned down to kiss her mother good bye she whispered that the five month old twins would be needing her care in about seven months. She then smiled and told her mother not to worry.

–*Not to worry? Another baby on the way and little Amanda Grace was not yet two years old with the twins only five months, this was too much. Worry will be my constant companion and of that I am sure.*

The only link would be letters, and Catherine intended to write every week.

Chapter 44
Susan's Hiding Place

News of death, missing or captured soldiers was delivered every week to families in the community. It was a fact they could not deny or run from. Not a week passed that at least one family learned of a loved one lost. The Stamper family grieved for the families in the neighborhood who had suffered. They wept for husbands, sons or brothers of their neighbors. And every week Catherine tried to visit either a widow or a mother who had lost her son. She brought each one honey and biscuits, practically the only thing left that she could share, as her pantry was almost bare. What if she received word that one of her boys had been killed, would she want comfort from outsiders? Her answer was an immediate yes.

Early one Thursday afternoon, Broughton Lazenby came walking up the drive carrying a satchel, doing his monthly duty of delivering mail. It was said that he was not quite right in the head, so he had been quickly eliminated from serving in the Confederacy. Rumor had it that he had run into some Yankees over in Catawba County. They spoke with him a few minutes and went on their way, recognizing that he was not quite right. Orphaned at fifteen, he had been taking care of himself for quite some time. All the neighbors were aware of his situation, and his mental state, so most would look in on him occasionally. Grinning from ear-to-ear, he banged loudly on the door and waited. Pulling open the door Catherine was glad to see him as he always brought letters and today was no exception. Broughton was very proud that he could read, so bringing the mail made him feel special. Handing over the envelope to Catherine, he waited.

Realizing that they needed to go through their usual ritual, Catherine asked Broughton if he was well; did he have enough to eat; was he warm, and did he know any news. This is what he was waiting for, the invitation to tell all he had heard that week.

Somewhat of a self-proclaimed historian, he claimed to know something about every family in the county. Catherine stood as he told of widow Paris' rheumatism and how old man Isenhour had all his chickens stolen. For the next five minutes, Broughton went on and on, all the while Catherine waited, nodding occasionally. Finally with all the news delivered, he turned to leave, with Catherine thanking him for all the news.

Looking at the envelope, Catherine recognized Susan's handwriting. Heading for the parlor and calling for everyone to come quick, she ripped opened the letter. Within seconds the family filled the room and settled in to hear the news from Susan.

"My Dearest Mama, Annie, Ellen, George and loved ones,
Where do I start? I am at a loss to truly express to you the depth of our situation. We have moved and no longer enjoy our home with Charles and Angelina in Columbia. Being the younger brother, Fate has had to bear most of the work for Charles, as he has aged and has become weak. Last month, the fever swept through our area and Angelina died. Fate's youngest sister, Sophronia also died as did her two children. We do not know where her husband is now, as there have been no letters received from his company. Later we heard that Charles' son, Vincent, had died in a battle in Virginia, so Fate only has Charles left from his family. Learning that Vincent had been killed was a terrible heartache for Fate as he and this nephew were raised as if brothers. For a day or two after Angelina died we feared Charles would die also, from his grief. The children are all well, however they are thin. Fate and Charles had word that the Yankee army would be upon us on their return from Georgia and we filled our wagon with food and two crates of chickens and started north. We knew that there had been cousins living in Laurens so we thought to go there and seek shelter. But when we arrived their home was burned and there was no sign of them. Charles remembered his childhood days spent in the area with his father in this area. There is a hunting shack, in the Blue Ridge mountains, above Merritsville where the family used to hunt. It is very secluded and cannot be seen. Fate climbed a tree with Oliver in tow to show him the state, as we are so high in mountains that you can see North Carolina and Tennessee. Our wagon is now hidden in the woods for later use. It took all of us two days to carry our belongings from the wagon to the hunting shack. Fate took both the horses and turned them loose as we had no grain and would not be able to feed them on the top of the mountain. Amanda Gray can now say all of her letters of the alphabet. I had hoped that one day she could advance in reading, but we no longer have books. Lavinia and Oliver are together constantly and remind me so much of how Ellen played with George at home. Little Renny is a wonderful baby and she now has six teeth. By our dire straits I do not think more children would be possible as it is difficult to find enough food now. If you are reading this, it is because Fate has traveled several days to find supplies and promised to post my letter to you. He is going to travel down the North Fork River in hopes of finding supplies in Travelers Rest, but if not he would go to Dacusville or Pickensville. Oh how I miss my home but my little

*ones are safe and that is most important. I will come home as soon
as the war is over and will kiss and hug you. Your last letter is with
me and I read it often and so wish I could hear from you but there
is no way to get a letter to us. We are safe. What a wonderful
husband I have who cares for us and sees that we are warm and
have some amount of food but mostly we still have each other. I
remain your loving daughter*
Susan Virginia Stamper McAlpine

With the last word of the letter read, everyone sat quietly, taking in
what they had just heard. Catherine stood and left the room, heading to
her bedroom. Within a few minutes she returned carrying her Bible.

–All our answers are here.

And then she opened her Bible and read aloud from the book of
Jeremiah.
*–Thus saith the Lord: Refrain
thy voice from weeping, and thine
eyes from tears; for thy work shall
be rewarded, saith the Lord; and
they shall come again from the land of the enemy.*

*And there is hope in thine end,
saith the Lord, that thy children
shall come again to their own
border.*
Jeremiah 31: 16 and 17.

Standing in the middle of the room, with her Bible still open,
Catherine read aloud the scripture once again.

*–This tells me that my children will come home again just like God
brought the children of Israel home.*
Then closing her Bible she announced that there were chores to be done.

Chapter 45
Letters

The war raged on and the days seemed almost endless. From the dawn till dusk, Catherine focused on making sure the family was provided for. Today George would take honey and eggs to town for trade. Hopefully he would be able to trade for salt and tea.

The town seemed almost deserted with very few people milling about. Now, there were mostly old men, visiting with one another and discussing the war. How tired George was of seeing this same scene week after week. Walking toward the mercantile, he said hello to several men, but did not care to stop and talk. The less he knew the better he felt.

Tying his bag of supplies to the side of Burt, George turned as his name was called. The postmistress was coming his way and waving.

–Your mama has a letter George, and I knew you'd want to have it now rather than wait. Give my best to your family.

Looking at the letter his heart began to beat faster. It was from Alex and Catherine would be so relieved to hear from him as it had been months since their last word of him. Gathering his supplies, George raced for home.

Pale and trembling, Catherine opened the letter and read aloud to the family.

My Dearest Mother,
I write to let you know that I am very sick and in the hospital not far away in South Carolina. A nice lady is writing this letter for me and for that I am grateful, as my hands are too shaky to write. Do not worry about me though the doctor says he will send me home when I am stronger and can travel. I will not have to fight anymore and this gives me much peace. Shooting at other men has made me terribly sick. The first time I could not keep down my food. I could see the man falling dead and it made my stomach turn. If there had not been boys from our neighborhood beside me I would have slipped into the woods to hide. Then I could have made my way home with hope that you would keep me hidden. But I know that is wrong and that I have to stay. All this fighting is not what I

had in mind. After our first big fight near the Tennessee line, when we searched the field for the wounded enemy and one of our men found his cousin among the Yankee dead. He lived in Kentucky and did not fight with our side. This made me think that I had cousins there and wondered if they were shooting at me. Mama, I need to come home now but am too weak to travel but know that you will pray for me. Tell the boys that I will come home and help them with the farm as soon as I can. I do not want to go back and work for other people anymore. I think of all at home every day and long to be with you.
Your loving son
Powell Alexander Stamper

The room was silent for several minutes. Then George spoke up and said he would go to South Carolina and bring him back in the wagon. Annie said it would be too dangerous and that George still did not have his total strength back from being sick with his lungs. Then everyone began tossing ideas around. Finally George's father-in-law Mr. Allen spoke up and said that he would go with George.

–No one's going to bother a raggedy old man with his idiot son.

Grinning as if he had found the pot of gold, Mr. Allen was quite pleased with himself. Although George carried his discharge papers with him at all times, there had been rumors of some men taken away, papers or no papers.

Late into the evening Catherine sat by the oil lamp, writing a letter to her sister Nancy. Although they were living only one county apart, the sisters had not seen each other in more than a year. Brooks had held on and was still at home, refusing to go fight, unless they dragged him off his land. There was not time for him to fight. There were five daughters to feed and Brooks' mother also lived with them. Oh, how Catherine missed her time with Nancy. In their old home, she was only ten minutes away and they spoke nearly every week, sharing their lives. Tonight Catherine could share her thoughts and worries to her sister only on paper.

....

The wagon was loaded with tattered quilts for Alex to lie on during the ride home. Mr. Alley strutted out of the house looking just awful. His suit was grease stained and smelled. Not far behind George presented himself in old pants and a dirty torn shirt. Pulled down over his head was an old hat three sizes too big, and he immediately looked like an idiot.

–Just remember not to say anything if you're stopped George. And

Mr. Allen, you will be in my prayers until you return.

Catherine felt a lump in her throat as she watched them turn on to the road. They would be gone perhaps as much as a week. Time to keep busy and hope that the days would go by quickly.

The road to Charlotte was well traveled, even in time of war, and George and Mr. Allen made good time. At sunset, they had just crossed the state line and decided to veer off the road and camp for the night. While George took care of the horses, Mr. Allen built a fire and sliced some bread for dried beef. Sitting around the fire the two men talked of anything that would keep their minds off possibly being in a dangerous place. Not having traveled this road before, George was uneasy not knowing what was around each curve. As the fire began dying, they stretched out on the ground under the wagon to sleep.

Night sounds were all around and they seemed to get louder by the minute. Lying on his back, George could not sleep and shifted to his side. Out of the corner of his eye he caught a slight movement. Mr. Allen was snoring, and the short jab that George gave him only stopped the noise, but did not wake him up. Sitting up George held his breath and listened. There was a faint scratching noise, then quiet. Trying to hold completely still, George listened but could hear nothing. Scooting from underneath the wagon he crouched beside the wagon wheel and looked around. Hearing nothing, he stood and headed toward the horses just to make sure they were secure.

That's when it happened. With his second step, George felt his boot brush against something. Within seconds, the mysterious noise was identified and George was yelling at the top of his lungs. Mr. Allen, startled out of his sleep immediately sat up, hitting his head on the bed of the wagon above him. By now George was running in circles shouting "Skunk!" but the smelly little critter had perfect aim. Crawling out from under the wagon Mr. Allen was bent double laughing.

–It's not funny. Oh, I think I'm going to be sick.

And with that George went into the bushes.

Sunrise brought the sight of an old man, driving a wagon with a man sitting at the very back of the wagon, his legs dangling. The driver held a handkerchief to his face and ever few minutes glanced to the man at the back of the wagon. People passing them on the road stared and sniffed the air.

By four o'clock Spartanburg, South Carolina was in the distance. George still smelled of skunk and even gagged at his own odor. For the last few hours, Mr. Allen had put away his handkerchief and now seemed immune to the strong odor. It only took a few minutes to find out where the field hospital was located, and the men headed in that direction. The scene was not unlike what George had seen before. A virtual city of tents, complete with wagon loads of followers. Homeless immigrant women followed groups of soldiers around the countryside taking care of washing and cooking, while earning very little. At the sight of George the women were pointing and hollering. Humiliated, George pulled his hat further down, trying to completely conceal his face.

The sergeant that met them immediately called for George to be taken somewhere and cleaned up. Producing a letter from Catherine, Mr. Allen handed the paper over to the sergeant. Reading the letter, the man's face suddenly went blank and he asked Mr. Allen for the full name of the soldier they were sent to bring home.

Leading the way, the sergeant escorted Mr. Allen to a large tent, where he introduced him to Captain Moody as he handed him Catherine's letter. After reading, the captain looked at Mr. Allen and said I know this man. Without so much as taking a breath Captain Moody announced that Alex had died, just that morning. Shock washed over Mr. Allen and his knees gave way and he sat down, hard, on the ground. The tent flap pulled back and George stood standing there, still smelling somewhat, from head to toe. Seeing his father-in-law sitting on the ground, his head in his hands, George dropped to his knees beside him and started to cry.

Not wasting time, Captain Moody extended his sympathies and asked if they were prepared to bury the body. This news was too much for George and he sat just shaking his head and mumbling that it could not be true. Taking the captain by the arm, Mr. Allen said that they wanted the body prepared for travel. Only recently had he heard that the military had a new way of preserving a body for travel that they called embalming. Mr. Allen was not exactly sure what it entailed, but knew that he wanted this child to go home to his mother.

Later that evening, a military wagon loaded the casket containing the body of Alex Stamper into the boxcar of a train bound for Statesville, North Carolina. George would ride in the car with the casket as Mr. Allen had agreed to drive the team home. Once in Statesville, George would transport Alex home. A telegram would be sent to Preacher Icenhour to meet the train.

Watching the scenery go by, George's thoughts were swirling with what to say to Catherine when he arrived home. She would not be expecting him for several more days, but yet at the end of today, he would have to look at her face and see her eyes cloud with emotion and how he dreaded this. The miles sped by with each clickety–clack sound that had now lulled George into a sound sleep.

Feeling the train lurch, George awoke to seeing signs of the outskirts of Statesville, through the door. Pulling on his coat he prepared for the stop. Several men at the station were waiting with baggage carts to unload the cars. Hopping down to the ground, George moved aside as men began moving the casket out of the baggage car and onto the cart.

The pace of the horses was slow and the ruts in the road rattled the wagon bed. George stared straight ahead, deep in thought. What would she say? Would she be able to take it? What should he do if she just went crazy with grief? Glancing over at Preacher Icenhour, George asked him how he thought this was all going to play out.

–Your mama is going to take it real bad. But she already knows. I know several men that work at the train station. One of them has a friend who works the telegraph office. He told him that a telegram was *sent this morning out to the farm and that he knew all about Alex* and *how you were bringing him back on the train.*

This was some comfort to George, as now he knew that he would not have to be the one to tell Catherine her son was dead.

The wagon swayed, wheels running in and out of ruts in the road. Just around the next curve they would be able to see the lane leading to the house. Sitting up straight, George adjusted his hat and pulled the brim down further, shading his face. Tears streamed down his cheeks as the lane to the house came in view.

Chapter 46
A Welcome Home

Standing at the edge of the road was Catherine, along with Ellen and two women from the church. Each held a small confederate flag in their hands. As the wagon drew closer, they lifted their arms and held the flags high as the wagon turned into the lane.

The horses slowed and the women fell in behind the wagon and followed to the house. Looking up, George was surprised to see that the front porch was full of people and there were many standing around in the yard.

The wooden coffin was gently slipped from the wagon bed and carried into the house. The air was silent, with only the occasional sound of the rustling of skirts as the women moved about.

Everyone was waiting for Catherine and she soon came into the room. Turning she looked at everyone, letting her eyes roam from one side of the room to the other.

–I want to be alone.

This seemed to take everyone by surprise but they all started for the door.

Calling out to George, Catherine asked that he stay behind. Once everyone was outside, she drew the draperies and lit the lamps.

–Now you can remove the lid. I want to see his face.

Prying the lid off the coffin, George gasped at the site of Alex. He lay as if in a deep sleep, with his arms at his sides. He was white, very white, not just pale. This must be the result of what the army did to preserve the body.

Placing her hand on his hair, Catherine dropped her head and began whispering. Then George realized she was praying. He looked at the body, moving from the head down. The stress of war showed in Alex's slight frame, which had been muscular when he left. Lack of food and constant marching had made him almost skeletal.

A tap at the door sent George flying in that direction. Opening the door he looked into the scared eyes of Ellen and Annie.

–Come in, she's praying. We'll wait until she's finished.

Minutes went by and they stood and waited for Catherine to give them some sign that she was finished praying, but she still stood, with her hand on Alex's shoulder, and whispering.

George took Ellen and Annie by the hand and started toward Catherine. Together they stood with their arms around her as she continued to pray.

Outside on the porch, Heath was peeking in the windows, trying to see in between the tiny slit where the drapes came together. It was useless as all he could see was light and no movement. George's wife Sarah moved to stand beside Heath, putting her arm around his shoulders.

–You know Heath, your Aunt Catherine is a strong woman. And although her heart is wounded, she will not die. The next few days are going to be hard and not something that any of us want to face. We will be strong for her in order to get through this. But one thing that is right to do, is cry and if you feel like you would like to shed tears, even big boys can cry.

Arms went around Sarah's waist and a small face buried into her apron, shoulders shaking with sobs.

....

When James had brought Annie home, and began having children, Alex was overjoyed, giving them lots of attention and playing with them. Always making time to tousle their hair, he was rewarded with grins and his heart beat happy when Heath would smile and say his name, only it came out as Wax. Heath was toddling around, but still small enough that he was always with his mother when one morning the men left the table to begin their work in the fields. The women were busily cleaning up the kitchen and the smaller children were sitting in the floor playing with a small wooden wagon and blocks. Turning around, Annie went to scoop Heath up, ready to change his clothes and wash his face, only he was not in the room.

Immediately everyone began calling his name and searching through the rooms. No answer and no Heath. Frantic, Annie went to the porch and began calling his name. Across the road in the field the men heard her calls and stopped to listen. Catherine was running all over the yard, searching behind bushes, calling Heath's name. Hearing this commotion the men began running toward the house. Alex had been at the far end of the field, and jumped over the deep ditch to the road. Hearing a familiar sound, he walked a few steps and listened, hearing the sound again. Crossing the road he peered down in the ditch and there sat Heath covered in mud. Looking up, he smiled a mostly toothless smile and said "Hey Wax". Laughing, Alex reached for the dirty little boy and hollered, "I've found something! There's someone trying to follow us to the field."

Laughing but with tears, Annie flew to her little one and hugged him close. James was relieved and laughed when Heath tried to reach for Alex. Taking the little boy he walked to the house with a happy Heath repeating, "Hey Wax! Hey Wax!"

The bond grew as Heath aged and he usually would be at Alex's heels, whether in the house or in the fields. It was not something that brought about jealousy in James, but rather an admiration for Alex, at how he guided this young boy, yet deferring any decision that needed to be made to Annie or James.

When Heath was around five years old, he took great pride in the fact that he could now recognize certain hymns and sing them during their church services. One Sunday fifteen inches of snow lay on the ground and the family held their own private worship in the parlor. James read from the book of Proverbs and they sang several hymns. It brought smiles to the faces of the adults as the children sang, loudly on each hymn. Finally Heath asked if he could sing Alex's favorite hymn. Smiling Catherine told him that she would love to hear him sing. Standing in the middle of the room, very straight and very serious, he began to sing.

> –On Christ the solid Rock I stand,
> All other ground is stinking sand;
> All other ground is stinking sand.

The laughter was deafening and Heath looked terrified. Crying he ran from the room when he realized they were laughing at him, not knowing why. Standing up so fast that his chair fell over, Alex shouted at them to "be quiet, it's not funny" and started upstairs behind Heath. Even James and Annie had been laughing, as it was just so special, not realizing how crushed Heath would be at their laughter.

This special bond between the two was more than kinship; Alex felt that a good part of himself was reflected in Heath, who was almost a small image of his younger self.

When the war began taking the men from the farms and sending them to battle, Heath became withdrawn. His daddy was leaving and that cut to the bone, but Alex left and without even saying goodbye. Then they were both gone.

Chapter 47
Dressing The Part

The clock on the mantle chimed three o'clock in the morning as the candles burned low at each end of the casket. Amelia Carriker shifted in her chair and smoothed her skirts as the clock chimed. Across from her sat Margaret Biggerstaff with Effie Franklin on the couch. Without words, all three women stood and walked to the casket and began replacing the candles with fresh, tall candles.

Sitting once again, they struggled to stay awake. Without announcement, Catherine came into the room and all three women stood.

   –It's all right. I just wanted to see him one more time.

Standing at the casket, she laid her hand on his arm and patted. Then reaching into her apron pocket, her hand closed around the small object that her mother, Elizabeth, had brought from England. Nestled inside was the dry soil taken from the rose garden that Elizabeth's mother had lovingly tended. Somehow carrying the box in her pocket, kept her close to her mother's memory. What would mother have done? How would she have handled this? Am I doing the right things?

Dawn brought about the bright sunlight. By eight o'clock the house was full. Women were in the kitchen putting out food, men lingering on the porch and the front yard. By nine thirty, Catherine came down the steps and everyone became very quiet, staring at her attire. Stopping at the bottom step and seeing their shocked expression, she looked at the faces of her family and friends.

   –When Alex was a little boy, I would let him look through my trunks. He loved seeing anything that I had kept over the years, especially loved the blue color of my wedding dress and hat. Each time he would say, "Put the hat on mama and let me see", and I would put the hat on and he would say, "Would you wear the hat for me?" and I would say yes. Shortly before he left, he helped me move several items to the attic and he spotted my old trunk. Lifting the lid he picked up the hat and said" Would you wear the hat for me?" and we laughed and I wore the hat the entire time we worked in the attic. Today I'm wearing the hat for Alex. I'm wearing his blue.

The procession from the house to the cemetery seemed to take forever. Most of the family had worried over Catherine as they thought she was too calm for all that was happening. Stepping from the carriage, Catherine raised her parasol and gathered her skirts, stepping across the damp grass. Everyone was still in shock trying to adjust to the spectacle of her appearing to be dressed for a wedding, but standing over her son's grave. Before everyone had even gathered around the grave, Catherine told the minister that she had something to say. Several of the women immediately placed their lacy handkerchiefs over their mouth to stifle their gasp. How could Catherine who was very respected act so disrespectful at the burial of her own son? Women simply did not speak out when they were distraught with grief and usually had to be physically assisted, but here was Catherine walking to the grave at the head of the crowd.

–I stood in my room this morning and relived the birth of this child, the *joy that I felt. I can still see the smile on my husband's face as this child was placed in his arms. John's first living son. A son who was gentle and thoughtful; a son who became a man, with a heart filled with compassion for those around him. He was someone you would want your daughter to marry. Someone you would want your son to be like. He was my Alex and we had a special bond between us such that he knew what I was thinking and I knew what he was feeling.*

I stood there thinking that I knew what Alex would want, so I chose blue dress and hat, his favorite. Tomorrow I will mourn and wear black. But today I want to remember how wonderful he was and his sweet smile and the shy way he had about him. I want his nephews to remember him with joy and not with sorrow. Alex would want you to know that he is with John and for that I find great comfort. My son served honorably and I am truly grateful. He met his destiny as God intended and now he is in heaven with God where one day I will see him again.

The only sound was the whisper of the breeze through the trees as everyone stood transfixed to the spot. Even Preacher Icenhour did not move. A full two minutes passed and no one moved or spoke. This moment of remembering, Alex was so moving that time seemed to be frozen. Standing beside his mother, Heath began to sing.

> *–On Christ the solid Rock I stand,*
> *All other ground is sinking sand;*
> *All other ground is sinking sand.*

Then everyone began to sing.

My hope is built on nothing less
Than Jesus' blood and righteousness,
I dare not trust the sweetest frame,
But wholly trust in Jesus' Name

On Christ the solid Rock I stand,
All other ground is sinking sand;
All other ground is sinking sand.

When He shall come with trumpet sound,
Oh may I then in Him be found.
Dressed in His righteousness alone.
Faultless to stand before the throne.

On Christ the solid Rock I stand..........

The funeral had been over for hours and the neighbors had left. In her bedroom Catherine gently folded the blue wedding dress and placed it in the cedar chest at the foot of her bed. Putting on her work dress, she sat in a chair by the window and looked at the sky but felt agitated. Quietly she left her room, walking down the hall, through the kitchen and out the back door she headed for the barn. Hoping that a ride would settle her anxiety, she saddled her horse and guided the horse to the road.

Heading back to the graveyard, Catherine wanted just one more moment alone, to stand beside Alex's grave.

She took comfort in knowing that Alex was resting close and that she could visit his grave every day. Just before sunset, Catherine mounted her horse and began the journey home. She pulled on the reins and looked over her shoulder.

–I'll be back tomorrow.

Chapter 48
Hiding Places and Deserters

The woods held secrets that hopefully no one would discover and before James left he was counting on just that fact. Cautioning Catherine, he told her what to expect if the war escalated. James truly did not believe that the Yankees would ever be on their land, but he also knew that with so many men serving, desperation would visit many homes. Catherine quickly decided that all but one pig should be taken to the woods for safekeeping. The Stamper land held miles of wooded areas, mostly behind the house.

James had trekked through their woods, over a half mile, before he found a spot he felt would be secure. There he marked out a perimeter for the boys to see. Within a month the boys had managed to clear the small area and build a fence. In the fall Jonathan, Heath and Jamie transported the squealing animals to their secret place. In a large tree beside the fence they built a small platform, about twelve feet off the ground. Here they could keep watch if the area were threatened. Behind the large tree they laid a stacked fence. If there was to be trouble and they had warning, the women would bring several of the cows and place them there. The worst part was dragging food for the animals through the woods.

On Saturday morning, after feeding the pigs in the woods, Jamie checked one of his traps, and to his surprise he had caught a small wild turkey. Brave enough to roam the woods alone for hours was one thing, but brave enough to slaughter the turkey himself was another matter. Dragging the very vocal bird back to the house, Jamie tried to come up with a reason as to why the bird was still alive. Now that he was twelve years old, it was expected of him to not only furnish meat or fowl for the table, but also present his catch ready to be cooked. As soon as he came into the yard, the bird put up a fight, struggling to pull its feet from Jamie's hands.

Looking out the window Jonathan came to his brother's rescue. Taking the bird he disappeared around the side of the shed, then just as quickly he was back. Thrusting the bird back to Jamie he whispered he would not tell who killed the bird. That afternoon Ellen plucked the feathers and put the turkey into a barrel of salt brine for an hour and then to the oven. By nightfall the aroma of turkey baking, drifted throughout the house.

The next day just at sunrise, Catherine found Ellen coming into the house with a basket of eggs.

– My but we're up early this morning.

Ellen's only response was a smile. All through breakfast Ellen was quiet, even to the point that her boys noticed. Excusing herself she said she had a headache and was going to lie back down and for everyone to go to church without her. Feeling her forehead, Catherine was relieved to find no fever. Offers to stay home with her brought objections and a response of "I'll be fine. Just go." Something was not right but Catherine could not put her finger on the problem.

Church services could no longer be the joyous bonding of neighbors. In every service, Catherine stood and listened to the names of those in the community recently killed or captured by the Yankees. Each time a name was read, her heart lurched knowing she had kin still out there. Looking around Catherine counted ten new widows with children. Dora Carter and her children sat with Catherine and after service they walked together to the wagon. The two women spoke of pleasant things and avoided speaking of their loved ones, now in battle. There were so many who no longer came to church. Unable to cope with their loss, they retreated and mourned in private.

Several of the women had asked about Becky Dagenhart, who was reported to have taken to her bed, with the pain in her back making her unable to stand. No one had seen Henry Dagenhart in several weeks or his two youngest boys, Emanuel and William. Being many years older than his wife, Henry had started showing signs of aging shortly after the birth of their last child. But he had seemed to age dramatically when three of his sons marched off to war. There would always be a place in Catherine's heart for Henry. Quietly helping those in need, he asked for nothing in return. Once her family was settled after Sunday dinner, she would ride over to the Dagenhart farm to see what she could do.

Having the turkey for their Sunday dinner was a real treat. Ellen served up sweet potatoes, turnips and cabbage along with cornbread. There was also a cobbler made from dried apples. The meal reminded Catherine of times past with everyone talking and laughing at the table, sharing stories. After the meal Ellen cleared the table and told her mother she would feel better with fresh air. Watching her walk towards the woods, Catherine had an uneasy feeling. Something was going on that Ellen was not revealing.

....

Climbing into the wagon, Catherine called to Burt and Simpson and they were on their way. The basket on the seat beside her was packed with turkey, cornbread and baked sweet potatoes. The Dagenhart farm was only a few miles over the hill and soon Catherine could see the smoke from their chimney. But there was something else that caught her eye, riders in the distance going in the opposite direction. Squinting, Catherine saw what appeared to be four or five men, riding fast. Slowing the horses she debated whether to continue on to the farm. What if it was a Yankee party out looting in the neighborhood? Shifting her weight on the seat, she felt the metal of the gun against her leg. Catherine knew she was brave, but she also knew to be smart enough to not leave her house without protection. Her son-in-law, Fate, had given her a small gun with a strap that she wore around her lower thigh.

Not seeing any other movement on the road, she called to the horses and continued on to the Dagenhart house. Pulling into the yard, she was immediately met by Emanuel Dagenhart. Helping Catherine from the wagon he was excitedly telling her that the Home Guard had just passed by their house and said there were Yankees nearby, and they had chased some confederate deserters into the area. There had been a battle called Bristoe Campaign some weeks past and some of the confederates had decided to desert and strike out for home. Catherine questioned the boy to see if he knew which company or regiment, but he did not. Handing him the basket, she climbed back into the wagon and asked him to give her best to his parents.

Back home, Catherine told of seeing the men riding the road. Maybe they should ask George what he thought. But if he thought there was danger in the neighborhood he would have come to tell them to prepare. Since George had just been to town the day before, there was no mention of concern, Catherine felt better. By evening Catherine became distracted helping Ellen decide on a nightgown pattern as they searched through their box of patterns. The visit to the Dagenhart farm was now put out of her mind.

Chapter 49
Yankees

Several miles over from the Stamper farm, the Carter's had been struggling to stay alive. Dora Carter had been managing to keep up their farm during these war years. With only young children to help work the land, Dora's efforts were slowly paying off.

It was just after dusk and Dora had settled her children for the night and was now sitting by the fire. A faint sound prompted her to put down her book. There was only the stillness of the house. At first she thought she was hearing things. Listening again, she was sure there was someone outside. Quietly she slipped into her children's room and woke her ten-year-old son, telling him that someone was outside prowling around.

Back in the main room, they listened for several minutes, but heard nothing so the boy went back to bed. Settling back in her rocker, Dora picked up her book and began reading. Thirty minutes passed and again Dora heard the noise. Quickly she went to the bedroom and woke her son once again.

With the boy carrying a rifle almost as long as he was tall, he stood behind his mother as she slowly opened the door. Lifting the lamp she called 'who's there' and immediately heard a moan. Looking down at the foot of the steps, they saw the dark shadow of a man lying on the ground. Stepping closer and raising the lamp, Dora caught the first glimpse of her husband, Samuel.

Dora along with her children managed to get Samuel in the house. He had been wounded at Bristoe Station and was now wheezing with infection in his chest. Settling her husband in their bed, Dora grabbed her cloak and left to find Doc Stewart. Walking in the dark, she kept to the side of the road, hoping that no one would be out this time of night. The Stewart family were bedded down for the night, when a pounding on their door woke the household.

Quickly Doc Stewart saddled his horse and lifted Dora to sit behind him. It seemed as if it took forever to finally see her house in the distance, and Dora immediately slid off the back of the horse before he was completely stopped.

The doctor dressed the wound and determined it was not as serious as he had previously thought. He mixed a poultice and rubbed on Samuel's chest and instructed Dora to build up the fire and then put pots on to boil. The moisture in the house, along with the poultice would help Samuel's chest.

For several days Dora nursed Samuel; he kept to the bedroom out of sight. Tomorrow would be Christmas. Dora knew that this would be the most special Christmas she ever had and wanted it to be so very special for Samuel. Everything they would eat on Christmas she would prepare the day before, thereby leaving the entire day to enjoy being with family.

Out in the smokehouse, there was only the smell of smoked meat, as it had been quite some time since there was the sight of hams hanging and curing. Looking around the only thing visible was grease spots on the wooden floor. The rafters held nothing but cobwebs and what appeared to be a squirrel nest on one side, right beside a small hole in the wall. Pulling a ladder inside the smoke house, Dora propped the ladder and began climbing to the top. She stretched and started pulling straw from the squirrel's nest. Just a few handfuls of straw removed and a large hole, leading to the inside of the wall was quite visible. Reaching inside she pulled out the ham. Yes, this Christmas would be the best ever.

By evening Dora had prepared the ham, sweet potatoes, greens, turnips and cornbread, setting the food on the table in the cooking room. The Carter house had almost burned from a cooking fire several years back, prompting Samuel to build a small building, just a few feet from the back door, where Dora cooked all their meals. Opening a drawer, she pulled out several beeswax candles and placed them in holders. Christmas Day they would light the candles and the house would be filled with this wonderful aroma. Tomorrow they would have a feast and sing hymns. They had much to thank God for.

Later that evening as they were sitting by the fire, horses could be heard coming up the road. Quickly Dora helped Samuel to the bedroom and closed the door. Sitting back in her rocker she waited and finally the pounding on the door began.

Cracking the door, Dora saw a Yankee colonel standing on her porch and with a dozen soldiers in the yard, still mounted on their horses. Squeezing out the door, Dora laid her hand on the captain's arm and told him she would like to give his men some water. Standing and watching her walk to the well, the Yankee colonel did not quite know what to think. A bucket of icy cold water was pulled from the well and several gourds were handed out to the men. Then Dora insisted on getting water for the horses and started drawing water for the trough. Twenty buckets later the men were quietly watching this small woman lead their horses to the trough.

Stepping forward, the colonel said gently that he needed to search the house and turned to step from the porch into the main room. With Dora on his heels, she quickly gained position in front of him and quietly said that he did not need to search. Seeing the closed door to the bedroom, the captain asked what was behind the door. Dora quietly said that she had something she wished to read to him.

Grabbing up her Bible she turned to the Christmas passage in the book of Luke.

–For there is born to you this day in the city of David, a Savior, who is Christ the Lord.......And suddenly there was with the angel a multitude of the heavenly host praising God and saying: Glory to God in the highest, and on earth peace, goodwill toward men."..........

Dora looked at the colonel and said again "peace and goodwill toward all men."

The room was so quiet, Dora wondered if the soldier could hear her heart pounding. Turning toward the back door, Dora told the colonel that she had already cooked Christmas dinner and would like to feed him and his men. Walking through the main room, heading for the back door, the colonel paused, and looked at the closed bedroom door. Then seeing the woman waiting on him, he stepped out on the porch.

Later that night, Dora stood on the porch and watched the Yankee colonel ride away with his men. Samuel slowly crawled from under the bed. Yes, this was the best Christmas they had ever had.

Chapter 50
Christmas Day

The morning was cold and the fire in the stove was beginning to heat the kitchen. Catherine had been up for hours, making sure all her plans were in order. In the parlor there were sprigs of greenery lying on the mantel and the side tables. Nestled amongst the greenery were holly berries. This was something Catherine had seen when she lived at Vanderburg Plantation. The air smelled of fresh cedar.

Bread was rising on the kitchen table and the smell of cider was wafting through the air. On a trip to town, back in June, Catherine had traded for two sticks of cinnamon, one of which was now floating in the heating cider. Stirring the heating liquid, she dropped in several huge spoons of brown sugar.

Pushing up her sleeves and dusting the table with flour, she kneaded the dough and began pinching off small pieces. Reaching into her apron pocket, she felt for the pennies, and laid them on the table. Carefully she placed a washed penny on the piece of dough and then folded the dough over, hiding the money. Each child would be given a roll that morning, brushed with butter and sprinkled with brown sugar. The surprise inside would be a special treat for them.

The house was still silent as everyone slept and Catherine quietly started up the steps. On the second floor she paused to listen. No one was stirring so she continued to the attic. Tiptoeing across the attic floor she went to an old wardrobe that had been Nanny Grindstaff's. It was a sentimental piece and really of no value, except that it had belonged to someone Catherine loved dearly. Quietly she opened the door and stood back smiling. Who would have ever thought to look here for Christmas dinner?

Brushing aside old dresses revealed a small ham Catherine had managed to hide. The family assumed that someone stole the ham from the smoke house and talked about it for weeks. But Catherine knew that if they had two hams, they would eat two hams, and she desperately wanted one of them for Christmas. So in the middle of the night, she stole her own ham and secreted it away in the cool of the attic.

By midmorning everyone had finished with their chores and the women were busy in the kitchen. The children were anxious to see what there was to eat as Catherine had told them it would be a surprise. For the second time since they had lived in the house the table was set with china and the center of the table held a bowl of pinecones, still smelling of fresh pine.

By one o'clock George and his family had arrived and the children could not stand the suspense any longer; thankfully it was time for Catherine to invite everyone into the dining room. On each of the children's plates, lay small flat little rolls, glistening with melted butter and brown sugar. Tearing the rolls apart, the children squealed in surprise as they found the pennies. The adults enjoyed the sight of all the children smiling. All settled in for the meal and Catherine came from the kitchen carrying the ham. They were surprised and clapped. Smiling she told them the secret of the ham and everyone laughed.

It was a joyous Christmas and after the meal, they sat by the fire and Mr. Allen, George's father-in-law, read the Christmas story and said a prayer. He prayed for all their loved ones still away and asked for everyone's safety. After the prayer they sang carols and talked of Christmases past. It was a wonderful time of sharing. Even Annie told a funny story about James on the first Christmas they were together. This time was for healing and remembering and there were no tears. They enjoyed one another's company, thankful that they had each other.

At four o'clock, George pulled the buggy around. He drove Mr. Allen and Sarah back to their farm. Tomorrow George would take his wife and Mr. Allen to Barringer Township to visit Mr. Allen's brother. The house was now quiet and Catherine watched Ellen as she just stood staring out the window.

Chapter 51
The Confession

By Christmas night the wind was now blowing freezing rain and snow. The house was drafty and Heath had the sniffles. Annie worried that her young son would get sick and insisted on putting a poultice on his chest. Tonight she planned on Heath sleeping on a pallet in front of the fireplace, where he could be kept as warm as possible. Catherine was also concerned for Ellen, who had been acting strangely for a week.

It was late and Annie had decided to come downstairs and sleep near Heath. She had roused Catherine and Ellen as Heath's breathing was labored. Catherine immediately told Ellen they would need to mix another poultice to put on Heath's chest and she headed downstairs to the kitchen. Gathering up a quilt and a blanket, Annie started down the stairs, she heard a rider coming fast into the yard. Before she could reach the bottom step, someone was pounding on the door. Then she could hear a voice calling for them to open the door. George was on the porch, pounding and yelling to hurry and open the door. Annie unlocked the door and George pushed his way into the room, covered with freezing rain and calling for Ellen.

Just as George was bursting through the door, Catherine and Ellen were coming from the kitchen where they had prepared the poultice for Heath's chest. Catherine looked from George to Ellen and asked what was happening here?

Not being gentle, George grabbed Ellen by the arm and said he wanted to know where her husband was hiding. With terror written on her face, Ellen tried to free his grasp, and began to cry. Grabbing her shoulders George began shaking Ellen and demanding to know where she had hidden him. Realizing what this was about Catherine went pale. Josiah, Ellen's husband, must be hiding somewhere close. Catherine turned and pushed at George's arm and told him to let go. When he did, Ellen crumpled to the floor, crying uncontrollably.

-Mama she'll get us all killed. Yankees came last night looking for Samuel Carter. His wife Dora managed to save him, but I don't know for how long.

There were ten soldiers that went to the Carter farm. Someone had told a Yankee colonel that three confederates were hiding in the neighborhood and suggested they start with the Carter farm. Staring at Ellen, George's fury was evident by his red face.

-*There's no telling who around us is a traitor and telling the enemy all our comings and goings.*

The entire neighborhood had been ignorant of the deserters so no one was on the lookout for them. This information was the first that anyone in the family had heard; they wondered who was living among them who knew about these men. Ellen was now lying in the floor, covering her head with her arms and crying loudly.

Gently Catherine urged Ellen to sit and then held her close.

-*It's all right and we're all fine, but you need to tell what is going on.*

Ellen had gone to the corncrib, preparing to feed the chickens, and when she opened the door, there sat Josiah in the corn, pale, dirty and with an open wound on his arm. Not believing what she was seeing, Ellen grabbed the door to keep from falling. Quickly Josiah grabbed her and pulled her into the corncrib, placing a hand over her mouth. By now her shock had turned to great joy and she hugged him tightly around the waist and cried.

Over the next few days Josiah moved about on the farm, hiding out in this storehouse, and then another outbuilding. Ellen had managed to sneak food as well as medicine for his arm. She was afraid to tell their sons, for fear they would somehow give him away. One night Ellen rose from her bed after midnight and quietly left the house. She spent the next two hours with her husband, listening to his tale of the war. Over the next week, Josiah slept in the potato cave and secretly met with Ellen during the night, each night telling her more about the war.

Their company had marched to Bristoe Station, Virginia, pushing northward toward Manassas Gap unaware that they would stumble across a large contingency of Union army in the process of retreating. Fighting began and the rebels suffered tremendous losses in two brigades and lost a battery of artillery to the Yankees. It was said that almost 2,000 men lost their lives at Bristoe Station. The Yankees continued their retreat and the rebels' offensive came to a halt.

It was the perfect opportunity to head for home and it would be days before the Confederate officers would discover some of their men missing.

Three men banded together and headed south out of Virginia

across the North Carolina line and straight to Iredell Co. Josiah along with Levi Dagenhart and Samuel Carter were finally home. Coming into the county the men kept to the woods, then split up, each going his own way. Levi had watched his parent's farm for an entire day before showing himself to his sister, Mime. Throwing her arms around him she cried and clung to him. Looking out the window, Henry Dagenhart jumped from his chair and ran from the house grabbing his son by the arm and helping him to the house.

For the next week, those riding up and down the road saw the same scene of a tall, gangly woman plowing and working the fields with another woman. Levi donned his sisters oversized skirts and bonnet and headed for the fields. The land was life, the future, and Henry was slowly becoming unable to work the farm. Becky would not hear of Emanuel and William working the field. They were both almost of an age to serve and it suited her just fine if everyone thought they were gone, because they were not seen. At the first word of the Home Guard being close by, the boys were sent to a cave in the woods, which they had dug into the side of a large hill.

Meeting one night, at the edge of the woods, Levi, Josiah and Samuel discussed whether to return to the fight. Staying near their farms meant placing their families in danger, not to mention the fact they were terrified of being caught. If they stayed it would be a constant job of hiding. Going back to their company meant a few weeks' punishment, but at least they would be alive. Tales of Yankees coming into areas and finding Confederate deserters, torturing their families before removing them as captives, helped in making the decision. Levi said he could not go, that he would just have to take his chances. His parents were in poor health and without him the farm would fail. Josiah and Samuel watched as Levi made his way back through the woods. Their decision had been made and they would go back and hope for the best.

With his haversack, new blanket, hardtack and a few cans of Underwood Deviled Ham, Josiah said his goodbyes and disappeared through the woods. Ellen had stood staring in the dark, awash with a feeling of dread. Placing her hands in her apron pockets, she held on to the letter that Josiah had written and that he had asked for her to read to his boys.

Chapter 52
Preparation

The following morning Ellen could not move from her bed. She was consumed with grief from seeing her husband, Josiah, leave once again. Giving Josiah's letter to Catherine, Ellen asked her mother to read it to the boys privately.

After breakfast Catherine told the boys that she needed to see them in their room. Slowly climbing the stairs both boys wondered what they had done wrong. It must be pretty bad if their mother had told Catherine to dole out the punishment. Entering their bedroom, they sat and waited.

Pacing back and forth Catherine finally told the boys that she had something to read to them. Sitting silently on the side of the bed, they waited. Seeing them sitting so stiffly, eyes filled with fear, Catherine's heart ached.

–*Let's get this over with boys, and then we'll talk if you want.*

Opening the letter, she began to read.

"Dear sons Jamie and Jonathan,
This is your daddy saying goodbye, as it may be a long time before I see you again. Your mother will not have my help to get by and you need to do what needs to be done. My company will take me back but not before they punish me then I will be sent to fight again. There will be big battles and it may be that I will not come home. But I cannot go away without you knowing that you are my boys and I hold you in my thoughts and in my heart. Keep the wood box full and help with the chickens. Take your turn in the woods watching the pigs and do for your mother the things she needs done. When you are grown men remember me with gladness in your heart and tell your children about me.
Your loving daddy, Josiah Stamper"

Standing in the middle of the room Catherine watched the boys, blank and staring. Asking if they wanted to talk about the letter, both boys shook their heads, no. Turning she quietly left the room. Moving down the hall to Ellen's room, she went in to check on her. Not moving or speaking the two little boys continued to sit on the edge of the bed.

By midafternoon Annie had sent son Heath to check on the boys and he found them both sleeping. They were exhausted from crying. An uneasy silence had settled on the house as if they were waiting for something.

Sometime during that night Ellen came downstairs and sat in the rocker where Catherine found her asleep the next morning. The rest of the week though, flew by with everyone returning to his routines. George came by nearly every day to check on them. Word had spread of the Yankee army advancing and there had been reports of a small skirmish at Cool Springs not more than ten miles from Statesville. Immediately Catherine put into motion the gathering of food to be moved to their secret place. George would go back and gather up his belongings and bring his wife Sarah and her father Mr. Allen to stay at Grindstaff House. Hopefully there would be no Yankees within miles. Plans for being safe today are better than being sorry tomorrow.

About a quarter mile into the woods a pit had been dug three feet deep and three feet wide with wooden planks covering the hole. Straw was laid in the hole and placed on the sides. Once their food and valuables were in the pit more straw was added and the planks pulled over the top. Next they shoveled dirt on the planks and then spread pine needles. Even if horses were to ride over the spot, the dirt would muffle the sound of the hooves on the wood.

Late in the afternoon, pulling a large wooden sled by ropes, Riley, Heath and George made their way into the woods heading for the food pit. Catherine and Annie stood on the back porch and watched until they could no longer see them. A nervous knot had formed in Catherine's stomach and she felt sick. Standing beside Annie, Catherine put her arm around Annie's shoulders. She immediately noticed Annie's frown.

–I'm so thankful that our James had the wisdom to tell us how to save our food. This is just one more thing that you can be proud of.

–I know you're right, but I just miss him so much.

Two days passed and they continued to hear of soldiers roaming their area. George was glad that he had decided to move Sally and her father to Catherine's house since it would be better to have all the family together. A neighbor stopped by to tell them that most of the boys in the area had been sent to the caves in the woods to keep them safe, reasoning that it would be harder for Yankees to kill old men, women and babies. Young boys were a dangerous threat to the Yankees. They were potential Confederate fighters.

Standing in the lane looking toward the house, George decided that the house looked barren and he could see no animals except for two chickens. Someone though, sat at the attic window or on the porch round the clock keeping watch. There were no riders on the road but there were sounds of gunfire in the distance.

George checked inside the house to see that everything was ready if visitors arrived. Earlier in the week he and Heath had prepared the area under the stairs. This particular space was walled in with wood paneling and at the center of the wall one panel was removed. The panel was just wide enough for an adult to turn sideways and slip under the steps. Under the stairs the floorboards were pried up to make an escape door to the underside of the house. When the boards were gently tapped no one would ever know that the hiding place existed. The back of the panel had two wooden knobs in order to place the panel back in its place from the inside. A small side table slipped in front of the panel helped the area look normal. Valuables could be placed under the stairs at a moment's notice and still have room for three people to hide. But if soldiers did come this exit would be their last plan of action because Catherine had made other plans to keep unwelcome visitors away.

At the end of the week black smoke could again be seen in the distance and gunfire could be heard. George knew that the time had come. Quickly assembling the family he gave instructions, then moved the panel under the stairs in case he felt the need to hide. The women changed into stained and dirty clothes. Mr. Allen sat in a rocker, while waiting in the parlor with his daughter Sally by his side. He reached into his pocket and placed dark glasses on his nose. Turning to Sarah he grinned.

-Look! Now I'm blind!

She swatted him on the sleeve of his jacket and told him "this is not a time to be merry."

The road was dusty and the riders moved slowly then stopped as they spotted chimney smoke in the distance. A tall soldier at the back called to the captain in front.

-Black smoke ahead captain!

-Well it looks like this could be where we requisition more supplies.

The Yankee captain kept his eyes peeled while glancing from one side of the road then the other side. This farm would not be the first southern house he had visited and he knew to be cautious. These southern belles were not all beauty and weakness. Rubbing the lower side of his jaw he felt the scar placed there by a knife held by a dainty white southern belle's hands.

Stopping at the entrance to the drive, the captain spoke to the men instructing them to wait for his lead.

–There will be no looting of the house. We are here only for food supplies and any medicine they might have on hand along with candles. Keep your eyes open because if there are any men they will be hiding and most likely with a shotgun aimed at your heart.

Nudging his mount forward, he led the men up the lane constantly keeping his eyes on the house.

Ellen and Annie stood on the porch ready to receive anyone who came up the road. The sound of horses could be heard as they turned off the road and headed up to the house. The Yankee officer quickly reined in his horse and shouted the command to "halt!" Staring at the house he nudged his horse forward only to stop again. From behind the house he could see black smoke billowing into the air.

Standing on the porch holding up a sheet, Ellen and Annie appeared pale and sick. On the sheet was painted skull and crossbones with the word 'Cholera' written in large red letters. Dropping the sheet, the women stepped aside to reveal Catherine sitting on the floor of the porch leaning against the wall. Jamie and Jonathan were lying on their stomachs at her feet not moving. The boys were pale as ghosts and Catherine looked grey. Stepping forward, Ellen held her arms out to the soldiers.

–Please help! We need help! If you would just bring us some water and leave it at the foot of the steps.

Ellen started down the steps speaking to the Yankee officer.

–We can't leave them alone for even a minute and we are now out of water. Our well has been poisoned and I can't go to the creek for fear they will die before I get back. We're trying to burn all that belonged to those who have died, but I fear that now we have put disease in the smoke that rises.

All the while in the background the boys are making moaning noises.

Backing his horse, the officer began putting space between himself and an advancing Ellen.

—Stop where you are madam! Do not come any closer.

Ellen persisted, stepping forward.
—We will do anything if you will just help us. It has been days and days since we have seen anyone. We are out of food and need a doctor. There are six more children inside and all are sick. Their mothers have all died and we have moved our own mother and children outside to protect them but as you can now see they are now sick too.

With every word from Ellen's mouth the Yankee officer continued to back his horse. Drawing a pistol, the captain pointed the gun at Ellen.

—If you come any closer I will have to shoot. Keep your distance!

At that Ellen sank to her knees sobbing, covering her face with her hands and the officer turned and gave the command for his men to follow. Peeking through her fingers Ellen began to wail while watching the retreating men gain speed on their horses putting distance between themselves and the dreaded Cholera. At the end of the lane one soldier dismounted and tied a black cloth to a tree limb to warn others.

Everyone stayed in position for a full ten minutes. They dare not chance that one of the men would sneak back. They stayed frozen where they were. Ellen sat in the dirt with her head dropped against her chest while Annie fanned the boys. Finally, George cracked the door and said that all was clear. Having gone upstairs, he looked out the window and could see that the soldiers had truly left.

The boys sat up on the porch and began to giggle and point to each other's face. Sally came on the porch with a wet towel and everyone began wiping off the rice powder and ashes from their cheeks and eyes. Catherine had gently touched under their eyes with ashes and then powered their faces. From a distance they looked deathly ill. Sternly, Ellen soon scolded the boys and told them this situation was not something to laugh about.

—We can't have cholera forever so the next time soldiers come we will most likely have to flee and lose our home.

At that sobering statement the boys lost their grin.

The sun was just seconds before setting when George came on to the porch and placed his arm around his mother.

–We'll get through this.

Laying her head over on his chest, Catherine thought of Alex and Gilbert. A tear of relief ran down her cheek and she turned and went into the house.

Chapter 53
Word from The Front

Weeks went by quickly and the tension in the neighborhood seemed to ease, that is for everyone except Catherine. Somewhere along the way she had lost her trust in people.

Their chickens had been raided several nights in a row and the following morning revealed tracks in the dirt leading to the next farm over. Facing the owner, Catherine asked for her chickens back only to be met with a bold stare of "if you want them come and get them."

–I would have given you the chickens if you had just asked.

And at that, she turned and mounted her horse.

Slowly she was finding out that the ravages of war had placed people in desperate situations. God fearing men stealing to feed their family was just one example. That night, their biggest dog was tied outside the chicken coop.

At the end of December 1863, three letters were delivered to Catherine. Her boys! She was finally hearing from her boys! There was one letter from Gilbert and two from Melmath!

June 8, 1863
Dearest mother and loved ones,
This letter is to tell you that I am fine although we are not getting enough to eat and I am now quite thin with my clothes hanging loose on me. Today I received six of your letters and hid in the brush and read each of them several times over. How I wish I was home with you and could give you a hug and sit at your table and sleep in my bed. One good thing has happened and I have been promoted to sergeant and my commanding officer tells me that I am very reliable and he can tell I was raised well. How is the farm doing and do you have crops? Some of the men in my company have had letters from home and their people don't have enough food to eat. We were in a big fight over at Frayser's Farm and Thomas Moose and his brother Garrett were killed. I saw Delbert Crouch and he is now without his left arm. I also saw Alex and hollered and hollered but he could not hear me and then I lost sight of him in the fight. Although he was not close I could see that

he looked well. After the fighting was over I searched for him but someone said his company had moved on. It would have been like being home to see him and talk with him as I miss him and wish I had joined his unit. There are so many boys   from our neighborhood that are not going to come home and I am scared that I will not see my beloved North Carolina again. Pray for me that I can come home.
Your loving son and brother and uncle
Gilbert Neil Stamper
North Carolina 33rd Reg. Company A

Sitting in the rocker, Catherine rocked back and forth, holding the letter to her chest.

–He must have written this the week he was captured. I wonder if he had my letters with him when they sent him to Maryland?

Slowly the tears began to stream down Catherine's face, and then Annie and Ellen both started crying. Baby Lina took in all this emotion and she too began wailing away. Quickly Sarah picked her up and left the room. George knelt beside his mother.

–Mama, he'll be all right. Gilbert knows how to take care of himself and he'll come back home to us.

Looking down at George, Catherine wiped her tears and began to read the letter out loud once again.

–He doesn't know that Alex is dead. Here is his letter and he doesn't know.

George gently enfolded his mother in his arms as Catherine finally let all her grief flow from her. Mr. Allen asked Jamie to take Riley and Heath to the barn. Jonathan was cleaning the stalls and probably needed the company. Understanding what he was being asked to do and why, Jamie grabbed Riley and Heath by the arm and ushered them out the door.

Catherine's sobs could be heard throughout the house. No one stopped her or tried to soother her; they knew Catherine's strength was not broken, but her emotions were being released to make room for more living. Wiping her eyes, she looked at George and Mr. Allen.

–We must get another package together for him and make sure it gets to him in Maryland.

Both men assured her that they would start immediately gathering things for Gilbert and making sure it was delivered.

The next hour, they sat in silence as Catherine rocked, her head laid back with hands folded in her lap, still clutching Gilbert's letter.

Hearing the sounds of the children coming into the back of the house, Catherine asked Annie to bring them all into the parlor. Once they were all gathered, she told them that they had to start preparing.

-*Winter is here and if we're careful we can maybe squeak by. But we can't go to town and barter any butter or milk, and we're going to have to stop taking as many eggs as we've been taking. The neighbors are not prepared for any more war. Butter and milk says that we have cows. And we're going to have to move them further back in the woods. I don't want to be able to hear them if they bellow loud. We're going to have to take turns guarding what little we have. We'll take turns, except for Ellen and Annie. George, you and Mr. Allen will have to build us a small shelter in the woods. People are getting desperate, and we need to keep safe what we have. So far, we've been lucky. Now, let's get on with this letter and see what Melmath has to say.*

April 14, 1863
To my dear Aunt Catherine and loved ones,
There have been so many things that have happened to me, I do not know where to begin. First let me assure you that I am enjoying fine health, although there is not enough to eat. Some of those around me are sick because of the lack of food, or maybe it is because of bad food. A man came by one day and had a big bag of dried peaches. They were not as ripe as they should be, but I ate them anyway and was sick to the point I laid in a ditch. My company had to move as we were headed to a place called Chancellorsville..My position was at the end of our detail as I continued to fall out with my bowels. It is my hope that our arrival there will allow me to rest and regain my stomach once again. Tonight I looked about me in the woods, hoping to see the herb that you used in tea for oursick stomachs but could not find anything familiar. Desard Bennett, who is Miss Meredith's nephew, has been with me now for three weeks. He joined us along with his cousin, Clark Bennett. They have told me that their aunt will have no one if they are killed and I wanted you to know so that maybe you could send the boys to check on her occasionally. Clark says that she is nearing ninety years old and I know that you would see that she has food. I think of you as we pass farmland and see women working farms. It will not be long surely before I can come home and help you. I promised James that I would help with the farm, as it seems like my home, my only home. Daddy wrote me a

letter and said that mama no longer walks or talks and that he
fears she will die soon as she refuses to eat. Please pray for her as
she is very sick in so many ways.
    Your loving nephew
    Melmath Stamper
Everyone sat staring at the paper in Catherine's hand,
comprehending that the words were written many months ago, while
Alex was still alive. Memlath also did not know of the death of James.
Shifting in her chair, Catherine opened the final letter.

September 19, 1863
Dearest Aunt Catherine,
I hope this letter finds you in good health and that all is well at the
farm. Today I thought of you and the land. Looking at the trees and
the colors makes me homesick for the woods behind the house.
Alex and I had good   hunting there and it will be good to hunt
there again and I hope that it is soon. This is the time of year that
we started looking for turkey tracks. I want to stand in the house
and smell your turkey baking in the oven and watch as you mix
together cakes and pies. Yesterday I showed several of the boys
how to make the snare for rabbits and this morning we caught one.
Although it was not big, we did get a few bites each and it was
good. Everyone gathered around while we cooked it, on a stick over
the fire. How I wish we had some of your good rabbit stew with
biscuits. All of my hardtack is gone but it is just as well as I have a
broken tooth in the back of my mouth. At next camp if there is a
barber I hope to have it pulled. We camped on a farm last week and
the lady there had a little girl that reminded me of Susan when she
was little. Their old coon dog would follow behind her and grab the
tail of her gown and pull until she sat down. Then he would lie
across her legs and she would laugh. The woman said that if we
went near the little girl that we would see the dog's teeth and feel
them. So for two days we watched as the dog followed the little girl
around, pulling her down so he could lay in her lap. One fellow,
that I know, from over near the Waugh farm, came too close and
the dog bit him on his backside. We laughed and laughed but the
woman was mad and she came out with a big gun and told our
captain that we had to move off her land so we did. As soon as I
can find more paper I will write again. Tell everyone that I am well
and want to be home and send my best wishes.
Your loving nephew
Melmath Stamper

Everyone sat silently taking in the words that Melmath had written
and pondering his fate and the fate of those loved ones, still out there
somewhere, fighting. Lina sat in the floor playing with a doll that Annie
had made for her. She looked so sweet and innocent and Catherine told

everyone how blessed they were that troops were not camped in their yard, with soldiers watching Lina play.

Chapter 54
Secret Revealed

It had only been two months since Catherine had buried her son Alex and her heart was still heavy. The family worried about her, as she had not behaved in any fashion that they expected. When she learned that Gilbert was in a Yankee prison, she was almost inconsolable. Little did they know of her restless sleep and tears throughout each night.

The house seemed unusually quiet. George tried each evening to start conversation at dinner and even Mr. Allen tried by telling funny stories. Somewhere the joy they had shared as a family had been stifled down. The women went about their daily chores as did the men and boys, but life seemed to have dulled. Two loved ones now gone. Sitting by the fire, Ellen sewed on a new apron. Her complexion seemed pale and her eyes lacked luster. Catherine had noticed this but she also was worried about Josiah. There had been no word of him in months, not since he returned to his unit. Both Riley and Heath had asked about their father and why they did not have word of him. They were answered with silence as Ellen just stared and shook her head.

The wind was picking up as Jamie carried two buckets of milk from the woods. Grumbling, he was not pleased at having to walk a half mile or more to milk the cows hidden in the woods. And then begin the walk back to the house, only now carrying heavy buckets full of milk. But at least they had milk, as most of their neighbors did not.

Softly making his way through the trees, Jamie could now see the house. From the back door he saw Ellen begin to run for the other side of the corncrib. Adjusting the buckets, he scooted over to peer around a large tree to see what she was doing. Down on her hands and knees she was brushing leaves into a pile on the ground. Standing she braced herself against the wall of the corncrib, and taking a cloth from her pocket wiped her forehead and then her mouth. Smoothing her skirts, she went to the front of the corncrib, opened the door and took out several ears of corn.

Walking out of the woods, Jamie called to Ellen and she turned and smiled as she thumbed the kernels of corn from the cob. The chickens were scattering around her feet chasing the kernels as they dropped.

-I saw you behind the corn crib, what where you doing?

–I was not behind the corncrib.

–Yes you were and you were doing something with the leaves on the ground.

Like a flash of lightning, Ellen grabbed Jamie's arm, pulling, causing the milk to slosh out of the bucket.

–I was not doing anything. You did not see me, you hear!

At the kitchen window Catherine saw the exchange between Ellen and Jamie and immediately went out the door.

–What is going on here?

Turning, Ellen marched past her mother and into the house. Immediately Jamie began telling Catherine all that he had innocently said and how Ellen became angry. Now she knew for certain that something was wrong as it was not like Ellen to storm around angry, and she had been exceptionally quiet for weeks. Mostly Catherine attributed all this to the death of Alex, as Ellen and he were very close.

–You go on in the house and put the milk on the table, and I'll be in shortly.

When Catherine came back in the house, Ellen and Annie were beginning to cook dinner. Sarah was setting the table and the men were on the front porch, laying out their plans for winter. Everything seemed normal.

Dinner that night seemed more normal that it had in weeks. The boys were excited about talk of having school in the spring. Ralph Carlton's old maid sister was going to come live with him in March. She was a schoolteacher by profession and had offered to teach for three or four months, providing that the war was not in their backyard. Most communities had totally given up on schooling their children. Ralph had six young children under his roof, he was not excited at having his older sister, Elvira, come live with him. Since the beginning of the war, she had been moving from one relative to another, hoping that the fighting would soon end and she could once again be on her own.

As the house settled down for the evening, Catherine snuffed out the last lamp and took her candle, making her way up the stairs. Once on the landing, she picked her skirts up and looked up to begin her climb. Sitting on the top step, starring down at her was Ellen. Her hair was in disarray and she was crying. Stopping, Catherine spoke softly to her.

–Do you know when this baby will be here?

Falling over on her side, Ellen lay on the floor at the top of the steps and sobbed. Reaching for her, Catherine gathered Ellen in her arms.

–What is done is done.

–But mama, everyone will think I'm a loose woman. No one knows that Josiah was here. I'll be a disgrace and it will be on the family too.

–Who said that no one knew Josiah was here?
With that statement Ellen drew back and stared at her mother.

–Do not tell anyone in the family. It will all be well, don't worry. I certainly don't want this little new one deprived because his mama is scared all the time.

The next morning Catherine announced that they needed some provisions and that for two days they would not eat eggs, so that she could have a basket of eggs to sell in town. Amidst groans and complaining, Catherine held her ground.

–No eggs!

Walking into Statesville, Catherine passed by many neighbors. Her egg basket was full and she lifted the cloth several times, looking at the eggs and figuring in her mind how much she should ask for each egg. Before going to the mercantile she would stop by to see her friend Lilly, who helped her husband run the mill. It was not only an opportunity to visit, but Lilly would also know what price staples were going for and she would also know who was in town.

Opening the door, Lilly smiled and gave Catherine a hug, welcoming her into the house. Lachland and Lilly had moved to Statesville over twenty years ago, and established their mill. They lived in the back of the mill and had raised their two boys there. One thing that Catherine so enjoyed when visiting Lilly was that she always had tea. In times when no one for two hundred miles had tea, Lilly would somehow have wonderful aromatic tea, mostly by bartering. She was very English and could not do without her daily tea, even if Lachland thought it distasteful. The women had visited for about thirty minutes, when Catherine heard Lachland call Lilly to say they had a customer. Smiling, Lilly patted Catherine's arm and asked if she'd like to walk down with her.

–They're here, just like clockwork, every week.

Entering the mill Catherine spotted Gideon Solomon unloading several bags of corn with Jemima standing close by. Smiling she waved to Jemima and called to Lilly.

–Thank you Lilly for being such a good friend and bearing my burden.

Watching Catherine walk down the street, Jemima walked to the door of the mill.

–You're a good friend to Catherine, and I so admire that in a woman Miz Lilly.

–Yes, she has meant so much to me through the years.

–So, she's got trouble?

–Oh if only Josiah hadn't deserted. OH! Jemima! You must swear to me that you will not whisper a word! I promised. How could I be so loose with my tongue? Poor Catherine had been so worried that someone would see   him while he was here, that she literally guarded the place. Poor man. He went back and now they haven't heard from him since, and it's been months and months.

–Oh Miz Lilly, you can trust me, I will not say one word. Why Catherine must be crazy with worry and I'm sure her daughter Ellen is distraught. When was it you said he was here?

–Please do not mention this Jemima. Never would I ever let Catherine know that I had broken my word. But it's been...well maybe as much as four months back. Remember when there were some riders in the neighborhood and there was a rumor of deserters?

–Well, no, I did not hear that. But I'm sure that someone possibly told my husband.

An hour later, the Solomon wagon was loaded and Jemima was nowhere in sight. Gideon pulled the team out on the road in front of the mill. Down the street he watched as Jemima left one shop and went into another. What was that woman up to now? Pulling the team up to the last place he saw her enter, he waited. Within a few minutes, Jemima was coming out the door.

–Jemima, I need to get this meal home.

–Gideon Solomon, you should be ashamed of yourself keeping news from me! Probably thinking to protect me, but you know that I can take even distressing news.

–What in the world are you talking about?

–I'm talking about why you did not tell me that Josiah Stamper had deserted and lived at the farm for a week, and then in a fit of guilt, returned to his unit. And it was months and months ago. They said there were riders out looking for deserters.

–Well, I never heard anything of the sort.

Shoving her elbow into Gideon's side, she leaned back with a scowl.

–Don't be fibbing to me Gideon Solomon. You certainly did know and did not tell me. Why, I could have been comforting poor Catherine. Just think. If they had been found out the Home Guard would have been down on them. Or worse, the Yankees could have followed them. When I think about all those poor people went through with him hiding on their farm. Well, it's just disgraceful. He should have thought about his family before he put them in such danger.

The next few miles Gideon thought about how much he wanted to be anywhere but in the wagon seat listening to Jemima go on and on.

Chapter 55
Facing The World

Sunday came and went with Ellen staying in the safety of her home. There were no words that could persuade her to go to church with the family. Standing at the window she watched as they pulled out on to the road and were on their way.

The morning was crisp but not too cold for February. Their Sunday meal had been cooked the day before, so there was really nothing for Ellen to do except read. Deciding to stay in the kitchen, she sat at the table reading her favorite book of sonnets. After only a few pages, she was sound asleep.

Arriving home from church, the family was met with the sight of Ellen, still asleep. Hearing everyone come into the room, Ellen jumped, awake and embarrassed. She had not put their food on the table nor made any preparations toward the meal. But not one person said anything about their food not being ready.

Weeks went by and Ellen seemed to finally relax. Several neighbors had been by the house for various reasons, and each had wished her well. Mrs. Garrett even told her that she hoped this one would be a girl for her. Realizing that everyone probably knew that Josiah had been home, Ellen felt her strength returning and her worry was now fading into the past.

When the next Sunday rolled around, Ellen was up early preparing for church. She had put on one of her old dresses that she had worn when she was expecting Heath and seemed not to mind that a small stomach was now visible. Secretly Catherine smiled and knew that Ellen would be fine.

That morning all the Stamper women, along with their children were present at church. During the first hymn, Catherine smiled as she could hear Ellen's alto voice strong and clear. The harmony of so many women was beautiful, but it only brought to mind the painful absence of most of the men.

Chapter 56
The Child Messenger

It had been almost three days since he left his home and the old mule he rode was winded and slow. Each night he managed to find shelter off the road, and sat on the ground wrapped in a blanket, too scared to build a fire. Several times he had moved from the road to hide in the woods as soldiers passed. Nathan Stamper was eleven years old and certainly too young to be traveling over eighty miles alone. His grandpappy had sent him on this errand and he was too scared not to continue on.

He looked at the paper his grandpappy had written on, and knew that he was in the right place. Stopping at one house he asked for directions and continued on his way. Feeling inside his shirt, he made sure that the letter was still there. His grandpappy had insisted that the letter be delivered by someone in the family. All he knew was that his grandmother cried most times and his mother was quiet, always watching the road.

Turning into the lane he stopped and looked at the house. Surely this house was not the right place. No Stamper he knew ever lived in a house like this. Kicking his heels in the side of the mule he moved forward toward the house. Looking out the window, Jamie hollered that someone's coming. Quickly shoving the bread in the oven, Catherine wiped her hands on her apron. Patting her skirts, she felt for the small pistol strapped just above her knee. Making her way through the house she opened the door and stepped on the porch, followed by Riley and Jamie. As the rider came closer, Catherine breathed a sigh of relief. It was just a boy.

Pulling on the mule to stop, Nathan slid off the animal's back and asked if this was the Stamper place.

–It is. I'm Catherine Stamper. Who are you?

–Well, you're my cousin, I think. I'm Hiram Stamper's boy from up in Ashe County, just the other side of the mountains. My grandpappy sent me to deliver a letter. He said it was important and that I could not stop until I got here and gave you the letter.

Feeling her heart begin to pound, Catherine came down the steps and held out her hand as Nathan placed the letter in her hand.

–You've come a long way and we have food. Please, go inside and the boys will take you to the kitchen and Annie will fix you something to eat.

It was almost as if she could hear her heart pounding as she looked at the writing on the envelope. No one would send a small boy, alone, such a great distance to give good news. Trembling, she stood at the foot of the porch steps and opened the letter.

"To Catherine Stamper mother of Ellen,
My son Hiram has been sent home, wounded, without a leg. When he came he brought news that my older son, Josiah, had been in the same battle with him. My heart is heavy to tell you that Hiram saw his brother fall on the battlefield and he is dead. Miriam cannot believe that her boy is dead because his body is not home. Hiram said that he was buried almost at the spot where he fell. I grieve for the sight of him, but I also grieve for the sight of Jamie and Jonathan, as they are big boys by now. It was my wish that Ellen stay near when Josiah left but I know that her heart wanted to be near her own kin for which I hold no grudge. This is not all my news and I am sorry to tell you that Joel and Polly are both dead and buried. Polly got worse with each month and finally would not eat. When he died Joel could not come out of his grief. Each day I sent one of the children to check on him. His daddy and my daddy, being brothers, were close and I feel a responsibility more than just a cousin. On Tuesday last, I decided to go myself to see if Joel needed anything. He was nowhere to be found and I searched the house and barn for him. Then I remembered that the boy had said he found him the day before at Polly's grave. Walking through the field I saw him at a distance lying on Polly's grave. But he was not mourning, he was dead. When I turned him over he was lying on his gun and the front of his face was gone. A neighbor helped me bury him beside Polly and my heart still hurts at the sight of seeing him. I am sorry that after so many years we have not seen each other since Josiah and Ellen's wedding and I am sorry that this is my letter to you. Miriam sends her love to Ellen and grieves deeply for our first son. We long to see Jamie and Jonathan and ask that they be allowed to visit as soon as all is safe.
Respectfully Joseph Nathaniel Stamper, Jefferson, North Carolina."

Sitting down on the steps, Catherine held her head in her hands. How much more death could they take? Or better yet, how much more death would there be? Ellen. What will I tell Ellen? Thoughts were flying through her mind. Laying her head on her knees she began to cry with a deeply felt grief. A son-in-law, who not only was dead but died not knowing he had another child on the way. Two little boys who would be devastated at hearing their daddy is dead. But Ellen, she would surely grieve to the point of losing the baby. Then she thought of Melmath. Wanting to come back to the farm, he did not know that he was now the only one left, as both his parents were now dead. For the first time in her life Catherine could not think of what to do or what to say. So she sat crying, holding the letter to her heart. Placing her hand in her pocket she felt for the small item and curled her fingers around the warm of the wood.

Chapter 57
A Healing

The afternoon had passed slowly. Every time the clock chimed, Annie glanced out the window. It had been four weeks since the afternoon of letters; of joy, then sadness and then the following day, learning about deaths of Josiah along with Joel and Polly. Two days of deep, deep sadness. Riley and Heath had retreated to the woods to tend the animals. But when they heard a woman screaming, they ran through the trees toward the sound. The entire family could find no solace in any word or deed for the depth of their hurt. Standing on the back porch Catherine watched as Ellen lay on the ground crying, with Annie and Sarah trying to comfort her.

That would be a day that remained in their memory forever. Poor George seemed at a loss and sought advice from Mr. Allen, his father-in-law. After conferring with Catherine, Annie and Sarah it was decided that George would take the wagon and follow Nathan back to his grandfather's house. And along with him would be Ellen, Jamie and Jonathan. By this time Ellen was in a daze and seemed not to care where they led her or if she ate or slept. At one point she was found standing in the middle of the floor and suddenly without warning, turned and slapped Jonathan and began screaming and crying. Terrified he ran from the room as she slumped to the floor.

Weeks passed and it was time for their return. No word or message had been received from George, but Catherine kept assuring Sarah that she felt all was well. Even Annie was on edge and would be overly glad when all the family was under one roof once again.

Another three days passed before they heard the sound of the wagon as it rolled up the lane. Standing in the bed of the wagon, behind George and Ellen, stood Jamie and Jonathan, smiling. Jumping from the wagon before it even stopped, they ran to the porch and embraced Catherine, then Annie and Sarah. They mussed the hair of Heath and Riley and even picked up Lina, swinging her around. Tears came to Catherine's eyes as she realized how happy they were at being home and hoped that this happy reunion was a good sign for Ellen also. Stepping from the wagon George embraced Sarah and then his mother.

-We've been driving since before dawn and could not wait to get home.

Feeling a hand on her shoulder Catherine turned to see the clear eyes of Ellen and her smile.

    —Mama, we're finally home.
With tears streaming down her face, Ellen embraced her mother.

    —Oh mama, it was the best thing anyone could have ever done for me. I needed to be with Josiah's people, my people. I needed to grieve with them. I needed for his mother to tell me once again all the stories she kept in her heart of his childhood. And the boys needed to see Pappy and go hunting with him and feel the presence of their own daddy through him. But we're home now. Even though my heart is broken, the new life within me moves strong and I know that Josiah would want me to raise his children to be strong men. And I can't do that without your help.

    Unloading the wagon George laughed and told of how they were stopped twice going to Jefferson. The first time, Ellen had the presence of mind to take the reins from him and explain to the Home Guard that he had been sent home from the war, wounded and now an idiot. Ellen spoke up and told them how George had drooled and crossed his eyes and made faces. The men on the road left them alone as they weren't sure if what George had was catching! Out of earshot, George and Ellen laughed for first time in a long while.

    Catherine stood and watched as George tenderly handed down a cradle to Mr. Allen.

    —Mama, this was Josiah's cradle and his mother wanted this baby to lie in his daddy's cradle.

It was very old, and obviously had been handed down for many years.

    —Come fall, before the frost, I expect Joseph and Miriam to come visit, if they are well enough. Hiram will drive them. His wife Jessie is due to have their fourth baby in the fall.

    Catherine thought back to Ellen's wedding, and all the Stamper men who were in attendance to see John's daughter wed. Now most were dead or gone to war, and possibly even those were not coming home.

    —It will be good to see John's kin.

Chapter 58
Family Addition

September breezes were blowing across the land and trees were beginning to show signs of turning color. The Stampers were busy preparing for winter and were now uneasy and cautious. There had been trouble the first of the month with an intruder. One night Jamie was asleep in the tree platform, guarding their animals. Startled awake he realized that the bellow of the cow had awakened him. Sitting up he listened as he heard someone talking softly to the cow. Reaching beside him, he picked up a large rock. Crouching at the side of the platform, he squinted to see in the dark, and then saw the man slowly moving. Someone was stealing one of the cows. Without thinking he threw the rock, striking the man in the back of the head, and down he went.

Racing to the house he woke everyone but Ellen. George along with Jonathan and Riley dressed and started for the woods. Catherine and Annie waited at the edge of the woods with a lantern for what seemed like hours. Soon she could hear George calling to her and she held the lantern high and waved it back and forth.

–I've never seen this man before, but he's out cold, not dead.

–Probably a deserter looking for food. He must have heard the cows and followed the sound.

Jamie told them that shortly before he went to sleep a raccoon had run across the cow pen and stirred them up.

–They did bellow and moo for a few minutes, but I got them calmed down.

Laying the man down on the grass they tried to decide what to do with him. Mr. Allen had now come outside and told them they should put him in the back of the wagon and move him off their land. Thinking that would take too long, George suggested that they just sling him over the back of their mule and gently lead the mule down the drive and out into the road.

–Chances are that by daylight, he will not be able to tell where he had been when he saw the livestock.

Mr. Allen agreed, as Heath ran to the barn, and quickly harnessed the mule. Leading him out, and holding his head steady, Heath watched as George and Mr. Allen lifted the unconscious man over the back of the mule. The women retreated to the house and waited in the kitchen for the men to return.

–*We'll have to move the animals and I just don't know where to keep them safe and us fed.*

Jonathan told Catherine there was a small ravine just west of where they had cleared an area for the livestock.

–*It's narrow enough that we can lay branches across the top. We can actually block the cattle off in the ravine and because there will be something over their head, they most likely will be more quiet. During the day we can lead them back to the field to   graze and at night hide them in the ravine.*

–*We can't take any chances. As soon as George gets back, we'll get started.*

Within the hour George had returned. He grinned saying that he propped the fellow up against the barn door at the next farm over. Daylight was beginning to break on the horizon and Catherine blew out her lantern.

–*He'll wake up before too much longer and won't have any idea where he is or where he has been.*

Jonathan told George about the ravine. There was an urgency to move the livestock and Catherine wanted to get started. Finally agreeing that it was probably a safe place, she asked Jonathan to lead the way. Once they had seen the sight, if it was suitable, they would begin moving the cows.

Inside the house, Annie and Sarah were cooking eggs when Ellen came into the kitchen. She was so heavy that she could hardly walk and had no idea that the family had been up since midnight. Settling into a chair, she sipped her tea and suddenly noticed no one was there except Lina. After asking where everyone was, Annie began telling her about their night and how they were all working at the ravine to move their livestock. Staring at her, Ellen did not move.

–*Are you all right Ellen?*

–*No. My water just broke.*

The sound traveled through the woods and everyone went very still.

-Mama it sounds like Sarah and she is calling for us.

George began making his way toward the sound of Sarah's voice. Shortly, he hollered in her direction and they soon made their way to each other through the trees.

Mr. Allen and Catherine were both securing branches across the ravine and had worked up an appetite and were talking of going home to eat. Catherine heard George calling for her and she started back toward the sound of his voice.

-Quick! Ellen is having the baby!

Pulling up her skirts, Catherine struck out in a full run through the woods. She burst out of the woods running across the field with the boys behind her. Running across the yard, she saw Annie on the porch.

-You're too late! This one came like lightning!

Stopping, Catherine could hardly breathe from running so hard and could not get her words out.

-That's right, you missed seeing your new granddaughter break into the   world.

By the time that Catherine had washed her hands and face, changed her apron, and was heading toward the stairs, Riley and Heath came running down the hall.

-Come see Mam Maw, she's beautiful.

Entering the bedroom, Catherine could barely believe what she was seeing. Ellen looked beautiful sitting up in bed holding the baby. Standing by the bed was a smiling Sarah and Annie. Ellen stretched out her arms and Catherine took the baby and looked into a tiny face that looked exactly like her mother, beautiful black hair, and smooth pink skin. She was beautiful and perfect. Then Ellen announced the baby's name.

-I'm naming her Margaret Alexandra Stamper. But we're going to call her Maggie.

Smiling, Catherine cooed to the baby and marveled at how pretty she was. The baby had long slender fingers and a pink round face. Snuggling the child to her shoulder, Catherine kissed her tenderly.

Chapter 59
Discovery

It had been several months since Catherine had been able to spare any eggs for sale. Today she had gone to Statesville, carrying her precious basket of eggs. Everyone had agreed to forego eating eggs for two days in order to have enough to sell. Prices were now outrageous, and it would be lucky to have money to buy salt, much less be able to afford sugar. The entire family was tired of chicory and she hoped if nothing else to find some coffee beans.

As she walked along the street, in the distance she spotted the bank, empty and boarded up for the last few years. When her son-in-law, Fate, had moved Susan and their children to be near his home place in Columbia, South Carolina the bank closed. In South Carolina he had the protection of an older brother and felt his family would fare better living there. And now they were gone even from there. How she missed Susan. Marriage had turned Susan into a totally different person. Catherine smiled as she thought of the change in her daughter, good changes.

Fate had been more than generous with Catherine's family. She still had supplies buried in areas around the farm. She was holding out until they could not survive without them. But Catherine was also sensitive to those around her. She did not want the smell of coffee coming from her house when her neighbors had none and knew that coffee usually could not be purchased within a hundred miles.

The war had effected every aspect of their lives; not only was the family deprived of everyday staples such as coffee and sugar, but now staples such as flour, meat and potatoes had to be used carefully to stretch out their provisions in order to survive.

Catherine had received a letter from her sister, Nancy, the week before. It has been more than two years since the sisters had seen each other, although they were just a county apart and now Nancy wrote of hard times at their farm.

"My Dearest Sister Catherine,
I looked at our tintype today as I had almost forgotten what we looked like together. How glad I am that James made us sit for the picture when the photographer came to Statesville. I will always cherish it. Brooks is working very hard but we are nearly starving.

Granny Stamper is still with us and in bad health, and we are all she has right now, as there has been no word from Margaret or Mary in Kentucky. We do not know if they have forgotten their mother or if they are dead. She still grieves over the death of Joel and worries whether he is in heaven or not since he took his own life. She talks about Melmath and how she wants to live to see him home from the war. She still carries a letter from James in her Bible and I see her read it nearly every week. It will be two years in November since we heard from either Margaret or Mary or any of their people. Brooks says that we should have gone to Kentucky when we first knew the war was coming, but his mother would not leave, and we could not very well leave her behind. She speaks of you often and still speaks of John. All five of the girls are well, although they are thin and I do so need clothes for the two oldest. Soon we will have six as I am going to have another baby in the fall. I pray that God will let this one be a boy. This time I have not had the strength that I felt with all the others. I think it is because we have not had as much food and I am older. The Home Guard came again last week and told Brooks that he had to join a regiment or they would take him to one. We do not know what to do and feel that surely the war is near an end. Cassie Stamper's brother, John Waggoner came to our house yesterday and delivered a note from Cassie. Her boy Lewis has been sent home and is dying. He married a girl named Louisa before the war started and now he will make her a widow. From the words that Cassie wrote there is no hope for him, only a matter of time. She said that Joseph is still in the fight and that she heard from him only a month ago. He is to marry a girl named Dovie when he comes home and had asked about moving near Brooks to help him farm. We saw both the boys before they left. Lewis looks just like Hugh looked at that age. Dear sister I am scared that they will drag Brooks off and that he might not return. I read my Bible every day but ask that you pray for me. Brooks has promised that when the baby comes and we can travel we are all going to come to see you. I was so excited that I dragged the trunk from the barn hoping to clean it up if we traveled. You will laugh. Inside on the bottom was stuck a small bar of pink soap. Remember our rose soap? It is too hard to use and no longer smells of roses but of barn. I love you very much and crave the time when we can see each other and that this war will be over soon.
  Your loving sister
  Nancy Stamper"

The family knew that they too were on the verge of being in dire straits as their provisions were running out. They were down to two pigs and the trips to and from the woods were wearing on them. But Catherine insisted that they continue as she felt it was their only hope.

That year their sweet potato crop had been unusually large, and they had plans to dig an extra potato cave farther away from the house. Even though several neighbors had stolen from the Stamper farm, Catherine took the neighbor on each side of her farm a bushel of potatoes, with a request not to steal from her. Dumbfounded they stood with their mouths hanging open and accepted her gift.

For a few hours, having Catherine out of the house was a blessing to Ellen. Her mother had hovered over her since the day Maggie was born and it was nice to have a pause from Catherine's attention. The baby was now two months old and Ellen felt as if she had all her strength back.

With Catherine out of the house, Ellen decided to clean and dust through the downstairs including Catherine's bedroom. Lying on the bed was one of Catherine's skirts and her mending kit. A small tear was marked for patching, and as Ellen picked up the skirt to see, she felt the huge weight of the garment. Lifting the skirt up and down, she started feeling around the waist, then looking inside. Finally she laid the skirt down and picked up the hem, feeling the bulge inside. Checking around the bottom of the skirt she felt ten more bulges.

–*Would you like to check the rest of my clothes?*

Turning and red faced, Ellen explained that she was dusting and saw the skirt, picking it up only to see the area of repair and felt the weight.

–*It's all right as long as this is between you and me. For almost four years I've dragged around skirts with weighted hems. Nanny left me gold coins with the instructions that I save them for when needed. And Fate also gave me coins. What better place to keep them?*

Hugging her mother, Ellen realized the sacrifice Catherine had made to make sure that they would survive now and even after the war.

–*I've used only two and George took each one to a different city to use for supplies. One went to Salem and another went to Charlotte.*

–*Oh. I won't tell mama.*

That evening Catherine announced that she was not able to barter any coffee. Looking at the disappointed faces she reversed her earlier decision.

–*Well, we don't have much but this family does deserve some comfort every once in a while. I can't bring myself to drink boiled chicory and hickory nuts tonight. And if the neighbors come snooping around and smell coffee, we'll just tell them it's some we saved and we won't be fibbing. George we have one last stash with coffee and I think you should dig it up today. That will leave us with only two stashes left, neither with coffee though, and we can't touch those unless we're starving.*

That night the smell of coffee floated from the kitchen. Mr. Allen smiled as he slowly sipped from his cup. Even the children were allowed a taste.

Chapter 60
Trouble On the Doorstep

George and Jonathan had finished digging out the remaining potato cave. They spent several hours placing the sweet potatoes in the cave, covering each layer with straw. When the bleak days of winter come, if nothing else, they would have potatoes.

Starting back to the house, George paused, listening. In the distance he could hear horses and laughter. Waiting at the edge of the woods, he sent Jonathan ahead to see what was happening. Within a few minutes Jonathan returned and told him that there appeared to be hundreds of soldiers at the house. At this news, George felt his heart begin to beat with fear.

Catherine was preparing to bake several loaves of bread when her front door was literally being pounded down. Running to the front of the house, she met Mr. Allen, holding his old gun and standing at the foot of the stairs. Opening the door, she faced a Confederate officer. Tall and slim, with hair so blond it was white and deep set eyes that were pale blue. His hat was cocked just so on his head, with a lock of hair sweeping across his forehead which hid a large port wine birthmark.

–Ma'am, I am Captain Bloomguard of the South Carolina 21st regiment and we are enlisting your land for our encampment until the first of the month.

The captain's voice was high pitched and annoying as he stood looking around as if searching for something.

–Oh no you're not! I'll not have your people on my land, stripping it and stealing everything we have.

Turning to face Catherine he touched his hat, ensuring that it was still at a tilt.

–I assure you that this will not be the case. My men have their own food and you will not be bothered. But we will not go elsewhere either.

Reaching to touch his hair, and smoothing it across his forehead, he turned and started down the steps.

Jamie had taken Riley and Heath hunting east of the house, and had the dogs with them. There had been no warning that anyone was even on the property, until the banging on the door.

Seeing she had no options, Catherine told the Captain that she would shoot any man who came into her home uninvited. The Captain in return told Catherine that if she was a Yankee sympathizer she was asking for trouble. At this declaration she turned red in the face and slammed the door! Why the nerve! Going room to room, she began pulling the drapes, shutting out the view of the soldiers.

In the kitchen, Jonathan slipped in the back door and called for Catherine. Telling her that George was at the edge of the woods, and could not figure out how to get back to the house without being seen.

By late afternoon Jamie returned with several quail, which immediately were taken out of his hand by a soldier stating that he was requisitioning the birds for his evening meal. The dogs were hysterical, barking and growling. Lina's favorite dog and playmate, Candy, lunged at one soldier latching on to his wrist. Inside Catherine heard a shot and flew to the door. Lying on the ground was Candy, dead, with a soldier still pointing his gun as if to shoot again. Another soldier sat on the ground beside the dead dog and was rubbing his wrist. Screaming, Catherine flew down the steps and pushed at the man with the gun.

–*Hold up there!*

Advancing on them the Captain appeared in his shirtsleeves, shaving cream still on his face. Without his hat, the red birthmark on his forehead was large and ugly.

–*You get off my land. You haven't been here three hours and already you've killed one of my dogs! Get out!*

Behind her on the porch stood a crying Lina along with Mr. Allen, Annie and Ellen, holding baby Maggie.

–*Get off my land! Today!*

–*You have no right to turn your dogs on my men and they have every right to shoot if they are in danger. I would suggest that you keep your family and your animals inside your house.*

Turning, he left with Catherine staring after him and several soldiers standing with a smirk on their face. Calling to Riley to come help her pick up Candy, they lugged the dead dog around the corner of the house. Catherine gave Riley instructions to find Heath and together bury the dog. But first they were to put all the dogs in the barn or they would find themselves without any hunting dogs before weeks' end. As Riley left to find Heath, Catherine grabbed the scruff of one dog's neck and began pulling it up the steps.

–Come on Belle. You always want to be inside so now's your chance. You're going to come and live inside.

Belle was a favorite of Catherine's. She was the great, great granddaughter of Biscuit and looked remarkably like him. Very quiet with the appearance of being timid, she would bite if felt threatened. Not exactly the size dog for keeping in the house, as she was huge and wiry just like Biscuit.

Turning to close the door, Catherine told the family that now they were in a fine mess. George stuck out in the woods and soldiers on three sides of their house. Going back into the kitchen she put on a huge pot of boiling water and sat down to plot how to get rid of the soldiers. Reaching into her skirt pocket, she felt for the small object. It became very quiet in the kitchen and Ellen faced her mother with her thoughts.

–Mamma, they're southerners and we can't just turn them away.

–Oh, yes, we can and we will. I don't care if they came from Robert E. Lee himself. This is our land and I'll not see them tear it up, taking all it has, leaving us to fend for ourselves and starving to death.

Several hours later a knock was heard at the front door and Annie went to see who was there. A soldier stood and told her that his captain had requested chicken for his evening meal and that they would be taking one from the pen. Slamming the door Annie ran to the kitchen telling Catherine what the soldier had said.

Calmly moving from the table to the stove, Catherine dipped a small pot into the boiling water. Walking to the back door she watched and waited. Soon a soldier was seen approaching the chicken pen and Catherine came behind him and threw the hot water on him. Screeching in pain, he ran in circles. Hearing his screams, soldiers came running around both sides of the house, along with the captain. Seeing his man writhing in pain on the ground with steam rising from his clothes, he turned and ordered that Catherine be taken as a prisoner. A gunshot exploded and everyone turned to see Mr. Allen standing with a long barrel gun pointed at the captain.

–She comes back in the house and you go without chicken for dinner. I can only fire one shot and it will be for you. Then your *men can do what they want with me, but you will not be here to see it. This is a peaceful family but you push too far. Move back and take your men with you, or be prepared because I might be old but it does not take youth to pull back on a trigger.*

All the men looked to the officer as he slowly backed away, instructing them to pick up the scalded soldier, and back around the sides of the house they went.

After the afternoon disturbance, Ellen and Annie had insisted that Catherine lie down. Standing at the foot of her bed both women began to draw the cover over her. Ellen moved closer and took her mother's hand.

–Mama I'm not saying that you're not taking good care of this house and all these people. But what I am saying is that you cannot do this again or we will be running the house without you. It makes me angry also that they're here, but there's nothing we can do about it. If they take our chickens, then they take our chickens. We'll get by.

Sitting straight up in bed, Catherine looked at them both.

–I don't believe what I'm hearing. You're giving in. You're just going to let them take everything that we've worked for and haul it off! Well, they're not going to do that and somehow we're going to see them off our land. I did not want this war and I'm sorry that we're in it! I've already given them one of my sons and a nephew and another son locked up in a Yankee prison. I'll not be giving them the food off my table, nor provisions that will keep us alive. Get Out! Get Out now! Both of you!

Quickly going out the door Annie began to cry saying that she had never seen Catherine so angry before. Ellen nodded in agreement and suggested they stay out of Catherine's way the rest of the day.

With soldiers surrounding the house, and two standing at each outside doorway, the family resigned themselves to retire early to their rooms. With darkness to protect them, ten soldiers slowly crawled through the back rows of the house garden, taking what suited them. Tomorrow would bring a pot of cabbage and turnips and the folks in the house would be no wiser.

No one slept that night. All the lamps were out but all the drapes on the upstairs windows were open so that they could see the movement of the soldiers. The field was littered with small campfires and the outline of tents could be seen. Belle constantly went from one room to another sniffing and looking out the windows. The next day the drapes stayed drawn the entire day. Soldiers milled around outside and constantly looked at the house. But there was no movement, nor was there smoke from any of the chimney's. Several times there were knocks on the door, but never answered. Trying all the doorknobs, the soldiers found the doors were locked tight. In the late afternoon Captain Bloomguard personally took his fist to the door. Hollering, he told them they had best open the door but his request was met with silence.

The following morning, just at dawn, Catherine climbed the steps to the attic; here she could view the soldiers without being seen. Opening the door, she was met with a swarm of flies literally covering everything in the attic. Brushing at the flies on her blouse, she made her way to the window, positioning herself close to the side curtain. There was over a hundred soldiers, with tents lined in neat rows across the field. To the right at the edge of the field, horses were corralled using wood that had been cut from Catherine's land. With this many horses, and all dropping their waste, the fly brigade had been born and was spreading quickly to the house, to the soldiers and all soundings. There was a stink in the air of manure, sweat and cabbage. Holding a handkerchief to her mouth and nose, Catherine decided that she would do whatever it took to run these soldiers off her land and she just might have a plan.

Chapter 61
Striking back

Crouching at the edge of the woods, George watched with Jamie as the soldiers settled down for another night. It had been a great delight for Jamie to fool the soldiers when he left the house undetected. In one of the attic windows overlooking the back yard, a rope ran from the house on a pulley for about twenty feet to the tree house where the children played. The rope was also used for airing out quilts. Catherine insisted that the bedding and laundry be aired even in the dead of winter. After many complaints about chapped and raw hands, George had come up with a brilliant idea. He would install a rope pulley from the house to the tree house. The women would go to the attic and hang the clothes without going outside. Last summer during a game of hide and seek Jamie discovered that the rope would hold his weight. At a few minutes after midnight, he hauled himself from the house to the tree house and down the back of the tree, then off to the woods.

Around two in the morning, George unlatched a door on the backside of the hen house. Quietly they worked over the next hour removing all but two hens. Jamie had climbed in the barn window and fed the dogs, and then wrapping strips of cloth around their muzzles, he quietly handed them out the window to George. Tying them together with rope, George led them off to the ravine. There he removed each cloth and fed them again. Now extremely full the dogs laid down and almost instantly fell into a deep sleep.

Deep in the woods the Stamper's livestock of pigs, cows and chickens were secreted away. There would be two days of constantly watching the animals and keeping them quiet. Also two days of keeping all the drapes pulled shut. Several times each day the captain would pound on the door calling for Catherine to come out. But each time he was met with cold silence and a locked door. The animals were gone but he knew that the family was still in the house. It angered him that somehow they had managed to remove their chickens without being seen.

....

At midnight, the soldier guarding the back door was sound asleep. Sitting on the porch was a bucket full of water laced with a sleeping potion, from which the soldier had taken several dippers, all was going as planned. Before most of the soldiers had turned in for the night, a young soldier had walked through the camp offering fresh water. At the captain's tent, he left a full bucket of what he claimed was pure sweet spring water. With gratitude the captain thanked the young soldier, smiling, but not able to place him within the company. Oh well, he thought, with so many men, there are probably more than a few that look unfamiliar.

Smiling, Jamie tried to stand tall and look official as he gave out the water around the camp. When Alex was brought home, Catherine wanted him buried in clothes he left behind and not an army uniform. Carefully hung in her closet, the uniform shirt was now being put to good use as Jamie walked about the camp. Because the shirt was too large, the sleeves were rolled up and the tail tucked in. No one seemed to notice that his military pants were sizes too big.

Soon the camp was still with only the sound of snoring. A ghostly figure seemed to float around the back of the camp. Long trailing robes of gauze like cloth, streamed from a white cloak, worn and old. White hair hung almost to the waist and whipped about the shoulders in the breeze.

Long white fingers clutched the knife and began the cut at the back of the tent. Slowly drawing the knife, top to bottom the figure stepped through the opening, stopped and looked about the tent. The captain lay sprawled on his cot with his mouth open, deep in sleep. Silently the figure went toward the sound of his breathing. Placing a hand on his chest the figure pressed hard, laying the other hand across the captain's mouth and nose.

Gasping, the captain sat up on his cot. Disoriented and feeling light headed he put his hands in his hair and then rubbed his face. He felt air on his face and turned in the direction only to see a white figure with no eyes. Running his fingers through his hair pulling it back from his forehead revealing his large blood red birthmark that stretched from eyebrow to hairline. Opening his mouth as if to scream the figure placed an icy hand over his mouth.

–Do not speak. Only listen and you will live to enjoy your grandchildren. You are walking about my grave and those I have loved, all buried on this land. I cry at night and walk the earth as your men pitch their tents over   the resting place of my loved ones. Do not stay or you will surely meet your fate..

The sound of a clanging noise rippled through the air twelve times.

With the last clank a light 'thunk' was heard as the captain slumped back on his bed, as he wet himself from fear.

At seven o'clock the next morning Catherine opened her door and stepped on to the porch. Not one soldier was stirring. By seven thirty several soldiers were seen sitting in front of their tents, stretching and trying to wake up. Back inside, Catherine began opening all the drapes on the first floor, humming her favorite tune. Going to the kitchen, she looked out the window. The chickens were all in their pen, pecking away at the corn on the ground. All five of their dogs were sleeping on the back porch, but tied to the railing. The soldier sent to guard the back door still sat, leaning against the porch railing, sound asleep.

Around eight-thirty, the family heard shouting and commotion. Going to the front door Mr. Allen stepped on the porch and witnessed soldiers scattering in all directions, dismantling tents and packing up to leave. Catherine stepped on the porch and started down the steps. In the distance she could see the good captain giving orders. He looked in her direction and she smiled sweetly and called to him, but he ignored her. Speaking to his orderly he pointed in her direction.

-'Morning ma'am. Captain has decided to press forward and not delay our arrival so we will be leaving today. He apologizes for any inconvenience.

-Tell your captain that I wish him God's speed.

She turned and walked back into the house, with Mr. Allen right behind her.

By ten o'clock that morning the Stamper farm was once again a farm and not an army camp. Annie and Ellen walked over the yard, picking up trash left behind by the soldiers. In the field the boys were shoveling manure and swatting at flies. As sunset, Catherine walked in the yard, viewing the flattened grasses around the house and trampled house garden. It was not anything that could not be fixed. She would start at daybreak.

Later that evening after the children were in bed the adults discussed the events of the last few days. No one found any humor in anything that had happened, only relief that the soldiers were gone.

Catherine hugged Annie and told her how proud she was of her and how brave she was to face the captain.

-Well, he would have known you Catherine but he had not seen me clearly and Ellen's idea of keeping my hand in a bucket of cold water till it shriveled did the trick. When I placed my cold hand on his mouth, his eyes rolled back in his head and I thought he would *faint. He was so scared that he did not notice that the hand on his mouth was not painted white.*

All afternoon in the attic the women had pieced together what they thought looked like an ancient burial outfit. Annie's beautiful hair was wiped with damp towels and then flour was sprinkled on her hair. She lay on an old daybed in the attic with her hair combed out behind her. For hours they worked to make sure that her hair looked dried out and white. The ashen face and arms were more rice powder put on in heavy layers. But Ellen thought that Annie should close her eyes almost completely and let them crush charcoal from the fireplace and darken her entire lid.

–If you keep your eyes shut, then they're black and look like you have no eyes!

As Annie stood in the presence of the captain, she spoke to him with her eyes almost closed. Keeping only a slit to peek at him. And the 'thunk' was a rolling pin that she used on the back of his head.

–He was so concentrated on looking at me that he never saw my other hand when I swung out with the rolling pin. Hearing George beat on that old pot, sounded like a large clock out of tune, announcing the bewitching hour.

The easiest part had been mixing herbs of lemon balm, chamomile and catnip into a strong tea. Straining the mixture they placed in the water and knew that it would induce sleep in all who drank it. One soldier did tell Jamie that it looked a little 'green' and he told the man that's just the way the spring water looks. Not questioning the boy, the soldier dipped his cup in the bucket and took a big swallow, then stating that it was right tasty. Their plans had been successful but they still had to be on guard.

Sitting in the rocker, Catherine said that they needed to pray that the war would soon be over and that Gilbert could come home.

Chapter 62
A Sister's Heartbreak

It seemed like the war would go on forever. The Stamper farm seemed to barely to squeak by each day. Sometimes it seemed as if the weeks just flew by and at other times when news of death came to the neighborhood, time stood still.

In the attic Catherine checked her herbs. They had been blessed with an abundance of herbs and hopefully there would be a way to sell some of the bundles. Opening her sewing box, Catherine took out small folded squares of cloth. Carefully opening each one, she checked the seed inside. Everything looked good.

Weeks passed and the small garden they had planted was now beautiful rows of green. In their secret hiding place in the woods George had cleared a twenty by twenty space. Here they planted Irish potatoes. From past experience they knew their kitchen garden would be raided so this small plot was really needed.

Several times Catherine had walked to town only to come home empty-handed. Prices were sky high and they would just have to find another way to get salt and soda. No way was she going to pay what the merchants were asking. Lately they were not even willing to trade for herbs, butter, or eggs.

The second week in June brought hot weather. Taking her turn in the woods Catherine had finished the milking, fed the animals and was now on her way back to the house. Coming out of the woods into the clearing behind the barn, she spotted a buggy parked at the side of the house, with the horse untied and grazing in the yard. Making her way back through the trees she headed for the springhouse.

Inside the house preacher Icenhour was telling George that he could not wait any longer and would he please give Catherine the letter. Walking with him to his buggy, George told the preacher he knew his mother would be sorry she missed him.

Sitting behind the springhouse, Catherine heard the buggy as it left and she scurried quickly to the back porch where Ellen was waiting for her.

-Mama! You just missed the preacher.

–I did not recognize his rig or I would have come right in. What did he want?

–He brought a letter from Nancy. Brooks has been killed at Spotsylvania.

Standing still, Catherine looked at Ellen in disbelief.

–But he has not enlisted! How could this be?

Rushing through the house, Catherine grabbed the letter and began reading aloud.

"My dear sister Catherine,
My Brooks is dead. He is dead and lying at a place called Spotsylvania Court House in Virginia. I cannot believe that I will not see his sweet face ever again on this earth. A man came yesterday with the news and at his words I fainted in the yard. Just that morning I had started a letter to you to let you know that Brooks had been enscripted. I had written to you right after he left, but the messenger that was to take our mail disappeared. Last week they found his body and that of his horse at the bottom of a ravine. When I had not heard from you then I knew that you surely had not received my letter and now realize it was at the bottom of the ravine with the dead messenger. My poor, sweet, Brooks. I can still feel his breath upon my face and hear his voice. Sister what am I to do with five daughters and another child kicking within me? Granny Stamper fell to the floor when she heard the news and could not get up. The older two girls helped her up and into the chair, but she could not speak and her mouth would not move. Our Neighbor Miss Mamie Strickland, came and brought her medicine bag. By nightfall granny tried to speak but the words we could not recognize. My heart is breaking and I feel that I will be torn in two pieces caring for my girls and Granny. Please come to me Catherine. I need to see you and to cry with your arms around me. Come quickly. My heart is broken and I am afraid.
　　Your sister
　　Nancy Stamper"

Everyone sat stunned at hearing Nancy's words. The first to break the silence was Jamie.

–I can go and help Aunt Nancy. I'm big enough to milk and chop wood and even plow.

George agreed that they had to go and Ellen said that Jamie could certainly stay with Nancy until they could figure out what to do.

The following morning the wagon was loaded with supplies and as George led the team down the drive, Catherine turned and waived to the family. Sitting in the bed of the wagon, with his feet dangling, Jamie waved good-bye.

It took several hours to arrive at the Stamper farm in Catawba County. Because they had left at dawn, there was no one on the road that morning. Had they left later in the day, they would have been stopped several times. There were some back roads they had also taken, taking them out of the way, keeping them shielded from passing many people.

Finally, Nancy's house was in the distance. At the sight of the wagon, the children bounded off the porch, calling to their mother that Aunt Catherine was finally here. Stepping on the porch, Nancy took one look at Catherine and collapsed. Jumping from the wagon George raced to her, scooping her up in his arms and into the house where he laid her on the bed.

Sitting by the bed, George gently held Nancy's hand as she wept. In the main room Catherine was busy spreading out food that she had brought. It had been more than two years since Catherine had been to Brooks and Nancy's farm. Four months. He had been gone four months, but the condition of the farm made it look like four years.

Sitting by the fire, wrapped in a shawl was granny Stamper, not moving, just staring. Gently Catherine took her by the arm and told her to stand because it was time to eat. Struggling with a cane, she took one step and dragged the next one. The old woman followed directions and sat at the table. Sitting beside her, Jamie took the spoon and put it to her mouth. She turned and looked at him calling him Brooks and saying how glad she was that he was in from the fields, speaking slowly and with a slur.

-My roses are blooming Brooks. The one's your daddy brought me last fall. After we eat, we'll cut some for the table tonight. Powell loves to have flowers on the table with his evening meal. He will be so surprised.

Smiling sadly, Jamie answered yes. At this brief exchange Catherine's eye's filled with tears and she turned so that no one could see. Mary Stamper was just a shell of the woman she had been at John and Catherine's wedding.

As if suddenly coming out of a fog, she looked at Catherine and smiled.

−You're my John's wife. Where are my grandchildren?

Softly and tenderly, Catherine told her they were well but did not begin to tell her about the war tragedies the family had suffered.

By three o'clock, Catherine had made up her mind that Nancy and the children, along with granny were coming back home with them. A few miles down the road from Grindstaff House stood Nanny's old house and Nancy could live there until this baby was born. George and the boys would check on her every day and Catherine could help care for granny Stamper.

By three fifteen that afternoon, George and Jamie were loading Nancy's wagon and their wagon. Hopping on the seat, Jamie took the reins. George helped Nancy up to sit beside Jamie and covered her with a lap blanket.

All five of Nancy's girls giggled and snuggled in the bed of the wagon directly behind their mother, excited to be going somewhere. In the second wagon Granny Stamper sat beside George and Catherine sat behind them on folded quilts.

That evening Catherine saw her sister, nieces and Granny Stamper settled into Nanny's old house. They were safe now and Catherine would see to their care. Her plan was to try and persuade Nancy to stay and to let her help raise her nieces.

The summer wore on and the families trudged through another hot summer with limited supplies. The double duty of tending two gardens and two barns began to show on George, Jamie and Jonathan and they were tired most of the time. Catherine had tried to get Granny Stamper to stay with her, but she would not. It seems that her security was being with Nancy. Each dawn brought a new plea from Granny to go home.

In only four more weeks the baby would be here. The family had prepared as best they could, but Granny Stamper was becoming a problem. Twice she had tried to walk home holding the hand of Nancy's youngest child. After a scolding from Nancy, she promised not to leave until the entire family could go with her. But Granny kept telling them that Brooks wanted them at home, and she needed to help him. She was always agitated and continuously walked from the house to the road and back. Constantly mindful of what Granny might do, Catherine's days were clouded with uneasiness.

Sweeping the front porch steps, Catherine looked up to see Jamie riding Nancy's old mule lickety-split up the lane. Hollering, he told Catherine the baby was coming early. Grabbing her bonnet and shawl she raced to saddle the horse and was off at a fast pace for Nanny's old place.

The labor was short but hard and Nancy was exhausted. But the sixth daughter of Brooks Stamper came into the world exercising her lungs. She was very tiny and Catherine knew that she was too early and she thought back to her second child. He had been too small and only lived a few hours. Wrapping the baby tightly she laid her in a large egg basket and placed the basket on a stool in front of the fire. Five sisters crowded around looking as Granny sat and rocked, looking out the window and commenting about the birth.

—When Brooks comes in from the field he'll be right proud. I'll write Mary and Margaret tonight, as I know they'll come quickly to see this new child.

Bowing his head, George felt a surge of pity for Granny Stamper. No one had heard from his Aunt Mary or Aunt Margaret in over 25 years. Deep down he knew that something tragic must have happened to them. Living with Brooks had been Granny Stamper's link to sanity and now that seemed to be gone.

Granny sat by the window with her tatting lying on a pillow in her lap. Her hands seemed to move the shuttles without looking, as the stand of lace grew longer each day. Every few minutes she would stop and lean forward saying that she did not see Brooks yet.

Catherine had no need to worry about the new baby who seemed to be growing, even from the first few days. By the end of the week Nancy had pink in her cheeks and she smiled and cooed at the baby.

—I'm going to name her Susannah Brooks Stamper.

Approving, Catherine told her that was a good name and that Brooks would have been proud of this new life.

When Susannah was three-weeks-old, George took Nancy, Granny and the girls back to their farm. He then went to see Cassie Stamper, Hugh's widow and Granny's daughter-in-law. Explaining to Cassie about all that had happened, George asked if she would check on Nancy and find help for the farm, to which Cassie agreed. There were several older men in the community near Nancy, and Cassie would have no trouble soliciting their help. With this promise, George left for home, filled with hope for Nancy and her family. He knew they would be taken care of and Granny was finally at peace as she sat by the window at home, watching for Brooks to come home hour after hour.

Opening her Bible, Catherine recorded the date of Susannah's birth. Rubbing her fingers over Brooks name and the date of his death, she closed her eyes and prayed for her sister and mother-in-law and all those little girls. She knew in her heart that they would be well and that the Lord would watch over them.

Chapter 63
Final Blow

The churchyard was full of buggies and wagons. Gathered around the open grave, brother McGill talked about Lydia Waugh.

-She was a fine, God-fearing woman who raised her children in the sight of the Lord. As the good book says, "Her children rise up and call her blessed; her husband also, and he praises her." Proverbs 31:28. Let us pray.

Catherine looked around at the large crowd gathered for the funeral, mostly women and old men. Poor Lydia. She had lost three sons in the war and two brothers. The pain and struggle had proved too much for her. Now her husband stood, staring at the deep hole in the ground, not crying, just staring.

After the funeral the women of the church returned to the Waugh farm and laid out food for the family. Among them was Catherine and she remembered how these same women had come to her house when they buried Alex. How many more times would she do this? When would this way of life be over? At the funeral there had been talk that Richmond had fallen and most thought that the South had definitely lost the war. Well, it could not be over soon enough for Catherine, and she wanted her boy home and safe.

Several hours later, she climbed in the wagon and headed home, mindless to anything, except the soft sound of the horse's hooves. Turning into the lane she looked to see George and Mr. Allen on the porch. Standing with them was someone Catherine did not recognize. Pulling on the reins, Catherine set the brake and started to climb down from the wagon. Immediately George was at her side.

-Mama we have bad news. It's Gilbert.

The world went black as Catherine sank to the ground. Jamie had watched from the window and came out the door and down the steps to help George. With tears streaming down his face George lifted his mother in his arms and started up the steps and into the house. Carrying her down the hall he laid her on the bed. Patting her hand and calling to her, Annie told the boys to quickly bring her a basin of water and a cloth. Placing the cool cloth on Catherine's forehead, Annie silently prayed for strength.

Opening her eyes, Catherine lay very still and stared at the ceiling. George was speaking and telling her that Mr. Miller from over at Millers Creek had delivered the telegram all the way from Statesville. There was still no movement from Catherine, only the occasional blink of her eyelids.

Several hours passed and George and Annie finally left Catherine's bedroom.

–She's most likely crazy. Struck dumb. Will never be the same again.

–Don't say that George. Catherine's always been a strong woman.

–Yes, but this is probably where it ends. She's now lost two sons, one nephew she loved as a son, heard that another nephew Lewis has died. She has no idea where Melmath is or if she will ever see him again. She has fought to keep the family together and fed. She did it all for him, for daddy, and he's been gone seems like forever. Well, she is tired and this will probably do her in for good.

George headed up the stairs to his room and left Annie standing staring after him. Entering the kitchen, Annie found Ellen with her head lying on the table and sobbing.

Rubbing her hand on her back, Annie spoke softly to her.

–Your mama is going to need your strength. And Maggie cannot live without you. If Gilbert were here he would not want you to grieve. He would want you to fight back.

For the next five days Catherine stayed in her bed, not speaking. Both Annie and Ellen brought broth to her and tried to spoon-feed her, but little passed her lips. She was pale, her hair matted and her body definitely needed a cleansing. As Ellen was trying to bathe Catherine's arm with a damp cloth, Catherine sat up and shoved at Ellen and shook her fist. She had never seen her mother act in such a way, Ellen ran terrified from the room.

The following day Catherine rose from her bed and sat in the chair. Dressed in dirty nightclothes with a ragged shawl around her shoulders, she looked demented. Staring, always staring. Late morning George came to her room carrying a bowl of soup and a glass of milk. Setting the bowl on the bedside table, he held out the glass to her and she knocked it from his hand. Without a thought, he lashed out and smacked her on the cheek and screamed 'enough! Kneeling on the floor at her feet he looked through his own tears at her face. With her face twisted in dismay, she stared at him as a tear slowly ran down her cheek.

-*Oh mama I'm sorry. I'm so sorry!*
Reaching out she placed a hand on his shoulder and patted.

Gilbert had been dead six weeks by the time word reached the family. Two weeks later a rider had stormed up the drive early in the afternoon to tell them that Lee had surrendered to Grant at Appomattox Court House the day before, April 9, 1865. The war was over. Gilbert had died eight weeks short of freedom.

Chapter 64
Life Returns

Since the end of the war, Catherine had slowly been making progress toward regaining her former self. The death of Gilbert took something from her that could not be explained. Something within her died with him. The sparkle had gone out of her eyes and she seemed to age before the family's eyes. No longer was she up before dawn and in the kitchen. Her pace had slowed and there were signs of silver in her hair. In the evenings she would sit on the porch, and watch the children play in the yard, but never offered to join the conversations.

In November of 1865, Henry Wirz, the superintendent of the Confederate prison at Andersonville, Georgia was hung at the very prison where he made life a living hell for thousands of Yankee soldiers. Somehow, this news peaked Catherine's curiosity. A neighbor had shared a Charlotte newspaper with George and he sat on the porch, reading the article aloud to Catherine and Ellen.

–Read that part again George. The one about what he did to the prisoners.

Surprised that she was even taking in the story, George read the paragraph again. Catherine smiled.

–Good. He got what he deserved.

The weather was now very cold and Christmas was only a month away. Things had not changed much by the war being over. Prices were still high and there were very few provisions to be bought at the mercantile. Slowly men were returning home but they heard nothing from Melmath and did not know if he was dead or alive.

Most days Catherine sat in the parlor, her hands lying idle in her lap. Maggie was now toddling around and would walk to where Catherine sat and would lay her head on Catherine's knee. Then look up and grin, turn around and toddle off. George had started to notice that Catherine would look for Maggie and once saw her smile at the child.

One morning Catherine lifted Maggie and sat her on the kitchen table.

–You're up early little lady.

The little girl lean over placed her hands on Catherine's cheeks and gave her a very wet kiss directly on the mouth. Then she belly laughed as if she had done something very funny. Catherine laughed also. Everyone turned at the sound, something they had not heard in a long time.

The healing had begun and heartache was being displaced by a growing fondness for a little girl with brown curls and big blue eyes. At the sight of the first deep snow, Catherine had the boys go to the attic and see if the sled was still there. Standing on the porch she waved and hollered as Maggie held on while being pulled through the snow.

On Christmas morning the family awoke to a mixture of smells coming from the kitchen. Quickly pulling on her apron, Annie rushed down the stairs and toward the kitchen. Standing in the doorway she smiled at what she saw. Catherine must have been in the kitchen for hours. There were some ginger cookies and pies cooling on the table, and she was just taking Christmas buns out of the oven.

–Well, good morning and Merry Christmas!

Annie grinned and returned the greeting.

Later in the morning they sang carols and ate the cookies. Catherine read the Christmas story from the Bible and then prayed, including a special supplication to bring Melmath back to them. It was the first time that it truly seemed like the old Catherine was in the room. Telling all the children they had to close their eyes, she gave each one a peppermint stick. Immediately Maggie drooled sticky saliva down her chin and on to her dress. Laughing her mother wiped her mouth and attempted to pick her up, but she quickly ran to Catherine. Swinging the little girl on to her lap, Catherine said that this day was the best Christmas they had had in a long time.

Chapter 65
A Stranger Visits

The land burst forth in bloom with grasses returning to green and leaves appearing on the trees. Days were pleasantly warm and the plowing had begun. Annie and Ellen had laid out the kitchen garden. Catherine sat mostly on the back porch, watching them as they dropped their seeds. This planting would be their first garden since the war, and they had hopes of having additional produce they could sell. Of course there was one person now in the house that had boosted her spirits like no other could and Catherine now seemed to be at peace. Final peace had come with the end of the war.

....

The year 1866 brought a partial return to a somewhat normal family life Early one afternoon there was a knock at the door, Sarah opened the door and looked at the stranger. Before her stood a ragged man with long hair and beard, carrying a small satchel. He wore an old tattered uniform and battered hat with sweat rings. Seeing the beggar, Sarah told him to come around to the back porch and she would bring him food.

–Hello Sarah. It's been a long time. I guess I've changed a lot.

At the sound of his voice, Sarah threw her arms around him and began shouting "Melmath's home! Melmath's home!"

After a bath, shave and a haircut, they viewed a very thin and aged Melmath. He embraced Catherine and kissed her on the cheek and she hugged him but seemed to not be able to find any words to give him.

After dinner Melmath and George walked the land as George filled him in on all the events in recent years, and shared his last journey. At the end of the war he went straight to Ashe County where he found the graves of both his parents. He had not expected to find his mother alive, but it was a shock to see that his daddy was also gone. He stayed four days with his aunt and uncle, Joseph and Meriam Stamper. Grieving for his daddy, he would not take the clothes they offered nor would he clean himself or shave. Months of walking had brought him to stand before two graves and he felt the need to leave as soon as possible. Wandering around the mountains and living off the land, Melmath continued to grieve for his loss. Fall came and went and winter was upon the mountain. Standing in front of his lean-to he watched as snow began to cover the pine branches. Moving inside he sat and thought of the times he and Alex had trekked through the snow following rabbit tracks and tears ran down his cheeks. He desperately wanted to see Catherine, to sit with his cousins at her table. Spring saw a tired Melmath heading for Iredell County. What he found was not the Catherine of his memory but an aging woman who seemed to have lost her very essence.

George was very pleased to have Melmath at home.

-*Now that you're here, mama will perk up.*

Placing his arm around Melmath's shoulder, George could feel his bones as they walked back to the house.

For the next four days Melmath ate and slept, secure and unafraid. In the afternoons he entertained everyone with stories. The children constantly asked him to sing his marching song. He had told them that a man named General Pike had written some new words to be sung to the tune of Dixie. Soon the children learned the words and were singing with him.

> *Southrons, hear your country call you!*
> *Up! lest worse than death befall you!*
> *To arms! to arms! to arms! in Dixie!*
> *Lo! the beacon fire is lighted!*
> *Let our hearts be now united!*
> *To arms! to arms! to arms! in Dixie*
>
> *Advance the flag of Dixie!*
> *Hurrah! Hurrah!*
> *For Dixie's land we'll take our stand*
> *to live or die for Dixie!*
> *To arms! To arms!*
> *and conquer peace for Dixie!*

Good changes came with Melmath's homecoming. Within four months since his arrival, the bloom came back in Catherine's cheeks and Melmath gained weight, though still relatively thin. Just having Melmath back in the house had proved to be a tonic for Catherine. She was beginning to sound like her old self, making sure all the chores were done. Some evenings Melmath would actually sit in the floor at Catherine's feet as they talked, just as he did as a child. He shied away from talking too much about the war, but did tell a few things he had seen and places he had been.

At the end of the month a man slowly rode up their lane. Stopping, he looked at the house and turning he started to leave. Pulling on the reins he turned the horse again and headed for the house. The boys were watching his actions from the parlor window and someone said they thought he was lost. Dismounting the man climbed the steps to the porch and knocked on the door.

Jonathan was quick to go to the door, and said hello. The man asked if this was the Stamper place and Jonathan said it was. Then the man said his name was Jake Lackey and that he was a friend of Gilberts and had wanted to see Mrs. Stamper. Hearing this Ellen stepped forward and told him that she was Gilbert's sister and she would be glad to speak with him. But he said no, he had to see Catherine.

Knowing that Catherine was working in the herb garden, Ellen invited Jake in and told him she'd be right back. Hurrying through the house she was out the back door and into the garden.

–Mama there's a man named Jake here to see you. He said he was Gilbert's best friend.

Seeing her mother's face, at first Ellen thought she was going to faint. Ellen
reached for her arm, but Catherine told her she was fine and would like to see this man.

Entering the house, Jake stood when Catherine came into the room.

–Are you Gilbert's mama?

–I am. Do you need to speak with me?

–Yes ma'am. I promised Gilbert that if he did not make it back I would come to tell you all.

Hearing those words, Catherine turned pale, lifted her skirts, excused herself and fled to her room.

–Please don't leave Mr. er, Jake. We would all like to hear about Gilbert.

Offering him a chair, Ellen sat opposite him and asked him to please stay.

–She just needs time to get used to the fact that she's going to hear about him.

Agreeing to stay, Jake listened while the family tried to make him feel welcomed. Sitting straight in his chair he kept his knees bent and the back of his legs close to the chair. Pulling at his jacket the women noticed how large it was on him and knew by his thin face that he was probably skinny all over. Jake's copper colored hair looked freshly cut and his beard was neatly trimmed but still hid his upper lip. His face was heart shaped and he had freckles across his rounded nose and cheeks. Nervously he shifted in the chair and constantly ran his hand through his hair.

At noontime the family gathered around the kitchen table to eat. Melmath had taken over Jake, making sure that he had food but mostly trying to be friendly in hopes that he did not leave before they heard about Gilbert. Soon they were all gathered around the table, laughing at funny stories Melmath was telling.

-We had this big bully in our company. Everyone was afraid of him. Even the sergeant was afraid of him. He was tall and solid as a rock. We always knew when he was around as he was filthy and made no attempt at cleaning up. His hair was dark and greasy and he had squinty little eyes that were green and were too small for his face and he was hairy all over. He had a big square chin with several scars and lots of rotten teeth. In other words, he was not real pretty to look at and he was mean. There had been a game of ball and this fellow was rough and did not play fair. Several of the guys decided it was time he got what was due him. The first thing that we did at a new campsite was to dig a new latrine. The big bully would not help and kept telling the fellows to hurry up that he needed to sit.

Usually we dug a deep hole about three feet deep and about two feet wide, all around. Once the hole was deep enough, a log was laid across the hole and we cut some limbs to stick in the ground, just for a little privacy. This guy was no one's favorite, even the sergeant was in on the joke, he called the guy aside and gave him an assignment that kept him busy for almost an hour. Meanwhile we were filling in the hole with horse manure. Then everyone took a turn at peeing down the hole and then we poured buckets and buckets of water in to make it really mucky.

By now it was about a third full. We lined up like we were waiting until the latrine was finished. The guy with the shovel hollered that it was ready and sure enough here came Mr. Bully pushing men aside and saying that he was going to be first. Parting the branches that were stuck in the ground, he stepped through and everyone got very quiet. It did not take but just a minute to hear the craaack and the man screeching "the log broke!" Down he went into all the muck. We broke the log. You could not see the break except on one side.

Everyone began pulling the branches from the ground and tossing them aside. Oh how we laughed. There he was sitting wedged in the hole with horse manure and wet up to his waist. He could not move. Screaming at us that he would show us what for if we did not get him out, we answered him by pouring buckets of dirty water on top of him. Sometime during the night he managed to turn himself and climb out of the hole. And that was the end of his being a bully.

Blushing Annie told him that certainly was not a story to be repeated in front of young children and ladies. But they all laughed. Hearing a noise, they turned to see Catherine standing in the dining room.

–I'm ready to listen.

Jake immediately came to his feet and told her that he was with Gilbert when he died. At hearing the word 'died', Catherine once again fled to her room.

Everyone was speaking all at once urging Jake to stay. Explaining that only within the last month had Catherine been able to be a part of the family again it would just take time for her to prepare herself to listen. Agreeing to stay he asked questions about Alex, as Gilbert was so sure that Alex would be waiting when he got home. Everyone seemed to look at George so he assumed it was his duty to give Jake some of the family history. Leaving the room Sarah and Annie went to prepare a place for Jake to sleep upstairs.

The day had passed quickly and everyone was busy with the evening chores. The smell of baking bread was in the air so Catherine knew that the girls were busy preparing their evening meal. She had watched from her window as George and Melmath, along with the boys walked through the yard, headed for the barn.

She had avoided Jake since he spoke the words she could not bear to hear. Now she had to know. How did this happen? Did Gilbert have pain and suffering? Where did they lay his body to rest?

Easing the door open Catherine finally left her room and crossing the main room, she stood at the foot of the stairs. Lifting her skirts she climbed to the top.

Jake sat on the bed holding a folded cloth on his lap, rubbing his hand back and forth across the top. When he looked up to see Catherine he knew she was ready to hear all he had to say. He stood up and she motioned for him to sit on the bed but he kept standing. Quietly she eased into a chair beside the bed.

Sitting in silence, Catherine watched as Jake stood holding the cloth to his chest searching for a starting point. The minutes passed and Catherine sat without speaking. Watching his struggle to find words she thought of how Gilbert had often paced trying to form his thoughts before he spoke.

Looking at Jake, Catherine decided that they needed to get this over with and get it over with quickly.

-*It's best to just get it said. There's nothing that comes from your mouth that's going to do me in because the letter has done that already. And if it will help any you don't have to look my way while you talk.*

Catherine watched as Jake paced. He was very thin and his copper hair showed the first signs of silver at his temples at only 26 years old. Tanned and with eyes that looked almost purple they were so blue; he was quite handsome. Jake looked down at the cloth he was twisting in his hands and Catherine noticed that his hands were freckled and small and his nails ragged.

Continuing to pace back and forth and with his back still turned to Catherine, Jake slowly began his story. Gilbert had befriended him the first month of his service.

Most of the Alexander County boys enlisted in groups and all of Jake's cousins had signed on with Company G. 38th Regiment. There were eleven Lackey men, all cousins, who joined together on November 02, 1861. Following them were four more Lackey cousins several months later. And then there was Jake who felt like the last man in Alexander County who had not enlisted.

Being the youngest son of a widowed mother did not foster his cause. Every day he felt compelled to join; every day he was eaten up with guilt because he wanted to join.

There were older brothers and sisters close by but Jake's mother depended heavily on him and he simply could not pull himself away. But then the decision was made for him and he was conscripted.

Before he hardly knew what was happening he was traveling north and had been engaged in some light fighting. At night he kept to himself and worried about his family back home. Then one night a soldier came and sat by his fire, quiet and with no words. This went on for a week. Every night the soldier would bed down at Jake's fire but never uttered one syllable.

Jake started wondering about the soldier and why he came to where Jake built his fire every night.

-*Why do you come over here?*

-*You looked like you needed someone close by, just to be near but not to talk. I miss my family and it looked like I saw that on your face too.*

After that Jake and Gilbert were inseparable. At night they talked about home and how much they missed their families. They were amazed at the similarities of their families and of themselves. The things they had in common seemed to make things bearable.

There was a young thirteen-year-old boy named Philip who took care of the horses. Anyone who was around him two seconds could tell that he was not quite right in his mind. He was fat and walked with a waddle but could move quickly when he wanted. Both of Philip's parents were dead so when his older brothers joined, he followed behind them. It was evident by his appearance that his brothers took no pains with his grooming. Tucking his hair behind his ears, he pulled a battered hat low on his head. From the front the hair was hidden but when he turned around his hair hung below his shoulders. Always smiling it was hard to miss that one front tooth was missing and several others showed early signs of rotting and he smelled like he hadn't bathed in a year. Shortly after Gilbert first met the boy he began seeking him out. Several of the older men in camp had taken to poking fun at Philip and it was something that Gilbert could not abide.

After several months into their service, Jake and Gilbert were constantly shadowed by Philip everywhere they went. At Gilbert's urging Philip agreed to let them cut his hair. Jake showed him how to chew on a twig to clean his teeth and both Gilbert and Jake introduced him to soap.

In May of 1862, the NC 33rd infantry became a part of the battle at Hanover Court House where Gilbert was nicked in the arm. He would not let anyone know as he just did not trust the army doctors and Jake helped him clean and bandage the arm. Sitting by his side Philip continued to ask Jake if Gilbert would live. The boy's lips quivered and he showed his fear at losing this friend. Placing an arm around the boy's shoulder Gilbert assured him that he was fine. Tears streamed down the boy's chubby cheeks and he fled to the bushes to cry in private.

Over the next twelve months they fought several battles one being called the Seven Days Battles. Then they were at Beaver Dam, Frayser's Farm, Gaines' Mill, Cedar Mountain, 2nd Bull Run, Chantilly, Harpers Ferry, Antietam....this is where Gilbert was promoted to Sergeant....from there their company was involved in a battle at Shepherdstown Ford, Fredericksburg and Chancellorsville.

Exhausted from battle and the constant marching Jake and Gilbert stayed to themselves but always with Philip nearby. He had told Jake that at the end of the war he was going to take Philip home with him.

Many of the men played ball, or cards, but they decided that the best thing they could do was eat, sleep and write letters to their loved ones. And that's exactly what they did. Gilbert wrote home every chance he got and hoped that his mama was receiving his letters.

Their first day in camp after Chancellorsville Gilbert slept eighteen hours straight. Several times Jake would check on him but each time could see that he was just exhausted and not sick. Philip sat outside the tent and waited. It was the end of May 1862.

By the end of June, they had received orders to move out and they were headed for a place called Gettysburg.

Chapter 66
The Beginning of the End

The soldier poked at him with his gun and then took a booted foot and nudged him. Turning he called to another soldier, "this one here's still living." Gilbert lay still and tried to control his breathing. Dawn had broken hot and humid that July morning in 1863. The NC 33rd Regiment, company A had seen their numbers dwindle and weaken. Gilbert had seen bloody battles and had survived it all in the twenty months he had been gone. Last May he took some shrapnel in this arm at Hanover Court House. And both feet had turned blue when he slept in freezing rain at the battle of Fredericksburg in December. How could he come this far through terror and blood and be alive only to see the true face of death at Gettysburg?

His regiment had moved on June 30th, under the direction of General William Pender, to within seven miles of Gettysburg, were joined by General Henry Heath's and General Richard Ewell divisions. Gilbert was tired and dirty. Now they were going to be on the move again. General Heath's men advanced first and were attacked by enemy forces, delaying any further advance. Seeing them leave camp Gilbert thought of the rest that he might be afforded for a few hours. But word soon arrived that Heath and his men had been attacked. When they encountered enemy fire in strength near Gettysburg a ferocious battle ensued. Heath's men suffered severe losses on McPherson's Ride.

Soon Pender and his men were on the move to assist. Gilbert was forced to forgo his rest and made his way toward Gettysburg. With the arrival of Ewell's men the fight became intense and the enemy began to yield. They were marched by Ewell's men right up the street to Cemetery Hill just south of town. The battle had not been won. The following day General Pender was killed. On July 3rd General Lee was attacked unexpectedly the enemy. Large numbers of Pender's divisions were either captured or killed and those remaining began to retreat. Gilbert did not retreat nor was he dead. Instead he watched through partially closed eyes, lying beside Jake, as Yankee soldiers combed through the battlefield inspecting the dead and looking for those still alive. Several feet away lay Philip, eyes open and lifeless. Now Gilbert was not only physically wounded but his heart ached looking at poor Philip.

Union soldiers poked and prodded their Southern captives into wagons, and headed to the train station. Gilbert and Jake lay in the wagon, quiet. The pain in Gilbert's leg was almost unbearable but he chewed on his lip to keep from uttering a sound. When he was loaded on the train, he almost passed out from the pain.

The train ride was longer than Gilbert expected. The car had been converted to berths and hammocks to hold the wounded. Sounds of the track beneath them with its constant clickety-clack soon lulled Gilbert to sleep as the train rolled toward what would become the last place on earth he wanted to be.

Thirty acres of land known as Point Lookout stood at the southern tip of Maryland surrounded on three sides by water. The wind blew cold and strong off the water causing the tents to sway. Once a grand resort for the rich and famous it now housed the sick and captive of the South. The elegant hotel was now home to officers and their staff, busy 24 hours a day ensuring that their captives were made as miserable as possible, in spite of the fact that the facility was intended originally as a prison hospital where the confederate captives could heal.

Major Brady was the Provost Marshall during the duration of the camp and answered to no one except Major General Benjamin "Beast" Butler. Equipped to house less than eight thousand prisoners, the camp grew to an unmanageable twenty thousand at one point in time. By the end of the war more than fifty thousand prisoners would have passed through Point Lookout.

The fourteen-foot wooden parapet wall stood menacingly around the perimeter of the camp. Large gates stood open as wagons loaded with confederate wounded passed through, jostling moaning men as the wheels slid in the ruts of the road. Prisoners stood close by and watched as the procession of wagons passed. No one moved toward the open gates, which held freedom on the other side. Armed guards stood atop the wall anxiously calling to the prisoners, "Go ahead and try it, it's only a few feet away." There was a deadline approximately ten feet from the wall, that although an invisible line, all prisoners knew of its existence and backed from the location. Any prisoner who crossed the line was shot with no questions asked and dragged to an area where the dead were stacked like cordwood until they could be buried. This is where Gilbert was headed.

Gilbert heard Jake moan, but he could not open his eyes. There was something wet dripping on his face. He had lain in the bed of the wagon for hours, feeling the splinters from the rough wood sticking through his shirt. His skin felt dry and hot and his tongue felt swelled. If only they would give him water, he knew that he would be able to kill the dry in his mouth. Turning his head to the source of the constant dripping he opened his mouth ready to receive the sought-after moisture, anything to stop this thirst. Dead eyes, wide with fear, appeared within inches of his face staring through the slats of the bunk above, and he stared as the blood and pus dripped from the man's nose and mouth. Frozen to the spot Gilbert closed his mouth and looked at the man and studied his face, the shape of his eyes, the arch of his brow, and the bruise on his nose where it had recently been broken. His mouth was slack and showed his lower teeth, black with decay and foul smelling. Slowly he turned his head and counted the drops as they hit the slat beside his face. An hour later, the train stopped and the prisoners were transferred to wagons for the final ride to their new home.

Pain shot through his leg when the wagon stopped abruptly and another soldier lost his balance, falling on Gilberts right side. Shoving he tried to remove the man but soon felt the weight lifted from him as rough hands grabbed at the man, pulling him from the wagon and throwing him to the ground. Struggling he tried to sit but felt the hands pulling his legs toward the end of the wagon. Kicking with his one good leg, he heard the tearing of what was left of the back of his shirt and felt splinters as they embedded in his skin. Before he could scream with his pain a huge fist slammed into the side of his mouth as he continued to kick at the hands. Closing his eyes he heard a "whack" as the back of his head hit the edge of the wagon bed as they dragged him out and the silence of a welcomed blackness swallowed him up.

The female voice had a sound that he had not heard before. The sound was high pitched and muffled, almost like she was trying to talk with something stuffed up her nose. Lying still with his eyes closed he mentally checked his body, moving each toe and then slowly moving each leg. "Thank God I got 'em both." Opening his eyes he tried to focus in the bright light of the room. Across the room he could hear a woman speaking softly with a comforting tone. Turning toward the sound he saw her, dressed all in black, standing with her back to Gilbert's bed. She was placing a bandage around what once had been a right arm. Her head was draped in black that looked like a mourning veil, streaming down her back almost to the bend of her knees. Patting the man on the shoulder when she had finished she lifted a cup to him and said something that Gilbert could not quite make out. Seeing the cup he called out for water and watched her turn in his direction, smiling, showing large white teeth.

The nun was sister Alice. At least that's what he thought she said. He tried watching her lips move to see if he could read her words. He gave up when he realized that they were moving too fast and continued to gulp down the water she offered. Her voice was pleasant, but sounded foreign. Every now and then he would catch a word like "Boston" or "home". But then again he was not sure. With deft efficiency she drew a wet cloth from a pan of cool water and began the arduous task of wiping the grime and dried blood from Gilbert's arms and face. After she felt he was halfway clean she checked the splint on his leg, then handed him a bowl of what looked like watery mush and walked briskly away.

The food smelled soured, but anything at this point was welcomed. He tipped the bowl to his lips and drank, shuddering at the foul taste and the strange texture of the mush, which seemed to have lumps and specks floating on the top. Dipping his finger in the bowl he swirled the mixture and watched as a black looking speck floated to the top. Holding the bowl closer he peered at the speck and recognized the shape as a small dead bug. With his finger he lifted out the tiny bug and with his stomach cramping from hunger, begging for food, he tipped the bowl once again and finished the mush. Dropping the bowl he grabbed the edges of the bed and pulled himself into a higher sitting position just as his stomach rebelled and rejected the food.

Eight weeks had passed since Gilbert had arrived at Point Lookout prison camp. His leg was pronounced healed, even though he still had constant pain from the haphazard setting of the bone. He was sent from the hospital to the grounds, to begin a life he never knew could even exist.

The Sibley tent was crammed with twenty-two men and was only meant to hold twelve. There was a boy from South Carolina, not more than sixteen years old, two men from Tennessee, one from Virginia and the rest from North Carolina, including Jake. At least you could understand what they were saying when they opened their mouths. All these Yankees talked so fast and clipped that it did not give you time to truly understand what was being said.

The tent was one of hundreds set up for housing and sat in the open on sandy soil without shade or windbreak. The smell of the river was in the air and at first seemed a pleasant enough smell, since he'd never before seen, felt or smelled this particular body of water. Most he'd ever seen back home was the Yadkin River. Now he could only see the water through the cracks of the fence. Soon the distinct smell of human waste took over what air there was to breathe. And the mosquitoes were bad. The constant scratching at bites left small-infected sores on his neck, legs and arms. His feet were so swelled that he took off his boots and left them in the tent, burying them in the sand for safekeeping. He decided that as long as the weather holds he could do without them.

The sun was high in the sky and the heat beat down on the men as they milled around the tents, discussing family and the war and trying to figure out what the date was. Men in ragged trousers and shirts roamed between the tents searching for those suffering with the fever. If they could find a man they thought might eventually die, then they had hang close by watching and waiting for the last breath to ease from his body. Those who were lucky enough to be on hand for a death clawed their way through their comrades fighting for shoes, shirts, pants, hat or anything the poor soul was leaving behind. If you wanted clothing, you had to get it the best way you could and death was just as good as any other way.

How odd, first they capture you and take you to a northern hospital. Fix you up. And then put you out in the open, and if you got sick again, well it was just a fifty–fifty chance that you would see the hospital again.

Gilbert and Jake sat with a man named Rufus and watched as a ragged band passed their tent trying to shove them aside to look inside. Rufus Alexander was thirty years old and had seen his share of robbing since coming to Point Lookout. His hair was cut almost to the scalp and his head showed scars and scratches, his face clean–shaven. This was all in thanks to a guard who took pity on him and cut his hair and beard. Sounding a shout, Rufus had warned the guard of another prisoner poised to jump him, holding the ragged edge of a tin can. To show his appreciation the man took him aside and gave him soap and let him use a razor. Being average in height Rufus was slight in frame, as were most who stayed at Point Lookout for any amount of time. He raised his fist and yelled at them.

–Get back! There ain't no sick or dying in this tent and what is in there is mine.

The group backed off but promised to be back.

Gilbert was sure he was starving and told Rufus that if they soon did not get some food he'd probably keel over right on the spot. The men had not been fed much that morning and it looked like they might have to wait till sundown for their next meal. Rufus pointed to the right where in the distance two men were slugging each other, pulling hair, biting and scratching. They fell to the ground and rolled round and round. Then they both jumped to their feet and lunged at a third man throwing him on the ground, smashing his face with blow after blow. Gilbert stood and stared asking Rufus what he thought was going on over there that set those boys in such a rage as he'd never seen.

–They're fighting over who has rights to the critter.

And Gilbert asked just what critter that might be.

–Well, the tall skinny feller found a sickly wharf rat and he killed it with a rock that the other feller handed him. Then when he *was fixing to eat the thing the other man went and grabbed it from him. While they were fighting that other feller, the one they're trying to kill, he reached in and grabbed it for himself. Happens all the time around here. When you find something, best eat it right quick like before anybody sees you or there'll be a fight for sure. There was a fight last week when a feller got hold of a sea gull. Found him floating in a mud puddle. Ate him raw they did.*

Suddenly the men began to run in all directions, falling and clamoring and clawing their way heading in every direction. Shots rang through the air as soldiers on horseback rode through the crowd cursing and some swinging blades at everything in their path. Led by Major General "Beast" Butler, he turned his galloping horse to overtake the stragglers in the crowd. Yelling commands to his followers, he swung his sword in wild abandon catching those nearest with slices to their backs, necks and arms. The prisoners that fell were trampled while others frantically grabbed the arms and torsos of those closest and tried to pull them out of reach. The "Beast" had made his position clear once again; as this brutality was not the first nor would it be the last time that he rode about the camp, slicing and hitting his way through the crowd. Soon a perimeter around him was clear and he sat erect still holding his sword in one hand and pulling on the reins with his other hand.

–Filthy Southern scum! You'll soon learn that you get no better here that what you gave out to others when you lived on your fancy plantations. You sacrificed poor helpless men and women for your life of leisure and fine clothes for your ladies. But you're not in the South any more boys and the sooner you realize who is in charge the sooner this war will be over. And if you live long enough you might even see your precious South again, if there's anything left when our boys are through. And just to make sure you know who is running things around here.

Nodding to a corporal he gave the command. Shots whizzed through the crowd and men fell where they stood. Panic seized those around them and they shoved and trampled one another in flight. Soon there was not a man to be seen as they scrambled for the tents pushing and shoving and cramming as many as ten men to a tent. Bodies lay bleeding in the sun and sand, and as if to prove the point even further, the general nudged his mount forward followed by his men as they rode back and forth at a clip over the bodies ripping and tearing flesh and clothes and mashing faces that were staring lifelessly at the sky.

In the back of the tent Gilbert held on to Jake's arm.

Chapter 67
Downward Slide

The months went by slowly and Gilbert lost weight rapidly. Although they were fed, the food was bland, sometimes verging on being spoiled. One week they received nothing but broth made from boiling beef bones.

But survival did not seem as if it was going to be a problem for Gilbert. His leg still bothered him and he walked with a limp but his spirits were high. In the winter, with the cold blowing in off the ocean, he would sit in the tent wrapped in his blanket, his leg throbbing from the cold. Jake and Gilbert had formed a circle of ten friends, and they kept their tents side by side and tried to stay out of trouble. However, trouble sometimes came looking for them.

The guards were mostly black men brought from the South. The prisoners could not move without permission from a guard and if you wanted to survive you had to learn quickly or the guards would be upon you, pounding your head with their rifle butts.

At one point Jake thought that Gilbert was going to give up. They had talked late one night and Gilbert told him that this was going to be his life forever. Inside he was setting himself up for the fact that this was to be his fate for years and years. Trying to talk him into a better mood Jake soon had him laughing and noticed that his gums were bleeding. Soon there were other signs. Gilbert had scurvy.

Gilbert and Jake both realized that the South was probably losing the war. And he was glad that there would be an end to this madness and they could go home. By now Gilbert was gravely ill and was actually moved to the hospital. For weeks Jake tried to get duty at the hospital mopping floors, doing laundry or just anything so that he could get a chance to see him. But he was told no.

One morning just after sunrise Jake heard his name being called. Several of the men huddled around him as a big black guard walked in their direction, calling Jake's name. Too scared not to answer Jake called out and the guard said he was to follow him. Fear ran over his body as he did not know what he had done or what he had not done that had surely displeased some officer.

Walking almost the length of the camp, the guard kept his gun pointed at Jake and an occasional command of "keep moving'." The guard walked Jake over to a door and knocked on the door, which immediately opened. Now Jake recognized a familiar face, a guard named Mason who used to patrol the lower area.

   –Come in Jake, I've been expecting you.

Now Jake was really worried as he could feel the tension in the air and knew that something unpleasant was probably about to happen.

   –Oh, don't look so downcast, I sent for you to do a special favor for me. Every week I can select someone to work in the prison hospital and for this week I've chosen you.

Jake could hardly believe what he was hearing.

   –Here, put on these clean clothes. You cannot go into the wards in those filthy, smelly clothes.

   Instructing the guard to get him cleaned up, they left the small building and headed toward another small tent. Inside was a bucket of water and lying on a chair was a towel and soap. The guard still stood with his rifle pointed at Jake as he striped and began washing his arms and legs. Once he was clean he put on the clean clothes and the guard motioned for him to leave the tent. Still pointing the gun at Jake, he followed him to the hospital.

   Handing the orderly an envelope the guard turned and left. Jake just stood and waited while the soldier read the orders.

   –You're to come with me for a special duty.

Walking down one hall they came to a staircase and climbed to the second floor, then down another hallway. Looking at the numbers on the door the guard finally stopped at one door.

   –This is where you'll be assigned for the next week. You are to keep the area spotless and do whatever needs to be done for any of the patients.

   Pushing open the door the man stepped inside the large ward and Jake followed. Walking down the aisle between the beds the guard began checking charts, as if he were looking for something.

   –Here soldier. This is where you are to stay.

Looking up Jake realized that they were standing at the foot of

Gilbert's bed and he began to cry silently, the tears rolling down his cheeks.

–Thank you sir.

Later Jake would learn from Mason that he had held a soft spot for Gilbert. He told Jake that his mother had been born in Iredell County. Her marriage was arranged to a cousin living in Pennsylvania. She moved immediately to the groom's farm after the ceremony; this is where she started her family and remained there. Although she never returned to North Carolina, she told him often how beautiful the land was and how she missed her people there. Two weeks before the war began, she passed away and Mason had pleaded with his father to let him take her to North Carolina and bury her on that soil but he was refused. Out of kindness to his mother's memory, Mason sought out the Confederates who hailed from his mother's precious home state and did what he could for them.

For the next four days Jake stayed by Gilbert's side. He tried to spoon liquid into Gilbert but he was so weak that swallowing was almost impossible. His gums bled profusely and Jake could see places on his arms and legs were blood would just appear under the skin. There were patches of ingrown hair on his arms and legs that were festering with infection, all results of the scurvy. Gilbert complained of pain in all his joints when Jake tried to move him.

They whispered in the night talking of their time together.
–Promise me that when this hell is over and you are free that you will go to my mama and tell her that even to the end she was in my thoughts. I could feel her prayers ever day as I have not been afraid and know that is where my strength was coming from. But I want you to tell her not to grieve for me as I will be with my daddy and will finally get to see his daddy, Powell. Tell her that I remember all my Bible stories and that I know that I am going to be with Jesus. When I get there, it will be peaceful and I will have no pain. Promise me.

With tears running down his cheek and holding Gilbert's hand, Jake promised.

–So here I am ma'am. Keeping my promise to one of the finest men I ever knew. But I want you to know that the entire last day, he slept and felt no discomfort. Right before he breathed in his last, he smiled. And the smile was still on his face when he was cold. There was a large burial ground at the prison and they buried him there that night.

Turning, Jake faced a dry-eyed Catherine.

–I thank you for coming all this way to tell me about Gilbert. You are a man of honor as you kept your word to him even though he is dead. Truly he was blessed to have had you as his friend.

For the first time Jake smiled and held out his hand. Looking, Catherine saw a dirty piece of cloth.

–This is yours ma'am. It's one of your handkerchiefs. Gilbert said that he took it from your drawer before he left. He wanted something of you, something of home with him. He asked me to bring it back to you.

Crossing over to Jake, Catherine embraced him and placed a kiss on his cheek.

–Please tell me that you will stay with us a few days. The family would like to hear all that you've told me.

–Thank you Mrs. Stamper, I'd like that.

Later that evening Catherine opened her Bible to the book of Psalms and gently laid the dirty handkerchief on the page. Leaning forward she kissed the cloth and said "One day I'll see you Gilbert. One day."

The day had been extremely busy. Wash hung on the line was dry and Ellen was busy taking the clothes pins out and dropping them in her apron pocket. She was hurrying as fast as she could. Earlier in the day Louisa Waugh had walked over to bring some quilting scraps for Catherine to help piece together. While visiting she happened to mention that the person taking the census was two farms down the road and she had to get back to her house soon. No one wanted to miss being counted. When the 1860 census was taken, Louisa had been a new bride just recently married to Lewis Stamper, Catherine's nephew. After Lewis died, she had married a widower named John Waugh who was thirty-four years older and they had started a family.

How could it already be 1870? Five years since the war had ended. The neighborhood was mostly widows raising children the best they could. But Ellen wanted to be in the house and ready when the census taker came. After all, he would know everything that had happened in every house, for miles and miles.

Inside the house Catherine was putting the final ingredients into pudding.

–Now Miss Maggie, would you like to taste?

Handing her a spoon Catherine watched as Maggie smacked her lips, then smiled a chocolate smile.

–That's it Mam Maw. That's it. When will it be ready?

–Well, we've got to cook it till it gets thick, and then I'll let you have some.

Getting up on her knees, Maggie stared down into the bowl. Smiling, Catherine thought of what a wonderful gift this child was and what joy she had brought to her life these last years.

The first year after Gilbert died, Catherine mostly just went through the motions. She dressed in the morning, worked in the kitchen and garden, but there always seemed to be a cloud over her. There was no joy in her eyes or in her speech and she went about each day as a requirement rather than a blessing.

Maggie was drawn to Catherine, almost as if she could sense as a toddler that this woman needed something. And what little Maggie had was exactly what was needed. Maggie began following Catherine around, hanging on to her skirt, reaching her arms up to her. Maggie was a magnet and Catherine was metal. Once Catherine agreed to pick her up, small arms would go around her neck and she would say 'Mam Maw'. Slowly over time the heart that had been so totally broken, began to mend. Everywhere that Catherine went Maggie was only a few steps behind. Now she was standing watching every move that was made and helping to stir pudding.

At four o'clock there was a knock at the door and Ellen rushed to open the door. A very tired looking man who was slightly dusty, introduced himself as Mr. Freeland, Assistant Marshall, United States Census Bureau. Inviting Mr. Freeland into the parlor he sat in the chair with a 'thrump' and leaned his head back. Ellen offered him something cool to drink and he smiled and told her, "yes that would be nice."

Within the hour, the entire family stood before the census taker, watching as he carefully wrote out their names and ages. Asking what they did for a living. Could they read, write? Where were they born?

The household was now small compared to five years ago. Remaining on the farm was only Catherine, her daughter Ellen and grandchildren Jamie, Jonathan and Maggie. Last summer Catherine's nephew Melmath had married Sarah Allen's cousin Martha and leased land near Vanderburg Plantation in Coddle Creek.

The end of 1866 had seen the first child born to Catherine's son George and his wife Sarah. A girl they named Dolly. Two years later they had buried stillborn twins but in 1870 they welcomed a son they named Gilbert Abraham Stamper. Sarah's father, Mr. Allen, still lived with them and helped them on their small farm located in Catawba County, just over the county line. Cassie Stamper, Catherine's sister-in-law, who was the widow of John's brother Hugh, still wrote faithfully. Cassie's son, Joseph, was living not far from George and Sarah's farm. He had returned from the war and married his childhood sweetheart Dovie and they now had two sons. Last year at Christmas Joseph came to visit Catherine and brought her a quilt his mother had made especially for her.

In 1869 Annie's mother died and she reluctantly agreed to return to her father's house. By now Annie's father, Angus, was old and in ill health. She would return to her birthplace, but made it very plain to all that it was her choice to do so, only to see Angus wipe his eyes and nod his head. Annie's sons, Riley and Heath, were in their late teens and her daughter Lina was now seven. The boys agreed to follow their mother, but did not want to go, as they considered Catherine's farm their home. For an entire week, Lina cried and begged her mother to let her stay with Catherine. On the first day of June, Annie's brothers arrived to transport her and all her belongings. Dry-eyed, she boarded the wagon and sat staring straight ahead with Lina squalling and the boys hanging their heads. It was a sad day for both Catherine and Annie but they faithfully wrote one another at least every three weeks.

That same year Catherine's sister, Nancy, relocated her family from Catawba County to Iredell County. Samuel Campbell had land that he gladly leased to her. Sam was the nephew of Hiram Campbell on whose land John and Catherine first lived. The Campbell family still stayed in touch with Catherine as they always remembered John and Catherine fondly from when they first moved to the area. Nancy's house was small and she was comforted, as she had the Campbell's on one side and across the branch in the back was Cassie Stamper's oldest brother, Daniel Waggoner and his family.

When granny Stamper died, Nancy wanted to remove herself from anything that reminded her of Brooks. She had promised him that she would care for his mother, whatever their fate and she was good to her word. The last two years she had watched as Granny slowly wasted away. There had never been any word from Granny's daughters living in Kentucky and Nancy grieved them as dead, even though they did not know for sure. The youngest daughter Susannah was now six, having only heard stories of her father and what a great man he was. Six glorious daughters, all sharing the same beautiful smile as their father.

Living only two miles apart, it was like old times for the sisters. Visiting sometimes as much as twice a week, they laughed and hugged each time they saw one another. And every Sunday they sat together in church. One of the first things they did after Nancy's move, was to make soap.

One weekend Catherine asked Nancy to visit, bringing all her daughters and they spent several days together. It was a wonderful time. The month prior Annie had allowed Lina to come and stay with Catherine for the summer. She was attached not only to Catherine but also Ellen. But her special favorite was Maggie. Never having a sister, she felt like a big sister to Maggie and missed her terribly.

The house was once again filled with voices and laughter. Jamie and Jonathan chose to stay in the barn as much as they could, complaining to Catherine that there was so many female voices you could not hear yourself think.

The summer had proven to be one of the happiest for Catherine since when her children were small. The farm was once again beginning to prosper, the house was filled with laughter and love and she was finally at peace with the past.

Chapter 69
Remembrance

In late summer, the heat in the attic was not the place to be but an unusually cool day brought Catherine to climb the attic stairs. She could no longer stand the clutter, and had decided to organize years of accumulation in the attic. Naturally Maggie was on her heels.

–What is this Mam Maw?

This phrase that would be repeated a hundred times or more. Twice Ellen came to the top of the attic stairs and called for Maggie to come down and leave her grandmother in peace. But each time Catherine told Ellen that Maggie could stay.

Looking behind several chairs, Maggie spotted an old trunk, and began pulling it out into the clear. Seeing the trunk, Catherine smiled and told her that of all the things in the attic, this was the most precious, as it had been Nanny Grindstaff's trunk. Opening the lid she lifted the gauzy fabric and told Maggie that this was what Nanny had worn when she was married. The dress was rotten in spots and practically fell apart in Catherine's hands.

–What are these Mam Maw?

Looking at the papers Catherine had almost forgotten about them. She began looking through them and remembering. Smiling, she told Maggie that these were things that Nanny Grindstaff had felt were important. There was a letter from Nanny's great grandmother that was written to Nanny's grandmother, several years before Nanny's own mother was born. Many times she had shown the letter to Catherine and kept it protected with a piece of cloth. The letter was over a hundred and twenty years old, yellow and faded. The penmanship was beautiful and although the ink had faded the words were still readable.

There was a small cloth sack and inside were two rings and a brooch that had belonged to Nanny's mother.

–This ring is small. It could have belonged to Nanny's grandmother when she was a young girl. Would you like to try it on?

Extending her hand, Maggie watched as Catherine slipped the tiny ring on her middle finger. Holding her hand out Maggie smiled and told

Catherine that now she looked like a real lady. Putting her hand in her apron pocket, Catherine felt the small box and thought of a true lady who had been her own mother. Smiling, she thought of how determined she was and then thought about how much she was like her mother.

Sitting on the trunk Catherine began looking through the papers and letters. One folded piece of paper was addressed to Nanny, and she carefully unfolded the paper. A drawing of a spring meadow, with beautiful flowers stretched across the paper. The detail of each flower was very distinct and you could actually see the wind blowing over the meadow. Below the picture was a very neatly written note.

"You are as beautiful to me as all the flowers in the meadow. I love you"

There was no signature but surely it had been drawn by Nanny's husband before they were married. It was obviously something that had been very special to Nanny.

Catherine was still looking at the drawing when Maggie began pulling at a small wooden box out to the center of the floor. Smiling, Catherine helped Maggie with the lid of the box. Sitting on the floor she began looking through the contents of the box. There were the gloves she wore on her wedding day, a book with a pressed flower, small baby gowns and a shawl.

The rest of the afternoon was spent telling Maggie all the history behind the items in the box. It was a mellow time of sweet remembrance for Catherine, an afternoon she would remember for a long time.

Chapter 70
Broughton

Not many communities could boast of having a local historian. But Broughton Lazenby would fit that description. Most in the community merely tolerated him, but Catherine genuinely liked him.

He was a gangly old man who walked as if his joints were not quite attached. Arms swinging wildly front to back and a stride that even the best tracker could not make out in the mud. Mismatched boots that were patched and slightly different shades of brown, scuffed down the dusty road. His clothing was the last remnants of his daddy's wardrobe, who had died and left behind this youngest son to fend for himself just before his fifteenth birthday. The faded coat was threadbare and two sizes too small. Ragged strings hung from the bottoms of his pant legs swishing along the ground and crudely sewn patches dotted his pants. Broughton Lazenby was quite a sight.

Striding at full speed with his head tucked and staring at the ground, Broughton could walk faster at age seventy than most men half his age. Always looking down as if he were counting his steps or searching for some unknown object.

Broughton could do most anything he set his mind to do and was honest to a fault. He served as the unofficial town crier and kept most of the area history inside his head ready to spout off at a moment's notice if asked. You could always depend on him to know exactly what was happening, to whom and where. There was not a joy or sorrow that he did not know about and was more than willing to share with anyone who would listen.

Every Tuesday he passed by the Stamper farm and would always stop to speak to Catherine. At first she was not sure exactly how to take him but now she was fond of him and looked forward to his visits.

This Tuesday was identical to all others. It started with Broughton waving from the road, then striding up the lane. He always stood at the bottom of the porch steps, but never actually came on the porch. Smiling, showing yellowed teeth, he told all that he knew was happening in the neighborhood. Joy and sorrow, that's what he says makes up life.

On one particular day Catherine felt inclined to ask Broughton about his personal life and he actually blushed. Telling her, "Why no one's interested in me." But she assured him that she was. Several people had told her about his parents, and she knew all the details, but was interested in what Broughton remembered.

-Oh Miz Stamper, my mama was a wonderful woman with beautiful hair and my daddy was tall and stately. They were both extremely well thought of throughout the neighborhood. And my daddy taught me all he knew which was a lot, I can tell you that!

And with that he smiled, sat on the ground and started telling Catherine what he knew about his parents. Of course he gave no descriptions but Catherine had already heard about the Lazenby's from several sources.

In the year 1783 Gerald Lazenby had traveled from Pennsylvania to North Carolina, settling in the Blue Ridge mountains. There he met and married Gazelda Broughton. The marriage was one of convenience as the bride was not considered young and beautiful nor the groom handsome but rather two people who were willing to carve out a life together. The first child born to them was Elijah but he failed to gain weight and died at four months. A year later another son was born and they named him Trevor after his mother's father. When he was two months old they found him dead one morning. Desperation set in and both Gerald and Gazelda thought they would never see a child born live.

Years went by and every day Gazelda grieved over her lost children and the fact that she did not conceive again. They gave up and contented themselves with the fact they were to be childless. Farming was hard work but they both put their back into their work and had a very small but efficient farm, seeing themselves through twenty winters together. But Gazelda felt she was growing old as she seemed tired all the time and occasionally lost her meal. Gerald insisted that she see the doctor and so one Monday morning they hitched up the horses to the wagon and headed for Asheville.

The ride took slightly over three hours and Gazelda asked to stop twice. By now Gerald was worried but felt hopeful that the doctor could give her something that would put her back on her feet. Patiently he waited outside the doctor's office until Gazelda came out to summon him inside. They paid their fee and left with Gerald carefully escorting her to the wagon while Gazelda held on to a bottle of tonic.

-What'd he say was wrong with ye?

-He thinks there's a late baby on the way and the tonic is to make me strong.

All the way home they smiled and talked about a baby. That night they knelt in front of the fire and prayed to God to give them one last chance at having a child. The decision was also made to move away from the mountain. Being wary of mountain folklore and superstition, they decided not to take a chance with this baby and would move further away. Within the month they sold their farm, left the mountain and never looked back. Settling on Fourth Creek in Iredell County, they established themselves as good, though slightly odd, neighbors.

Months passed, Gazelda glowed as she grew huge and fat. All the neighbors smiled when they saw the older couple expressing their excitement over the coming child.

On the coldest day in January, Broughton Lazenby pushed his way into the world and was greeted by his parents. He was long and gawky looking even as a newborn. The couple doted on him and soon they were taking him out in the community and even to church. Folks smiled and congratulated them but rolled their eyes behind their backs. Broughton had to be the ugliest baby anyone had ever seen. Tiny eyes that were close set with a large pointed nose. His ears stuck out and his mouth was huge.

By the time Broughton was five–years–old his long gait was evident. He walked as if trying to place his feet in the tracks of someone much taller and slinging his arms as he stretched on each step.

Shortly after Broughton's seventh birthday Gazelda dropped dead in her tracks one day carrying eggs into the house, she simply flopped on the ground like a rag doll as the eggs rolled in all directions. Gerald grieved deeply for her but he had Broughton and that was a big comfort.

Following his father around Broughton soon learned all the aspects of carving out a living on their small plot of ground. School was not something that Gerald felt was necessary for his son as he could teach him all he needed. The boy grew tall and seemed to reflect the worst facial feature of each parent on his face. But he was always smiling and speaking to everyone that he passed. He took time to say hello to old ladies and listened to them as they complained of this ache or that ache, always seeming truly interested.

A few weeks before he turned fifteen Broughton came in from slopping the hogs to find his father lying dead in the yard. The word grief cannot describe the boy's condition. For miles around folks heard of the boy and how he was inconsolable over his father's death.

It was three months after Gerald's death when neighbors began seeing Broughton walk up and down the road dressed in his father's clothes. Several neighbors dropped by occasionally and left him food but he seemed to be surviving. Years later he was considered a permanent fixture of the county. There were some weeks when he would walk from one end of the county to the other over several days sleeping along the side of the road. He could boast of literally knowing every farm in Iredell County and could tell you the name of all who lived on each farm. If you needed to know something___anything___you found Broughton Lazenby for your answer. The same was true if news needed to be spread, you found Broughton Lazenby.

Every week he stopped to visit with Catherine and felt close to her. She remembered him on his birthday and at Christmas, always taking time to listen to him with genuine interest. Catherine was one of the few people in the neighborhood to treat him with respect and true kindness.

Chapter 71
Moving Along

It was Maggie's fifteenth birthday and she was not too happy. Her mother moved her to a small house with only a few acres and a small barn. Both her brothers were now grown and married. She did not care if her brothers lived in the same house or a thousand miles away, but she did care that Catherine was no longer a part of their household.

One morning in the fall, Catherine did not come out of her room. Very quietly, Ellen knocked on her door and heard nothing. Cracking the door, she saw Catherine lying on the bed with her mouth drawn to one side, the victim of a stroke. The doctor said it was not a bad one but that she simply could not keep trying to hang on to such a large farm. So the decision was made for her and the farm was sold. Catherine now lived with George and his family and it did not sit well with Maggie.

Every other day she detoured from her route home from school and visited with her grandmother. Even seeing her four to five times each week, she still was not comforted. Maggie found her new situation lonely without being able to talk to Catherine, share secrets and just generally be there whenever she needed her.

One day on the road she stopped and talked to Broughton Lazenby. Seeing the young girl's distress at being separated from her grandmother, he promised her that he would check on Mrs. Stamper every day. And if there was ever a day that she was sick or needed something, he would seek Maggie out.

Somehow this plan calmed Maggie. There was something about the man that you knew you could trust him and that he would be good to his word.

George now had five children with a sixth on the way. There was never a day that the house was not filled with children's voices and laughter. This was a good time for Catherine, but she missed Maggie so much. Not that she did not love the grandchildren now surrounding her, it was just so hard not see her precious little Maggie every day.

After the war ended, Susan and her husband Fate McAlpine had returned to Iredell County with their children. Several years later, they moved to Hickory, North Carolina to start a business. Catherine had been to visit them several times and Susan was faithful to write her mother and to visit nearly every month. The McAlpine children were almost grown and Susan and Fate had done a wonderful job raising them. They were educated and well mannered. The oldest girl, Amanda Grace was older than Maggie but the two of them would squeal with delight at seeing one another each time they were together. Whispering and sharing secrets, they spent hours sitting in the swing that hung from a tree in the side yard.

Lavinia, who most resembled Susan, loved to sit and hear all the stories that Catherine could offer and constantly asked for them to be repeated, over and over. The only boy, Oliver was going to be taller than his father and was a handsome young man. The baby was now almost ten, and was a beauty. Named for Catherine, she was called Reeny, and always had a smile and a hug for her grandmother.

On one visit, Fate helped George begin construction on a small cabin at the back of the house. It was to be a place for visitors, since the small house would not accommodate more than were already living there. It would simply be a place to sleep with bunks lining three walls. Catherine sat in the yard watching the construction with Lavinia close to her side. It would be good for her family to visit and be able to stay several days.

The end of September brought about the beginning of beautiful color splashing through the Brushy Mountains. A surprise was coming on this beautiful crisp Saturday morning and a request was made by George that Catherine wear her new print dress as he was expecting company. Sitting in the parlor, Catherine waited to see who was coming. Age was definitely showing on her, and her head soon rested on her chest as she napped.

Several times Sarah checked on Catherine and was pleased that she was still dozing in her chair. Around 10:30 they heard a buggy turning off the road. Coming from the porch, George gently shook his mother telling her that his company had arrived. Sitting up in the chair, Catherine smiled saying she did not realize she had dozed off.

-Well, that's fine with me, because I will visit with you whether you are awake or asleep!

Hearing the voice, Catherine opened her eyes and George stepped aside to reveal a smiling Annie with Riley, Heath and Lina at her side. It had been almost a year since the family had been together all at one time.

By noontime Susan and Fate arrived with their brood. Other buggies began turning off the road and into the yard. The men set up tables under the trees, with the women covering them with cloths. Baskets of prepared food was laid out on the tables. Children were everywhere, laughing and running through the yard as they played tag.

Still confused about all the people, George told his mother that they had decided to have a family reunion and he had volunteered to host the very first one.

–We're all getting older and it's a time when we should be together, to remember and honor those who've gone on ahead of us. I want all my children to know where they came from and to be proud of who they are.

Reaching up, Catherine hugged George and told him how pleased she was and what a happy day this would be.

At one o'clock, Catherine sat in a chair under the large tree in the front yard. There were people she had not seen in years surrounding her and some she saw each week. Sister Nancy was there with all her daughters, the two oldest bringing their husbands and little ones.

Sitting and looking at all the people, Catherine watched as one woman made her way through the crowd of people, walking toward Catherine. Stooping down she smiled and asked if Catherine remembered who she was. Looking at the woman's face, especially the eyes, she lightly touched her cheek.

–Yes. Yes, I know who you are. You're my dear sister-in-law, Cassie.

Hugging her close Catherine told her how very glad she was to see her after so many years.

During the afternoon Catherine was able to visit with Cassie and Annie for several hours. She was especially interested in hearing all about Cassie's life after Hugh died. The only surviving son of Hugh and Cassie was Joseph and he was in attendance and glancing several times in his direction, Catherine remarked how much he looked like Hugh and even reminded her of John. After Hugh's death Cassie stayed with her parents and helped her mother. Peter Waggoner had welcomed his daughter and her sons into his home. They grew up strong and were taught well by their grandfather. After her son Lewis died, Cassie said that her father aged right before her eyes. He lost his will and it seemed as if his strength just ebbed from him. Only two months after Joseph returned from the war, Peter Waggoner died peacefully in his bed.

The day saw generations gathered together, laughing and talking.

To everyone's memory there had not been a time in well over twenty years since they had all lived within the same vicinity, seeing one another on a regular basis. By the end of the day everyone was saying that gathering together should be a yearly event and George had agreed to host the event again the following year. As the sun was setting the day came to an end. It had been a day of memories, sweet and sad, but a day they would all remember with many hugs and promises to write. Catherine sat on the porch and watched Broughton striding up the lane. Smiling, she knew he had come to hear all the stories of the day. And she was glad as she really liked him and wanted him to feel needed.

Chapter 72
The Dance

There was to be a dance, for Miss Edwina Cloninger and Jessup Moore, in honor of their forthcoming marriage. Excitement rippled through the neighborhood and most of the young ladies could think of nothing else. This was "the" event of 1878 and everyone wanted to be a part of any celebration for Edwina. Maggie Stamper was no exception and she begged her mother for a new dress and slippers, to which Ellen smiled. Remembering how exciting it was to be young and involved, she promised they would go to Statesville to look for fabric.

During the next few weeks Maggie visited with Catherine several times, always talking about the upcoming dance. How good it was to see such happiness and smiles. Every visit made Catherine feel younger and more alive. Sitting on the porch, she waited, as she knew that Maggie would come to visit after school today. And right on schedule, Maggie appeared, walking up the road, swinging her books and humming. Seeing her grandmother on the porch, she began to run and wave, Catherine smiled.

Sitting beside Catherine, she told her all about her day at school. But mostly she talked about what all the girls were going to wear to the dance. Her dress was almost finished and was a beautiful shade of green.

–I have something for you to wear with your new dress.

Reaching into her pocket, Catherine brought out Nanny Grindstaff's brooch. Maggie was speechless. She had seen the beautiful piece of jewelry once before and knew that it was very valuable.

–You know, during the war I sewed anything of value into the hem of my skirts. Nanny's brooch was one of the things I padded and sewed into my hem. I would always think about her when I wore the particular skirt with her brooch in the hem. Walking I could feel the heaviness at the bottom of my skirt swing out with each step. And I would think of her and how blessed we had been by her goodness. She would be so very proud to see you wear her brooch.

–Nanny was so very special to me and she saved our family with the coins she left to me. If we had not had the coins after the war,

we would have lost everything we had worked so hard for.

With a tear glistening in her eyes, Maggie hugged her grandmother and promised to take extra care with the jewelry.

The night of the dance was finally here and Maggie looked beautiful in her new dress. Her best friend, Miranda Miller, had offered Maggie a ride and she quickly accepted, not that it had anything to do with Miranda's brother driving them. Robert Miller was the most handsome boy in the neighborhood even if he was almost ten years older than the girls. Ellen had a strict rule that Maggie could not go alone, but even worse she could not go with a boy. Miranda's mother had come up with the perfect solution. And so Robert was now escorting his sister and her best friend to the dance, which in his mind was all he was doing. He certainly had no intention of dancing with little girls.

It was a wonderful night, clear with a full harvest moon lighting the landscape. The Cloninger house was very large and all the furniture had been removed from the parlor for dancing. Musicians from Statesville had been employed to play in the upstairs gallery, which overlooked the main hallway. The music drifted down the stairs and could be heard as if they were playing right there in the parlor.

Stepping into the entry of the house, Maggie's eyes were wide taking in all the beauty of the house and all those in attendance. There were flowers and silk ribbons at every turn. Tall wicker stands with huge ferns were everywhere. Never had she seen such elaborate decorations. Mr. and Mrs. Cloninger stood at the doorway and greeted each guest. Robert excused himself saying he would get the girls some punch.

Standing to the side the girls watched as several couples waltzed around the room. Maggie began looking around at all of the people and realized that there were many there she had never seen before. Asking Miranda if she knew who these people were, she learned that most were friends of the Cloningers were from when they had lived in Alexander County. One boy in particular caught her eye. She turned and saw him staring at her and blushing she quickly turned around.

Before the night was over, Miranda and Maggie had met many new people and danced with the boys from Alexander County. Press Lackey had made sure that he danced with Maggie and gave her his biggest smile. It would be a night she would forever keep in her heart.

The following week, while helping Ellen weed the flowerbeds, Maggie turned to see Press Lackey riding up the lane to their house. Quickly going inside, she brushed her hair and wiped her face. Putting on a clean apron, she returned to the porch where she found her mother and Press talking.

-Maggie, Press has asked my permission to call upon you. And I have said yes.

Blushing, she could not look at him.

-Could I come by this Sunday afternoon?

Not looking up, she nodded and smiled, Press turned and mounted his horse and was on his way.

It was the beginning of true happiness for Maggie and she told Catherine all about him. How wonderful he was, what beautiful brown eyes he had, how large his family was and how nice they were to her. All of which Catherine listened to carefully. Her little girl was becoming a woman and she just hoped that she lived long enough to see her married and with children.

The years were sweeping by and Catherine felt helpless to stop time. Looking in the mirror she saw an old woman with wrinkles and grey hair. Last year she had seen Susan and Fate's oldest daughter, Amanda Gray, married. Her first great grandchild had arrived with Ellen's son Jonathan being the proud papa, followed a few weeks later by a great grandson, with Jamie naming his first born, John. Both men continued to return for visits bringing their families with them and wrote when they could not visit.

By 1880 the family had grown to major proportions. Each year the family reunion seemed to grow with an addition of a child, bride or a groom. It was becoming increasingly hard for Catherine to climb steps and George had made a cane for her. At first she refused but then realizing how helpful it was, used the cane without any more complaining. Now during the reunions, she never left her rocker, and her meal was brought to her, as she sat under a shade tree. Throughout the day she welcomed folks and enjoyed visiting with everyone, many taking turns sitting with her. A photographer had been hired and he arranged the family around Catherine and took several photographs. This was only the third time, in her life-time, that Catherine's likeness had been captured on film.

Not only was Catherine aging, but Nancy was also showing signs of old age. All of her daughters were now grown with three of them married and presenting her with a combined total of twelve grandchildren. It was not easy for the sisters to visit now so they constantly exchanged letters. In 1881, Nancy had traveled by train with her oldest daughter and son-in-law to Virginia. Here she was able to see the spot where Brooks was killed and had been buried. She knelt in public and prayed out loud thanking God for letting her see his final resting place.

Catherine was not able visit or go to church, all of the family visited often, sometimes having worship in the front parlor. The little cabin George and Fate built behind the house saw much use. Melmath came and stayed a week bringing with him his wife and three little boys, Clarence, Archie and Caleb. Almost every other week, Susan and Fate came to visit and Catherine was always so happy to see them. Their youngest daughter, Reeny stayed one entire summer and doted on Catherine. It was a time for her to hear again all the stories that her grandmother had stored up. Telling her all about her grandfather John, and how they had met, their marriage and the first little cabin. In her old age, Catherine was serenely content.

Chapter 73
Bearer of News

The heat had been oppressive and the large oaks shading the porch provided a somewhat cooler place to finish shelling the peas before the heat got any worse. Press would soon be in from the field, tired, dirty and hungry. Rocking back and forth on the porch with a lap full of peas would be the only sitting time today. Methodically shelling while watching a slight breeze stir the tall grass, swaying the wild daisies and Queen Anne's Lace. Maggie watched a small dust cloud kick up and swirl along the dry dirt road. Hands that were calloused even at an early age quickly slit open the peas while enjoying the peace of the sights around her. You did not need to look at peas to shell, just needed to feel for the ridges.

The four-room house sat off the main road some two hundred yards and was surrounded by good farmland. Plain and simple but sturdy it had been constructed by a twenty-two-year-old, soon-to-be groom, with no experience at building houses.

Thinking back about the past years, Maggie remembered the early days of her engagement to Press Lackey. How shy she had been after their first meeting and how persistent he had been in courting her until he had won her heart.

Maggie Stamper had sat under the shade tree for hours on end watching Press split the wood that would become shingles for the roof. Propped against the giant poplar tree with skirts spread carefully, she watched with fascination and love at the man who would soon become her protector, her world. With her bonnet adjusted just so, keeping a slight shadow upon her face, she was able to glance in his direction without detection. An older copy of a Godey's magazine lay in her lap, which helped perpetuate the illusion that she was reading. She watched day after day as the house took shape and would lean back on the tree, eyes closed, and envision her life with Press.

Returning to the present Maggie thought about the events since that day back in 1879. There had been hardships and illness and lots of good times and love. Of course there was more joy than she ever expected and life was good. Simple. Quiet. The only sounds were the creaking of the rocker and the 'ping' of the peas as they hit the bucket along with the soft muffled sounds of children playing. Once the peas were shelled it would be time to stoke up the fire. How she hated the heat and that wood stove. And cooking would only deepen the sweat stains on her plain cotton dress.

In the distance their old coon dog barked and the hens out back began singing their song. She stood and laid her lap cloth holding the peas on the porch and reached for the bonnet lying beside the rocker. Stepping down the steps from the porch and tying on the bonnet, she walked a few paces while shading her eyes with both hands from the noon sun. She looked to the road to see the figure of a man coming in the distance.

Broughton Lazenby was coming down the path, swinging his arms as he took long strides. Well into his 80's, he still walked the county.

Walking to the end of the path Maggie waited for him to come within speaking distance. It was not every day someone came down the road during the day. The men were always in the fields and the women were busy trying to hold together what little harvest was placed at their feet to feed hungry children. It was good to see someone in the middle of the day. Even an occasional salesman was cause for excitement. Broughton was bound to bring the latest gossip. Recognizing the old man their old coon dog came racing through the field, wagging his tail. Falling in step, the dog escorted him the final distance, wiggling and making little yipping noises.

Stopping just short of five feet from Maggie, Broughton squared his shoulders and removed his battered dusty hat revealing thinning hair that was greasy and matted. An air of solemn dignity showed in his stance, as he looked her in the eye as if preparing to give a grand speech.

-*Your grandma's dying and they sent me to fetch you. Stopped at your man's old home place to let them know. His sister Mary's girls will be here shortly. Mighty sorry for you Miz Maggie, but she's an old woman who done seen all she can see in this ole world. You want I should go find your man in the field?*

Standing in the bright sun and heat, Maggie felt chills run down her body. She looked at him and asked if he was sure. He was. Turning without speaking, she walked back up the path to the porch, climbed the few steps and sat down in the rocker. Catherine was dying and everything around her seemed unreal. She slowly began rocking back and forth. Broughton just stood at the end of the path and stared, not knowing what to do. Then without speaking he started off across the field to find Press.

Tears finally came to her deep-set eyes and rolled down her dusty cheeks to drip off the end of her chin onto folded hands now resting in her lap. Her heart began to race. Suddenly she was hot again and felt she could not breathe. Rocking faster increased what little breeze there was and she took deep gulps of air and felt her heart begin to slow. The air seemed thick and stifling and her clothes felt damp. Her rocking motion slowed and her breathing became easier. She reached down and gathered up her lap cloth full of peas and began shelling again, dropping the peas in the bucket, rocking but seeing Catherine in her mind's eye. Shelling peas was not going to stop what she was about to face.

Then the tears began again. If only I did not have to watch her go. The thought was almost unbearable, but Maggie knew that she needed to see her grandmother one last time. Best to pack a few things in the satchel and get the children ready to go with Mary's girls. Maybe Mary would loan her their buggy, then Press would have the wagon. She wanted him to be able to come to her when Catherine died.

Chapter 74
Preparing to Go

The freshly washed sheets smelled of sun and clean air. All this fussing about would drive her to the grave for sure. Catherine lay in her bed and watched as Maggie placed a pitcher of water by the bedside table. Eyelids that had grown heavy slowly closed and the constant fatigue gave way to sleep. Maggie laid her hand on Catherine's head brushing away a stray wisp of fine white hair.

Catherine had been ill for over a month and Doc Stewart had told the family that she was just worn out. After all, she was up in years now and her time on earth would not be long.

Looking at Catherine sleep, Maggie's eyes filled with tears. Here was the one she loved most in the world, wasted and frail. Quietly moving a chair to the bedside, she sat and reached for her yarn satchel. Hook and yarn were comforting at times like this and helped to pass the time. Reaching in the satchel she drew out a shawl she had been working on for a week. Fall would be here before you knew it and she wanted to have the shawl finished before cooler weather set in.

As Maggie sat vigil, others came to the door and peeked into the room. Always acknowledging their presence, she waved them away. Goodness knows Mam Maw needs rest, not company. Looking at Catherine resting so peacefully she placed her hand on the frail hand lying atop the quilt. Looking at the older woman's hand she studied the pattern of veins and turning the hand over inspected the still visible calluses. These hands had taught her to knit and crochet, sew, to cook and clean, to slaughter hogs, milk and churn butter, preserve their food, tend to cows and hold small babies.

Opening her eyes, Catherine watched as Maggie slowly studied her hand.
    –It can't be dirty, 'cause you've washed it a dozen times.

Smiling Maggie shook her head.

    –No Mam Maw, I'm just thinking about all the strength this hand
    has used through the years. How you used your hand to show me
    how to make do for myself. And how many times that hand laid on
    my head when I was sick, my backside when I was bad, or my

shoulder when I was good. But mostly how I love that hand.

Feeling the gentle stroking on her hand was nice and relaxing.

–John used to stroke my hand. First time was when all the skin had about come off from working the fields. Did I ever tell you about that? He was such a fine man. Big man. And he used to tell me how proud he was that he had such a strong wife to help. Shame he was gone by the time you came along. Will you do something for me?

–You know I will.

–Open that top drawer over there.

Standing and crossing the room, Maggie pulled the drawer opened and looked back at her grandmother, waiting to see what she wanted out of the drawer.

–Bring me that small box.

Picking up the small box, Maggie handed it to Catherine and waited.

–My mother was an English Lady. A true Lady. Lady Elizabeth Falsworth. She was born in the English countryside. Her mother was a beautiful French woman and her father was from a long line of aristocrats. My grandfather worshiped my grandmother. Everyone talked about her great beauty. But she died giving birth to my mother, my grandfather never forgave my mother for that. That tiny box holds the earth from my grandmother's rose garden. My mother knew that she would never see her home again when she left to come to America. One thing that she loved most was the roses that her mother had planted. So she took the earth from the garden and put it in this small box. I never remember a day in my life when I did not see her occasionally put her hand in her pocket and feel for the small box. She carried it with her every day until I got married and she gave it to me. And I've carried it nearly every day. When my mother died, I was expecting my last child, a little girl who did not live. I would sit and hold the little box and feel my mother's hand on mine. Her death left me broken, as she had sacrificed so much for me. Now I want you to have the box and I hope that someday you will give it to one of your daughters.

Seeing the signs that Catherine was once again slipping into that dreamland where her one true love was always waiting, Maggie waited. Catherine lay very still, watching through half closed eyes. Scooting her chair closer to the bed, she laid her head on the quilt, as Catherine slowly laid her hand on Maggie's hair. Just like when she was a child.

–I remember what you told me about my grandfather and I tell my children his story often. He will never really be gone Mam Maw, as long as we talk about him. I remember what you said about how it all began.

Catherine's eyes grew misty with almost a glassy look. She could see John. She could see her love. He was here now and her mother Elizabeth, stood behind him.

Chapter 75
Going Home

Maggie pulled the quilt up to Catherine's shoulders. Smiling, she looked down on the elderly sleeping woman, and then lit the lamp. Knowing that Catherine would sleep for the rest of the night Maggie slipped out the door and started down the hall to the kitchen.

The family had eaten several hours earlier and were all sitting on the front porch taking in the sounds of night and enjoying a cooling breeze. Taking a biscuit from the warming bin on the stove she forked a piece of ham and wrapped them both in a napkin. Then pouring a glass of milk she headed for the porch.

The porch was the best place to be after a long day. The adults shared stories of the day and the children chased lightning bugs on the lawn. An oil lantern sat at each end of the porch gave just enough illumination to see to get around but not enough to read.

George Stamper sat in the big rocker and smoked his pipe, slowly rocking back and forth.

–How's she doing? Still reliving the past?

Maggie sat down on the top step and nodded her head at her uncle.

Everyone knew of Catherine's storytelling. It was almost like she had to say the memories out loud or they would disappear. Afraid that her family's struggle to make their mark would be forgotten, she constantly told anyone who would listen, memories of her early years and her marriage to John. The heritage of her family was foremost in her mind and she was determined that her great grandchildren would know and pass along to their great grandchildren.

Sitting in the semidarkness of the porch, Maggie told the others of hearing again the story of how Catherine met John. Not that she minded but during the last few weeks, it was practically all she had heard. George nodded and puffed on the pipe. Many of the memories were his own and some not too pleasant.

....

Sunrise brought activity around the farm from every direction. The men were in the field as the sun rose. In the back yard the wash water was almost boiling over in the big black pot for the endless dirty laundry from the sick room. Arriving at the house early Maggie was in the kitchen stirring oatmeal that she would soon take to Catherine. Getting her to eat was not easy. And then it would be time to bathe her and change the bed.

The room was cool and the breeze could be seen lifting the curtains. It had all come down to lying in the bed, in and out of sleep, with no appetite or thirst. Sounds from the yard told Catherine that the children were playing and she could smell pies baking. It must be getting near suppertime. And then she slept again with another day passing.

The following day Doc Stewart gently closed the bedroom door behind him and faced the family.

−She won't make it till sunset. Her kidneys just don't work anymore, poisoning her own body. I'm sorry, there's nothing that will help. Catherine is well over eighty years old and her body is begging for rest.

George bowed his head and his shoulders shook but there was no sound. Standing in the hallway were his sons Abe and Lum, there to support their dad. Gently Lum laid a hand on George's shoulder and asked him to come sit on the porch. Maggie sat on a stool beside the door and told her uncle that she would watch Catherine.

She felt a lightness, with a feeling of peace, as if she could float along in rest and well-being. She knew that she was dying. Finally she would go home and see all her loved ones. John. She would see John. Opening her eyes, she turned her head to stare at the ceiling. Maggie quietly slipped into the chair beside her grandmother's bed and gently took her hand.

−I'm here Mam Maw.

She reassured her as she stroked the small frail hand.

Stirring slightly Catherine looked again to the ceiling focusing on the corner. A slight smile was on her face. Maggie put another light quilt on the bed, as she realized how cold her grandmother's arms and hands felt.

−They've come and I can see them.

Maggie asked who was there. But Catherine lay still and smiled, not answering.

—My baby is so beautiful and she is holding her hands out to me and calling to me. My baby. My baby. John is holding her up. My John......he's here.......

The last breath escaped her lips with a small 'whew' sound. Catherine Stamper was dead.

Throwing herself across the bed Maggie cried and hugged Catherine to her chest. Soon the room was full of people and they all took turns giving her one last kiss. All her children and grandchildren were present for the last day of this life. It was almost as if Catherine knew that the last child had arrived, and she felt it safe to leave.

That evening Annie and Maggie prepared Catherine for burial. Gently they washed her body and dressed her. It seemed fitting that the beautiful blue wedding dress would be the perfect thing for her burial rather than black. Both women knew that there would be much talk about the selection being disrespectful but somehow it was the only thing that seemed right.

Several neighborhood men carried the casket into the parlor and placed it between two candle stands. From her pocket Maggie took Nanny's brooch and pinned it to the front of Catherine's wedding dress.

—She looks beautiful. This is what she would want.

As Maggie stood looking at her grandmother, she slipped her hand into her pocket to feel the comfort of the small box. Press came to stand beside Maggie and placed his arm around her shoulder.

—I don't think it could be any other way.

Throughout the night family members sat with the body and at daybreak women from the church began arriving to take their place. Throughout the morning people arrived at the house to pay their respects and view the body. Not one comment was made about the blue dress.

Chapter 76
Final Rest

There were over one hundred people who stood listening as the life of Catherine Stamper was eulogized. Men and women dressed in black, standing silent as the service was conducted. Three women sang the hymn Rock of Ages

Rock of Ages, cleft for me,
Let me hid myself in Thee;
Let the water and the blood,
From Thy wounded side which flowed
Be of sin the double cure;
Save from wrath and make me pure.

While I draw this fleeting breath,
When my eye-strings break in death
When I soar to worlds unknown,
See Thee on Thy judgment throne,
Rock of Ages, cleft for me
Let me hide myself in Thee

Throughout the crowd could be heard muffled crying and sniffling. Maggie stood straight not moving. Her mourning veil had been lifted back over her hat revealing her tear streaked face. Clinging to her skirts were her daughter's, Addie, Della and Oma Lee, not fully understanding all that was happening. Next to them was Lina with her husband and son.

Stepping forward, Press Lackey began to speak.

-Catherine was a strong woman, a God fearing woman. Every person here today has been touched by this woman's life. Even as she was dying she thought of others. Her honesty was known by all, and her kindness to those in need was seen throughout our neighborhood. All of Catherine's children and grandchildren were so blessed to have her in their life.

With the eulogy over, the pastor read his scripture and offered a prayer. Lina and Maggie stepped forward, stooped to gather a fist full of dirt and released it into the deep hole. Then they stood and listened as the dirt landed on the coffin.

....

The night air was sweet and cool with the sound of cicadas singing in the trees. Sitting in the porch swing, Maggie and Press quietly passed the remainder of the evening. The last of the mourners had left some time ago and Maggie felt that she needed to be outside. It had taken the girls over an hour to settle down and go to sleep and now she wanted just to rest and be with Press.

The hooks attached to rings in the porch ceiling squeaked with the swing going back and forth.

–How am I going to get along without her? She gave me strength when nothing else could.

Press placed his arm around Maggie and she laid her head on his shoulder.

–She's never left Maggie. If you look in the mirror you can see her face. When you speak you will hear her voice. Every time you cook, she's there. No, she's not gone. Her spirit will be with you in everything that you do because she so carefully taught you all that she knew. Just as you will teach our daughters and maybe even their daughters. And she will live on, even through them.

Settling back in the swing, Maggie looked at the porch ceiling and watched the hook slide in the ring as the swing moved forward and back. The air was filled with the soothing fragrance of honeysuckle. Placing a hand in her pocket, she felt the small box. Suddenly she felt very peaceful and content. Press was right, Catherine would always be with her.
s

Wrapping her warm hand around the box in her pocket, her thoughts were how she had known about the box all her life, but only now was she beginning to understand. The box did not represent the connection to England, not the coveted inheritance of aristocracy, nor a reminder of the great Falsworth mansion in England. The box contained more than a sample of dirt from her great great-grandmother's rose garden, it was invested with the heritage of family, not necessarily family name or prosperity. Now the box was linked to Maggie; to the goodness, love and strength of Catherine and of Catherine's mother, Elizabeth. A legacy she would pass on to the next generation.

The End